00401133108

D0119561

THE YEAR OF
DANGEROUS LOVING

By John Gordon Davis

Hold My Hand I'm Dying
Cape of Storms
Years of the Hungry Tiger
Taller Than Trees
Leviathan
Typhoon
Fear No Evil
Seize the Reckless Wind
A Woman Involved
The Land God Made in Anger
Talk to Me Tenderly, Tell Me Lies
Roots of Outrage
The Year of Dangerous Loving

Non-fiction
Operation Rhino
Hong Kong Through the Looking Glass

THE YEAR OF DANGEROUS LOVING

JOHN GORDON DAVIS

HarperCollins*Publishers*

This novel is entirely a work of fiction.
The names, characters and incidents portrayed in it are
the work of the author's imagination. Any resemblance to
actual persons, living or dead, events or localities is
entirely coincidental.

HarperCollins*Publishers*
77–85 Fulham Palace Road,
Hammersmith, London W6 8JB

Published by HarperCollins*Publishers* 1997
1 3 5 7 9 8 6 4 2

Copyright © John Gordon Davis 1997

The Author asserts the moral right to
be identified as the author of this work

A catalogue record for this book
is available from the British Library

ISBN 0 00 223666 4

Set in Postscript Meridien by
Rowland Phototypesetting Ltd,
Bury St Edmunds, Suffolk

Printed and bound in Great Britain by
Caledonian International Book Manufacturing Ltd, Glasgow

All rights reserved. No part of this publication may be
reproduced, stored in a retrieval system, or transmitted,
in any form or by any means, electronic, mechanical,
photocopying, recording or otherwise, without the prior
permission of the publishers.

To Buck and Diana Buchanan

PART I

1

'Send a policeman to arrest me – I've just shot my husband!'

That was the dramatic announcement Elizabeth Hargreave made when she telephoned Jake McAdam at the Foreign Correspondents' Club that hot Friday night. McAdam thought she must be drunk and he asked to speak to Hargreave.

'He's driven himself to hospital,' Liz said, and hung up.

Then McAdam took it seriously. He went back to the bar and asked Max Popodopolous to go to her immediately and keep her away from the police while he went to look for Hargreave.

McAdam traced him at the Jockey Club Clinic. Ian Bradshaw was in attendance, and said that Hargreave would be all right: the bullet missed the lungs.

'Thank God for that. How did you get involved in this?' McAdam asked. Ian Bradshaw was an expensive surgeon who did not hang around casualty departments of hospitals.

'Called me at the yacht club – he refused to let a government doctor treat him, he doesn't want any official reports. You can't see him, he's still under anaesthetic.'

'Did he tell you how it happened?'

'Says it was an accident. Gun went off unintentionally. Don't say anything to the police. Nor to the press.'

'Of course not. But the press are going to love this.'

'How embarrassing,' Ian said. 'Did you know the marriage was rocky?'

'No.' McAdam added in Liz's defence: 'She sounded as if she'd been drinking.'

'Al had been drinking too. We all drink too much in this town but we don't wave guns at our spouses. He doesn't play around, does he?'

'*No*,' McAdam said, 'nor does Liz.'

'What will the police do about this?'

'Nothing, if it was an accident.'

'But pointing a gun at somebody is a crime, isn't it?'

'Yes, but it's the sort of thing that can happen in a marital row. The police can't do anything if Alistair doesn't lay a charge – which he certainly won't; he'll want it hushed up.'

'I hope you're right, I like Liz. And Alistair. Amazing, isn't it, what can go on in a marital bedroom without anybody else suspecting? Just goes to show, marriage can be one of the most stressful of undertakings. Well, I'll go'n finish my dinner. You can see him in the morning.'

McAdam then telephoned Hargreave's apartment. Max answered.

'Okay, she's gone to bed with a sleeping pill, the neighbours have been looking after her. I've fended off the cops, told them she's not in her sound and sober senses and can't make a statement.'

'Any press around?'

'Somebody alerted them; they've been clamouring at the door. I fended them off too.'

'And what's the scene-of-crime look like?'

'The bullet hit the book Alistair was reading before hitting his chest. Another bullet-hole in the wall above the bed.'

'Jesus, she fired two shots?'

'After the first shot Al grabbed the gun, they struggled for possession of it and it went off a second time, hitting the wall.'

'Al was *reading*?'

'Apparently he was lying in bed, pretending to read, ignoring her. They'd been quarrelling.'

'Did you find out what about?'

'Not really, she was crying. Bits about how infuriating Al is, how he used to be life and soul of the party, now he doesn't want to go anywhere, just work work work, et cetera.'

'So she pulls a gun on him? There's more to it than that.'

'Oh, she's convinced he's seeing another woman, that's all I got out of her before she passed out. She was furious because he was drinking in Wanchai this afternoon – she found lipstick on his ear. And he disgraced himself at the Chief Justice's dinner party by falling asleep. They were both the worse for drink probably, Al's been hitting the bottle of late – overwork. Do you think there's another woman involved?'

McAdam sighed. '*No*. Al's too honest a soul to lead a double life. Too much of a worrier.'

'But how did he come by the lipstick?'

'In Wanchai? Easy. I've come by a bit of it myself down there over the years. He probably picked it up dancing.'

'Al dance? In Wanchai? Come on. Anyway,' Max sighed, 'I'll spend the night here to make sure she doesn't blab to the police when she wakes up. Will you look after Al in the morning?'

'Sure, first thing.'

'And Jake? Don't go back to the club now, you'll only be asked a lot of questions by the press boys.'

History is confused on the earlier events of that afternoon, avid gossip making hearsay more confounded.

One version of the story has Alistair Hargreave carried shoulder-high into the Pussycat Bar in Wanchai by the police after the jury returned a verdict of guilty in the big heroin case he had just successfully prosecuted; another is that the police even instructed the manager to get the bar-girls out of their beds to entertain the Director of Public Prosecutions because Wanchai does not warm up until night; another is that he was so drunk that he took several off to bed at once; yet another is that his wife found him in bed with one of them and shot him *in flagrante delicto*.

None of this is correct. The truth is that, after the jury returned their verdict, Hargreave went with the police investigation team to have a Chinese meal in Wanchai to celebrate; that a good deal of booze was drunk and that later they adjourned to a nearby bar called the Pussycat to have just one more; that the place was jumping, despite the comparatively early hour, because a shipload of American tourists had arrived; that Hargreave met some of his journalist friends there and had several drinks; and that he somehow acquired some lipstick on his ear whilst successfully resisting the blandishments of a bar-girl. When he finally emerged into the garish Wanchai sunset, he couldn't remember where he'd parked his car and ended up taking a taxi home. His wife was very angry because he was late for a dinner party, because he had been drinking in Wanchai, because he was drunk, because he had lost the car, and she became angrier still when she discovered the lipstick. They arrived in a borrowed car at the Chief Justice's party when everybody was already seated, and Hargreave promptly fell asleep, because he had been up most of the previous night preparing his closing address to the jury. He had to be kicked awake several times before his wife took him home in disgrace: and then, ten minutes later, two shots rang out.

The next morning the front-page headline of the *South China Morning Post* read: LEADING LAWYER SHOT.

Mr Alistair Hargreave QC, the Director of Public Prosecutions, last night drove himself to the Jockey Club Hospital suffering from a gunshot wound to his chest.

Friends immediately rushed to the Hargreave home where a spokesman for the family, Mr Max Popodopolous, also a lawyer, refused to allow Mrs Elizabeth Hargreave to answer questions from either the press or the police. At the hospital another spokesman for the family, Mr Jake McAdam, told both police and the press to 'get lost'.

Police enquiries continue.

Mr Alistair Hargreave is a former Commodore of the Royal Hong Kong Yacht Club, a fine tennis player, and a leading member of the legal community. Last year his yacht, *Elizabeth*, won the Hong Kong–Manila race under his captaincy in record time in very bad weather . . .

The front pages of the *Hong Kong Standard* and the *Eastern Express* were in similar dramatic vein. Hargreave had them all on his bed when McAdam arrived the next morning.

'Thanks, pal,' Hargreave said, 'for pulling me out of the soup. Max too.'

'How you feeling?'

'Just a flesh wound, Ian says I can go home next week. *Home* . . . ?' He snorted softly.

'You can stay with me,' McAdam said, 'until this blows over, whatever it is.'

'Thanks, but I don't think it'll be necessary. Just before the fireworks she announced she was going home to the States forthwith.'

McAdam sat down in a chair. 'What's the story?'

Hargreave slapped the newspapers. 'The police were here earlier. Told them to take a powder, it was an accident. They didn't believe me but there's nothing they can do if I won't testify. She won't blab anything to the cops, will she?'

'No, I've just spoken to Max on the phone; Liz is all weepy and remorseful. The cops have called again and Max fended them off.'

'Remorseful?' Hargreave closed his eyes. 'What's Max talking to her about?' He shook his head. 'No, don't tell me, I don't want to hear what a shit I am.'

'You're not, you're a hell of a nice guy.'

'Sure.' Hargreave was silent a moment, then: 'Old Liz, you know, she's not such a bad old stick. In fact she's a very good old stick. She's just unhappy.'

And she's not an old stick, McAdam thought, she's damned attractive. He waited, then said: 'Why's she unhappy?'

Hargreave sighed. 'Don't want to talk about it. You playing marriage counsellor?'

'You've got a bullet wound – we don't want you to get any more.'

Hargreave sighed again, eyes still closed. 'Accident. Won't happen again.' There was a silence; then he continued with reluctance, 'She's unhappy because the marriage has been going downhill for several years. And that's my fault.'

Downhill for years? The Hargreaves had always presented a solid matrimonial front to the world. McAdam waited again, then asked, 'How is it your fault?'

There was another silence. Then: 'Oh Lord, how can one summarize marriage failure in a sentence? Don't want to talk about it.' He sighed. 'It's my fault because I'm bored with life here, because I don't want to have anything to do with the bullshit Hong Kong social scene any more. So she's bored, because I'm boring. The *marriage* is therefore boring. Worn out. Don't do anything together any more. And that's all I want to say.'

'You're not boring.'

Hargreave snorted softly. 'I even bore myself. I'm *bored*, Jake. I'm bored with the Law. Been there, done that, every case is just more of the same old guff. I'm bored with lawyers and most of all I'm bored with His boring Lordship. I'm bored with witnesses, with juries. I'm bored with *Hong Kong*.' He sighed. 'About the only thing I'm not bored with is booze.' There was a pause: then before McAdam could say anything Hargreave continued: 'What else is there at our age? Got all the money we need – even if we'd like more – but we've got enough. We've got the success we strove for. So what else is there?'

'Climbing the Andes? Sailing round the world in your yacht? Buying that ranch and raising those cattle?'

'But that's several years down the line, till I've recovered from my last stock market misadventure. Meanwhile I have to soldier on.' He grimaced, eyes closed: 'And that's why old Liz pulled the gun on me. To shake me up, give me a fright. It went off, that's all there is to it. Don't want to talk about it.'

Like hell that's all there is to it, McAdam thought. 'Well,' he said, 'boredom happens in marriage.'

Hargreave did not open his eyes. 'Does it? Or just happens to me? I think it just happens to me. Out there all the other guys who've been married twenty years are still happily screwing their wives every night. And old Liz, you know, she's a very attractive woman.'

Oh dear, McAdam thought – so this is it? He ventured: 'I doubt all those married men out there are still doing it every night, Al, I was married once myself.'

7

'And evidently I've got unhealthy appetites. Like booze and gambling.' He paused. 'How can you make love to a woman who's always fed up with you? Always telling you what a washout you were at the dinner party last night, you don't tell funny stories any more, all you talked about was politics.'

McAdam wasn't sure what to say. 'Well, maybe you should spend more time together, take her out for a few romantic dinners.'

'Bit late for that – don't feel very romantic with a bullet in my chest.'

'But you love her.' He added: 'Don't you?'

'Ask me another one. Right now I'm angry, mortified. Whole town knows. Wish the earth would swallow me up.'

'Do you think she loves you?'

Hargreave snorted again. 'She's too angry with me for that. Fed up with me. *This* fed up –' He indicated his chest – 'even though it was an accident. When people do that, raise their hand to strike, or pick up a weapon, it means they'd really like to do it, even if they stop themselves.' He sighed grimly. 'I almost wish she'd had an affair, maybe that would have made me less intolerable.'

'You told her to have an *affair*? Last night?'

'No. She accused *me* of having an affair. Oh,' he shook his head, 'I don't want to talk about it. Utterly untrue. God, who with? Friends' wives? Don't want a guilty conscience as well as being bored.'

McAdam hesitated: 'Apparently she found some lipstick on your collar?'

Hargreave groaned and opened his eyes. 'Oh Christ. That was just some Wanchai whore trying to be persuasive. Nothing happened, didn't even buy her a drink. The cops were with me, they'd bear me out.' He closed his eyes again. 'But Liz was furious, yes, accused me of having it off down there, accused me of all kinds of womanizing for years.' He sighed angrily. 'Utterly untrue.'

'So what happened with Elizabeth? You told her you were innocent. Then?'

Hargreave sighed. 'Furious with me for being late for the CJ's dinner party. And drunk. I wasn't really drunk, just exhausted after the case. Fell asleep at dinner. Snored, apparently. Gave me hell coming home, particularly about the lipstick. I refused to fight, went to bed, started to read while she ranted on about Wanchai whores. Next thing she's standing at the end of the bed with the gun shouting "*Answer me!*" Then, *bang!* Bullet knocks the book out of my hands and hits my chest. I sat up with a certain alacrity. Couldn't believe it.'

'Jesus. So?'

'So I leap off the bed, spouting blood. Grabbed the gun. We wrestle for it. Thing goes off again, punches a hole in the wall. She runs to the telephone and calls you. Drama. Then the neighbours come rushing in. While I stagger out and drive myself to hospital. Now the whole fucking town knows.' He slapped the newspapers. 'What did she say to you?'

McAdam hesitated, then said, '"Send a policeman to arrest me, I've just shot my husband."'

Hargreave groaned. 'Drama. She knew the cops weren't necessary – that gun's got a light trigger.'

'I didn't know you had a gun.'

'Hangover from our days in Kenya. When we were seconded there ten years ago I bought a gun in case of burglars. It's quite kosher, fully licensed.'

'Where is it normally kept?'

'My bedside table. Didn't notice her get it, she was striding up and down giving me a bollocking.' Hargreave sighed. 'She didn't intend to shoot me – just being dramatic.'

'Okay, but this doesn't look good from a police point of view. She fires, then she struggles to retain possession of the gun? That would sound like serious intent to the jury.'

Hargreave took a deep, tense breath. 'No jury, no cops. Natural reaction to struggle over a weapon once you've produced it to be dramatic. I just hope she goes back to America and cools off.'

'Well, when I spoke to Max an hour ago he said she was packing her bags.'

Hargreave opened his eyes and raised his head. 'Really?'

'But it might be bravado. Want me to go around there and pour oil on troubled waters?'

Hargreave looked at him, then slumped back. 'No,' he said tremulously. 'It's for the best. Let her get out of this bloody awful town for a while . . .'

2

In the Hong Kong summer your skin is oily, your hair is oily, the sun beats down oily maddening hot on this teeming city on the South China coast: on the frantic money-making, the towering business blocks and the apartments crowding along the manmade shores and up the jungled mountains; on the myriad of resettlement blocks and the squatter shacks, beating down on the sweeping swathes of elevated highways and byways and flyovers and underpasses, on the buildings going up on the mountains that are chopped down to make more land for teeming people, on the mass of factories and the shops, the jampacked traffic carbon-monoxidizing everywhere, the narrow backstreets and ladderstreets and alleyways, the jostling sidewalks, and the signboards fighting each other up to the sky. It blazes down upon the mauve islands and mountains surrounding the teeming harbour, with its container ships and freighters from around the world, and its cargo junks and sampans and jampacked ferries, beating down on the noise and work and money-making. But it is China's money-making that comes first and foremost in this clamorous, anachronistic, capitalistic, British colony on the crazy-making China coast: Hong Kong is Communist China's capitalist colony – it is only Great Britain's in name. Hong Kong is a very unusual, dramatic place.

And this year it was even more dramatic because the question on everybody's mind, the question everybody had to answer was: 'Shall I go or shall I stay? Shall I leave this crazy place and start life over again, or shall I take a chance on China and trust in the Lord?'

Ten years ago they had trusted in the Joint Declaration – in which Great Britain and China agreed that 'only the flag will change' when the territory reverted in 1997 – ten years ago they had trusted in China's avowed policy of 'One Country, Two Systems', trusted in the internationally-binding agreement that the new Special Administrative Region of Hong Kong that would come into being would be autonomous and governed democratically, that British law would continue to apply, trusted in the Basic Law which China had drawn up enshrining these principles. Ten years ago there had been hope, and that hope had got stronger when Communism collapsed in Russia and eastern Europe, stronger yet when Premier Deng of China declared that 'to become rich is glorious'. In those days even Alistair Hargreave, who trusted Communists only as far as he could kick them, had resolved to stay after 1997. And then had come the massacre in Tiananmen Square, Beijing, where thousands of Chinese were gunned down by the People's Liberation Army tanks for demanding democracy; Hong Kong's hope was trampled into the blood of Tiananmen.

'Communism is dead,' Hargreave had said. 'Long live the fucking Communist Party!'

There was little hope after Tiananmen; thousands of business people left Hong Kong for Canada, Australia, England, America. And now, in that long, hot, maddening summer of 1995, Great Britain was timidly trying to enforce the Joint Declaration by holding the first fully demo-cratic elections for the Legislative Council, and China had announced that she would destroy the new Council when she took over, Joint Declaration or no. There is no democratic nonsense in the paradise of the People's Republic of China and there would be none in the Special Administrative Region of Hong Kong: there would be no independent judiciary and no freedom of the press either, Basic Law or no Basic Law, United Nations or no United Nations.

It was a bad time for Hong Kong, that long hot summer of 1995. Shall I go or shall I stay?

It was a bad summer for Alistair Hargreave, although it had nothing to do with China's treachery. Within a week of being shot by Elizabeth he was back at work, showing a brave face, but he was very embar-rassed. Lord, he hated the solicitude, the polite circumlocution, he hated people feeling sorry for him: most of them believed that Liz had shot him deliberately, that he had come by the lipstick the usual way. He went to work early, came home late and did more work with the help of whisky. He declined all social invitations. Occasionally he had to meet Jake McAdam or Max or Bernie Champion for a drink, and even those encounters were embarrassing: these guys were his closest friends and expected him to open up to them, but Hargreave did not want to open up to anybody, he wanted to turn his face to the wall. As they said, there were plenty of women out there who would be pleased with his attentions, but he could not bring himself to go through the bullshit involved; he would feel a fraud. And, oh yes, he missed Elizabeth, even though he knew the marriage was a certifiable failure now. Sometimes, in the long hot nights in the empty apartment he considered taking some leave and flying to California to see if they could try again: but in the cold light of hungover dawn he knew it couldn't work. Finally, towards the end of that long bad summer he decided what to do: pull himself together, stop feeling sorry for himself, take early retirement after he had had his next annual leave and get the hell out of this bloody embarrassing town whether he could afford it or not, and start life anew somewhere. He felt better after he had made that decision. Then the letter from her Californian lawyers arrived.

It was the usual hostile stuff that lawyers prefer, advising him that they were instructed by Elizabeth Amelia Hargreave to institute divorce proceedings against him in the Supreme Court of Hong Kong, reminding him that in terms of the law of California, where the marriage was solemnized, the said Elizabeth Hargreave was entitled to half the matrimonial assets. The grounds for divorce were his 'mental cruelty', his 'persistent refusal to lead a normal social life', his 'unnecessary dedication to work at the expense of his home life', his 'excessive drinking and gambling', his 'embarrassing attentions to other women', his 'unreasonable withholding of conjugal rights' and his 'mediocre performance of same'. No mention of her shooting him. Fuller particulars of his cruelty would be provided in the petition that would be served on him shortly: meanwhile it would expedite matters and reduce expenses if he would indicate whether he intended to contest the action.

Lord, it hurt him. And mortified him. But no way would he contest it – *Unreasonable withholding of conjugal rights and his mediocre performance of same* . . . No way could he wash his dirty linen in public; no way was he going to stand in the witness box and argue about any of it, let alone his lousy sexual performance. Anything rather than that – let Elizabeth take him to the cleaners, let the divorce slip quietly through undefended, just let the earth swallow him up, let him resign his post immediately, fold his tents and steal out of this bloody awful town.

That letter arrived on a hot Saturday at the end of that long, tormenting summer, six weeks after Hargreave came out of hospital. He had intended venturing out socially for the first time since the shooting incident, and had arranged to meet Bernie Champion at the horse races in Happy Valley, the first meeting of the season: but the letter changed that. He could not face his friends with that letter ringing in his ears, nor the yacht club crowd; but neither could he face the empty apartment. So that left only one place to go, to get the hell out of himself, out of this embarrassing town: Macao.

And so it was that Alistair Hargreave, on impulse, took a taxi down to the hydrofoil jetty and boarded a vessel to the Portuguese colony of

Macao, forty miles away, on the other side of the River Pearl: and his life took a very serious turn.

Many events in life are mere coincidences, in that something happens only because something else has just happened to happen. Had the lawyer's letter not arrived that very day Hargreave would have gone to the races in Happy Valley, not to Macao, and he would not have made a fistful of money by betting recklessly on greyhound races – he knew nothing about greyhounds and didn't bet on animals whose form he had not studied. Had that letter not arrived that Saturday he would not have got drunk in the process of making a fistful of silly money and he would not have gone on to the clamorous floating casino to blow it. Hargreave, being a cautious, serious gambler, believed in quitting when he was ahead, and furthermore he eschewed games of pure chance. Had he not gone to the casino he would not have found himself throwing silly dice at the crap table, winning more money, and standing next to the beautiful Olga Romalova. Had the letter from Elizabeth's lawyer not arrived that very Saturday, had Hargreave gone to Macao the following weekend to drown his sorrows, even if he had ended up at the very same floating casino, he would not have met Olga Romalova, for her work permit expired that week and she would have returned to Russia. Had he not been winning silly money, the beautiful Olga would not have followed his bets, jumping up and down in excitement and planting a big fragrant kiss on his cheek. Had she not done that he would not have rubbed the dice against her for luck and felt her magnificent femininity as she hugged him in delight when he won yet again, he would not have been emboldened to invite her for a drink. Had he not done that, his life would have been very different.

Despite all the whisky inside him Hargreave was surprised that she accepted: he had presumed that elsewhere in the clamorous casino was a husband or a boyfriend about to reclaim her. When, at the noisy bar, she looked into his eyes and said she was totally unattached, Hargreave thought it was his lucky day. *What a beautiful, magnificent girl . . .* So when he invited her to dinner, thinking that beat-up Alistair Hargreave had made a conquest, her reply disappointed him greatly.

'Thank you, that would be very nice, but I am a singer at a night-club so we must first go there so you can arrange to take me out.'

Bitterly disappointed, was Hargreave. A prostitute – what kind of night-club singer can you 'arrange' to take out? So it wasn't his lucky night – it wasn't true love after all. A prostitute, a smashing girl like this . . . But night-clubs, and prostitutes, were simply not Hargreave's scene – he had not been to bed with a bar-girl in twenty years. So he mumbled an excuse and watched her walk away to work with regret.

It was watching her walk away that did it: those long golden legs, her silk dress sliding over her beautiful buttocks, her tumult of blonde hair down her back, the dazzling smile and cheery wave she threw over her shoulder: she was pure sexuality. If he had not watched her walk away, if he had shrugged off his alcoholic disappointment and gone back to the crap table, his life would have been very different: but for the next hour, while he drank another row of whiskies midst the Chinese clamour, that image of her sexuality steamed in his mind. Maybe she really was a singer, not a prostitute? Maybe arranging to take her out meant nothing more than advising the manager she was going to be absent for a while, perhaps it simply meant rescheduling her performance? And when he finally scraped together his drunken resolve and set out into the teeming Macao waterfront to look for her, coincidence continued to play a vital part, for he did not know which night-club she worked in. He could have wasted hours looking in the Troubadour or the China Nite or the Pearl, and given up: but he went first to the Heavenly Tranquillity because it was a well-known place he remembered hearing about over the years. And if he had been even five minutes later he would not have found her, because she was a very popular prostitute.

'Hullo, Alistair,' she murmured behind him as soon as he had sat down at the crowded bar in the glittery tourist joint, 'so am I *very* lucky tonight?'

Even then Hargreave had no actual intention of trying to go to bed with her, despite the drink: he had looked for her only out of an intoxicated desire to see that female sexuality again, and maybe to hear her sing, to admire her, to lust after her from afar. But when he turned and saw her again, that lovely face, those big blue eyes and the sparkling smile, those perfect breasts, those long golden legs, he was lost: if she was a prostitute he simply had to have her, he simply had to possess that magnificent body just once.

'Olga. What a surprise!'

'Is it? You didn't look for me? I am disappointed.'

'Will you have a drink?'

'Will you have a dance with me first?'

Oh yes . . . Alistair Hargreave was not a dancing man, but he had to feel this glorious woman close against him immediately, he just had to hold her in his arms.

Her dress was mid-thigh length to show off her long legs, her lovely

14

breasts swelled against the low-cut bodice, her smooth skin warm through the slippery silk. They danced close, and he could feel her body-heat against him, the warmth of her belly and thighs, he could feel the cleft of her buttocks under his hand, her mound of Venus pressed against him.

'You want to make love,' she whispered.

Oh yes please. Hargreave was smouldering with desire. He did not ask, 'How much?' He did not care how much.

3

It was very expensive: five hundred American dollars bar-levy to buy her out of the club for the night, plus five hundred dollars 'for me'. Hargreave knew it was an outrageous sum, that he could have her for half if he protested, but it would be ungentlemanly to bargain with a lady. He paid unflinchingly at the bar, with his winnings. He had not had a woman for a long time, and he simply had to have this glorious girl splayed out beneath him tonight.

And what a wonderful night it was. When he woke up beside her in the Estoril Hotel that Sunday morning to the sound of church bells, hungover and exhausted, he felt no remorse. He was not concerned about having been recognized in the Tranquillity club: it was a well-known tourist venue and anyway there had been nobody he knew. He did not flinch when he remembered he had not used a condom, he felt no moral guilt at the sound of those church bells.

When he woke up he was thinking of her golden nakedness, the breathtaking beauty of her as she had slipped the silk dress off her shoulders: her glorious curves, her jutting breasts, her soft hips, her long perfect legs. She was the most naked woman in the world. Then came the wildly erotic business of showering together, the glorious soapy feel of her, her breasts and buttocks and thighs gleaming, slippery: he had wanted her so much that he had not been able to produce an erection. That's how come he had not used a condom: he remembered her leading him to the bed, her riotously golden hair splayed across his loins as her wide mouth did its magic on him. That's when he had thrown caution to the wind, toppled her over and clambered on top of her nakedness, thrusting frantically up into the sweet hot depths of her.

No; no regrets. And when he woke up that sultry church-belled Macao morning with Olga's sleepy nakedness against him there was no question about an erection. And after it was over, in a crescendo such as he had never known, he had no doubt about how he was going to spend today. Lying beside her, exhausted, he said:

'Don't go. Stay.'

She sat up, tousled, and beamed down at him: 'Yes? Lovely!' Then she added apologetically, 'But I regret you must pay.'

Hargreave grinned. Of course she didn't regret it, but the solemn way she said it was endearing. 'How much?' He did not care.

'The same as last night?' she said with an anxious little frown.

'On a Sunday? Surely there's a discount for a Sunday; no night-clubs do big business today.'

'No,' she said earnestly, 'every weekend in Macao is high season. Monday to Thursday is low season, but Sunday is full price: I'm sorry, darling.' It seemed she almost meant the endearment.

'But the night-club won't know – tell them you spent the day in bed with a headache.'

She said earnestly: 'They know everything, and if I do not pay they will punish me.' She widened her eyes, made a guttural noise and drew her finger across her throat.

Hargreave grinned. 'And such a beautiful throat. Okay, but I haven't got five hundred US on me.'

'Credit-card!' She scrambled up on to her knees and hugged his head against her glorious breasts. 'I'm so happy!' She reached for the bedside telephone, punched the buttons, and spoke rapidly in Russian.

They were lying squashed up together in the bubble-bath, drinking champagne sent up by room service, when there was a knock on the door. Hargreave heaved himself up and draped a towel around his waist.

A tall white man stood outside, smiling politely. He had slick black hair, was athletically built, and carried a briefcase. 'My name is Vladimir. I have come about Olga, sir. I am the accountant.' He walked in, opened his briefcase and pulled out a credit-card machine.

Accountant? Very fancy name for a pimp. He was the guy to talk to about discounts. 'I get a different price on Sunday?'

'Will Olga return to the club at seven o'clock?'

Oh, he wanted her tonight. 'No.'

'Then it is full price, sir.' He ran the machine over the card, wrote 'Goods' on the slip, and gave it to Hargreave to sign. It was made out to Gorky Enterprises. 'You are satisfied with Olga's service, sir?'

'Oh yes.'

Vladimir produced a visiting card, printed in English on one side, Chinese on the other: there was no address but it gave a Macao telephone number. 'If you have any complaints, please call immediately. We have many girls, all very good, all speak English, sir.'

17

Lord, a thousand dollars. But Hargreave signed the slip without second thoughts.

'Thank you,' Vladimir said. 'Have a nice day.'

It was a lovely day. Afterwards, when he was to look back, it seemed the happiest day of his life to date, the start of the happiest period of his life. After finishing the champagne in the bath – her happy, slippery nakedness all over him felt like love – they had a late breakfast on their balcony overlooking the waterfront and harbour, with another bottle of champagne, while downstairs the hotel's casino hummed and tinkled.

'So tell me about yourself, Olga.'

'Where do you want me to begin?' She grinned. 'And what do you want me to leave out?'

'Nothing.'

'Not even about my profession?' She added, with a twinkle in her lovely eyes, 'You must not worry about Aids, you know. I always make love only with a condom. You were the first time I did not.'

He was thankful to hear that, though he had not thought about it since the sound of the church bells. 'Why didn't you?'

She clasped her hands under her chin. 'Because . . . I wanted to do it like that. I wanted it to be natural. Because I like you. Because I was –' she searched for the word – 'reckless about you.'

He wanted to laugh, and squeezed her hand. 'Yes, I also felt reckless. Because I like you too.' He felt like a teenager.

'Because you think I am sexy?'

'Because you are *very* sexy, and very beautiful, and because you are a very nice person.'

'How do you know? All I did was take your money and say let's fuck, like a prostitute.' She smiled: 'Because you *wanted* me to be a nice person? Because you are unhappy with your wife?'

Her perspicacity surprised him. 'How do you know I even have a wife?'

'In my business you learn about people. You looked like a man who is not experienced in talking with prostitutes, you were very polite, so I thought you are probably a nice married man and such a man must be unhappy with his wife if he has followed me to my night-club when he should be at home with her.' Before he could respond she added, 'Is she nice, your wife?'

He was surprised that he wanted to talk to her about it: he had never confided in anyone except Jake McAdam, and for the last seven weeks he'd been too embarrassed about the shooting incident to show his face socially, yet here he was sitting over breakfast with a Russian prostitute and it felt as if he wanted to open his heart. But he only said:

'Yes, she's nice. However, she's gone back to America now, we're getting divorced.'

'Oh, I'm sorry.' She looked concerned. Then she snapped her fingers. 'Of course! That scar on your chest – you said it was an accident. But she shot you, your wife! I read it in the newspaper.'

He was surprised and embarrassed. Even a Macao prostitute knew about his humiliation? 'You read the Hong Kong newspapers?'

'And your photograph, I recognize you now!' She pointed a scarlet fingernail at him. 'You told me you are a business man, but really you are a big lawyer!' She swept both hands down over her golden locks. 'That big English wig!'

Hargreave smiled wanly. 'So you do read the papers.'

'For my English. So,' she smiled, 'you are a lawyer. So your nice wife is asking for lots of nice money in her divorce?'

'Something like that.'

'And now you are spending so much money for me!' She took both his hands across the table and sparkled mischievously: 'So I will make it a very good day for you, don't worry, darling! We will make love as much as you like. Any way you like! Tell me how you like to do it.'

Hargreave seemed to feel his loins turn over. He grinned.

'Let's check out of here and go to the Bella Mar Hotel, it's more secluded. And I'd like you to go home and change into a daytime dress. Bring a bikini, they've got a nice pool at the Bella Mar. I'll meet you there. Know where it is?'

'Of course I know the Bella Mar.'

4

Of course she knew it – she was a Macao whore. But that did not trouble Hargreave – he was going to have a nice day for a change. A lovely day! Nor did it worry him that he might be recognized – in an appropriate dress Olga would be just another tourist. Nonetheless he checked the hotel register when he signed in and was relieved that all the guests were foreigners; nor was there anybody he knew in the bar or on the terrace.

The Bella Mar is a grand old Portuguese hotel on the knoll, over-looking the tree-lined esplanade and the Pearl River estuary. The floors are polished wood, the ceilings are high and a sweeping staircase leads up to airy, old-fashioned suites with ceiling fans. The blue swimming pool is on the terrace below the verandah.

Olga Romalova dived and swam the length underwater, her long blonde hair streaming silkily behind her. She broke surface at the shallow end, her hair plastered. 'How much?'

'Nine seconds. You're improving.'

'Once more.'

She climbed up the ladder, gushing sparkling water, and walked back to the deep end in her tiny bikini. Hargreave, seated at a table under a beach umbrella drinking a Tom Collins, watched her every movement. She was truly beautiful. There were other couples at other tables, all watching her. The Chinese waiters were watching her. They doubtless knew her, but Hargreave did not care: they didn't know who he was and he was happy – surely every man here must envy him, every woman must surely envy her exuberant beauty. Olga came to the deep end of the pool, held up her finger and demanded, 'Ready?'

'Ready.' Hargreave looked at his wristwatch.

'*Now!*' She dived in like a goddess and streamed frantically under-water, her feet kicking. She gushed up at the shallow end. 'Yes?'

'Yes – eight seconds flat.'

A man at a table clapped, then everybody was clapping good-naturedly. Olga climbed out of the pool, beaming, gave them a wave and flopped down in her chair under the umbrella. She picked up her vodka and grinned: 'I am improving, last week my best time was ten seconds. It is because I have stopped smoking.'

'You come to the Bella Mar often?'

She shrugged. 'Sometimes. It depends.'

'I wanted to be an athlete,' Olga said, 'a swimmer. Athletes make good money in Russia. But there was no pool on the collective, so I swam in the river. So *cold*. For a pool I must go fifty kilometres on the bus. So expensive. So I thought, I will be a gymnast. I could walk on my hands, do backward somersaults. At my school we had parallel bars, a springboard, climbing ropes. I practised like crazy. But my teacher told me I am too big to succeed.'

'Can you still do backward somersaults?'

'Yes. Want to see?'

'Later,' Hargreave grinned.

She continued: 'My mother always told me that the farm is not good enough for me, I must leave when I grow up – so little money, so much work. She died when I was ten. So I looked after my father, he was a sick man – he was a foreman, a very good farmer, but he was always sick, with tuberculosis, he died when I was fourteen. My big brother, he left many years before to work in the mines. So I went to an orphanage. I wanted to study to become a vet, but there were many difficulties, so when I was sixteen I went to work in a factory in Yekaterinburg. Do you know where that is?'

'No.'

'In the Urals. Very cold in winter. Big city, grey skies, grey buildings. I worked in an aluminium factory. We made plates, cups, pots, knives, forks. Millions and millions. But nobody buys them because people do not like the taste of aluminium. But still we make them, because Gosplan says so, because of the mines and the big hydro-electric stations producing the power. You know Gosplan? It is our big ministry for economics.'

'Yes.'

'Nobody buys our aluminium plates. Our wages are very little, and always late. Then we heard that some KGB men are stealing our plates and cups and making them flat with a steam roller and selling it to the West for much money. We were angry. But still we went on making plates for the KGB to steal because Gosplan said we must. Then one day the factory director sends for me. In his office is a man I haven't seen. He says, do I want to be an actress, because I am pretty.'

'He was wrong. You're beautiful.'

21

'I said, "Yes, of course!" So immediately I go to Moscow. Many days by train. So exciting. In Moscow they say to me: "We are the KGB, Mosfilm does not really want you, *we* want you to be a diplomat."'

'A diplomat? How old were you?'

'Eighteen. Of course I was not going to be a diplomat, they were cheating me from the start, I was going to be one of their girls who sleeps with foreigners to get information. And for blackmail. But I did not know then. They said: "To be a diplomat you must first learn how to dress nicely, Western ways." So they began to train me.'

'What did they teach you?'

She grinned. 'Mostly how to make love. And I already knew that, most Russian girls learn that very young because there is nothing else to do. I was kept in a hostel like a student, but I was really a hostess for KGB officers. I was taught to cook and entertain, even to sing Western songs, how to dance, very sexy, but after the party – there were always many parties – after the party I had to go to bed with one of my trainers.'

'How did you like that?'

She shrugged. 'I hated it, but they said it was part of my training. One of them I liked, the others I didn't like.'

'Were you paid a salary?'

'Yes, I was working for the state. Then after only six months Gorbachev disbanded the KGB. Everybody was very anxious, and angry also. Then my trainers told me I was being sent to Istanbul to continue my studies. But, of course, when I got there I had to be a whore.'

Oh, Hargreave was so glad to learn she had been tricked. 'Istanbul? Did you protest?'

'At first I cried and cried, and argued. But what can I do? They hit me. The other girls told me the KGB would kill me if I tried to run away. They said a girl called Natasha had been killed, as a lesson. And I had no passport, no money. No job in Russia. And we were kept in this big house with high walls, and there were guards.'

Hargreave thought, *Oh, you poor child.* 'And? Who were your customers?'

'Rich Turks. Rich Arabs. And some Westerners, businessmen, English, Italian, Germans.'

'How did you feel?'

He felt a stab of anguish when she shrugged. 'Afterwards I got used to it. It was a nice big house, nice rooms, nice bar, nice garden, good food. The madam saved your money for you, every month you got paid, you could send it home or buy things, or put it in the bank. So

I thought, this is better than Yekaterinburg, better than the KGB hostel where I got fucked for nothing.'

Hargreave didn't want to hear that. 'Were you allowed out?'

'Only when the KGB trust you. But if you run away they will catch you. And how can you run away without a passport?'

'Did you try?'

'Not then. Natasha tried. They killed her.'

Lord. You poor child. 'So the KGB were still functioning despite being disbanded?'

'No, the Mafia was controlling us. But many KGB are Mafia now.'

Yes, Hargreave thought, that was common knowledge. Right now the Hong Kong police were trying to deal with the Russian Mafia who were using Hong Kong as a staging post for international smuggling. And here he was sitting in the Bella Mar Hotel with one of the Mafia's girls: in principle he was compromising himself. But he did not care, he was happy for the first time in a long while, he was having a lovely day with this exotic girl, and she had nothing to do with smuggling – prostitution in Macao and smuggling in Hong Kong were far removed from each other, the one almost legal, the other not. Nonetheless he said:

'Please don't tell any of your friends who I am.'

She smiled. 'Of course not, darling. In my business you must be discreet. You would be surprised what important Hong Kong people come to us, but I won't tell even you.'

Even him? That felt like a compliment. He said, 'Vladimir, the guy who came with the credit-card machine this morning, he wouldn't know who I am, he wouldn't read the papers, would he? He's got my name now.'

'No. And even if he knew he wouldn't do anything, he only wants business.'

'Is he a big noise in the Mafia, or is he just a pimp?'

'A pimp. He says he was KGB, a big man, but he is nothing.' She squeezed his hand. 'Don't worry, darling, I won't let anybody hurt you, I like you.'

He liked her too, he just didn't like a pimp knowing his name. But he put it out of his mind. For heaven's sake, the Triad societies con- trolled most of the girlie-bars and brothels in Hong Kong, did that mean every government official who went to a girlie-bar in Wanchai was compromising himself?

'And how long were you in Istanbul?' he said.

'Almost three years. Then I was sent back to Moscow. That is when

I tried to run away. One of my girlfriends was from Estonia, which had become independent from Russia, she said it was nice there, we can make a new life. But I had no passport, the Mafia had it. So I bought a gun, and we went on the train and I tried to hide when we crossed the border. But the Estonian police found me and sent me back to Moscow. I was very worried. I got a job in a café but the Mafia soon found me. They punished me because they said I had not finished my contract, and they kept me in an apartment and made me work.'

'Your contract? Had you signed a contract?'

'Yes. I signed many forms when they said I was training for diplomatic work.'

'For how long was this contract?'

'Three years. But now I am on a one-year contract.'

'And how did they punish you?'

'They beat me with their fists. But not too bad because I had to be in good condition to work. But they said next time they would kill me. So I did not try to run away again.'

Oh you poor child. 'So they made you work in a whorehouse?'

'No, I was sent out to customers in the big hotels, like the Metropole. That is a famous Moscow hotel. But I always had a guard with me. Then, after two months, they sent me here, to Macao. As a "dancer".'

What a sad history. 'How do you like it here?'

'I like it. Here we are free, because we cannot escape to China, or Hong Kong. I like Macao.'

'And the work?' Please God she didn't like the work.

She shrugged. 'I am used to it. It means nothing now, to me it is just like being a gymnast, or being a tennis player. What else can I do?'

Oh dear. But it had meant something last night, and this morning, hadn't it – all that hadn't been faked, had it? 'And how long will you stay?'

'Until next Thursday. My Macao work-permit is finished then.'

Next Thursday? Hargreave stared at her. And what he felt was *No* . . . Oh, no, she couldn't just disappear, this gorgeous girl.

'Where are you going?'

'Back to Russia. Moscow.'

'And in Moscow you go back to work? Where?'

'I don't know. In the big hotels.' She smiled. 'Will you visit me, darling?'

Jesus. 'But do you want to go?'

'No. I would like to stay here.' She grinned: 'Then you can visit me every weekend?'

'Can't you get your work-permit extended?'

She raised her eyebrows. 'The Portuguese police? They will want a lot of *cumshaw* to extend it. And Vladimir's boss says it is important to change the girls every year.'

'How much *cumshaw* will the Macao police want?'

'I don't know. Perhaps a thousand US dollars.'

Lord, was he mad to be thinking like this? It was on the tip of his tongue to say 'I'll pay it', but instead he asked, 'And would Vladimir agree?'

She beamed at him. 'Oh darling, do you really want to do it? So I can work –' she made her eyes sparkle – 'really *work* with you?'

Oh Lord, Lord . . . He grinned weakly. 'Would Vladimir agree?'

'Vladimir, yes, but I do not know about his boss.'

'Who's his boss – where is he?'

'He is in Moscow, I have never seen him. But I think he will agree, why not? Oh darling!' She squeezed both his hands. 'Is this really true?'

Hargreave sat back. Oh God, what was he doing? He smiled.

'I must think. It's a lot of money.' He hated saying it – a gentleman does not talk about money at a time like this. And that's only the start of it, he thought, she would expect him back each weekend.

'Yes, a lot of money, I understand. And now your wife, too.' Then she brightened: 'Do not worry, darling – we still have a whole afternoon and a whole night!' She grinned: 'And I am going to make it so wonderful for you that you will say yes! What do you want? Do you want handstands? Backward somersaults? Belly dancing?'

Hargreave threw back his head and laughed.

And, oh dear, it almost felt like love. He knew it was not, of course, but that was how it felt.

She did make it wonderful. Afterwards, lying on the big four-poster bed under the ceiling fan she whispered, 'And you were wonderful. Last night you were drunk, and you had no dinner, but finally you were okay. This morning you had a big hangover, and you'd had no breakfast yet, but you were good. But this afternoon you had your breakfast *and* your lunch, and you were wonderful! I had a lovely orgasm, darling.'

'Did you really?' He felt very pleased. *Mediocre performance of same*, huh?

'Yes.' She leaned on her elbow and looked at him earnestly. 'Didn't you know? That was *real*. Oh, okay –' she swept her hair from her eyes – 'prostitutes always pretend, huh? To make the man finish quicker?

25

Right, that's what I do – but with *you*? No. That was real. You know why?'

'Why?'

'Because you are a very sexy man. And because I like you so much.'

Him, a sexy man? He grinned – he wished Liz's lawyers could hear this. Olga flopped down beside him again. She snuggled against him.

'I was going to say I love you. That is what I sometimes have to say. It is bullshit, of course, but that is what they like to hear, maybe. But I will not bullshit you. So I say, I like you, *very* much.'

He squeezed her golden shoulders. 'And I like you, very much.'

'Okay. So now I let you go to sleep, and when I wake up I give you another triple-A blowjob so you like me more, then I do a belly dance, then some backward somersaults, then we have a nice dinner. *Oh . . .*' she squeezed him, 'I do not want to go back to Russia.'

He woke up in the sunset. She was still asleep, spreadeagled on her belly, her hair flamed across the pillow, her lovely buttocks naked. And, no, he did not want her to go back to Russia next Thursday, never to be seen or heard of again. Looking at her lying there made him want to mount her again, it seemed he couldn't get enough of her. Yes, but what about the money? It's not the thousand bucks up front for the Portuguese police, that's easy enough, what about every time you come to see her, even if it's only twice a month – what are you letting yourself in for? How can you afford it, even *once* a month? Of course you shouldn't do it – it's crazy to even think about it, so put it out of your mind. But he looked at her lying there, and he could not put it out of his mind. He got off the bed carefully so as not to wake her, went to the bathroom and turned on the shower.

Fuck the money? You'll make a deal with her? Live dangerously? Cross the bridges as you come to them?

Yes, and fuck Elizabeth's lawyer as well, with his law of Community of Property? He stepped under the shower. Yes, cross the bridges as you come to them! Live dangerously! You've never lived until today!

When he emerged from the bathroom she was sitting on the bed with the telephone to her ear, speaking in Russian. She gabbled for another ten seconds then banged down the receiver, jumped up beaming, arms wide, and laced her hands behind his neck. 'I have done it!'

'An extension to your work-permit?'

She was delighted with herself. 'At first I thought I make a deal with you – I give you a discount every time until you have got back the thousand dollars *cumshaw* for the police. Then I thought, no, this is my business not yours, so *I* will pay the *cumshaw*! *And* I will give you a discount every time! And so I telephoned Vladimir and told him!'

Hargreave wanted to laugh. 'And it's arranged?'

'Vladimir agrees, and the police will agree. Vladimir will telephone the boss in Russia tomorrow. Oh darling –' she jumped up and down – 'I am so happy! And you?'

Yes, he was recklessly happy. Fuck the money! 'But Olga – I will pay the thousand *cumshaw*.'

She turned out of his arms, her palm up. 'No. Not fair.'

Okay, thank God. 'And you think Vladimir's boss will agree?'

'Why not? But I will pray!'

He grinned: 'You're religious?'

She put on a mock frown, placed her fists on her lovely hips. 'What do I look like? A *Communist*?'

Hargreave threw back his head and laughed.

PART II

5

All the next week it seemed he could not get the image of her out of his mind. Her glorious nakedness, the sweet smell and taste and feel of her, and the memory of her standing at the immigration gates at the hydrofoil jetty that Monday morning, midst the clamour and jostling, the smells of diesel, of China, smiling all over her lovely face, her hair still wet from the shower, waving energetically: *'Goodbye – goodbye . . .'* Hargreave went aboard the hydrofoil and slumped back in his seat. He could not wipe the smile off his face as he sat back in the air-conditioned first-class cabin skimming across the hazy South China Sea. And when the distant islands of the British colony loomed on the horizon, the myriad of ships from around the world at anchor, then the skyscrapers rearing up along the harbour front of Hong Kong and Kowloon, the most expensive real estate in the world with its mad money-making and its dense traffic and swarming people, it seemed he could not bear to wait to get back to sleepy little Macao next Friday, to Olga. He did not care what the weekend had cost him.

He disembarked at the ferry terminals, queued up to pass through the congested immigration barriers, then joined the sweating crowd along the walkway above Connaught Road. He hurried along the raised thoroughfares, past the marbled stock exchange with its fountains, where he had lost so much money the year before, past the elevated turn-offs to teeming Central with its hotels and shops and alleyways and towering business houses, until he descended through the crush towards Statue Square. *Lord, give me sleepy Macao every time.* Statue Square was teeming with pedestrians hurrying to work, cars and taxis and buses pouring out pollution around it. He hurried past the grand old Legislative Council building that used to be the Supreme Court, through the park that was the cricket club in the good old days, and crossed into roaring Queensway with its sweeping flyovers. Three hundred yards ahead the Supreme Court building reared up bleakly amongst the skyscrapers. He reached the basement parking area and rode up in the elevator to the first floor. He crossed the big atrium and entered the Crown Prosecutor's chambers.

31

He was almost an hour late. There was the usual Monday morning bustle, his lawyers heading off for the courts in their wigs and gowns. He hastened down the long corridor, greeting his staff, and entered his chambers. There were several policemen waiting to consult him, and both his secretaries were speaking on telephones. He signalled to Miss Ho, entered his big office and closed the door. He slung his overnight bag on the long conference table and went to his desk. There were half a dozen telephone messages from policemen asking for an appointment, his in-basket high with files.

Miss Ho entered. 'Good morning, Mr Hargreave.'

'Morning, Norma. What problems?'

'No problems, Mr Hargreave. Nobody sick.'

What a wonder! Over a hundred lawyers to worry about, and this Monday nobody was sick – it had to be a good omen.

'Well I'm sick, Norma, sick and tired of this job, so treat me gently today.' He slapped the pile of files. 'I've got all this to read. Those policemen out there – send them to Mr Downes and Mr Jefferson and Mr Watkins, and if you're stuck send them to Timbuktu.'

'Yes, sir,' Norma said, 'but what about Superintendent Champion? He's just telephoned for an appointment.' She added: 'The uranium case?'

Hargreave sighed. 'Okay, I'll see Mr Champion, but nobody else today.'

'Where were you on Saturday?' Bernie Champion complained, big and sweaty in his suit. 'You said you'd be at the races. And I was going out for a Chinese chow last night, thought I'd invite you, I wanted to pick your brains.'

'Which you're doing now?'

'Which I hope to do now. You look like death, where were you?'

Hargreave felt wonderful. 'I was sailing.'

'Like hell, your boat was in the yacht club all weekend, large as life. Who is she?'

'I went to Macao.' Hargreave smiled.

'Macao, huh? Hope you wore a condom. How's the chest?'

'Healed very well. What's the problem with the uranium case?'

Champion sighed. 'Okay,' he said, 'you don't want to talk about it, but I'm your friend and I'm asking you seriously, how are you?'

Hargreave hated this solicitude. 'I'm fine, Bernie.'

Champion grunted. 'Haven't seen you around for a while, that's all. Max, Jake and I, we were expecting you at the races, said you'd come.' He raised his eyebrows: 'And Liz?'

'She's fine too. She's divorcing me, I got the letter on Saturday.'

Champion looked at him. 'Divorce? I heard she was coming back.'

'*What?*' Hargreave stared.

'Rumour at the yacht club. She phoned somebody and said she's coming back, don't know who. But listen, pal.' He sat forward. 'If you want her back, fine, I'll play violins. But I've seen plenty of domestic strife in my thirty years in the cops, and if there's going to be any more, don't have the gun around. We nearly lost you. Imagine if she'd really hit you? You'd be six feet under and she'd be in jail. We don't want that, for either of you.'

Oh God . . . Hargreave massaged his forehead. Liz returning, just when he was starting to feel he could show his face again? 'She's not coming back, it's just a rumour. Her lawyer's letter was only written last week, and it was very explicit.'

Champion said sympathetically, 'And how do you feel about a divorce?'

'Please, I don't want to talk about it, Bernard. Now what about this case?'

The uranium case – Hargreave was sick of it. It wasn't a case, it was a big amorphous file of theory and hearsay, mostly Investigation Diary reporting rumours which came to little. But it was Bernie Champion's pet investigation. The only hard evidence was that a year ago the German police had arrested an elderly man called Wessels at Munich airport carrying a small sample of radio-active weapons-grade uranium in a glass jar. Enriched uranium is the basic ingredient in the manufacture of nuclear weaponry. Mr Wessels had just arrived from Moscow when he was arrested, and he had been about to board an aircraft to Hong Kong. He had refused to tell the German police how he had acquired the uranium in Russia, or to whom he was going to deliver it in Hong Kong: then, whilst being interrogated, he had died of a heart attack, leaving everybody none the wiser. The German police had sought the cooperation of the Hong Kong and Russian authorities. The Hong Kong police suspected that the notorious Chinese Triad societies were involved, intending to purchase large quantities of uranium to re-sell to terrorist organizations or warmongers like Gaddafi of Libya or Saddam of Iraq: but no evidence was uncovered, only rumours. A certain Colonel Simonski of the Moscow police had tried to trace the source of the uranium, without success: Russia was in chaos following the collapse of Communism but the government and all the personnel at nuclear sites insisted that none of their inventory had been stolen, every gram being accounted for and stored under tight security. Simonski had filed a detailed report to his superiors alleging, inter alia, that

33

corrupt Russian bureaucrats were hand in glove with Mafia gangs to export nuclear material to Third World countries: he had promptly been removed from his post in the Organized Crime Squad and assigned to administrative duties. But his investigations were continuing, unofficially. There were some statements, forwarded to Champion by Simonski from Russian informers, who reported that this Russian crook had reported to this other Russian crook that this Russian bureaucrat at this godforsaken Russian nuclear plant had a deal with this unnamed Russian scientist who had not been paid his salary for six months to flog uranium for a staggering amount for export to Mr Gadhafi or Mr Saddam to blow us all to Kingdom Come in World War III. All serious stuff – but all hearsay.

'So what's new?' Hargreave said.

'Read the last page of the diary.'

Hargreave read it. More forgettable Russian names reporting rumours of a delivery of uranium to Moscow for shipment by air to the Far East.

Hargreave nodded. 'Bad news. But where exactly are they going to ship it to?'

'Right here,' Champion said emphatically. 'Hong Kong. Because we're a huge duty-free port. For onward shipment to somewhere like North Korea, or the Middle East.' He sat forward. 'So I want your recommendation for more investigation money, I want to go to Vladivostok and Moscow and pay for information and get some statements from witnesses, so we can nail the Russian Mafia when they fly into Hong Kong. But the Commissioner of Police is worried this is a wild goose chase. However, he'll allow me the funds if you recommend it.'

Hargreave was inclined to agree with the Commissioner. 'But this is an offshore investigation so far, in Russia. How can I recommend paying out Hong Kong taxpayers' money?'

'Because,' Champion said, 'it *ain't* offshore. Because when this stuff arrives in Hong Kong, who is receiving it, working with the Russian Mafia? The 14K. Terence Chang himself.'

Hargreave sighed. He'd heard all this before from Champion. Yes, everybody would love to nail the 14K, the biggest, strongest, nastiest Triad society in the world. And Terence Chang, the grand master. 'But where's your evidence?'

Bernie Champion tapped his head. 'Trust me. Recommend the money and Simonski and I will get the witnesses' statements in Russia, the plans for the shipment, who's going to receive it in Hong Kong, the works. Then when that uranium leaves Russia we'll do an Entebbe raid on the airport and catch everybody redhanded. Work backwards from there and uncover the whole murderous network – World War Three averted.'

'Which airport will you raid?' Hargreave demanded. 'We don't want radio-active uranium flying into Hong Kong!'

Champion said irritably, 'How do I know which airport? I haven't *seen* a Russian witness yet!' He waved a hand. 'Hell, man, this is the biggest, most important investigation imaginable – nuclear weapons to blow us all to smithereens, and you want to know which airport I'm going to catch the crooks at?' He shook his fat face. 'I don't know, do I, until I've done the investigation with Simonski. But that takes money. Simonski hasn't got access to police funds because he's been removed from Organized Crime – and the Russian police have no money anyway.'

'How much do you want?'

Champion pointed at the file. 'It's all itemized in there.'

Hargreave sighed. 'Right, I'll read the file again. But I'll have to discuss it with the Attorney General.'

'Why? You're the Director of Public Prosecutions.'

'Because he's my boss.'

Champion snorted. 'Notionally. Jesus, Al,' he appealed, 'can't you see how important this is? Imagine if the Islamic Jihad or the IRA could build nuclear weapons!'

Hargreave put the file on top of his in-basket. 'I'll read it.'

'How about dinner tonight?' Champion said.

'I won't have an answer for you by tonight, Bernie.'

'No, I meant just dinner. Haven't seen you for ages.' Champion looked at him appraisingly. 'You need to get out of yourself, have some fun. You look exhausted.'

Fun? Hargreave had never had so much fun in his life – that's why he looked exhausted. 'Better not, Bernie, I've got a lot of homework to do and I need an early night.'

Which was certainly true. He was tired when he got home; all he wanted to do was have a few drinks and something to eat and hit the sack. But suddenly he was determined to do something about himself physically, to get into better shape. For Olga. So he went jogging.

He had not jogged for months and he certainly did not feel like it today, but he forced himself to do four kilometres round the mid-Peak roads, sweating in the sunset. It was agony but he kept it up. Olga was twenty-three, for God's sake, and if he hoped to keep up with her he had to pull himself together, get some muscle-toning. Preserve the remnants of his youth. Tomorrow he would go to the gym. And he must do something about his diet – eat better: three meals a day instead of one and a half. He jogged doggedly to the supermarket at the bus terminus and bought some liver. He walked back to his apartment block with it. While the *amah* prepared it, he made himself go through the Canadian Air Force exercises that he used to do: press-ups, sit-ups, stretching. He was exhausted when he finished, sweating, but he felt good.

And virtuous. He showered, and he felt glowing. He looked at himself in the mirror. His pallor had gone. Forty-six years old – and she's twenty-three. Oh, those breasts. Those legs. That creamy smile . . . *You've got to get in shape or you'll just be another old guy trying to hang on to a young chick.* No whisky this week – and get some vitamin pills tomorrow. He drank only two bottles of beer before dinner, and although he did not like liver, he ate it all. He went straight to bed afterwards. His last thought was of Olga, what she was doing. He groaned – he could not bear to think of her with another man.

The next morning he did more than buy vitamin pills, he telephoned Dr Bradshaw. 'Ian, I want a tonic, can I come to see you?'

'Sure, what kind of tonic?'

'Something to give me a boost, I'm on a health-kick. Jogged four kilometres last night.'

'Hell, take it easy,' Ian said. 'How do you feel now?'

'Just fine. Stiff but good. And I want some advice on diet.'

'Don't overdo it on the exercise, we're not as young as we used to be. What brought this on?'

'And Ian – can you give me something to improve my sex-life?'

'*Hey!*' Ian said. 'This is good news! Look, I'll give you a course of vitamin B shots, but health is the best aphrodisiac. Good food – but watch the cholesterol. And watch the exercise at your age; don't jog, buy a mountain bike.'

At his age. At lunchtime, instead of going to the Hong Kong Club for a beer and a sandwich, Hargreave went to the gymnasium near the Peak tram terminus, with Ian Bradshaw's vitamin B shot buzzing in his system. He bought a season ticket.

It was years since he had been to a gym and he was not sure how to use all the equipment correctly, but he watched the next guy and followed suit. Lord, it was hard work. The gym was milling with sweating, muscled young men who knew what they were doing and Hargreave felt self-conscious: he was not flabby, but he was out of condition. And so pale – it was weeks since he had been sailing and he had lost his tan – and he wouldn't be sailing this weekend, no sir. Then some older men came in, and he did not feel so bad – they were out of condition too. Then he felt worse – *they* knew how to use the machines, they weren't sweating and puffing like he was. Hargreave watched them furtively as he doggedly slogged his way through the equipment. He was exhausted when he reached the end of the circuit, his legs and arms trembly. But by the time he got back to his chambers, after a hot shower and a nutritious lunch at the gym's health bar, he felt great. He wanted to tell everybody where he'd been. Then the telephone rang.

'A Miss Romalova for you, sir,' said Miss Ho.

'Put her through! Olga! Are you all right?'

She chuckled. 'I am very well, except for my poor pussy. And my heart, my heart is very sore also.' Hargreave was blushing. 'Will my heart get better on Friday?'

'Yes.' Oh yes, he could not wait for Friday. 'So your work-permit is okay?'

'Yes, the police have extended for three months. And the big boss has agreed also.'

Oh, *yes*. 'Well, I'll be there on the seven o'clock ferry.'

'Lovely! Which hotel do you want to stay in?'

'The Bella Mar.'

'So expensive. Why not another hotel, not so much?'

'No, the Bella Mar.' He had to have her in one of those airy, exotic suites, beauty like hers deserved the Bella Mar.

'Shall I reserve? Maybe if I reserve I can get a small commission.'

'Fine.' Hargreave grinned.

'I will give it back to you.'

'No, you keep it,' he laughed.

She seemed to accept that as reasonable. 'I cannot meet you at the ferry, darling, because I must be at the club. But do not come there because then you must pay entrance, and the drinks are so expensive. Telephone me there when you are ready, and I will come to the hotel. But you will have to pay the bar-levy, I'm sorry.'

'That's all right.' Talk of money made him uncomfortable.

'But I will give you a discount for me, darling, don't worry. And we will have a lovely weekend, I promise.'

Hargreave grinned, blushing: 'And I promise *you*.' He wanted to tell her about his health-kick but he felt silly.

'Oh darling, I am so excited. I thought about you all last night at the club.'

Hargreave didn't want to hear about the club. 'I thought about you too.'

'Did you really? I am very pleased. Okay, I must go to sleep now, I have to work tonight.'

Work. He did not want to think about it.

After he hung up he slumped back in the chair, and tried to make himself think about it. Lord, what am I doing, feeling like this about a . . . ? Say it – a *whore*? Feeling possessive . . . romantic . . . smitten. Feeling . . . over the moon about her. Aren't you making a bit of a fool of yourself? Don't forget she's a whore.

But I wouldn't be the first man to get smitten by a whore. Whores can be fascinating. Exotic, romantic, even, you wouldn't be the first man to fall in love with a whore.

Fall in love? What are you talking about, man? You're not in *love*, you're just in *lust*. You've had a bit of a tough time with Liz, unloved, sex-starved, so it just feels like love, you just feel sorry for yourself. Whores are for *fun*, not love . . .

Okay, so have fun. Enjoy it, stop analysing it. Stop thinking about her 'work', and her 'customers', stop flinching about 'discount' and be grateful for it, grab every discount she gives you because this fun is going to cost you plenty if you keep it up. A three-month extension on her visa? How can you keep up with this for three months? And you won't want to, you'll burn the whole thing out soon and she'll go back to Russia and you'll be relieved. So be cavalier, just *enjoy* . . .

But cavaliers were fit, cavaliers could keep up with their lovers, they did not fall by the wayside just because they were forty-six. He felt tired when he got home from chambers, and he wanted a stiff whisky, but he made himself go out to jog again. But he only managed two kilometres before his heart and his knees told him to stop: the image of her nakedness could not beat the ache in his legs today. *So, you gave yourself a workout at lunchtime, don't overdo it.* He walked back to his apartment block on Mansfield Road. He had one beer, one whisky, two boiled eggs, and went to bed. He was asleep before eight o'clock.

The next morning he could hardly stand. His knees were not swollen but they were giving him agony.

'Cartilage inflammation,' Ian Bradshaw said cheerfully on Wednesday. 'From jogging – told you not to do it. Buy a bicycle, I said. Or an exercycle, one of those stationary things that executives use. And buy yourself a pair of proper running shoes – but don't run, go for walks. Get the best, with springy soles. And for the next week that's all you can wear on your feet.'

'But I can't wear running shoes to chambers.'

'You're the boss, aren't you? Get a black pair, to go with your pinstripe suit, I'll give you a medical certificate saying you're a stretcher-case without them. Wear them to court, to cocktail parties, or you'll have a cartilage removal operation – want that?'

'No,' Hargreave said sincerely.

'Otherwise you're in good shape,' Ian said. 'Heart fine. Got some colour again. Let's look at my scar?'

Hargreave peeled back his shirt. Ian peered.

'You're healthy. Getting older, that's all. I did a good job on that bullet, what's left is pretty sexy. Tell the girls it was a jealous husband, makes them feel protective.' He sat back. 'What news of Liz?'

Hargreave pulled his shirt back on. 'We're getting divorced.'

Ian nodded. 'Still in San Francisco?'

Hargreave buttoned his shirt. 'I think so.'

'No truth in the rumour she's coming back to town?'

Jesus. 'Who told you that?'

'Yacht club. Don't know the source.'

Hargreave's heart sank. Just when he was going to have some fun. 'I've just received her lawyer's letter. If she's coming back it's just to pack the rest of her things.'

'You can come and stay in my guest room while she does,' Ian offered. 'You don't want any more scars. Did you marry under Californian law?'

'Yes.'

Ian shook his head. 'Same with me and Janet. Community of Property, half of everything you own. If Janet divorced me I'd be in trouble. Okay!' He slapped Hargreave's arm and stood up. 'Just remember you're forty-something, not thirty-something, come back for another vitamin B jab next week, and eat your wheaties. And whoever-she-is should have a smile all over her face. But no jogging. Buy an exercycle if you don't want a bicycle.'

6

He ended up buying both. He went to Lane Crawfords for the super sports shoes – they didn't have his size in black, he had to take a white pair – then he went to buy an exercycle. There were all kinds. Hargreave went for the most expensive model, with various speedometers and clocks and mileometers and calorie-counters. State-of-the-art. Made in America. And expensive, compared to similar machines made in China, Korea, Hong Kong, Japan. 'But much better everything.' Hargreave wanted much better everything. For Olga? No – for *himself*. About time he spent some money on himself. He arranged to have it delivered to his apartment, and he was about to go back to his chambers when he spied the mountain bicycles.

They were impressive. So gleaming – all the colours of the rainbow, all the gear, all the variations. Hargreave spent another hour with the salesman, asking searching questions. 'What about knee-impact?' He ended up buying the latest Canadian lite-weight fibre-glass super 36-Shimano-gears job, a machine which, judging by the salesman's account, would take him over the Himalayas with ease. Nothing but the best for Hargreave! Then he had to buy the latest in crash helmets, metallic red – he fancied blue but they didn't have any. Then gloves. Then a rainproof tracksuit. And goggles. And two sweatbands – 'You must have *two*, sir . . .'

Hargreave arranged for the whole purchase to be delivered to his apartment and walked stiffly back through the crowds to his chambers. He was pleased he had grasped the nettle of his ageing body, which no lesser savant than Ian Bradshaw had said was not too bad, which Olga evidently thought was pretty damn good. *And she would know . . .*

His own wit made him grin widely.

'Enjoy,' he said to himself. 'Just enjoy . . .'

But it was hard work to enjoy.

His exercycle and bicycle were resplendent in the middle of his living room when he arrived home, his red helmet and other gear draped on the sofa. (Ah Moi, his *amah*, was both mystified and amused.) Hargreave decided not to ride his new bicycle today: he was stiff all over, it was hot outside, the rush-hour was still on, all good reasons for the Great Indoors. With determination he got into his tennis shorts, pulled on his new sports shoes, switched on his television, mounted his new exercycle, checked that all his dials were on zero, and began to pedal.

He pedalled hard, staring at the television; within moments he was exhausted. He stopped. He looked at the mileometer: some four hundred yards. He looked at the clock: thirty-two seconds. He looked at the calorie-counter – not a sausage. And so *boring*.

Well, so these things take time – he had found the exercycle at the gymnasium hard work too. Maybe he should start with the mountain bike.

Hargreave put on his flash red helmet and descended in the elevator with his flash new Canadian Super-lite, Shimano-36-gear, hot-and-cold-running-water mountain bike. He mounted it, and set off. 'Into the Unknown . . .'

And, Lord, it *was* the unknown. It was thirty years since Hargreave had ridden a bicycle; he had forgotten what hard work is required of the legs. The area immediately surrounding his apartment complex was flat, but within two circuits his legs were aching. He came to the exit and stopped for a little rest. From here he had the choice of three directions: the steep, winding road up towards the Peak, or a more gentle incline around the Peak, or the road that led downhill towards Central. Rush-hour traffic was using all three roads. Hargreave got the ache out of his legs and chose the road that inclined gently around the side of the Peak. He adjusted his helmet, selected second gear, waited for a gap in the traffic, and went for it. He pedalled flat out across the road, then swung right, uphill.

He pedalled furiously as traffic overtook him. The ache came crashing back into his legs, his heart started pounding. He pedalled and pedalled, feeling nervous now midst the sweeping traffic roaring up from behind. He pedalled and pedalled, standing now, toiling, teeth clenched, desperately trying to keep to the extreme left of the road, out of harm's way. He pedalled and pedalled, trying to think of Olga to obliterate the pain; then he just had to stop. He wobbled to a halt beside the kerb.

He was exhausted: his whole body was trembling, his legs crying out; even his arms ached. His head was hot in the helmet, and he took it off. A legal friend passing in his Jaguar recognized him and shouted 'Go, Al, go!' Hargreave managed a sheepish wave. So now he was self-conscious as well as exhausted. If they knew why he was doing this, for a twenty-three-year-old Russian whore, they would kill

41

themselves with laughter. He looked backwards. Maybe he had done threequarters of a mile.

But a Hargreave does not give up easily. When the pain in his legs subsided he took a deep breath and toiled on.

But *toiled*. This gentle incline was not gentle at all. And it went on and on. He knew the road well, he thought he could visualize the turns and gradients ahead, but it all looked very different from here. He tried to put the machine into a lower gear, shoving the levers like the salesman had shown him – which made the handlebars wobble dangerously. A passing car hooted at him, swerving. Desperately he pushed both levers simultaneously and the gears crunched and jerked and then spun, in no gear at all – suddenly Hargreave's legs were whirling, he wobbled, his front wheel hit the kerb, and he crashed.

Fortunately he was going very slowly. Hargreave only toppled off his bicycle. But he landed with a nasty thump, on his side. A passing motorist hooted and laughed. Hargreave clambered up, embarrassed.

'Oh Lord . . .'

When the ache subsided in his legs, he examined the gear mechanism, cussing.

He did not understand what he was looking at, though it had seemed intelligible in the shop: there were layers of cogs on both the pedal contraption and the rear wheel: the selection of which particular cogs the chain operated at any given moment was determined by the little levers on the handlebars. Right; understood. But now the chain hung lifelessly. Hargreave gingerly lifted it with forefinger and thumb and tried to put it back on the cogs. Any cogs. The chain refused to oblige. In exasperation he wrenched, and finally the chain reluctantly took its place. Wearily Hargreave remounted, shoved off and trod on the pedals.

And fuck me if the infernal machine was not now in top gear. He wobbled to a halt again, another motorist blaring at him. 'Oh fuck off!' Hargreave muttered. He retreated to the kerb and glared down at the cogs.

'Okay, that's it!' Hargreave said – he simply did not understand the gears. He wasn't going to fuck about with the fucking chain again. So there was nothing for it but to return home – mercifully downhill – and get one of those kids in the apartment block to explain the gears to him. Grateful that his ordeal was almost over, he awaited another gap in the traffic, then wheeled his bicycle across the road. He reached the other side with doubtful safety, took a deep breath, faced his machine downhill, and mounted.

Alistair Hargreave, Director of Public Prosecutions, was about a mile uphill of the entrance of his apartment complex when he set off. Downhill, in top gear. He wearily trod on the pedals, once, twice, and the machine leaped forward like an enthusiastic pony. And off he sped.

And this was more like it! This was what he imagined when the salesman had eulogized about the Shimano 36-speed gears, making it sound as if he would whiz gracefully everywhere. Hargreave went swooping down the hill effortlessly, cool wind suddenly on his sweating face, the sunset caressing instead of beating him – this was almost like sailing! There was no other downhill traffic and he had half the swathe of road to himself. He trod on the pedals harder, and the machine surged again, going faster, and faster, the uphill traffic flashing by now. Hargreave pedalled joyously, effortlessly, gracefully, the wind whistling in his ears, drying his sweating face; harder he pedalled, and harder. And, oh, he would love to just keep going down this steep winding peak all the way down to Central, fun fun fun all the way. That's what he'd do tomorrow, by God – ride down to the Supreme Court and then take the Peak tram home with his bike and then it was downhill once more from the top of the Peak to his apartment.

That is how Hargreave was feeling on his new Canadian mountain bike as he approached the entrance to his apartment complex. Halfway down the hill his speedometer told him he was doing thirty miles an hour, threequarters the way down he was doing thirty-five. When he was a hundred yards from the entrance he was doing an exhilarating forty, and he felt twenty-three years old, like Olga. When he was fifty yards from the entrance, Hargreave began to apply his brakes for the turn.

First he applied the rear, and the machine slowed somewhat, screeching. Twenty yards from the entrance Hargreave felt he was going too fast to make the turn and he jerked on the front brakes as well and the machine lurched. Ten yards from the entrance Hargreave panicked: he had to make a ninety-degree turn into a blind gateway at terrifying speed. He wrenched on both brakes with all his might and rang his bell frantically. He hurtled towards the entrance. Two yards from it he filled his lungs and bellowed *'I'm coming!'* and he clenched his teeth and swung the handlebars.

Hargreave swung into the blind entrance at a breakneck fifteen miles an hour, slap-bang into an oncoming car. All he knew was the terrifying wobble of his hurtling turn, his wheels juddering, then the bonnet of the car looming towards him, the skid of its wheels as the driver slammed on the brakes, the blast of his hooter, the radiator roaring towards him, then *crash*! Hargreave smashed into the car head-on with a blinding jolt, his front wheel buckled and his rear wheel bucked, and he flew through the air. He went sailing over the handlebars, hit the bonnet, skidded along it, and smacked head-first into the windscreen.

The windscreen was fucked. The bike was fucked. 'And so am I.'

7

That was Wednesday. Hargreave took it very easy on Thursday. He did not go to the gym. He did not ride his exercycle. He did not have a drink. He did not even go to his chambers – he stayed in bed. But he re-read Champion's uranium file, finally making a note in the Investigation Diary that he recommended the expenditure of further police funds 'in view of the international importance'. It eased his conscience that he had done some work.

But when Friday dawned he felt wonderful. He still had some stiffness, but he was rested, he had been off the booze for thirty-six hours, his body felt wide-awake: and tonight he was going to Macao! He swung out of bed in the sunrise, to get the day by the tail good and early – and he winced. He had more than some stiffness: the wonderful feeling was only in his head. He walked to the bathroom very experimentally. His knees were still painful and he had a big bruise on his hip. He lowered himself very carefully into a hot bath and lay there, eyes closed, thinking of Olga.

After a moment he felt as excited as a teenager again, his aches and pains did not matter a damn. He knew it was crazy, but that's how he felt.

It felt even more like that as, in the sunset, the hydrofoil sped across the South China Sea towards Macao. The whole world was exotic, the haze, the mauve islands, the junks, the Pearl River mouth, and he was going to the most exotic girl in the world. He was smiling with anticipation as he swigged his cold San Miguel beer in the first-class cabin, his first drink in forty-eight hours: it was going down into his system like one of Ian Bradshaw's vitamin B shots. He was impatient with the delays at the immigration counters, but he loved the crowds, the noise, the smell of the place. He had a grin all over his face as his taxi sped and honked and swerved him along the teeming waterfront, then wound up the knoll to the gracious Bella Mar. He strode into the picturesque old hotel, and he loved every creaking floorboard and pillar and potted palm and smiling Chinese. It almost felt as if he had come home. He checked in with a flourish and hurried up to his suite with hardly a hobble. He dumped his bag, snatched a bottle of whisky out of it, poured a big shot, then picked up the telephone and dialled the Heavenly Tranquillity Nite-Club.

'Hullo, darling!' Olga cried. 'Are you really here?'

'In the flesh. In the hotel. In the bedroom. In the bed.'

'Oh darling, do not go anywhere!'

Twenty minutes later he heard her running up the staircase. He flung open the door as she burst into it. And there she was, even more beautiful than he remembered, her mass of golden hair piled up on her head, her big blue eyes sparkling, her lovely bosom bursting out of her dress, her wide laughing smile. Hargreave's heart turned over at the sheer glory of her. *'Olga . . .'*

He clutched her joyously, felt her fulsome young womanness against him; and he turned her as he kissed her and jostled her towards the bed, laughing into her mouth. She collapsed on to the bed, making giggling noises, and he fell on top of her, one hand wrenching up her dress, the other grappling with his belt. *'The door –'* He scrambled off her, his trousers halfway down, hobbled painlessly to the door, slammed it and turned back to her. Olga was laughing, her dress up round her waist, her lovely long legs bent as she raised her hips and wrestled her panties down. As Hargreave blundered towards her she hooked them on to her big toe, pulled back the elastic, then let go. They sailed through the air over his head as he collapsed, laughing, on top of her.

They had a wonderful time that weekend. For a week he had fed on the image of her beautiful body, and now he truly had her again. And despite his aches and bruises, his health-kick had paid off: it seemed he wanted to make love to her all the time. And it felt like love. It had almost felt like that last weekend when he left her waving on the jetty. For at least half the week it had still felt like that as he laboured at his exercises; only sometimes had he managed to convince himself that it was only a crazy case of lust. But this glorious weekend he knew that it was not just that, it was better – it was besottedness. He was besotted with her, her tumult of golden hair, her fragrant loins, her magnificent breasts – it seemed he could not get enough of her, there was no feeling more magnificent, more lovely than her body under his, her legs locked around his, thrusting, *thrusting* into the sweet hot depths of her. Every position she adopted was wildly erotic but the most magnificently important one was to feel her full naked beauty splayed out underneath him.

But there was plenty of laughter, too, and plenty of other fun. She loved jokes. They had the same sense of humour, the same sense of the ridiculous. She thought his health-kick was a hilarious story, and when he came to the bit about writing off his new mountain bike she went into roars of laughter. That established him as a raconteur, and thereafter, whenever he started to tell her a joke she began to giggle, even before he reached the funny part, and when he came to the punchline she threw back her head and guffawed, her lovely eyes wet.

'The way you tell a story!'

He was a scream, apparently. Hargreave knew he could tell a good tale when he felt like it, when he was in the mood, but it seemed a very long time since he had felt like that; he had forgotten how enter-taining he could be. Now he was happy, and it was lovely to be in lust with somebody who laughs a lot and thinks you're very amusing, it was delightful to laugh at his own jokes again. She was a good story-teller too. She was a natural mimic, her imitation of the English and American accents was very good. She was a born actress, and told a story with her hands and eyes and face and body-language. He was delighted to find out that Russians and English laughed at the same things, that many of his jokes had Russian versions which were often funnier.

'Darling, Russians tell lots of jokes because they drink so much because that is all there is to do, jokes and drink is all we have to laugh about.'

And it was fascinating, exotic, that she was Russian; from behind that Iron Curtain, suddenly let loose in the big wide world. He wanted to know all about her life in Russia, about her parents, her home, her schooling, her work, her friends. He built up a long series of images of her, hoeing the collective fields in the spring, harvesting in summer, the sweat running off her, her lovely girl-thighs steamy, dust and grit in her flaxen hair, her sexy hands coarsened; he imagined her bleak schoolhouse, hot in summer, cold in winter, smelling of unwashed bodies and chalk and books.

'I always sat at the very back of the class so I could cheat easier – everybody cheats all the time in Russia, darling, it is the only way to get anything –'

He imagined her swimming with her friends in the muddy river in her underwear.

'– and sometimes we swam naked, when there were no boys, that was great fun, oh that made us want to be free, to run away from Russia, swim in the lovely blue sea in the sunshine with palm trees on

47

the beach, and Coca-Cola and icecream, and then dance and fuck like crazy, like the Americans do –'

The image of a dozen Russian schoolgirls romping naked in the river was erotic, even if it was muddy. 'What made you think Americans did that? Did you have access to American books and magazines?'

'Of course, they were forbidden, but somebody always had some old magazine that had been smuggled, or from the black market, and of course we were taught at school that Americans were terrible people who only thought about eating food that makes them fat, and making money and making war – and that they fuck like crazy. Anyway, we studied the magazines and saw the fashions and the beautiful girls and the beautiful cars and the beautiful food and the white beaches with the palms and the Coca-Colas and the icecream and beef-steak, and the blue sea, and it looked pretty good to us.'

He grinned: 'And did you? Fuck like crazy?' He was not sure he wanted to hear the answer.

She shrugged. 'That's all there is to do in Russia, darling. But we were only schoolgirls, we didn't have much experience yet.'

Her candour was endearing, almost. She was a very honest soul. 'So how old were you when you first went to bed with a man?'

'Man, or a boy? I made love to my first boy when I was fourteen. Not too bad, huh? I'd had big breasts for two years. I was driving a tractor. I was having an orgasm, because the tractor seat was vibrating between my legs. This boy saw me and he said, "Come here and I'll give you a better one".'

'And he did?'

'He did.' She looked at him, her eyes sparkling with mischief, then she laughed and hugged him to her breasts. 'Oh darling – the look on your face! Do I make you jealous?'

'Yes.' Hargreave grinned sheepishly. It was almost true.

'I'm so glad!' She rocked him, then collapsed back and stroked her fingertip across his eyebrow. 'Oh, you're such a nice man. Such a nice English gentleman. I think I love you . . .'

It seemed that his heart turned over. It felt as if he loved her too.

And his mind formed images of her working out in her school gymnasium, leaping off springboards, flying through the air, doing somersaults, cavorting on the parallel bars.

'Can you really do all that stuff?'

'Oh, yes, I was in competitions. I was quite good, but not good enough to be famous, my breasts were too big, even when I was fifteen. But I won some prizes. Shall I show you how I can walk on my hands?'

'With all that wine inside you?'

'No problem.' She got off the bed, did a cartwheel across the room, then sprang on to her hands. She balanced there a moment, her body straight, her legs rigid, her toes pointed, her hair sweeping the floor: then she bent her knees and walked across the carpet on her hands. 'Yes?' she grinned at him, upside-down.

'*Very* good.'

'And now . . .' She stopped, straightened her legs again, then parted them into a Y; then she dramatically raised one hand. She lifted her arm out sideways, her fingertips pointed. 'Yes?'

'Amazing!'

She carefully replaced her hand on the floor, brought her legs together, and did a nimble spring. She landed on her feet in a flash of golden locks, her face flushed. 'You want to make love like that?'

'I can't wait!'

'Here I come!' She ran across the room and took a flying dive on to the bed, laughing.

'*Oh . . .*' He looked at her lying there beside him in the elegant room, her hair awry across the crumpled pillow, the China night out there, and it was hard to imagine her in a sexless smock toiling in an aluminium factory in the winter making pots and pans, living in a tiny grey apartment in a vast, smog-bound, joyless city: she was an exotic creature of the sun and sea and glittering nightlife, how could such beauty be caged in a factory?

'I could not live like that any more. And that is why I decided to fuck my way to freedom.'

Fuck her way? He had not heard this last weekend.

'What other way is there for a girl in the aluminium works? Everybody was fucking everybody anyway, what else was there to do? But I did not fuck my shift-boss and my floor manager like the other girls just to get a little more overtime on my ticket, not even the factory manager, although he begged me many times. No, I fucked the Party Secretary, because I wanted him to help me get to school to study to be a vet. That is how everything works in Russia – you must know somebody in the Party who knows somebody in veterinary school. And that is how the KGB man got to hear of me, saying he was from Mosfilm.'

'Did you have to go to bed with him too?'

'Of course. It was all a trick. But I thought I was going to be a movie star.' She fluttered her eyelashes. 'And here I am, darling, in bed with you. What secrets have you got to tell me?'

49

It was even exotic that she was a courtesan, a woman of the flesh, doubtless one of the most beautiful of her trade in the world, that she came from that earthy, sultry other-world, that she possessed a wealth of carnal expertise. What she was giving him would be the envy of any red-blooded man, and it did not even seem that he was paying for it. It did not spoil the atmosphere a jot when there was a knock on the door on the first morning and there stood Vladimir, looking annoyed.

'Oh, I'm sorry, darling,' Olga said to Hargreave, 'I forgot – the money.' They had just finished making love and she was dressing for breakfast, screwing an earring into her lobe. She delved into her weekend bag and produced a credit-card machine. 'I was supposed to leave the credit-slip downstairs last night for Vladimir, but I got – ' she made her eyes sparkle – 'excited.'

Hargreave was not embarrassed but he did not like Vladimir standing there in the doorway like a hood.

Olga ran the card through the machine, filled in the amount, and gave him the slip to sign. He noticed she had only charged him for two nights. He did not query it, but Vladimir did.

'How many nights you pay for, sir?'

'Two,' Olga said emphatically, 'last night and tonight.'

Vladimir said to Hargreave: 'Do you go home on Sunday?'

'Maybe,' Hargreave said. He had no intention of leaving until Monday morning.

'No, he goes on Monday,' Olga said archly. 'But this Sunday is my day off, I can do what I like on my one Sunday a month. Thank you, goodbye.'

Vladimir began to argue in Russian, Olga replied rapidly and closed the door on him. She turned to Hargreave. 'What cheek! He says if he sees you here on Sunday you must pay for another night. I told him to go to hell.'

Hargreave did not want any trouble. 'I'll pay.'

'No! Tomorrow is my one day off in a month.' She smiled at him dazzlingly. 'I told you I would give you a discount and I have – thirty-three per cent! You get three nights for two!'

'It's a bargain,' Hargreave smiled, 'but I don't want trouble; I think I'd better pay.'

'*No*, I told him it was against your principles to make love on a Sunday!' She entwined her hands behind his neck and smiled. 'But I think we will, huh, just to cheat Vladimir? We're going to have a lovely time!'

* * *

They did have a lovely time. The previous weekend he had thought was wildly erotic, enchanting, exotic, he had felt smitten: but this weekend it really felt as if he was falling in love. Hargreave knew enough about life to know that this could not possibly be true; he knew it was only a case of wild infatuation, of joyful lust, but love is how it felt and he did not want to analyse it, he did not want to question his happiness.

That Saturday they did not leave the Bella Mar. He wanted to take her out and walk along the esplanade with her hand-in-hand, to ride in a trishaw, take her to a smart bar, a fashionable restaurant, to parade her, show her off. That's how Hargreave felt; he wanted people to turn to stare at her beauty, he wanted the whole world to know she was his girl, to envy the fun they were having being together. But it might have been unwise: Olga could be anybody, just a tourist, but they might meet a friend of his and though Hargreave was now a free man who could do as he damn-well liked, perhaps it would be unwise for the Director of Public Prosecutions to flaunt his affair just yet. And he did not want to waste the time that could be spent making wildly erotic love.

It was almost lunchtime when they went down the sweeping old colonial staircase to breakfast beside the sparkling pool. There was nobody he knew. When she shed her robe to dive into the pool all eyes were on her magnificence. To Hargreave it was the happiest thing in the world, almost incredible, that that beautiful body was his, that an hour ago this gorgeous girl had been naked beneath him – it was almost unbelievable how lucky he was. When she took a running dive at the pool, her flaxen hair flying, all eyes were on her, riveted by her femininity, smiling at her exuberance. And when she had swum her ten lengths and heaved herself out, the water gushing off her, her long hair plastered, and walked unselfconsciously towards him, a spectacle of young womanhood, he no longer wanted to take her out of the hotel to show her off, he did not want to go any distance from that suite upstairs with its big double bed. So the champagne breakfast evolved into a long lunch while they talked and talked, and laughed, telling each other about themselves, undergoing the delightfully important business of getting to know each other. When they were full of good food and wine and sun she said, 'Let's go and make love,' and as she walked across the terrace he could feel all eyes on her, he could almost hear the men sighing, and he was immensely proud of her. It did not feel as if she was bought and paid for; it felt as if she was really his.

Later, lying spent on the bed in each other's arms, in the quietness

51

of afterlove, she said: 'Are you worried that one of your friends will see you, with a prostitute?'

No, he just felt happy. 'Nobody is likely to know anything about you, and even if they did, so what? This is the Far East, not Whitehall in London; we're not very judgemental out here. Anyway, don't talk of yourself like that.'

She was silent a moment: 'You are right. With you I am not really a prostitute. Because I *want* to be with you. I am sorry you must pay for today – if it was up to me you would not pay. And tomorrow,' she squeezed him, 'you will not pay, tomorrow I will not be a prostitute.'

'You don't feel like one now.'

She feigned indignation. 'You mean I am not expert?'

'Oh, you are.'

'You don't want your money back?'

'Not so far.'

'Okay.' She snuggled against his shoulder and smiled. 'I don't feel like a prostitute either, with you. I feel I am your girl.' She sighed. 'Wouldn't it be lovely to go away on a real holiday together, so I really was your girl, not the slightest bit a prostitute? Stay on a beach with palm trees and blue sea and tropical fish. I have never seen a beach like that, except in pictures. Macao's sea is so brown, from the river. And we could live in a hut and swim all day, with snorkels, looking at the tropical fish. And maybe rent a little sailboat.'

It was a pretty thought. 'We can do that. I can take some leave.'

'No,' she sighed, 'Vladimir has our passports, in case we run away. I cannot even go to Hong Kong for a day because it says on my Macao identity card I am a "dancer". The Hong Kong immigration people know what that means. I tried one day and they sent me back. "You are a prostitute," they said, "we do not allow you people in here!"'

Hargreave snorted. What hypocrisy – Hong Kong was full of prostitutes, the girlie-bars of Wanchai and Tsimshatsui were world-renowned tourist spots. 'What did you say?'

'I made a fuss. I said: "I am a dancer, sir! What dance do you want me to do? The rumba, the samba, the tango, rock-'n'-roll? Come out of your silly box and I will dance with you!" But they sent me back on the next ferry. I was so cross – and embarrassed. But maybe I can visit Hong Kong now because when my work-permit was extended they gave me a new identity card which says I am a singer.'

Hargreave smiled. 'Can you really sing?'

'Yes, not bad. Every night at the Tranquillity I sing some songs, with the band. Western songs.'

Hargreave looked at her. She had told him the first night he met her that she was a singer but he hadn't believed her. But if it really was true, this put a rather different complexion on their relationship. 'And what does it say on your passport?'

'Singer.'

Hargreave grinned. 'So that's what you are – a professional night-club entertainer, not a prostitute!'

She smiled. 'Okay, that's me from now on. A famous Russian singer, like Madonna.'

'Right, that's what we'll tell my friends. Do the other Russian girls at the Tranquillity sing too?'

'No, I am the only one with a good voice. But I'm not *very* good, darling. But,' she added, 'I can also play the guitar.'

'What songs do you sing with the guitar?'

'I can only do about twenty-five well – Western love songs. The manager likes me to do it, if I am not busy when the other singers are resting.'

'And does he pay you to sing?'

'Oh yes. Fifty patacas a song. Sometimes more if the people clap loudly.'

'Well, then, you're a paid professional entertainer! Can you really do all those dances?'

'Yes. The KGB taught me at my training school, so I could dance with all the foreign diplomats and steal their silly secrets. Even Scottish reels I can do, with swords on the floor. And American square-dancing, and the can-can, even belly-dancing. Next time I will show you, I will bring some music and my belly-dancing stuff. Even the ruby for my navel.'

Oh yes, he would love to see her do all that. And he was impressed by her accomplishments. She said: 'Are you a good dancer, darling?'

The foxtrot and the waltz were about Hargreave's speed. 'Liz did try to teach me the tango. But she gave up.'

'I will teach you to tango, darling, it is my favourite dance – so dramatic. I have all the music, on my cassettes, I will bring them next time. Would you like to go dancing tonight, I'll start teaching you?'

Hargreave wanted to do whatever she wanted. 'Only trouble is I don't want to get out of this bed. And I don't want you to put clothes on.'

'But I better get dressed for dinner, darling, in case we meet somebody you know!'

That Saturday night they did meet somebody Hargreave knew. They were sitting at the bar off the reception hall, having a drink before dinner, when Jake McAdam and Max Popodopolous came in with Judge Peterson. The judge slapped him on the back in passing.

'Hullo, Dave!' Hargreave said. 'Hullo, Jake, Max!'

They waved and went on their way. They all glanced at Olga appreciatively. They sat down at a corner table overlooking the terrace.

'Does it matter?' Olga asked.

'No.' He grinned. 'Anyway, you're a professional singer, remember?'

'But will they guess what I really am?'

They might guess but he didn't give a damn: how were they to know she wasn't a legitimate night-club singer? He almost believed it himself now. It was possible one of them had been to the Tranquillity and remembered her – she wasn't easily forgettable – but what the hell, they were all his friends.

'No, they won't guess.'

'The fattish, Portuguese-looking one, I've seen him at the Tranquillity.'

Yes, Max was a bit of a bon vivant who let his hair down occasionally in questionable night-clubs. Hargreave said: 'He's one of my closest friends, in fact he's my personal lawyer, he won't talk – or care. I'd like you to meet him, and Jake McAdam, too, the tall one.' In fact he'd like her to meet all his friends; he wanted to say, 'This is my girl Olga Romalova, she's a night-club singer, maybe she used to be on the game but not any more, take her or leave her but she's my girl.' He said: 'Jake, he's got a tragic story. He fell in love with a smashing American girl about ten years ago, a newspaper reporter from New York who came out here to write a story about Hong Kong corruption. She was killed in a typhoon.'

'*Oh*. What a sad story.'

And there was an even sadder story that he couldn't tell her because of the Official Secrets Act. Long before the American girl, Jake had fallen in love with a Chinese Communist schoolmistress, and that had also ended in tragedy because Jake had been a senior policeman in Special Branch.

Olga said: 'And now, is he married?'

'Used to be. Twice, to the same woman. But it ended in divorce both times.' He nodded over his shoulder. 'And the other one, Dave, he's a judge, also divorced. We stick together, us bachelors. Go to the races together.'

'And Jake, what work does he do?'

'He's a businessman. Builds boats. And he's got an import–export

54

business. Does quite a lot of business with Russia, everything from pins to diesel engines, I gather. And now he's gone into politics. He's one of those idealistic diehards who think that Britain should never have agreed to surrender Hong Kong to China in 1997. He thinks we should only give them back the New Territories when the lease expires and hold them back at Boundary Street. He says we can survive like Gibraltar does. Of course, it's too late now, because the handover has been negotiated, but he thinks the British Government shouldn't have mentioned the subject, that Maggie Thatcher made a mistake. But having started negotiations, we should have stuck to our guns at Boundary Street.'

She nodded pensively, stirring her pina colada. 'And what do you think?'

Hargreave shook his head. 'China wouldn't have backed down like Spain did because it's a matter of "face". Hong Kong is the holy soil of China stolen from the Celestial Kingdom during the wicked Opium War, et cetera. Do you know about that?'

Olga sucked the pina colada off the end of her straw. 'Sure. 1841. I've read some books about China. It's true – Britain *did* steal Hong Kong to force China to accept the opium trade. It is a shameful story, to force people to buy drugs like that.'

'Well, it was a long time ago, and people thought differently then.' But Hargreave was impressed. This was your ordinary prostitute? No, a thousand times no. How many books had he read on Russia? None. 'Anyway, now Jake is a vociferous democrat – he's campaigning for a seat in the Legislative Council elections and his platform is we must have complete entrenched democracy to withstand the Chinese Government after 1997 and that Britain must support us with a garrison stationed here.' He added, 'Jake's one of the few non-Chinese standing in the selection. As an independent.'

'Do you think he will win?'

'He's very highly thought of. But it won't do him much good – when China takes over he's likely to be one of the first to be thrown in jail as a subversive.'

'What kind of trouble will he make?'

Hargreave sighed. 'China has already announced that she'll throw out our Legislative Council the day she takes over Hong Kong. Jake and others like him will refuse to accept that because it will be contrary to the Basic Law and the Joint Declaration. That'll land him in jail.'

'Oh dear,' Olga said. 'Such a brave man. Oh dear. And you, darling – what are you going to do in 1997?'

Hargreave did not want to think about it. Ten years ago when the

Joint Declaration was signed he'd had hope that English law would survive in Hong Kong, that there would be democracy, but the massacre in Tiananmen Square in 1989 had proved that was a pipe-dream and he had decided to quit in 1997, go somewhere like Spain where he could live modestly on his pension. Three years ago when things started going badly between him and Liz and there was talk of divorce, he felt like doing that even sooner. But now her lawyer's letter had arrived, the reality of divorce under Californian law of Community of Property was upon him and his investments would be very modest when cut in half. So he would have to get a job somewhere. The only alternative was to continue to work under the new government and hope that China didn't throw him in jail for refusing to bend the Rule of Law when they demanded. That was the bleak prospect he had faced last weekend when the lawyer's letter arrived and he had jumped on the hydrofoil to Macao.

'I don't know,' he said. 'I want to leave, but divorce is an expensive business.'

She said sympathetically, 'Could you get a job as a lawyer in England?'

'I could, but I'm a colonial boy now, used to the sun. Cold, grey, rainy England? And the dreadful cost of booze?'

'I understand. I love Russia, but it will be grey for a long time, and I am very tired of grey, I am a sun girl. But you know what I think I would do if I was a businessman? I would invest in Russia.' She raised her eyebrows. 'Russia needs *everything*. Communism was so bad that Russia has nothing, not even enough food to eat. You can sell anything in Russia.'

'I couldn't sell a damn thing. But Jake McAdam does well there.'

'You know what I will do with my money?' She took his hand earnestly. 'I have over thirty thousand US dollars saved. I am going to buy an apartment in Moscow, on the west side. Because Moscow is going to go *voom* –' she exploded her hands – 'because so many foreigners are coming now that Communism is finished. And I am going to make a lot of profit when I sell it. And you know what I am going to do with it?'

'What?'

'Buy some farmland. My father was such a good farmer, and he taught me. And the Russian Government is saying, buy land and be good farmers. But my father was frightened of the responsibility because he only knew the Collective where the state pays for everything. My brother was the same. But I am going to buy some land for my stupid brother and me, and we'll have our own ducks and chickens and cows and pigs and rabbits and vegetables and we'll sell them in the market for the real price – and you know what else we'll have?'

'What?' Her enthusiasm was endearing and infectious.

'Horses! I love horses. And we'll build a nice, proper house, with a real toilet and bathroom! No more kettles for the tub on Saturday. No more shitting outside in the little house.'

Hargreave grinned. He glanced over his shoulder to see if his friends had heard, but they had moved. 'Say that again, not everybody heard it all.'

'What?' Then she smiled. 'Okay, a bit loud, huh?'

Hargreave grinned: 'Was it really like that?'

'*Shit* yes!' Then she clapped her hand over her mouth and burst into giggles. 'Oh, I'm sorry.' They laughed together so everybody looked at them. When they subsided she leant forward and whispered in his ear:

'Let's go'n dance downstairs . . .'

And did they dance?

Hargreave had no intention of dancing more than just enough to humour her, to be romantic, but Olga had her own ideas. 'I've got my dancing feet on!' The Bella Mar, with its dance-floor beside the pool, was a rather sedate Old China-Hand place, the elderly Chinese band given to waltzes and a bit of modest rock'n'roll occasionally just to show they weren't totally old-fashioned. But Olga Romalova, after the first rock-'n'-roll – which Hargreave performed quite well – called across to the band: 'Hey, can you do a tango?'

'The tango!' The Chinese bandleader beamed, and his men struck up.

'*Der-der-der-DA!*' Olga cried, and she swept back into Hargreave's astonished arms and leant back so her blonde hair swept the floor. '*Der-der-der-DA –*' and she swung upright and clasped him dramatically; then she swirled away – '*Der-der-darra-darra-der-der-Da!*'

And so Olga Romalova taught Hargreave the tango. Everybody left the floor when they started – nobody knew the dance, it seemed. But Olga Romalova sure did. At first Hargreave was mortified and tried to lead her off the floor but she had cried 'No way!' and pulled him back. And so Alistair Hargreave, Director of Public Prosecutions, was forced to dance the tango with the most beautiful woman in the world – and he found he could.

He could! Liz had declared him a failure, but with this glorious woman in his arms, laughing into his eyes, whispering instructions, everything that Liz had tried to teach him came flooding back with the drama of the beat, and with Olga leading him it seemed he knew what to do. So there was Al Hargreave sweeping earnestly round the terrace of the Bella Mar, doing the tango very creditably with the most exotic of partners, her hair sweeping, her breasts jutting, her long legs stalking, her back arching. And when the number ended, and fifty tourists burst into applause, it was Olga who led it, clapping her hands and laughing to the crowd.

'Didn't he dance good?'

There were shouts of 'Yes' and Hargreave was blushing as he laughed. Up there on the balcony McAdam and Judge Peterson and Max were clapping.

8

The next day, after an early breakfast, they went for a walk. It was the first time they had ventured outside their secluded hotel: but they would meet nobody he knew at this hour in this part of Macao and even if they did they would not know Olga – even if they recognized her, so fucking what? She was a night-club singer, that's all. And if they didn't believe that, fuck 'em, he was a free man!

It was a hot Sunday morning, the church bells pealing. They walked hand-in-hand along the old stone Praia Grande, under the trees, past the gracious old Leal Senado, the legislative council, past the governor's residence. Out there land-reclamation barges were at work building big dykes to hold back the muddy River Pearl, to turn the bay into fresh-water lakes with artificial islands where giant modern buildings would go up, hotels and shops and offices, all connected with the old shore by sweeping thoroughfares. Hargreave had difficulty understanding it: for centuries Macao had been a small, sleepy, faded Portuguese enclave on the China coast, thoroughly neglected by Lisbon; now, four years before the joint was to be handed back to China, in 1999, there was this frenetic burst of staggering investment that would transform the place into a mini-Hong Kong.

'Has Lisbon suddenly acquired a guilty conscience?'

'No,' Olga said, 'it is all local taxes from the casinos, it's called the Infrastructure Programme, to make Macao survive after 1999.'

'How do you know all this?'

'It is in the newspapers.'

'You read the Portuguese newspaper too?'

'I try. It is interesting to know what is going on. The same is happening in Hong Kong, not so?'

Yes, the same was happening in Hong Kong and Hargreave had diffi-culty understanding that too. One and a half years to go before the handover to the Comrades and Hong Kong businessmen and overseas investors were pouring billions into land reclamation all along the waterfronts to make more of the most expensive real estate in the world for more towering buildings: even the highly successful Hong Kong

Hilton, in Central, was being pulled down to be replaced by another towering office block. And now the colonial government was building a massive new international airport on reclaimed land off Lantau Island, and when it was finished the old runway jutting out into the harbour would be sold as more real estate to be crammed with yet more skyscrapers; and all along the old flight path into Hong Kong the existing height restrictions would be repealed, old buildings would be torn down and replaced by yet more high-rise development. Lord, was there no end to the optimism and sang-froid?

'It is the China fever,' Olga said, 'now that Communism is dead, China is going to go *vroom*. Imagine: one thousand million new customers for the world! Russia can be the same.'

'But,' Hargreave said, 'just up the coast are Shanghai and Swatow and all the other China ports, and just up the River Pearl is Canton, a huge port – fantastic development is going on in all those places too. Shanghai is going to become the biggest industrial centre in China, not Hong Kong. A businessman could build in Shanghai for a fraction of the cost.'

'It is because Hong Kong has the experience,' Olga said sagely, 'and British laws.'

Hargreave snorted. 'It doesn't take a Chinese long to learn anything; Shanghai will soon catch up on experience and I think a lot of Hong Kong investors will burn their fingers. And I wouldn't bank on there being British law for very long – China will throw it out the window as soon as it suits them. And,' he added, 'I wouldn't bank on Communism being so dead, either.'

'Oh, it is dead, darling! Finished, *kaput*! Look at Russia. Capitalism has proved it is the only way to succeed.'

'But it only takes a military coup to put Communism back on the throne and then everything's ruined again. And China's massive army is all the Party faithful. There was a coup against Gorbachev, and against Yeltsin. And what about this New Communist Party in Russia?'

'No,' Olga said, walking along with head lowered pensively, 'the spirit is out of the bottle, the people will never accept Communism again.'

'China put the genie back in the bottle very effectively at the Tiananmen Square massacre, didn't they?'

Olga tapped her head. '"Genie", that is the word, not "spirit". Yes, but that was the political genie, not the money genie. A thousand million Chinese will not let the genie go back into the bottle with their money.'

'Mao Tse-tung,' Hargreave said, 'and the Bolsheviks made a pretty good job of it. The guy behind the machine-gun is always right. And it doesn't take much imagination to see them doing it in Statue Square, Hong Kong.'

Then they came around the corner of the Praia Grande and there, towering up thirty storeys high, dwarfing all the buildings around it, was the new steel and glass tower of the official Bank of China. '*There*, darling,' Olga pointed, 'is the reason they will not go back to Communism!'

Yes, it was reassuring, like the new Bank of China building in Hong Kong; it tended to show that the Chinese took commercial stability seriously now that Deng had proclaimed, 'To become rich is glorious' – but if Hargreave were a businessman he would wait and see before investing his millions. Olga said: 'And have you seen all the factories just beyond the Barrier Gate?'

No, he hadn't, but he'd heard about it – and he'd seen the same thing across the Hong Kong border, in the new Shenzhen Special Economic Zone in the Samchun Valley where a few years ago there had been only sleepy paddy fields. Now the valley was covered in factories and apartment blocks and businessmen from around the world were setting up industries there because land, building costs and labour were so cheap. Yet just over the border, in Hong Kong, only ten or twelve miles away as the crow flies, on the most expensive real estate in the world the same damn thing was happening. It didn't make long-term sense. Hargreave was no businessman but it seemed to him that there had to be a levelling of the two sets of values, and surely Hong Kong's had to go down?

Olga said: 'And now let's go to my old Macao, where I live; I love it.'

They walked hand-in-hand up the narrow, crowded streets, the grubby Chinese tenements on both sides, their signboards fighting each other up to the sky, the shops selling everything from silks and hi-fi gear down to lizards' tails, through the smells of gutters and restaurants and spices and butchers and incense and smoke and urine, through the coolies and shopkeepers and urchins and mangy dogs and scrawny cats and the hammering and the yammering and the clattering of mah-jong, until they came to a tailor's shop near the old Central Hotel. Olga pointed up at the top floor of the joyless tenement building opposite.

'Those are my windows. It is old-fashioned but nice inside. I would take you in but my girlfriends are asleep now. I like it here because it is the old China, so much life everywhere. And I would like to show you my cats.'

'Cats? How many have you got?'

'About twenty, but they are not really mine, they live on the roof. Every day I feed them there and they are very grateful. I will show you another time, darling, when I cook you a nice Russian stew. But –' she held up a finger – 'I am learning Chinese cooking too; perhaps I must give you that, to impress you.'

'I'm already impressed.'

'Yes, but that is in bed – I mean in the kitchen.'

Hargreave grinned. 'Do you like your flatmates, the girls?'

'Oh yes, they are very nice. Yolanda is my good friend, she comes from Vladivostok, she spent all her life in the orphanage, since a baby – I was lucky. But she is so *stupid*, always falling in love with silly men.' She grinned: 'Not like me, who only falls in love with very important *lawyers*.'

She led him through the narrow, jostling, odoriferous streets, till they came to a squat, modern, white building with sheet-iron gates guarded by two lucky red flag-ensembles draped in yellow flowers. A small white sign on the wall read: *Missionaries of Charity*.

'This is my favourite place. *This* is where the Sisters of Mother Teresa work.' She looked at him. 'And a few years ago Mother Teresa herself came here, and said it was her best mission in the world!'

Hargreave was taken aback by her enthusiasm. 'So you're really not an atheist?'

'Yes, I am an atheist, that's what I was taught at school, but Mother Teresa is wonderful because she is so kind – she won the Nobel Peace Prize! She gives her life to the poor people. Such sacrifice! So good. Here they look after anybody, food, clothes, bed, find a job. I always give money to Mother Teresa, and any old clothes the girls don't want, even stockings and suspenders! Look.' She burrowed her hand into her brassière and pulled out a hundred-pataca banknote. She marched through the open gates, up to the door, and slipped it in through the letterbox. 'See? Even though I don't believe in gods.'

'None at all?' Hargreave grinned.

Olga cupped her hands to her mouth and gave a whisper-shout at Mother Teresa: '*That's from both of us this week.*' She giggled and put her arm around him and then led him off down the street. 'Do you?' she asked.

'Yes. One.'

'The Christian one?'

'Yes.'

'Not the Buddhist one?'

'No.'

'Not at all?'

'No.'

'Not the littlest bit? Even the possibility? Such Christian arrogance, darling! So only you are right, all the stupid Orientals are wrong? What about Allah?'

Hargreave smiled: 'God and Allah are the same god. Just different names given by different prophets.'

'But only *your* prophet is right? Poor Mohammed and Buddha, they made a big fat mistake? So you all fight each other, to prove who is right, ever since the Romans. Ever since King Henry VIII chopped the head off his poor wife to make himself the highest priest of England! And now today you are still fighting the Arabs who say you are infidels. Really,' she squeezed him, 'you religious people surprise me. Such arrogance, darling!'

'That's what they taught you at school?'

'It's not true?'

'So you reject all of it, because of its gruesome history?'

'*Pathetic* history, darling! *Shameful*. But . . .' She stopped and pointed up at the sky as Chinese thronged past them: 'See that up there? That is infinity! It goes on for ever. No end. With millions of worlds? With billions of millions of creatures. Who made all that?' Her eyes widened. 'It is so amazing to think about it that you must decide that *somebody* made it. And that is what men call God. Or Allah,' she added. 'Or Buddha.'

'And who made God?'

'Ah!' She held up a finger. 'That is the answer! *Nobody* made God – He was *always* there, that's why He is God.'

Hargreave grinned: 'But I thought you didn't believe in God?'

'Not the God you Christians and Jews and Arabs are always fighting each other about. You are so *cruel* to each other. Such bullies. How can a sensible Russian girl believe in that? But . . .' She held her finger up at the sky again: 'There is Somebody up there, I think.' Then she wagged her finger under his nose. 'So you be nice to Mother Teresa!'

They climbed the wide stone steps leading up to the ruin of Saint Paul's Cathedral, only the beautiful façade remaining, towering up, with carvings and colonnades. 'This was also the very first university in Asia,' Olga informed him. 'Did you know that? Started by the Jesuit missionaries nearly five hundred years ago.'

Hargreave didn't know that. 'I thought it was just a church.'

'No. The Jesuits were very rich because they taxed all the ships that

63

came to Macao to trade. They wanted money to convert the whole of China to Christianity. But then the Duke of Pombal took power in Portugal and banished all the Jesuits and took all their money, but when the soldiers came to this cathedral they found everything gone, all the gold and silver and silk, even the library. The Jesuits were sent to Goa in chains, but the treasure was never found. So where is it?' She tapped her toe on the stone steps. 'Under here. People say there are secret rooms under these steps leading to the harbour, the treasure is buried there. Exciting, huh?' She added, 'When China takes over they will probably dig all this up, to look for it. That would be terrible.'

'How do you know all this?'

'I got books from the library. So interesting. There are some nice little museums here, I will take you one day. Have you been to the new University of Macao, on Taipa?'

'No.' Hargreave smiled. 'Should I have?'

'It is very important because now there will always be Western education in China. Like the University of Hong Kong. That's good, huh, good for China, good for the rest of the world, it will stop China being so . . .' She put her hands to the sides of her eyes, like blinkers. She added: 'One day I would like to go to a university.'

'And study what?'

'There's so many interesting things to learn.'

Oh, this lovely girl was no prostitute, not in her heart, nor in her head . . .

They stopped at a Chinese restaurant in the narrow crowded streets of the old quarter, where Portuguese wine was served. It was noisy and pungent with a multitude of cooking smells, all the Chinese talking loudly, young girls circulating with trays of dim sum, small plates of Chinese delicacies, and there were glass tanks of fish and crayfish and crabs with their claws bound. Olga sat with her back to them so she couldn't 'see their unhappiness'. She did not know that the restaurant also served snakes, puppies and monkeys – when Hargreave went to the toilet he saw them in their cages in the kitchen, but he didn't tell her. They drank a bottle of vinho verde while they picked at a selection of dim sum as an aperitif before returning to the Bella Mar for lunch.

Olga said: 'So you don't know whether you will continue to work after 1997?'

Hargreave sighed; he was at a loss where to begin. 'Do you understand what the Rule of Law means?'

She shook her head.

No, there was probably no such thing in Russia either. 'The Rule of Law means that everybody is equal before the law, and the law always rules, not the politicians. It is the fundamental principle of the English legal system. The courts are not afraid of the politicians. But in China the Communist Party rules, the only law is what the Party wants, and that can change from week to week, day to day. And when China takes over in 1997 it will be the same in Hong Kong – despite the Joint Declaration which says that English law will continue to apply.' He shook his head. 'I couldn't practise law like that, it's against everything I believe in.'

'So are the people in Hong Kong worried?'

'Oh, the poor old average Chinese worker has no choice but to hope for the best – and pretend to be patriotic when China comes marching in. But thousands upon thousands of middle-class Chinese have emigrated to Canada and Australia and the US. And most of the British civil servants are worried as hell about whether China will pay their pensions, and there are very good reasons to think China will not, no matter what she promises – once they see these vast sums leaving every month to pay capitalist foreign devils who made a career of exploiting the holy soil of China, they'll put a stop to the outflow, and there'll be a lot of poor pensioners. Yes, they're very worried. But the big business houses are staying because all they're interested in is trade and most of their assets are safely offshore – they don't care about democracy and the Rule of Law.' He shook his head. 'But they *should* – because Hong Kong is prosperous only because there *is* British law here to give them justice. Take that away and Hong Kong will be a dangerous place to do business.'

Olga said pensively, 'I do not believe it. I look around and I see all the big business, all the new buildings, the big new Bank of China, and I do not believe China will eat the gooses who lay the golden eggs.'

Hargreave sighed.

'Lord, they've *already* broken the Joint Declaration half a dozen times. Look, the Joint Declaration is a legally-binding international agreement between China and Britain, and it says, amongst other things, that when China takes over Hong Kong will be an autonomous region and that there will be democracy. So in 1985 Britain began to introduce democracy, and China immediately protested, before the ink was dry, and has been threatening us ever since, vowing to throw out our legislative councillors.' He looked at her. 'How's that for breaking the Joint Declaration?'

'But,' Olga said, 'it is understandable, Hong Kong never had democracy before, now Britain introduces it – '

'How can it be understandable when China said that "only the flag

65

will change", that her policy was "One Country, Two Systems", that there would be a "through-train" on which the civil servants and the legislative councillors would travel smoothly from being a British colony into the new era?' He shook his head. 'The only thing we can understand from her behaviour is that China simply does not understand the law because they think the Communist Party *is* the law and can do what it likes – that is how Communists think. They have never had democracy or human rights in China, so they simply do not understand the real world – *that* is all that's understandable about them.'

'But,' Olga argued solemnly, 'they will change because they want trade.'

'But only on their lawless terms. Do you know that thirty-one foreign banks are presently trying to recover debts of six hundred million US dollars owed by China's state-run companies? And they owe millions to numerous American companies. Like McDonald's – the world's biggest fast-food chain? They signed a twenty-year lease with China for a prime site in Tiananmen Square, and after a while China just evicted them.' Hargreave frowned at her. 'They're simply not like us, Olga, they simply don't feel that the everyday laws of contract are binding on them, let alone strange international treaties made with foreign devils about this strange thing called *democracy* . . . *And*,' he held up a finger, 'China will suffer dearly for it. What China needs is what Hong Kong has – the Rule of Law. Last year Fortune Magazine voted Hong Kong the best place *in the world* to do business in, better even than New York or London. Why? – because of our free trade, of course, but particularly because of our Rule of Law: the international business community knows they can rely on our courts. But that will go when China starts interfering – Hong Kong is going to go to the dogs.'

'What does that mean, go to the dogs?'

'Go into a decline. But that's only part of the godawful story, Olga. The rest is even worse. Because what about human rights?' He waved a hand. 'China has agreed that our Bill of Rights will continue to apply, and they even wrote it into the Basic Law – but what does China now say? That will be thrown out along with our democratically-elected legislative council!' He spread his hands: 'Lord, how can anybody trust these guys on anything? And freedom of the press?' He snorted. 'Do you know that freedom of speech is actually enshrined in China's constitution? Well, we all know what that means in China – life in jail, more likely the executioner's bullet for speaking out against the Party. Tiananmen Square massacre, that's what happens.' He snorted again. 'The Basic Law also says there will be freedom of the press – but what happens?' He spread his hands again. 'China's propaganda chief has recently warned Hong Kong journalists to "be wise and bend with the wind", and "to watch out". And now China has banned television satellite dishes because she is terrified of her people learning what is going on in the rest of the world. Because information, general knowledge, is power, it empowers the people.' He shook his head. 'The press in China is just a propaganda machine, Olga, and it'll be the same in Hong Kong after they take over. And that'll be the death of our open, free-market culture that has made us so prosperous.' He looked at her. 'How can one do business with a country like that?'

Olga sighed. 'But then I look at all the new business going on, the new skyscrapers going up –'

'That's called *optimism*, Olga. That's called sang-froid, which has always been a characteristic of the China coast. That's called dollar-signs in the eyes of businessmen who know that a thousand million customers are wonderful – the businessmen will roll with the dirty punches and smile as long as they make their dollars, they don't care if democracy and human rights are trampled underfoot. Even though Hong Kong will go to the dogs they'll get their money back before it does.' He held up his hands. 'Oh, there may be a sort of honeymoon period while China tries to find its feet, but after that the bamboo guillotine will come down. And chop the heads off anybody who disagrees with the Communist Party.'

Olga shook her head solemnly. 'Communism is dead.'

'Yes, and long live the Communist Party of China – where it is alive and well. Not necessarily as a Marxist economic philosophy any more, because it is a proven failure which even China can understand, but as a diehard, tyrannical regime that has been in power for fifty years and doesn't intend to let go – like Russia did with such attendant chaos.'

Olga sighed. 'Do you know Martin Lee, the big Chinese politician in Hong Kong? He says the same as you.'

Of course, everybody knew Martin Lee, but Hargreave was impressed with her general knowledge. 'Martin Lee is a good friend of mine. Excellent man, and an excellent lawyer. Yes, he says the same as me – we must have democracy, so we can stand up to China and insist on the rule of law. Or rather, I say the same as him. I'm just a civil servant who can't say anything publicly; he's the courageous politician who is standing up to China as the leader of the United Democratic Party.' He added: 'He's going to win the elections, but he's going to lose his freedom in 1997.'

'Will he get his head chopped off?'

Hargreave snorted. 'Martin is probably too high-profile internationally for China to dare shoot him. But he's a sitting duck for being thrown in jail as a subversive – along with Jake McAdam and the likes.'

'And you, darling?' Olga said anxiously. 'What would they do to you?'

Hargreave sighed, weary of the question he and his fellow lawyers were asking themselves.

'I'm not a politician; I'm just a government servant whose job is to administer justice. However, if the new government wants me to pervert justice, to bend the Rule of Law, to prosecute people who are innocent, or if new laws are made which violate the Joint Declaration or the Basic Law, or if the new powers-that-be insist I do not prosecute somebody who is guilty I will *have* to speak out, refuse to cooperate, I will have to set an example – and that will doubtless land me in jail, yes.' He shook his head. 'I don't want to practise law under conditions like that. So I want to quit in 1997, yes. But,' he sighed, 'I've got to think carefully about the financial aspects. Divorce is a costly business. So? At this moment I'm not sure.'

Olga grinned: 'We'll find out. Finish your wine and I'll take you to my favourite fortune-teller!'

Hargreave didn't go a whole bundle on fortune-tellers – he didn't like messing with mumbo-jumbo and preferred not to know the future. Olga thought that was hilarious – 'My fortune-teller is beautiful!' Hargreave was reassured to find that the soothsayer was a little old Chinese man squatting on a corner and his paraphernalia consisted of a canary and a deck of little cards. Hargreave paid ten patacas and Olga squatted to observe the ritual closely. The man opened the cage door; out hopped the canary, picked a card out of the pack with its beak, presented it to the fortune-teller, was given a pinch of birdseed as a reward, and hopped back into his cage cheerfully. Olga was delighted. 'Isn't that clever!'

The fortune-teller gravely presented the card to Hargreave. Chinese writing was on one side, the translation in English and Portuguese on the other. He read aloud: 'You must work hard because you will have many sons.'

Olga thought that was very funny. 'So you'll have to be a lawyer, darling! Many sons!' She stood up and hugged him. 'And maybe I better get a job too?'

That Sunday night, as they lay in each other's arms, she said, 'Will I see you next Friday?'

'Yes.' Oh yes, he had to see her next weekend. But how much longer could he afford to keep doing this? It was as if she had read his mind, for she said:

'But what about all this crazy money you are spending? Crazy money. I will speak to Vladimir about a special price. Why don't I come to you, in Hong Kong? We save the hotel bill and all the dinners – I will cook for you, darling!'

Hargreave smiled. The China moonlight was streaming through the French windows, dusting her naked goldenness in silver. He loved her for her concern about his money; that showed she wasn't a whore at heart. But he hesitated: he wasn't sure about her coming to Hong Kong yet – he didn't care what people thought, or guessed, her alibi as a singer was good enough for Al Hargreave as an individual – but was it good enough for the Director of Public Prosecutions? And even if it was – which it *was*, for Christ's sake, plenty of Hong Kong bigwigs were known to have mistresses, and a good few were known homosexuals – even assuming he could get away with her alibi, was he ready to make that kind of commitment? Wasn't it quite a step, from a discreet hotel in Macao to taking her home to his apartment for all his neighbours to see? And even if that was okay, was it a wise thing to do when Elizabeth was suing him for divorce? And even if that didn't matter – which it didn't, because the marriage was over, whether he was shacked up with half a dozen girls or none – was it quite fair on Liz to have it known that her husband had a Russian girlfriend in residence? And most importantly, was it fair on Olga to take her into his A-grade government apartment and start the mental process that she was going to become the mistress of it? Was *he* ready for that yet? And was she, this Russian girl who had never had a real lover, who had been forced into prostitution – was she ready for the heady business of being taken into his privileged life, even if only for a weekend? What would she expect the following weekend, and the next? Oh, Hargreave knew what he wanted, he wanted her every weekend, but how would she feel when he simply couldn't afford her any longer – which was surely going to happen sooner rather than later. All these questions flashed through Hargreave's mind, then he said:

'Yes, come to Hong Kong. We'll go out on my boat for a few days.' The boat was the answer.

She sat up. 'You have a boat?'

'In fact we'll go sailing for a week,' he said. 'Next Monday is a public holiday, so I'll take leave from Tuesday to Friday; we'll have eight or nine days on the boat.'

'Oh how lovely!' Olga cried. Then she frowned anxiously. 'But supposing they won't let me in with my new identity card – the immigration man may remember me.'

Hargreave had forgotten that detail. 'Then I'll bring the boat to Macao to fetch you. I'll check you through Hong Kong immigration formalities at the Marine Department as crew.'

'Oh, *wonderful*, darling! And I will tell Vladimir to go to hell, he must drop his price!'

Hargreave smiled. Yes, it would be very nice to get Vladimir down. 'And what will he say to that?'

'He will finally do it – he knows he is getting a bargain because you are a good customer. And for me you don't pay, ever again, I will give you back my share!'

Hargreave grinned. Oh, this was ridiculous – the D PP getting a kickback from the Heavenly Tranquillity! She could keep her share, but he loved her for offering it. And he would pay the going price if he had to – he didn't want any trouble from Vladimir. But yes, something had to be done, he couldn't afford this much longer. But for the moment he could afford it, and a whole week with her on the yacht was going to be wonderful.

'Oh darling,' Olga said, 'I can hardly *wait*!'

9

And nor could Hargreave.

He worked hard, to leave his desk clear for the holiday ahead. Every morning before dawn he drove down to his chambers and put in three hours' work before his staff arrived, before his telephones started ringing. He kept his consultations to the minimum and declined all invitations to lunch. At lunchtime he went to the gym and pushed himself hard through the circuit of exercise equipment, then had a sauna and a hearty meal at the health-bar. He was getting fit and he felt good. He worked until about eight o'clock, then went home and rode his exercycle for half an hour whilst he watched the news and the weather report on television. There were no storms brewing nearby. He drank only a beer or two before Ah Moi served him another hearty health meal with plenty of salad: he was saving up his drinking-time for next week. Oh, he was so looking forward to the trip. He went to bed early with half a dozen different vitamin pills inside him and slept soundly. He woke up before dawn, eager to start the new day – one day less to wait. It was going to be a lovely adventure with his lovely girl on his lovely boat around Hong Kong's many lovely islands. On Thursday night she telephoned him.

'Hullo, darling! Are we really going sailing tomorrow?'

'Really!'

'Oh – all the girls are so envious, I'm so excited! Okay, I must go and work now. Is there anything I must bring?'

Work. The only thing he wanted her to bring was some good news from Vladimir. 'Only your sweet self.'

'And I've told Pig Vladimir to go to hell because I'm taking a holiday next week, there will be nothing to pay after Sunday, darling, next week is free.'

He was very pleased to hear that. 'And what did he say?'

'To hell with Vladimir. If I went back to Russia last week when my permit ended I would have some holidays before I started work, not so? Darling, I must go and sing now, goodbye. Know what I'm going to sing?'

71

Sing. That's better. 'What?'

' "Slow Boat to China". For us.'

Hargreave grinned: 'That's a lovely song.'

'For us. I must go now – but darling?'

'Yes?'

'I love you! Okay,' she giggled, 'goodbye!' The telephone went dead.

He woke up next morning at dawn feeling rested, fit and excited. He drove down to the gym, gave himself a quick workout, got to his chambers and finished clearing his desk. At nine o'clock he telephoned the Asia Company and asked them to deliver a week's supply of meat to his chambers immediately – there was plenty of booze and canned food aboard. He telephoned the yacht club and instructed his look-see boat-boy to hose down the decks, open the portholes, check the oil, batteries and water tanks. He sent one of his clerks down to the Marine Department with his passport and ship's papers to do port-clearance formalities for him: international destination Macao! With a hey-nonny-nonny and a hot cha-cha! He sent another clerk to the Hongkong & Shanghai Bank to cash a modest cheque – how delightfully cheap after the Bella Mar! He did a few pressing consultations, then, at noon, he summoned his three deputies, delegated the remnants of his files amongst them, discussed briefly the points of law involved, blew a jolly kiss to Miss Ho and Miss Chan, his secretaries, which sent them into fits of blushing giggles – *Mister Hargreave had never done that before* – and set off carrying his sailing bag. He rode down in the elevator to the parking basement, and drove out into hot, teeming Queensway with a song in his heart. *Slow Boat to China, yessir.* He drove through the steamy, congested thoroughfares of Wanchai to Causeway Bay, and turned out to the yacht club. He parked beside the clubhouse and strode down to the departure jetty. The good ship *Elizabeth* was waiting. Ten minutes later he was steaming down the fairway towards the international lane, a smile all over his face.

It was good to be alive! It was lovely to be steering his yacht across the South China Sea to fetch his beautiful Russian girl to go sailing around the myriad of islands – *how exotic can a love affair get?* And look at this magnificent Hong Kong, look at that breathtaking waterfront with its new skyscrapers towering up, look at that magnificent Peak, at teeming Kowloon with its Mountains of Nine Dragons beyond – look at all that land reclamation along the shores, all those ships from around the world, the freighters and junks and ferries and sampans. Lord, this is a wonderful triumph of human endeavour, a splendid tribute to Chinese industriousness, to sheer guts and sang-froid. This tiny colony on the China coast was a magnificent monument to British law – he was proud of it, although he hated the social nonsense, the one-upmanship. For all he was sick and tired of the law, he was proud of the high standard of justice, proud to be one of the standard-bearers, and he hated all that being trampled underfoot when China took over in 1997 . . .

He cleared the fairway, then swung between the mass of anchored freighters, into the international lane. There was no wind; the sea was flat, a haze hanging over the islands. He steamed past the end of big Lantau Island, measured off the compass course to Macao on his chart, turned the helm and pushed the automatic-pilot button. He went below to the saloon, down the alleyway to his aft master-cabin, stripped off his suit, and pulled on a pair of shorts. He went back to the galley, switched on the refrigerator, put a dozen beers in and opened one. He took it up to the cockpit. The sea ahead was empty but for the string of China islands: oh, this is what he would like to do with the rest of his life, with Olga – throw away the calendar and sail the world!

It was sunset when he reached the cloudy waters of Macao. He chugged past the ferry terminal, under the high Taipa Bridge, between the junks and sampans, and edged into the Club Nautico. He tied up, hurried ashore and checked in with the Portuguese authorities. Then telephoned Olga.

'Hullo, darling!' she cried.

He was grinning with anticipation as he waited for her. When he saw her running down the jetty, laughing, it seemed he had been away a long time.

She was enthralled by the yacht: by the mellow teak, the brass lamps, the spacious saloon, the galley with the little bar, the cosy sleeping cabins. 'Such luxury! And that nice big bunk in our cabin, oh boy, so sexy! And *two* bathrooms!' She was very impressed by the galley: 'A deep-freeze *and* a refrigerator! Wow – in Russia we are lucky if we have one small fridge, very old! And such a stove! I can show you what a good cook I am, darling, then you will think I am wonderful!'

'I think you're pretty wonderful now.' He was delighted with her pleasure.

She was fascinated by the wheelhouse: the radar, the satellite navigation system, the sextant, the charts, the radio, the automatic pilot. '*Air-conditioning* . . . You told me you had a boat, not a palace!' She went scouting around the upper deck, examining winches and cleats and ropes and halyards, demanding the function of each item. '*Two* steering wheels, *two* compasses . . .' She held a finger up at his nose: 'But only one Olga, sir! No girls with big tits on my boat!' Hargreave laughed with her. 'With this boat can we sail around the world?'

'Of course, she's built for it.'

'Oh, let's do it! Would it cost a lot of money?'

'The wind is free.'

'And love is free! And catching fish is free. And then money is unimportant! Oh darling –' she hugged him tight – 'can we please do it, I have some money saved! *Around the world . . .*'

That night they anchored off Coloane Island, not far from the Westin Resort Hotel. They lounged in the spacious cockpit in the moonlight, drinking wine. They could hear distant dance music coming from the hotel.

'Would you like to go ashore in the dinghy for dinner?'

'When we have our own palace for free? This is so exciting for me!'

She cooked up a storm of prawns followed by sweet and sour pork. They ate in the teak-panelled saloon by candlelight. Later, lying in the big double bunk in the aft cabin, spent, the moon beaming through the porthole, she stroked his eyebrow and said:

'I am so happy. You mustn't worry about Vladimir, darling.'

He wasn't worried; he'd cross the bridges as he came to them – for the time being he could afford this happiness. 'What did he say, exactly?'

'Oh, he thinks he's such a tough guy. He tried to make me bring the credit-card machine but I refused. Imagine such bad manners, going on your boat with the machine! I said we would pay for this weekend but no more, next week is my vacation. He protested so I wrote in my paybook, ''Olga is making her holidays from Monday to Sunday'' and I walked out. The girls all agreed with me, even the Chinese manager who likes me to sing said it was okay. And for this weekend I am giving you back my share, I have cash in my bag.'

Hargreave loved her for that. It was on the tip of his tongue to tell her to keep it, but he stopped himself – he didn't want to establish any precedents he might later regret. Moreover, whilst he was paying her he had control of the situation, the relationship. All he wanted was her, but it was early days yet for a commitment. 'He knows you'll be with me all next week?'

'No, only this weekend. He suspects, of course, but I said I was resting and going shopping and going to the beach. If he looks for you in the hotels he will not find you, will he? He does not know about this lovely boat! So I've tricked that pig.'

Hargreave doubted her trick would work, but he was glad she'd tried it. 'Is he so bad?'

'Such a pig, all the girls say so. And always trying to fuck us.'

He wanted her out of that life. 'And have you?'

'*Me?* Vladimir? I would rather die!'

Thank God for that. 'Does he pester you?'

'Now he's stopped, he knows what I think of him.'

'Does he dislike you too?'

'Pigs like him don't have feelings, they're just greedy.'

'Does he know who I am?'

'No. I haven't told anybody, not even Yolanda, she thinks you're a businessman.' She put her arm around him and squeezed. 'I wouldn't betray you, darling, please don't worry; I am very proud of you, I would like to tell everybody, but I know this life.' She hugged him. 'And now shall we stop worrying about Mr Vladimir and think about the lovely time we are going to have? Can I catch a fish tomorrow?'

The next morning they woke up late because they were making love much of the night. There was hardly a breeze but Olga wanted to sail: Hargreave would rather have stayed in bed with her but he wanted to please her. There are few places to sail around Macao because it is ringed by China's islands and mainland, so he headed back to the Club Nautico, went to the Marine Department to complete port-clearance formalities, then headed back into the international lane. He unfurled the genoa. The breeze had improved, the big sail filled and wrenched, and he cut the engine.

The yacht creamed along at a graceful four knots in the silence, slightly heeled. Olga was enthralled. '*It is so thrilling . . . !*' She examined the sheets and halyards carefully, asking the function of each. 'So to make the sail smaller you wind it up with this rope?'

'On that electric winch.' He pointed.

'Electric! And to make it bigger you give out more rope?'

'Right. And to trim the sail, to tighten it, you heave in with this rope, on this winch.'

'Right. Very good. Now how do we work the big sail?'

He operated the electric winch and the mainsail came sliding out of the mast. It filled and the boat heeled a little more.

'Oh, wonderful. Now explain how you did that, captain.'

She climbed around the boat studying the system, pointing out parts to herself and figuring out their function. Hargreave watched her from the cockpit, charmed by her enthusiasm: he looked at her clambering around in her bikini, at her golden curves and he felt he was the luckiest man in the world. *And* she didn't get seasick. He had been concerned about that possibility. The hydrofoil overtook them and she waved energetically and laughed with glee when its wash sent the yacht pitching. Macao was dropping over the horizon astern when she came back to the cockpit, declaring herself conversant with all the gear. 'It is so understandable if you use your head.'

She wanted to understand the navigational equipment. He took her into the wheelhouse and showed her the chart. 'Here's Macao, here's Hong Kong, forty miles apart, and here's the international shipping lane connecting them. Outside of this lane is China's waters and we can't go there. All those islands over there –' he pointed – 'are China's, and over the horizon is the mainland. If we enter their waters we'll be arrested.'

He explained the satellite navigation system, read off the latest fix and drew in their position on the chart with his parallel rulers. Olga was fascinated. 'So we can never get lost?'

'Of course, between Macao and Hong Kong I only need the compass. But on the high seas I wouldn't get lost, provided the sat-nav keeps working. If it breaks down I would use this.' He produced the sextant from its box. 'Elementary geometry.'

'Oh, you are so clever!' She meant it.

'A junior schoolboy could do it, after he'd read this book.' He produced Mary Bluett's *Celestial Navigation for Yachtsmen*, forty pages long, including the big diagrams.

'Then I must study it.' She reverted to the chart: 'And where are we going to sleep tonight?'

'Well, it's getting late, the Marine Department headquarters will be closed. So we'll anchor off one of the islands and check in tomorrow. Means we can't go ashore tonight.'

In the middle of the afternoon they cleared the end of Lantau Island and the magnificent colony opened up before them. He furled the sails and they cruised slowly through the anchored ships and into the fairway. Olga was enthralled. She sat on top of the wheelhouse, binoculars to her eyes, elbows on her knees, swivelling around, studying one side of the harbour, then the other. 'So much business . . .'

Hargreave was seeing the wonders of Hong Kong afresh through her excited eyes. 'That's the Ocean Terminal,' he pointed, 'and that's the Star Ferry terminal, and behind it is Statue Square with the old Supreme Court building. And see that big glass skyscraper to the left – that's the Bank of China.'

'So much money?'

'It owns most of the best real estate in Hong Kong. That tall building beside it is the Citicorp Bank, one of the biggest in America. And over to the right, that big grey monstrosity is the Hongkong & Shanghai Bank, one of the richest in the world, where I keep my money. And behind it is Government House.'

'Is that where you live, darling?'

'When I'm in town. And see that ugly tall building to the left? – that's the new Supreme Court, where I earn my money.'

She peered through the binoculars. 'Wow . . . So that's where you're the boss?'

'Well, the Chief Justice, the Attorney General and I kind of share the joint. And ahead is the famous Wanchai where all the girlie-bars are.'

'*The World of Suzie Wong*, I read the story! So nice! I feel she is my friend! Except I am luckier than Suzie, huh?'

'Absolutely.'

'Absolutely, poor Suzie, no director, no yacht. Oh darling –' she flung her arms wide – 'I'm so happy!'

Hargreave grinned. 'And so am I.'

She smiled at him, eyes suddenly moist, then raised the binoculars again: 'I'm a tourist!'

Hargreave pointed. 'And see all those junks over there – in there is the yacht club where my boat lives, and over there is our famous Kai Tak Airport, one of the most dangerous in the world. The aircraft have to fly straight towards those Kowloon mountains, then do a hairpin turn and skim over the rooftops to that narrow runway jutting out into all those boats.'

She studied it through the binoculars. 'Those pilots are almost as clever as you, darling.' She swung back to the Peak. 'Can we see where you live?'

'Not from here. All right, it's getting late, let's go'n find a nice anchorage.' He swung the wheel and turned around.

The sun was getting low when they returned to Lantau Island. They were on their third bottle of wine. He dropped anchor a hundred yards offshore in a deserted bay. There was a small crescent of beach between two rocky points, and a new middle-class housing development up the coast, a few miles away. To the north Hong Kong island loomed. 'Can we swim even though we haven't been through immigration control yet?'

'Provided you don't set your pretty foot ashore.'

But first they lounged in the cockpit in the sultry sunset, watching the lights of distant Hong Kong come on, drinking another bottle of wine. Olga was captivated all over again by the beauty of the place. The moon was coming up, and Hargreave was on his second whisky when she took it into her head that it was time to go for that swim. She pulled off her bikini and leaped up on to the wheelhouse top, silvery-golden in the moonlight. She dived into the moonlit sea, in a flash of streamlined femaleness. She broke surface, gasping, her hair swirling about her shoulders. 'Come on! It feels so sexy naked.'

Hargreave did not greatly enjoy swimming – in and out just to get cool was about his speed. And he didn't like swimming in the dark – he imagined sinister marine creatures bent on discommoding him. But in all his forty-six years Alistair Hargreave had never swum naked with a woman, and it was that erotic notion that galvanized him into action – plus, no doubt, all the booze sloshing around inside him. He put down his glass, unzipped his shorts, clambered up on to the wheelhouse and dived in to join his glorious girl down there. Olga gave a squeal and began to thrash away into deeper water, away from the island she'd been forbidden to set foot upon. Hargreave thrashed after her, to get that silvery loveliness in his arms. Olga swam away from him, legs and arms flashing in the moonlight: they were about thirty yards from the yacht when she let him catch up with her. And oh, the glorious slippery feel of her in his arms, writhing against him as she trod water and thrust her laughing mouth against his: then the stomach cramps hit him.

One moment Al Hargreave was laughing in a sensuous embrace, the next agony struck, a spasm that doubled him over, clutching his guts, holding him in a vice, wrenching his head underwater – all he knew through the agony was the terror of gasping in bitter salt water, the terrifying panic of strangulation. He thrashed back to the surface and gasped in another mouthful of choking water; he gagged and coughed, trying to spit it out. Another spasm wrenched him down, and Olga pulled him back to the surface. She grabbed him by the hair and hauled his head up, shouting, '*Don't panic!*' She pulled him over on to his back and thrust her hand under his chin to hold his face uppermost – '*Don't panic – don't struggle – take deep breaths!*' She trod water desperately as Hargreave gasped, trying to tread water through the agony of the cramp, choking and gasping again, his heart pounding. '*Kick your feet while I pull you . . .*' She started swimming with one arm, the other supporting his chin. She looked over her shoulder for the boat, and was horrified to see how far it was – and then she felt the current.

The tide was going out, sweeping around the tip of the island; the

78

boat was fifty yards off, and within a minute Olga knew she could not swim with Hargreave against the flow. She looked desperately at the other side of the bay – the rocky point was two hundred yards away. That was the only way she was going to get him out of this crisis, by using the current. Olga turned and started swimming desperately towards that point, on her back, frog-legging, one arm back-stroking, gasping; *'Kick – kick like a frog!'* Hargreave tried to kick, the agony shooting through his guts, his arms desperately working, his chin clasped above water by Olga's hand, gasping, coughing, retching.

Olga swam and swam with the tide, desperately trying to steer towards the point, her heart pounding, and then the exhaustion began to take hold. She thrashed and thrashed and thrashed, and the pain came screeching into her arms and legs and pounding heart, exhaustion that built and built to agony, and still she thrashed, gasping *'Kick – kick . . .'* Hargreave kicked and kicked, water slopping into his rasping mouth with each jerk, coughing and gulping in more: and then Olga could fight no longer; she just had to stop to get the pounding out of her heart; for a moment she went limp, gasping *'I can't go on!'* Hargreave's head went underwater and he floundered panic-stricken, and Olga cried *'I'm here,'* and wrenched his head up. She started swimming again, flailing and gasping.

Now the moonlit point was only ninety yards off, now eighty, the current threatening to carry them past it into the open sea beyond. Olga screwed up the last of her desperate strength and gasped *'Nearly there . . .'* She thrashed and kicked with all her crying-out exhausted might, trying to steer across the treacherous current, and Hargreave was racked afresh by cramp and his head twisted out of Olga's hand and she shrieked and grabbed his chin again. She thrashed as Hargreave tried to kick through his gut-wrenching agony, and then Olga could not fight on. She simply could not go any further, and she looked wildly at the point: it was only thirty yards off, and she cried *'We're there – kick!'* Hargreave kicked and kicked with the last of the agonized endurance, rasping, gasping, coughing, gagging, drowning. Then Olga's exhausted foot found the sand.

It was the sweetest feeling in the world. She trod on the sand, sobbing, trying to say *It's okay – I've got you –* but no words came out. She thrashed and plodded and dragged Hargreave to the rocks.

10

She lay flat out on her belly in the moonlight, long hair matted in sand, gasping her breath back. Hargreave lay spreadeagled beside her, trembling with exhaustion.

'You saved my life . . .'

'My fault . . . Shouldn't swim . . . with so much booze . . .'

'Never had cramp like that before . . .'

'I have. I should have known better . . .'

She rolled over on to her back, arms outflung, and looked up at the stars. Her breasts and belly and thighs were covered in sand. After a minute, she said, 'How are we going to get you back to the boat?'

'I'll swim.'

'No, you risk your life. *And* mine.'

Hargreave sat up wearily. 'You could fetch the dinghy,' he said.

'Yes. Of course.'

'Can you row?'

'I can learn.' She heaved herself into a sitting position.

Then Hargreave realized that he had forgotten to put the swimming ladder down before he dived in. 'Oh Lord . . . You won't be able to get aboard, the gunnels are too high.'

Olga stared out at the yacht lying out there in the moonlight, registering this information: then she dropped her head and giggled. 'Oh no! And we are naked on the beach.' Then Hargreave saw the funny side of it despite himself. Olga laughed: *'So the only solution is to walk naked to the village and borrow some clothes!'*

'Borrow us a sampan while you're about it.'

'Me?'

'You're the pretty one!'

Olga threw back her head in the moonlight and guffawed. She collapsed back on the sand, arms outflung. 'This is so *funny*. Naked in Hong Kong! But what are we going to do, darling?'

Hargreave stood up, grinning. He walked into the water and washed the sand off his hands. 'Climb up the anchor chain,' he said.

Olga sat up again. 'Of course!'

'Haven't done it for years; it's damn hard, but it can be done.'

'Not you – *me*,' Olga said emphatically. 'At gymnastics we had to climb up ropes, my arms are very strong. Look!' She bent her elbow and made her biceps hard. 'So impressive! I am not letting you swim out there and drown.'

'In an hour the tide will have turned and whatever causes cramp will have gone away.'

'No, I am not letting you . . . !'

'Al Hargreave may be unathletic but he's not a complete prick. Would Errol Flynn have let his girl swim out there alone to climb anchor chains? Sean Connery would do it in his dinner jacket.' He spread his arms. 'Relax. You're marooned in the hot China night on a deserted beach with your very own yacht out there – all we've got to do is climb up the fucking anchor chain. What could be more romantic?'

'With my own true love?'

'So come here and let me wash that sand off your beautiful body.'

She did not have to save his life again when they finally swam out to the boat when the tide had turned: she stayed beside him but the cramp did not return. She was as good as her word about rope-climbing: while he clung to the anchor chain she put one foot on his shoulder, grabbed the chain above his head, stood, then went hand over hand up the short distance to the bows. She grabbed the gunnel, then swung one leg up under the rail, lost her grip and crashed back into the water with an undignified flash of naked flesh. Giggling, she tried again. This time she succeeded. She wriggled under the rail, and got to her feet.

In the morning they sailed to the yacht club. Hargreave left Olga aboard while he took a taxi to the Marine Department and completed port-entrance formalities: he got her admitted into the colony as his crew-member without a hitch – the young Chinese immigration officer recognized him and did not query Olga's profession of singer recorded on her Macao identity card. 'Have a nice sail, Mr Hargreave.'

They had a lovely sail, for the next week. That first day he circum-navigated Hong Kong, to show Olga the bustling industrial development and the beautiful bays and luxurious apartment complexes on the other sides of the island. 'So much money – so much work!' He anchored in Repulse Bay for the night amongst dozens of yachts and pleasure junks out for the long weekend. They sat on deck in a beautiful sunset, the jungled mountains looming up, the shore lined with the lights of gracious apartment blocks, music and laughter wafting across from the boats.

'We were told at school,' Olga began, 'that the West was terrible, only very few people were rich, all the rest very poor, without enough food, dying of cold. Our teachers showed us movies of New York in the winter, the hoboes freezing while the rich people ate in restaurants and all their children took drugs and all the pretty girls had to be prostitutes. The American army were well-fed because their only job was to conquer Russia to make us slaves. And the whole of Europe was the same, our teachers told us, and England was worse, because you have a queen. I remember, when I was a little girl, when Prince Charles married Diana, we were shown a movie of them at Buckingham Palace after the wedding, on the balcony, the crowds of people outside, and our teacher told us the crowd was demanding bread.'

Hargreave smiled. 'And you believed your teacher.'

'Of course, I was only about ten. Even my father and mother believed it. I wanted very much to be a soldier for Communism to help those poor American and English people, to give them food, so their children could grow up happy like me. And when they showed us pictures of the Berlin Wall to keep out all the nasty West Germans and Americans, I clapped. I was very patriotic, darling, when I was ten.'

'And then?'

'And Africa – our teachers showed us such pictures of little black babies crying with nothing in their stomachs and flies on their noses and their mothers' breasts all empty, and we were told this was the fault of the capitalists who were making them work in their factories and mines, who killed all the wild animals and chopped down all the trees for firewood in London and New York. And we saw many pictures of brave Russian and Cuban soldiers fighting to free them from such misery. And, oh, I wanted to be a soldier. I was going to be a parachutist, darling!'

'A parachutist?' Oh, he loved her.

'Jumping out of the sky with my machine-gun and shooting all those nasty capitalists. And when we saw movies of the Americans fleeing out of Vietnam – oh boy, I wanted to marry a soldier so much!'

Hargreave laughed. 'And when did you change?'

'When I started to get tits, I suppose. When all us girls started to look at black-market magazines from the West – fashions and icecreams and motor cars. And one of my friends had a brother who had come back from the army and he told her many things. My mother was dead and my father was very sick now, and my brother had left to work in the mines. Then suddenly Mr Gorbachev was the new boss and he was talking about *perestroika* and *glasnost*. I was living in the orphanage now and I was very interested in boys, and clothes, and all this was very exciting to us. We only understood that the West was maybe not so bad, but to us it meant being pretty girls with rich husbands. So romantic. Then I went to work in the aluminium factory, but there were no pretty clothes, everybody was poor except the apparatchiks; things got worse not better because there was so much confusion, so many criminals now. Then I was offered the job at Mosfilm, like I told you, but it really was a KGB job. Then everything went crazy when the old Communists tried to take Gorbachev's power, and I was sent to Istanbul. I was very confused.'

'And now?'

She spread her arms. 'Now I am the happiest girl in the world, with my knight in shining armour. Now I am not confused, even if I am still a whore.'

'You're not, you're a singer.'

She smiled. 'Yes, with you I am not a whore. And I never want to be a whore again, that is what I have learned, that is one of the things I am not confused about.'

He believed her; but what would she do the week after next when this holiday was over? He felt the happiest man in the world, too – but was this the real world?

'And another thing I am not confused about: now I really know what I want to be. I always wanted to do it, but now I am really determined. Study to be a vet. I like animals very much. On the collective farm I often helped the vet, and I was very good at school with chemistry and biology, so interesting. So after I have bought my brother a farm I will study to be a vet.'

He was very pleased to hear that. She was no whore in her heart! But it raised a number of questions. 'But where? In Russia?'

She wanted to say, Wherever you are. She smiled: 'Wherever I can, darling, I will find a way to do it.'

Oh, yes, he wanted her to do it, he wanted to ensure she did it, pay for her to do it, but it was too early yet to consider the implications of all that. At that moment the two-way radio rasped in the wheelhouse: 'Yacht *Elizabeth*, this is *Kingfisher*, come in.'

Hargreave went to the machine and picked up the receiver. '*Kingfisher*, *Elizabeth*, good evening, Jake. Pick a channel.'

'Seventy.'

'Seventy.' Hargreave turned his control switch from the mandatory Channel 16 to Channel 70. 'Where are you, Jake, over?'

'Anchored about two hundred yards astern of you. Want to come over for a drink? I've got some friends aboard for the weekend.' He added: 'Including some very pretty ones.'

Hargreave hesitated. It would be nice to see Jake but right now it was much nicer being alone with Olga, and he didn't want to face questions about her; they hadn't even worked out a proper alibi yet.

'Not now, thanks Jake, we're just making supper, maybe tomorrow. Where're you going from here?'

'Thinking about having lunch on Lamma, join us if you like. After that just wandering up the islands, probably to Sai Kung area.'

'Good, we'll look for each other on channel sixteen, huh?'

'Roger, we'll be listening. Have a good time. Out.'

They had a good time. They slept late the next morning. Repulse Bay beach was full of people; there were many more pleasure-craft anchored when Hargreave and Olga left, lots of topless girls sunbathing on decks. They did not go to Lamma for lunch: it is a pretty island, with a quaint Chinese village with excellent seafood restaurants and Hargreave indeed intended taking Olga there sometime this week, but not today: today was a public holiday, there might be many people he knew and he did not want to start tongues wagging about Olga, and why Liz shot him. So after a late champagne breakfast they set sail up the island-studded coast towards Sai Kung area. The sun shone hot out of a clear sky, the blue sea was flat but there was just enough breeze to fill the sails and keep them cool. Hargreave was very happy: this is what he would love to do for the rest of his life, sailing, messing about on boats, living on his own boat, maybe even making a bit of money out of it – he would be perfectly happy for the rest of his life in the Caribbean, taking the odd charter party out for a week's cruising around the islands to augment his pension, he would be perfectly happy living like that with Olga. Look at her – she was loving it as much as he, revelling in the quiet *shh-shh* of the sea, loving the gentle slop and surge of the sails, the feeling of freedom, of free power, of working with nature, having an adventure, sailing to distant islands, sailing anywhere you like, to faraway places with strange-sounding names.

'Darling, this is so beautiful . . .'

And *she* was so beautiful: she was sitting topless on the roof of the wheelhouse, sometimes studying the islands through binoculars, sometimes flopping on to her back, arms spreadeagled, just looking up at the sails towering above her.

'Alistair, I could do this for ever.'

He was sitting on the wheelhouse roof near her, his legs dangling over the end, looking aft, drinking beer. 'And what about being a vet?'

She rolled over on to her stomach.

'You see, when I am a vet I will make lots of money. And you will not have to be a lawyer any more. You can look after the boat, you see, and maybe the chickens and ducks too, and then every weekend we can sail this boat. *But –*' she held up a finger – 'at the end of every month I do not work for the next month, because I have made so much money and anyway I am such a good vet all the animals are very healthy, so off we go sailing for a month!'

It was a pretty scenario. 'And where's your surgery going to be?'

Her reply astonished him. 'Cuba.' She added: 'Anywhere you like: maybe Florida is better for you Englishmen, but I like Cuba.'

Hargreave grinned. 'Why?'

She rolled over on to her back again and looked up at the sails.

'Because,' she said solemnly, 'Cuba is like Russia, starting all over, only much better. So exotic. Beaches and palm trees. And rum! Cuba is soon going to collapse, like Russia, and then it is also going to need *everything*. And then Cuba is going to go *vroom*, because the Americans are going to put a lot of money into Cuba, oh boy yes. And Cuba is a very big agricultural country, many farms, many animals and they will need many vets. But all the fat American vets will not go there, because they are making so much money looking after cats and dogs in Miami, and New York, and all the Spanish vets are making too much money in Madrid, and anyway Spaniards do not love animals because they have those terrible bullfights. So they will need plenty of vets in Cuba. And Cuba will be like America was fifty years ago – many opportunities.' She held up her finger at the sails: 'And *that* is when Doctor Olga Romalova arrives!'

Hargreave grinned. 'And when are you going to start studying?'

She looked up at him seriously, upside-down.

'When I leave Macao. I already have enough money, even after I have bought a farm for my brother and me – I have decided I will not buy an apartment.' She paused. 'But, of course, if you do not tell me to go away, I will start after you leave Hong Kong.'

Tell me to go away. Oh you poor girl. Before he could respond she twisted on to her stomach, scrambled to her knees and flung her arms around his shoulders. 'Oh, don't be frightened of me – I am not putting pressure on you! I am so sorry! Oh darling, of course you are not responsible for me, we are just discussing and the truth is I love you

85

so of course I want to do what you say, but I am not a crazy girl who thinks everything is decided, I am just telling you what *I* have decided about my life because I do not like to be a prostitute any more!'

'I didn't look frightened, did I?' Hargreave grinned.

'Oh –' she waggled her sweaty breasts against his head and hugged him – 'your face, so funny, so worried! Darling, there is no problem for you, I am just telling you my exciting future now I am almost not a whore any more. And I have already written a letter to the University of Moscow, and the University of Miami, asking how much it costs, soon I will know something. Oh darling –' she clasped his face to her and rocked him – 'do not be frightened of me – now let's stop talking about it.'

No, he was not frightened of her: he was enchanted. Her enthusiasm and energy seemed as boundless as her beauty.

That afternoon they anchored in an empty cove on Tap Mun Chau and went ashore with goggles and snorkels. They swam along the rocky shoreline, looking at the marine life: Olga led the way, and Hargreave was not watching too much marine life; he was entranced by the beautiful form ahead of him, her buttocks, her lovely long golden legs smoothly working the flippers, her long blonde hair streaming silkily behind her: she was the most sensuous creature in the world. They walked along the deserted beach together, looking at the shells and seaweed and jetsam, Olga crouching to examine bits of this and that, holding them up to the sun to admire the colours: she caught a very worried sandcrab and held it up for Hargreave to admire.

'Look how perfect this animal is. Look at his shell, to protect him. Look at his little claws, to catch his food – so strong. Look at his little breathing place – and look at his eyes! How can eyes so small have all the lenses and nerves and things to tell him what he is seeing?' She put the crab down and watched it scurry away gratefully. 'God is very clever, even though I don't believe in Him.'

'I think you do.'

'Yes? Then why is there so much suffering?'

'Because long ago God decided to let us do our own thing and not interfere, so we would develop our characters, become strong.'

'But if He decided not to interfere, why do you pray for help?'

'In the hope He will grant it.'

She mused, walking along, head down, very dissatisfied with that answer. 'But God knows *every*thing. So He knew long ago whether you would pray or not, and He knew long ago He would not interfere because He wanted you to be strong. So what is the hope in praying? You cannot make God change His mind by praying because He already knew before the world began what He was going to do.' She stopped to pick up a shell. 'I wish I understood that. If I did, I would pray.'

Hargreave wished he understood it too. 'Maybe by praying we harness some of His strength to ourselves.'

'Hmm,' Olga mused, 'I must think about that. Like the yogis. Maybe that is the solution to the puzzle.'

They were swimming nude, about twenty yards from the yacht, when Jake McAdam's junk came around the point and turned into their bay. There were three girls sunbathing topless on the foredeck, Jake and a dozen people on the big afterdeck. Jake shouted: 'Come over for a drink!' He steamed past them and dropped anchor about a hundred yards away. Hargreave and Olga swam back to their yacht. She mounted the swimming ladder and put on her bikini and he pulled on his swimming trunks.

'Remember you're a singer.'

'That's me. At the big hotels. And I'm making my holidays.'

'And we met in the floating casino, because Jake knows I don't go to night-clubs.'

They clambered down the ladder into the inflatable dinghy. He started the outboard motor and they chugged over to Jake's junk and tied up to his swimming ladder.

'Welcome aboard!'

Hargreave need not have worried. Jake remembered Olga – 'How could I forget that tango?' – but nobody else had seen her before. The party was going strong and everybody was very jolly. Jake was with a physiotherapist called Monica with whom he had a long-standing affair of convenience: Hargreave knew most of the fourteen people aboard, at least casually: they were a mixed bag, as Jake's parties usually were, from highbrow to low-brow: Doc Dobson, a bachelor from the government clinic whose 'tiresome duty' it was to keep tabs on the venereal health of Wanchai bar-girls; Jack-the-Fire, a senior fireman with his ageing live-in girlfriend, Nancy Smythe, who was a teacher; Harry Howard, the stockbroker with his imperturbable Chinese mistress, Petal, who was a psychiatrist ('He's crazy, even more than me'); Denys Watson, a very successful barrister whose weaknesses were whisky and women, who had left his long-suffering wife at home; Whacker Ball, a misogynist who was the editor of the *Oriental Israelite*, a caustic weekly digest of Hong Kong news owned by Jake; Isabel Phipson, the very attractive headmistress with her lesbian lover, Penny, who was Jake's bookkeeper: though there were some new faces, Hargreave counted these people as his friends – and Elizabeth's – and they all seemed pleased to see him. Nobody mentioned Elizabeth or his bullet wound – his dramatic scar was exposed – although there were many interested looks cast at Olga. ('*Wow*,' Isabel Phipson joshed him, 'lucky boy, Al, where did you find her?' 'Hands orf!' Hargreave grinned, and Isabel went into giggles.) 'What a lovely girl, Al,' Denys Watson murmured, 'where's she from?'

'You hands orf, too, Denys!' Isabel giggled, and they all laughed. Hargreave liked Denys, who stoically excluded his friends' women from his weakness.

'She's from Russia,' Hargreave said, 'she's a night-club singer in Macao.'

'How do you do, I am Olga Romalova from Russia,' he heard her say above the music and chit-chat, pumping hands energetically with Whacker Ball.

'And what brings you to our part of the world, Olga?' Whacker boomed.

'I am a singer, now I am making some holidays . . .'

Doc Dobson put his hand on Hargreave's shoulder and whispered, 'What a charming girl. Even Whacker likes her.'

Charming – that was the word for her. Hargreave watched surreptitiously as he circulated around the big afterdeck: now Olga was the centre of a small circle of people, the formerly-topless girls and Harry Howard: they all laughed uproariously at something she had just said. Jack-the-Fire, who was getting along with the whisky, murmured, 'Good on yer, Al – I hope she's not going back to Russia too quick.'

'I hope so too.'

'I hope she goes back tomorrow,' Petal twinkled, 'just look at that crazy man of mine, eating out of her hand!' She held a finger up at Hargreave: 'So, maybe she's young, Alistair, but that doesn't matter if her heart is good, and that girl has a kind heart, I can tell.'

Hargreave felt proud of her; she was the centre of attention and she was handling the task admirably. He knew everybody was being kind because they felt sorry for him because Liz had left him in a blaze of embarrassment, but he also knew they were genuinely charmed by Olga, and he was delighted.

'Interesting woman,' Whacker Ball rumbled beside him. 'Telling me about the Roman ruins in Istanbul.' Whacker liked Roman ruins.

'She was working in Istanbul before she came here,' Hargreave said.

'One of my favourite watering-holes,' Denys the Menace slurred. 'Which nightclub?'

'I'm not sure,' Hargreave said, 'I think she mentioned the Trocadero as one of them.'

'Trocadero?' Denys said. 'Don't know it.'

Jake put his hand on his shoulder. 'Nice to see you looking happy, pal; how long is she around for?'

'Her agent's trying to negotiate another contract for her in Macao, in the Estoril, I think.'

'Where's her agent?'

'Moscow.'

'Congratulations on that heroin case,' Whacker rumbled. 'Twenty years – that'll keep Edward Lo out of mischief for a while.'

'Will it stand up on appeal?' Denys asked. 'Evidence mostly circumstantial.'

'It'll stand up,' Hargreave said. 'There was nothing wrong with the judge's summing up.'

'The Chinese will probably shoot convicts like Edward Lo when they take over,' Denys said, 'appeal or no appeal. That's what Mao did when he took over China. Oh, justice is going to be such fun after 1997.'

'Are you staying on?' Hargreave asked.

'Where else can a beat-up lawyer like me make money like this? I'll stay until they make life too uncomfortable, like shooting defence lawyers as subversives. And you?'

'I don't know yet.'

'I thought you were definitely quitting?' Isabel Phipson said. Isabel didn't know about Californian divorce law and Community of Property.

'Why don't you go up on to the bench, Al?' Denys said. 'You'll probably be safer from the Comrades up there.'

'Until I hand down judgements they don't like?'

'Oh, justice is going to be such fun,' Denys said again.

'And what about our pensions?' Isabel said. 'We better save like hell in the next eighteen months, chaps, I don't see the Comrades letting our pensions flow out of the holy soil every month. Are you leaving, Whacker?'

'Me leave?' Whacker growled. 'When the Comrades take over is when the *Oriental Israelite* really starts getting bitchy – it'll be an honest journalist's dream.'

'Until they close you down,' Hargreave said. 'And shoot you, for "literary hooliganism".'

'Amen,' Denys said. 'And us for defending him. And the judge for acquitting him.'

'If there's a trial at all,' McAdam said. He turned away to recharge his glass.

'Hullo, my dear,' Denys murmured to Olga as she joined them. She looked radiant, the sunset on her golden hair and face. Hargreave smiled at her proudly.

'I'll go down fighting,' Whacker growled. 'I'm almost seventy, for Christ's sake, what else is there to live for at my age but the truth? And I'll defend myself, thanks, really give 'em an earful. No, I'm staying. I wouldn't miss the fun for the world.'

'Do you really think,' Monica asked Hargreave, 'that China will get rid of people like Whacker? And Jake? And Martin Lee?'

'No doubt about it,' Denys said.

Hargreave said, 'China probably won't shoot them, but a trumped-up charge to throw them in jail after a show trial is quite likely, to silence them.'

'I've *begged* Jake,' Monica said, 'to pull his punches in his electioneering, but he won't. I think he's being very foolish, antagonizing China so.'

Whacker growled, 'Courageous yes, reckless maybe, but foolish never. He's got to tell the people the truth.'

'He can't tell the truth for long if he's in jail,' Monica said.

'What is the difference,' Olga asked, 'between Jake and Martin Lee?'

Monica grinned: 'Martin Lee is richer, smarter and better-looking.'

Everybody laughed.

'Richer, no doubt, smarter, probably,' Jake said, returning with his glass recharged, 'but personally I've always wondered about the better-looking.'

'I mean,' Olga grinned, 'why is Jake an independent, not working with Mr Lee, what is the difference?'

'None,' Whacker said, 'except Martin Lee is a gentleman who only calls a spade a spade; Jake calls it a fuckin' shovel.'

Everybody laughed again. Jake said to Olga: 'No difference except, as an independent candidate I can say things he can't because I'm not bound by party rules.' He added: 'However, I won't win a seat – my eyes are the wrong shape. I'm only really interested in making a lot of noise so the people hear what I have to say.'

'And what is that?' Olga asked.

McAdam sighed. 'What Martin Lee says: we *must* have a strong democracy in place so we can stand up to China when she takes over.

We must show China we are a voice to be reckoned with, we must insist that Britain – and the United Nations – enforces the Joint Declaration, forces China to abide by its international undertakings, forces China to abide by the agreement that our Court of Final Appeal will be made up of respected Western judges, not party toadies appointed by Beijing who can't read English, let alone understand English law and who will do what the party instructs –'

'Hear, hear,' Hargreave said.

McAdam made a fist: 'We must insist that Britain punishes China when she sweeps aside our elections, insist the world comes down like a ton of bricks with all kinds of economic sanctions: freeze her foreign assets, close down her embassies, throw them out of the United Nations, treat them as untouchables – really *hurt* them. Even threaten war – Christ, there're six million Chinese British subjects in Hong Kong who're entitled to Her Majesty's protection.'

'Hear, fuckin' hear,' Whacker growled.

'But what is Great Mother Britain doing? Appeasing China at every turn, so as to not rock the boat, *appeasing* "in the interests of a smooth transition". By the Joint Declaration China must not interfere with the running of Hong Kong until 1997, and our autonomy after 1997 is guaranteed but China is interfering all the time, announcing they'll kick out our Legislative Council and abolish our Bill of Human Rights, threatening our business community with reprisals if they don't toe the China line, throwing Hong Kong journalists in jail, telling our press they had better "bend with the wind". And they've slandered our Governor for introducing reforms, calling him a "liar" and a "criminal", "a prostitute", a "Buddha's serpent", "a villain condemned by history for a thousand years".' He looked at Olga. 'And what does Great Mother Britain do? Does she shake a stick and say: "We *insist* you adhere to the Joint Declaration or we'll make sure the whole world kicks your arse"? No. Britain simpers and whines and does a hand-wringing exercise and appeases and compromises, all for the sake of,' he made quotation marks with his fingers, '"a smooth transition". The result? We face a Communist tyranny here in eighteen months.' He ended grimly: 'Britain must realize that the only way to protect her subjects is to be *tough. That*'s what I'm telling the people.'

'You can't tell them a damn thing if you're sitting in jail,' Monica said. Her eyes suddenly moistened. 'Excuse me.' She headed away abruptly to the booze table.

Everybody glanced at McAdam. Denys, to fill the brief silence, said to Olga: 'And tell me, my dear, what's it like in Russia these days?'

'Alas, it is very bad,' Olga replied. 'So much chaos . . .'

Jake McAdam murmured in Hargreave's ear: 'She's a knockout, Al. Now, are you guys going to stay for dinner?'

'Thanks, Jake,' Hargreave said, 'but I think we'll go back, we've got some nice fresh oysters waiting.'

'Oysters?' Jake joshed him. 'Go for it, pal, happy sailing . . .'

11

And it was happy. Sailing around Hong Kong's multitude of islands, anchoring in deserted bays for long boozy lunches and sensual siestas: they meandered through the archipelago of Sai Kung district, went ashore in the dinghy to explore Chinese hamlets with little smoky temples to Tin Hau, goddess of the seas, where the people seldom saw a white man. They lived as they had before the battles long ago, and had come from the age of warlords to the age of television without a revolution. Hargreave bought fish and prawns and oysters from them. On up the crooked coastline they sailed, across Tolo Channel to Wong Wan Chau, then up to Crooked Harbour and Kat O Chau, overlooking Mirs Bay which brave Chinese lads and lasses swam to escape to Hong Kong, the 'Golden Mountain Where Men Eat Fat Pork'. They sailed through Starling Inlet to Shatau Kok where the border runs through the middle of the road that is called Chung-Ying Street, Chung being an abbreviation of Chung Kwok which means China-country, Ying an abbreviation of Ying-Kwok meaning England-country. Olga was enthralled. Hargreave knew all the islands very well, they were old-hat to him, but now he was seeing them afresh through her eyes, and they became exotic all over again. They swam in deserted little bays, splashing around and playing the fool, snorkelling along the rocks exploring the underwater world, beachcombing, climbing grassy hills just to see what was on the other side: it seemed to Hargreave he had never been so happy.

And, oh no, he did not want her to go back to Macao next Monday, he could not bear the thought of her going back to 'work'. Anyway, how could he afford to keep paying for her? He would have to make a final settlement with Vladimir and take her away from all that, or forget about her – and he could not forget about her. So there was only one realistic thing to do.

It was on Friday, the second-last day of their sailing idyll, that Alistair Hargreave finally made up his mind. They were at anchor in a little cove on Kai Sai Chau, in the hour after love; he said, rehearsed:

'I've got some leave accumulated, about four weeks – I didn't take it all last year. Why don't we go to the Philippines, you and I, sail this boat down there, spend some time cruising those islands?'

There was silence for a moment, then Olga scrambled up on to her knees and looked at him. 'Oh, can we *really*?'

Hargreave grinned, delighted with her delight. 'It's only six hundred miles to Manila, I've sailed it often, and the islands are lovely; hundreds and hundreds of them, white beaches and turquoise water. And if we get bored we can go ashore and explore inland.'

'Oh, darling . . .'

Hargreave looked at her and made the commitment. He said soberly, 'And meantime I don't want you to go back to Macao, Olga. I don't want you to go back to the Tranquillity. I want you to come to stay with me in my apartment until we sail for the Philippines.' *There – he had said it.*

Olga stared at him, her blue eyes shining.

'Oh darling!' She knelt forward and hugged him, her beautiful breasts squashed against his chest, her shapely bottom up in the air: 'Oh, *darling*, how *wonder*ful!'

Hargreave grinned. 'So what we're going to do is this: tomorrow we'll sail over to Macao to fetch your things – I don't want you doing that alone, coming back on the ferry and perhaps falling foul of our immigration clerks again. Anyway, I'll have to see Vladimir and tell him what's happening, clear the air.' He left out 'and settle my bill once and for all'.

Olga sat upright. 'Oh, you don't pay him any more, darling! Only for last weekend, and that is *it*. Finished! Don't talk to Vladimir, let me do it, he'll try to cheat you!'

'But what about your so-called contract with him?'

'I haven't got any new contract with him! Yes, when I came from Russia I had a year's contract so it would be legal with the Portuguese, but I finished that contract three weeks ago. All I did was extend my visa, I didn't sign any new contract. Yes, I continued to work in the Tranquillity, but I did not sign anything, I can walk out any time I like!'

Maybe, but he didn't think Vladimir would see it like that: Hargreave would rather make a deal than have trouble. 'I want everything cut and dried with Vladimir, so I'll have to see him. And we've got to get your passport from him, you're going to need it to go to the Philippines.'

'I'll get my passport, don't worry, even if I have to steal it from him. I'll tell him he won't get paid for last weekend unless he gives it to me. Just you leave Vladimir to me, darling!'

That was fine with Hargreave, if it worked – the less he had to do with the likes of Vladimir the better.

Olga hugged him joyfully: 'Oh, I'm so excited! A whole month sailing in the Philippines!'

That's what they were going to do. They were going to have a lovely time. But after the month was over, then what? Hargreave did not care; a lot of things would become clear in a month, he would know what to do. All he knew right now was that he could not let this happiness go, that he could not let her go back to work on Monday.

And then they were struck by Sod's Law of the Sea.

Any experienced sailor will tell you about Sod's Law, how crises never come one at a time at sea but in twos or threes or more. In Hargreave's case they came in eights.

That Friday afternoon they were heading back to Hong Kong Island to clear port formalities on Saturday morning so they could sail on to Macao: they were in a strong wind when a faulty fitting on the backstay parted, the mast broke with a crack like a cannon and came crashing down on the rails, the sails falling into the sea. The second crisis was set in motion by Hargreave unwisely starting the engine to give him control over the boat while he cut the steel rigging with bolt-cutters: as the shattered mast finally crashed free into the sea the sails billowed under the keel and got wrapped around the churning propeller. The third crisis came when the mast, which was still attached to the tangled sail, hit the rudder and damaged it badly. By the time Hargreave had dived over the side with a carving knife to free the propeller, the mast had bent the drive-shaft as well. That was the fourth crisis: now they had no sails, no engine power, no steering, and no radio because the antenna had been at the top of the mast. Crisis number five was that darkness was falling and the wind and swells were buffeting the stricken yacht towards the shore. Sod's Law number six struck at midnight when they were driven aground on the beach of Clearwater Bay.

Their lives were not in danger, they would have escaped in the dinghy if they looked like going on the rocks instead of the beach, and Hargreave was not concerned about the expense – he was insured. What bitterly disappointed him, and Olga, was that they would not be setting sail for the Philippines soon: it would take several weeks to repair the boat; a mast would have to be made to specification, new sails and rigging had to be made, a new propeller shaft installed, the rudder-stock rebuilt. There would be no sailing for a month: that was Sod's Law number seven.

But Hargreave was determined that they would still go away together on holiday. They would fly to the Philippines and stay in a hotel on a palm-fringed beach instead. But then came Sod's Law number eight: because the yacht was out of commission, Olga had to return to Macao by ferry to fetch her clothes and passport.

It was late Sunday night when the big fishing junk which Hargreave hired towed them into the yacht club. His car was where he had parked it ten days ago: they could have driven to his apartment, but they were too tired to make the effort. Early next morning he drove Olga to the ferry. She left her weekend bag with him so she would have less to carry when she returned. Outside the terminal he gave her a cheque to give to Vladimir, 'in full and final settlement'.

'But above all get that passport from him, even if I've got to pay the bastard some more for it. Telephone me if there're any problems, let me speak to him.'

'Leave Vladimir to me, darling, this business I know better than you.'

'Just don't put his back up. Take your bags to the Macao ferry and leave them there *before* you go to see Vladimir, so you can make a fast departure if necessary.'

'Yes, darling, don't worry.'

Of course he worried. 'Phone me when you know what ferry you're on and I'll meet you. And if you don't have a chance, just take a taxi up to my apartment.' He scribbled the address.

'Yes, darling,' Olga grinned. 'And now I better go, the people are getting on board.' She kissed him hard. 'I love you,' she sparkled.

It felt as if he loved her too, but to tell a woman you love her is a very serious business and he had plenty of time for that kind of seriousness in the next glorious month in the Philippines. He kissed her and said, 'I'm so sorry about the sailing but we'll have a good time, I promise.'

'Darling, there is plenty more time when your boat is fixed, if you still want me.' She scrambled out of the car. She blew him a dazzling kiss through the window and hurried away.

If you still want me. Lord yes, he would still want her. He watched her hurry away in the crowd and those lovely legs, that tumult of blonde hair had the same effect on him as that first night on the floating casino. *More* – and she was as nice as she looked. As he drove away from the thronging terminal and made his way over the hurtling flyovers on to the road up to the Peak to shower and change before hurrying to his chambers, he was tingling with anticipation of her return tonight.

But he did not reckon with the fact that the world is a cruel place that does not care about lovers.

When he got to chambers he telephoned Maggie Brooke, his travel agent, and asked her to reserve their flights to the Philippines on the coming Saturday and book them into a paradisaical hotel. Then he telephoned his yacht insurers and gave them the bad news, then the yacht builders and asked them to order a new mast, new rigging, new sails. His next call was to the secretary of the yacht club, to arrange to have his boat hauled out on to the slipway so the engineers could go to work on her. Then he called his *amah*, Ah Moi, and broke the news that they were having a house-guest for the next few days, a relative of his from Europe – would she please prepare the guest room. Ah Moi would not believe the blood relationship once she clapped eyes on Olga, but at least that gave Olga (and Elizabeth) some face. Then he summoned his chief deputy and told him he was taking a month's leave as from next weekend, and handed over most of his responsibilities to him. Then he got down to work, with a song in his heart, to clear his desk before he did his disappearing trick.

And then, at four o'clock that afternoon, Olga telephoned, in tears.

'Darling,' she sobbed, 'I am in Macao. Pig Vladimir refused to give me my passport so I took a chance and went on the ferry with just my identity card, but your stupid immigration men sent me back again, they said a singer is really a prostitute, and they put me on their computer as a prohibited immigrant!'

Hargreave stared across his chambers, his heart sinking; then his blood rose, and he said, 'I'll fix it with our immigration department! I'll come over on the ferry to fetch you, day after tomorrow, I'll deal with Vladimir myself and get your passport from him! Now go back to your apartment and wait there; don't go anywhere near the Tranquillity.'

12

However, when Hargreave went back to Macao it was not to fetch Olga, but to stay. That Tuesday he threw all caution to the winds, because that day Elizabeth came back.

Tuesday was tough for Hargreave. He telephoned Percy Wallace, head of the immigration department, to plead Olga's case but the old codger was on leave. He did not know the deputy personally so he telephoned Max Popodopolous to ask him to take up the matter of Olga's status unofficially on the old-boy network, but Max was in court until mid-afternoon and by that time the deputy head of the immigration department had left his office: nor was Max happy about approaching the department in this way.

'For Christ's sake, Al, think straight, you're the DPP, do it above-board!'

'Then do it officially,' Hargreave instructed, 'but do it fast – we're supposed to be leaving for the Philippines on Saturday! And remember she's not a prostitute, she's a singer, it says so in black and white on her identity card *and* her passport.'

'But I can't do much without her passport in my hand,' Max said, 'and her identity card, you must get those documents.'

'Oh *Jesus* . . .'

It was a tense day; he was very worried about Olga being defenceless against Vladimir. And then, when he got back to his apartment that evening, he found Elizabeth had returned.

'Liz!' Hargreave stared. His knocking heart was sinking.

Elizabeth was sitting in an armchair, silhouetted against the big window. At her feet was Olga's sailing bag, the contents strewn on the carpet: her scanty panties, her cosmetics, her tiny bikini, two dresses.

'Whose,' Elizabeth demanded quietly, 'are these garments?'

Hargreave walked grimly to the bar and reached for the whisky bottle. 'A friend of mine.'

'I didn't imagine,' Elizabeth said, 'that she was your adversary. Which friend in particular? Or can't you remember? Let me remind you.' She picked up a number of credit-card slips and leafed through them. 'Bella

Mar Hotel. Bella Mar. Gorky Enterprises. Gorky Enterprises . . . Thousands of dollars.' She raised her eyebrow at him. 'Ring any bells? Yes? No?'

Hargreave took an angry swallow of whisky. He did not care any more.

'She's a Russian girl who lives in Macao.'

'Ah. That explains the "Gorky" – Gorky Park being in Moscow, I believe? But not "Enterprises". What kind of enterprise is she involved in, this friend? Let me guess. I know!' She snapped her fingers. 'She's an academic! She's a law professor from a Moscow think-tank, having a sabbatical in Macao researching Chinese law, and you're helping her! So you stay at the Bella Mar every weekend to be close to the *library*. Yes? *But,*' she frowned, puzzled, 'why are you paying her, if *you* are helping *her* research? *Ah* – I get it!' She smiled brightly: 'It's the other way round! She's helping you, so you're paying her a thousand dollars a day for her academic services! Of course, silly me.'

Hargreave began to cut through all this. 'Elizabeth, why have you come back?'

'Silly me, would you believe that for a moment it crossed my tiny mind that she might be one of those Russian prostitutes we hear about – but of course, Gorky Enterprises is only the name of her think-tank.'

Hargreave said grimly, 'Actually, she's a singer.'

'Ah! And she's giving you singing lessons! Yes, you used to sing funny ballads at parties before you turned into a workaholic stick-in-the-mud – I'm so glad you're snapping out of your dull self, dearest Alistair.'

'Elizabeth,' Hargreave said grimly, 'I'm not going to fight with you. Please tell me why you've come back.'

'And that accounts for this contraption –' she pointed at the exercycle standing guiltily in the middle of the carpet – 'you're exercising to improve your breathing for singing. And all that yoghurt and health-food in the fridge, even though you hate yoghurt – one has to be in shape for singing.' She frowned: 'But that doesn't explain how your expensive Russian singing teacher's *interesting* garments –' she indicated the panties with her toe – 'happen to be in my home.'

My home. Hargreave felt his blood rise but he controlled his voice. 'I wasn't aware this was your home any more, Elizabeth – you left this home and instituted divorce proceedings against me. From that I was inclined to deduce that our marriage is finally exhausted. But to answer your question, Olga's clothes are here because she went sailing with me last week – she does not stay here. Now, please tell me why you've come back – if it's to fight, you'll find no takers. If it is to discuss financial arrangements concerning our divorce, you'll find me fair and reasonable!'

Elizabeth flared: '*Olga*, huh? Thank you, you've saved me hiring detectives, my lawyers will be pleased!' Her angry eyes narrowed and she hissed, 'I came back to give us one last chance, labouring under the wan hope that our little ding-dong may have brought you to your senses! But no – I see my cautious optimism was entirely misplaced. And thank God I've found out in time – I was about to suspend divorce proceedings. Silly me again. Not now – they're going ahead full-throttle. And my lawyers –' she snatched up the credit-card slips – 'will be very pleased to have these interesting documents as evidence. Now the grounds are not only mental cruelty but adultery, loud and clear. And with a Russian prostitute, at that. First Wanchai bar-girls who leave lipstick all over your face, now Russian whores at a thousand dollars a day! Beautiful.' She got to her feet furiously. 'But you can tell your floozie –' she kicked a pair of Olga's panties – 'that she's not moving in! I'm here to stay in my lawful home as long as I damn-well like, until the divorce, Alistair!' She glared. 'I am not being a dog in the manger, Alistair – there is a lot for me to do, packing up my life, and I'll take my own good time about it! I refuse to be harassed by Russian tarts! And you and your Olga can go and stay in the Bella Mar! Or in hell!'

She started striding out of the room, then she shoved the exercycle over so it crashed. 'And take this *contraption* with you! Do your exercises together. And take these –' she kicked a pair of Olga's panties so they sailed through the air – '*damning* garments with you! *And* –' she turned purposefully for the kitchen – 'your nourishing yoghurt!'

Hargreave strode furiously out of the room, down the corridor to the main bedroom, slammed the door. He grabbed a suitcase out of the wardrobe and started packing. From the kitchen came the sounds of his yoghurt, liver and vitamin pills being hurled from the refrigerator. He hurried down the corridor with his suitcase, snatched a bottle of whisky off his bar, and walked out into the sunset.

He had not raised his voice during the encounter, but the neighbours had probably heard the Director of Public Prosecutions having a hard time again – and Ah Moi. Jesus, it was embarrassing – and he had had enough. This really made him see how happy he had been for the last four weeks, what fun life could be!

He drove down to his chambers angrily and signed a form, as head of department, authorizing himself four weeks' leave immediately. He would get that passport from Vladimir by hook or by crook! He wrote a note to his senior deputy saying he was 'going abroad forthwith'. Then he walked out on to Queensway and flagged a taxi to take him to the Macao ferry wharf.

He was still shaken from the encounter with Elizabeth, but he was not angry any more, only grimly determined to do what he had to do. Indeed, now that he was out of her enraged presence he felt sorry for her. It wasn't her fault that the marriage had turned sour, that he had turned off from the Hong Kong social scene, that he had become a workaholic, a bored husband whose only social life was horse-racing, whisky and sailing – it wasn't her fault that she got seasick and didn't like gambling. And he was sure she had not intended to hit him when she shot him, – she had only meant to give him a fright, shock him out of his infuriating inaction. But the fact remained that the marriage was over – finished, worn-out – and as a consequence he had met Olga Romalova, and now he had to do what he really wanted to do – You can't have a chance of such happiness and not go for it.

Two hours later Hargreave arrived in Macao. He took a taxi to the Bella Mar Hotel, and checked in, then he telephoned Olga at her apartment.

Coincidence again: if Elizabeth had not taken it into her head to return to Hong Kong unannounced, Hargreave would not have gone to Macao unannounced. Had he not done that he would not have found that Olga Romalova had gone to the Heavenly Tranquillity Nite Club to work, that she had been booked out by a client 'for dinner', and he would not have made the decisions he did: he would have got the Macao police to get Vladimir to surrender her passport, then Max would have lodged a formal appeal with the Hong Kong Immigration Department for a reversal of their decision against Olga, which would very likely have succeeded, and then, once that was achieved, they would have proceeded to the Philippines as planned: they would not have stayed in Macao, and this story would have been very different.

Hargreave slammed down the telephone when he was told she had gone to work. His face was suddenly throbbing, he felt sick in his guts. God, he could not bear this! He had specifically instructed her not to go to the Tranquillity! He had refused to confront this question so far, he had pushed the ugly thought aside, told himself it was ridiculous in the circumstances to be jealous, to imagine, to wonder what she was doing during his absences. But he had just spent a glorious week with her, he felt he was truly in love, and now confronted with the stark evidence he could no longer refuse to think about it – and he could not bear it.

Could not bear the thought of her fucking another man, the image of her laughing and dancing and being seductive, talking him into hiring her for the night, walking out of the glittering club beside him, being groped by him in the taxi – did she smile and flaunt herself as she undressed? He could not bear the vision of her nakedness, as she walked to the bed. And oh no, no, he could not bear the image of her fucking.

The time had come for him to confront the facts – and he could not endure them. He had thought the problems would resolve themselves during their month in the Philippines, but he had to deal with them now, he could not leave them unresolved while Olga's immigration status was sorted out, he could not bear the thought of her going to the Tranquillity while they waited. So he would have to put a stop to those facts right now, or forget her – and forget her he could not. So he would have to stay in Macao while her problem was sorted out, and he had to get her out of that night-club immediately, out of her whoring, and keep her for himself!

Until when? He took a deep, tense breath and faced another fact: until he was sure he really loved her, because that was what this was about now – *love*. It felt as if he loved her madly, but he had lived long enough to know that real love takes longer than this. But, by God, he had to give it a chance!

Hargreave opened the bottle of whisky he had brought, poured a shot, quaffed it, and poured another. Oh, he wished he could telephone her, pull her off that bed and tell her . . .

Hargreave swallowed his whisky and refilled his glass. *Okay, that's decided.* Now think through how you're going to do this, face another of the facts: namely, what is Vladimir going to do about all this?

One guess.

Hargreave paced across the room with his glass of whisky: tomorrow he would go to see Vladimir and demand her passport. And Vladimir wasn't going to let his star money-maker go cheap. At the least he would demand payment for the last seven days Olga had spent sailing with him – he had only paid 'in full and final settlement' for the first weekend. So Vladimir would claim seven thousand dollars at least. And then some. Ten thousand? Fifteen? That was a lot of money – no way would he pay it, he would hand the whole problem over to Max and the Macao police. But seven thousand? Yes he would pay that, to get rid of the problem, even though Olga insisted it was not owing because that week was her holiday-time. Seven thousand to get rid of the passport problem was a sensible investment in peace of mind.

But it was still a lot of money, particularly taken on top of what he had spent already. And the money it was going to cost to stay with Olga in this hotel whilst he waited for Max to sort out her immigration status. If that process took longer than expected? The divorce was going to take him to the cleaners . . .

Oh fuck the expense! You can afford it, Liz can't get more than half, you've got a good salary, Directors of Public Prosecutions don't come cheap either! Cross the bridges as you come to them!

He took a grim breath and considered the next fact, the one he would have faced after their idyllic month in the Philippines. After you've sorted all that out, then what?

Hargreave stopped pacing, and stared out of the window at the South China night. *And, oh, that exotic night out there was her . . .*

You *live* with her, that's what – that's what being madly in love is all about. You'll live with her, right here in Macao until Liz has packed her things and left, until Max has pulled the strings to get her into Hong Kong – you rent a small apartment in Macao and commute to work every day on the hydrofoil! And then Olga will come to live with you in your apartment, and you'll say to your friends in the establishment: 'This is my girl, Olga, look at her, and I'm here to tell you that she's as nice as she looks, so take us or leave us, but let one bastard say anything about her past and I'll break his jaw . . . !'

Hargreave threw himself down on the bed and stared up at the ceiling-fan. Oh, it felt good to know what he was going to do about this beautiful girl.

But, meanwhile, where were they going to stay until he persuaded Vladimir to surrender her passport – here at the Bella Mar?

No, get her as far away as possible from the Heavenly Tranquillity and Vladimir, take her to the Westin Resort on Coloane Island, across the bay.

He snatched up the telephone and dialled the Westin.

Yes, they had a room. Two hundred US dollars a night, sir. Yes, they had weekly rates and if the guest were to stay two weeks or more a better discount was offered.

He threw himself back on the bed. It was expensive but what the hell. He reached for the whisky bottle and took a swallow. And, God, he wanted to snatch up the telephone and tell her what they were going to do.

Then he thought of her writhing on that bed under that nameless man and he wanted to bellow. He rolled over on to his stomach with a groan of anguish.

13

He woke up before dawn, hungover and unfed, but grimly determined to carry through his decisions of last night. The dreadful image of Olga beside that unknown, horrible man immediately besieged him, and he swung out of bed, desperate for the new day to start. He pulled on his shorts and running shoes, clattered down the sweeping staircase, and set off into the China dawn.

Ian Bradshaw had told him not to jog, but he jogged. He had to get the air coursing through his body, to flush out the image of her in that bed. He ran down the knoll on to the esplanade, the junks and the land-reclamation vessels silent in the sultry bay: he jogged along the old colonial waterfront in the humid sunrise, panting, sweating out all last night's booze, trying to expel the image of her early-morning duties. He passed the Leal Senado, Government House, passed the Estoril Hotel where he had spent his first blissful night with Olga. He turned off the waterfront, up into the labyrinth of back streets; and thus he found himself passing her apartment building.

Hargreave had not set out to go there: it was an unformed desire to be near her that made him turn up her street when he recognized it, and stop opposite her building. He retreated to a shop doorway and leant against the frame, getting his breath back, staring up at her bleak windows.

Their silent emptiness shouted her nakedness in that hotel bed with that horrible bastard, and he wanted to bellow his outrage to the sunrise, shout that he was taking her away from all this, far away from this sordid apartment and the awful Heavenly Tranquillity Nite-Club and dreadful Vladimir, far away where everything was clean and graceful. Hargreave was filled anew with his resolution, and he shoved himself off the shop doorway to start walking back to the Bella Mar, when a taxi swung down the dark, deserted street, and Olga was in it.

He glimpsed her blonde hair against lamplight as the vehicle took the turn. There was another figure beside her in the backseat. Hargreave retreated into the doorway, and stared. His heart was knocking, and he did not know if he could bear this.

The taxi pulled up almost opposite him. As if in a dream he saw Olga talking to the man, then he heard her familiar laugh. Then she got out of the taxi with a flash of perfect legs, and gave the man a wave through the window. She walked around the back of the car, her hips swinging and her golden hair jouncing, and mounted the steps leading into her dingy Chinese apartment building. At the entrance she turned, with a brilliant smile, waved again, then she was gone.

The taxi drove off, and as it passed Hargreave recognized the Honourable Mr Justice Hackman in the back. Hargreave stared; then he slumped against the doorway, sick in his guts.

Oh God . . . that was awful. To actually see her coming home from a night's work, and with his colleague. *Judge Fucking Hackman* . . . One of the biggest lechers unhung, that prick who had only made it to judge by doing fuck-all for twenty years except screw other lawyers' wives, that odious, worthless, sanctimonious fool who made it to the Supreme Court bench only by never making a contentious judgement in his life lest he be reversed on appeal. Hargreave felt the vomit rise up.

He came out of the doorway to the gutter, and retched. But there was nothing to come up.

He leant against the pillar, hating, hating this. Olga and Hackman – it was too awful to imagine. He shuddered, swallowing back his bile. Then he turned and began to walk down the quiet street, head down, sick in his guts, trying to think it through.

It was touch and go whether Alistair Hargreave stayed on in Macao after seeing that.

You can take the girl out of the whorehouse, but you can't take the whore-house out of the girl . . . Oh Lord, what was he doing? Was she worth it – worth the money he was spending, worth this shocked heartache, this black jealousy, this sickness in the guts? Wouldn't it always be like this, every time he turned away she'd be back to her whoring? How could he instruct Max to appeal to the immigration department claiming she was of good character, a singer? Shouldn't he just slip away into the dawn and put his heady, brief relationship down to life's rich tapestry, a bitter-sweet memory, doomed to failure. Surely it was best just to laugh at what had happened, what he had just seen, shake his head regretfully and forget about her?

That was how Al Hargreave was thinking as he walked back in the dawn to the Bella Mar, as he sat on his bed staring at the sunrise. Gone were his drunken convictions of last night.

Paradoxically, it was the question of her worth that decided him to stay. Yes, she was worth it. Worth the paltry few thousand dollars he had spent on her for the happiness, the fun she had given him: yes, she was worth the modest expense of a holiday in the Philippines or, now, in the Westin Resort Hotel. Because despite what he had seen this morning he was convinced, or almost convinced, that she was in love with him, or almost loved him, as he was almost in love with her – and what was he worth to *her*? What had he given her but a few payments for her services, which she could have got from any other man – the rest she had given to him for nothing, like any other girl in love. Indeed she had lost money through him: how many respectable girls would sacrifice their income? And she had defied her pimp for him – which was courageous.

She had shown her courage in other ways too. She had risked her life to save his when he was drowning – she had beaten her exhaustion and fought the tide when most people would have given up to save themselves. And when the mast broke she had concealed her fear – she had admitted afterwards she was terrified but she had kept calm and been very helpful, even cheerful, trying to console him about the damage to his boat. By comparison what had he done for her? True, he had offered her a month's holiday in the Philippines, but that would have cost her more income – he could well afford the expense involved, but to her the loss would be a serious matter. He had made no promises about what would happen when the holiday was over – he may have dropped her and she would have been in big trouble with Vladimir. So, when the holiday fell through, who could blame her for keeping her irons in the fire and going to work last night? For all she knew her deportation from Hong Kong might frighten him off her, he might not have kept his promise to come to deal with Vladimir, then what could she have done without a passport but go back to work?

Yes, she must love him, she had put a lot at risk for him. But all those financial considerations aside, she was worth it because she made him happy. He had never had so much fun in his life. And, oh, the physical bliss she had given him with her beautiful body, the sensuousness of just looking at her, just being with her. She was worth it because he was besotted with her, she was worth it because he was so in love with her that he was black with jealousy.

But, by God, he would have to have it out with her about last night.

He got off the bed and started to pack his bag. He paid his bill and took a taxi to the Westin Resort, over the long new Taipa Bridge across the muddy bay, getting the hell away from downtown Macao with its hateful images. The road wound across Taipa Island with its Chinese

107

jumble of old houses, shops, shacks, workshops, market gardens, garbage scattered amongst the subtropical verdure, then across the long causeway towards Coloane Island. The taxi climbed up into the green hillside on the other side, then turned into the gracious grounds of the Westin Resort Hotel.

It stopped under the big portico. Hargreave strode up into the spacious marbled reception, checked in and hurried up to his room. He snatched up the telephone and dialled Olga's apartment. It rang and rang before a strange voice answered.

'Let me speak to Olga, please.'

'She is asleep.'

'Wake her up, please.'

'No, it is important for us to sleep!'

Important for us whores. 'Wake her up, please! Tell her it's Alistair.'

The girl muttered something in Russian. A minute later Olga burst on to the telephone: 'Hullo, darling!' she cried.

Hargreave closed his eyes, and they burned.

'I came over on the early hydrofoil,' he said. 'I'm in the Westin Resort. I want you to pack your bags – pack everything of value – and take a taxi here straight away. You can go back to sleep when you get here.'

'Oh, that's wonderful! And I don't want to sleep if you are here! But I must bring all my things? How long are you staying?'

'Until we've sorted out your immigration problem, then we're going to the Philippines. I'll speak to Vladimir today about your passport. But don't tell anybody, just come immediately.'

'Darling, this is so exciting!'

He hung up and clasped his face. He was getting her out of that fucking apartment, out of that fucking night-club, out of that fucking *life*. He took a deep breath, forcing out of his mind the image of her leaving John Hackman. *No more of that!*

He breathed out, and telephoned room service: he ordered two bottles of champagne and a toasted liver sandwich. *And no more fucking liver after this either*. He strode into the bathroom and slammed on the shower.

He felt he was over the anguish when he had showered; his hangover was gone and his body was glowing from the jogging. He was doing what he wanted to do! And it was a beautiful day and any minute the most beautiful girl in the world was going to walk through that door. He dressed, went to the refrigerator, ripped the cap off a can of beer and drank it down. It flooded his system like a balm. Then the champagne arrived: he gulped down the liver sandwich, trying not to taste it. He uncorked the first bottle, and gave himself up to the excitement of waiting for her.

Twenty minutes later there was a rap on the door. He flung it open, and there stood the most beautiful girl in the world, beaming. 'Hullo, darling!'

She rushed into his arms, laughing, and hugged him. He clasped her tight, and he did not care about this morning any more – *just thank God she is here.*

PART III

14

'Until we've sorted out your immigration problem,' he had said – but that could take Max a week after Vladimir surrendered her passport.

'So let's relax and make the most of it – then we'll go on our real holiday to the Philippines.'

'It feels like a honeymoon, darling!'

The Westin Resort is a lovely place, the spacious, gracious, terraced building hugging the hill, all the rooms overlooking the sea, surrounded by lawns and gardens. Around it are the brooding mauve islands and mainland of China. It was more discreet for an illicit honeymoon than the hotels in downtown Macao: those were substantially cheaper places where most Hong Kongers preferred to stay when they came to do their gambling and wenching: the Westin was mostly patronized by overseas tourists.

Hargreave had intended having it out with her immediately about last night, but he was so pleased to see her he put off the confrontation. That entire first morning they spent in bed. It seemed he could not get enough of her, he had to possess and repossess her to establish his ownership of her, to drive out the images. She grinned:

'You health-kick has done wonderful things, darling, but you are not getting much relaxation. Oh,' she sighed, 'it's lovely here . . .'

He had not intended to ask but he could not resist the question. 'Haven't you been here before?'

'Yes, but never on a holiday.'

Only to work. Hargreave flinched inwardly. But then he smiled despite himself: what the hell – he had know what he was getting himself into when he fell for this girl. But there was one unpleasant subject that could not be avoided.

'Did you bring the credit-card machine?'

There was a moment's silence, then she turned to him. 'No.' She frowned. 'We were going to the Philippines. If we had done so would I have brought the credit-card machine and said, "Thank you for your nice holiday but can you please quickly sign?" *Huh?*'

Thank God. 'I hope not.'

'You *hope*? Did I bring the machine last week when we went on our lovely sail? No. Because it was a holiday and I am not a prostitute any more with you!'

Oh, this was so good to hear. But it begged the question of last night and he had to pursue it now. He said carefully, 'Was Vladimir satisfied with that cheque I sent?'

Olga lay back and snorted. 'Satisfied? No, he protested very much. He said you owe him for the whole of last week too, but I told him to go to hell, it was *my* holiday.'

'And what did he say to that?'

'He was very angry, that pig. So when I asked for my passport he laughed and said I will never get it until you pay.'

Hargreave sighed. Of course. If he'd been there he would have paid and they would have been in the Philippines by now. But Sod's Law had prevented that. 'Did he ask why you wanted your passport?'

'Yes, he knew it was so I could go to you in Hong Kong.'

'Does he know where you are now?'

'No. But he will soon find out when I do not go to work tonight, there are not very many hotels in Macao.' She paused, then turned her head to him. 'I had to go to work last night, I am sorry. I telephoned you to explain, but you were out.'

Hargreave closed his eyes – thank God she had confessed to that. Thank God she had telephoned him. 'Did anybody answer?'

'Yes, a woman. She was not very kind.'

Hargreave sighed guiltily. 'What was said?'

'I said, "Hullo, can I speak to Alistair?" She said, "Who is this?" I said, "My name is Olga." She banged down the phone. Who was she?'

He wasn't going to tell her about Elizabeth yet. 'Just a neighbour who sometimes comes in to use my fax machine, I'm sorry if she was rude.' He paused. 'But why did you have to go to work?'

She sighed. 'I know you had forbidden it but I had just been arguing with Vladimir, if I did not go to work he would look for me and make trouble, and beat me. Then I would have black eyes when you came.'

Jesus, he was going to get Vladimir off her back! He dreaded asking the next question. 'And what happened at work?' *Please God she doesn't lie*.

'It was awful. I was thinking of you, and I was so anxious about my passport. And I had to go to dinner with a man I did not like.'

Dinner? He knew what time she had returned home from dinner. 'Why did you go out with him if you didn't like him?'

'Oh, that is how this business is. I thought, I am miserable, so I might as well have a nice dinner if I have to talk to this man all night. Of course I did not go to bed with him, darling, of course he wanted to, but I said I had my period but he didn't believe me so I said I had to go back to the Tranquillity to sing after dinner. But he came back with me and sat there all night, making a nuisance, he was hoping I would change my mind if he bought lots of expensive drinks. He even took me home in a taxi, still trying to change my mind. Oh, he was such a fat old bore.'

Thank God – she hadn't lied. He believed her. He loved hearing that prick John Hackman described as a fat old bore. And he was so glad he was putting an end to this dreadful work of hers.

'Well, I'll see Vladimir tomorrow,' he said, 'and get your passport back even if I have to pay for last week. We'll get to the Philippines, I promise you.'

Olga said emphatically, 'Darling, don't you go to see Vladimir – let him come to *you*. If you go to him you will seem too worried, too eager, and he will demand more money. Tomorrow or the next day he will find us here, and then we will bargain with him, tell him we don't talk about anything unless we have my passport first. Then when we have it we maybe pay him something, just a little – you must *not* pay for last week, that was my holiday.'

He loved her for saying that. But he would pay for last week rather than have trouble, rather than delay the trip to the Philippines. 'So Vladimir will come looking for me, demanding money?'

'Exactly. He will be worried if you refuse to pay anything, so his price for my passport will come down; finally he will be begging you to pay something.' She added, 'Leave him to me at first, darling, I know this business better than you, you will be too soft with him.'

Hargreave smiled. Hard to imagine Vladimir begging, but she was probably right that he would be too soft. Olga continued earnestly:

'But even when we have my passport they may not let me enter Hong Kong to go to the airport to catch the plane to the Philippines.'

'My friend Max is sorting that out for you as soon as we've got your passport. Tomorrow's Thursday – we'll wait for Vladimir until Saturday, then I'll go to him. Max can't do anything until Monday, anyway. So, we'll just lie low here for the weekend and enjoy it. This is a nice hotel to lie low in.'

'It's lovely! We'll make it like a honeymoon.'

So they made it a little honeymoon, and it was as good as the Philippines. At noon they made it out of bed and went down to the swimming

115

pool terrace for lunch. There were a lot of people but they were all tourists, there was nobody Hargreave knew. Olga's arrival in her bikini had the same effect as at the Bella Mar: she was a conversation-stopper. Hargreave enjoyed that; he loved the furtive stares, and when she walked to the water to dive in he could only marvel at her youthful beauty. He felt immensely proud of her, he enjoyed being envied by every man in the place, he did not care that the waiters probably knew who she was – all that was over now. They had lunch beside the pool and he looked at her, the sun glistening on her golden skin, her lovely lines and clefts and curves, her long hair in damp tresses, her happy smiles and laughter as she energetically chomped her way through a lobster, thoroughly enjoying herself, and she was so gorgeous it was hard to believe that this girl really belonged to Alistair Hargreave. But when, later, he lay on top of her abandoned nakedness, feeling her fierce kisses, he knew she really was his, knew she was not a whore any more, whores don't kiss at all, let alone like that.

'I love you,' she whispered, and he whispered back, 'I love you too.'

That night they dined on the patio by candlelight, the moon shining silver on the South China Sea. And, dancing close to her, her skin warm through the silk, her belly and gliding thighs against his, her smooth hand on his neck, her face dreamily against his, he could feel in her body she was not being a whore, she was just a beautiful girl dancing tenderly with her lover.

Thursday went like that too.

He had not told her about Elizabeth; he did not want Liz to sound like an unreasonable bitch – she really was not like that. Her anger at finding Olga's clothing and the credit-card slips was understandable, even though she had left him. She was an unhappily-married woman who was going through a mid-life crisis, as he was – or used to be. Liz was bored, the children grown up and gone, she had nothing to do but plan the next cocktail party and dinner party and bridge evening, her next game of tennis or golf, and she didn't really like tennis or golf: she had never liked sailing. Liz felt purposeless now, while he, on the other hand, had his work even if it bored him; he was at the zenith of his career. All poor Liz had to look forward to was a bit of charity work – and he had opted out of the colonial social scene, that drove her up the wall. And then there was the sex-thing: clearly that was his fault because he was sure proving he was far from past it. Poor Liz, he wanted her to be happy, but he wanted her to divorce him as she'd threatened. Sure, he felt guilty about her back in Hong Kong now, but he did not let himself dwell upon it – he was head-over-heels happy, and he just wanted her to be happy too.

He did not let himself think about the other things either, about Olga's past, nor about that awful morning when he had seen her with that prick John Hackman – that jealousy nonsense was truly over. And he did not want to worry about Vladimir. It was lovely here, and he could cheerfully have forgone the trip to the Philippines – but he had to get her passport and regularize her situation. Thursday passed and Vladimir did not show up. Friday passed. At sundown Hargreave announced he was going to telephone him at the Tranquillity to arrange a meeting.

'No,' Olga said. 'Let him worry, make him come to *you*. Wait one more day and then let me deal with him first.'

And then, on Saturday, there was a sharp rap on the door. Olga opened it and there stood Vladimir-the-Terrible.

'*You!*' she hissed. She stepped through the doorway and banged it closed behind her.

Hargreave was getting out of the shower. He draped a towel around his waist, went to the door and listened. He heard nothing. He opened the door: nobody was there. He looked down the corridor.

Olga and Vladimir stood at the end, in silhouette against the big window: she was jabbing her finger against his chest. Vladimir grabbed her finger and bent it backwards, and she cried out. Hargreave started angrily down the passage to her rescue – then Olga kicked Vladimir's shins, he gasped and let go. He turned with a Russian curse and strode off around the corner. Olga came storming back to the room, breathing fire.

'What happened?' Hargreave demanded.

'I told him to go to hell, that's what happened!' She swept past him into the room, smiling maliciously. 'He wanted five hundred dollars bar-levy for each night and five hundred for me. I told him go to hell! I said we will not even talk to him until I have my passport in my hand.'

'And what did he say to that?'

She snorted. 'He said he will *fix* me. I said I will fix *him*. I can do karate too, you know?'

That was a new detail, but it didn't surprise him. 'Then?'

'Then he said he will cancel my visa if you do not pay. I said go to hell, the police gave me the visa. Then he attacked me, so I kicked him and he ran away!'

Ran away? Her reportage did not quite accord with his observation.

117

He started pulling on a shirt. 'I'm going to talk to him right now.'

She grabbed his arm. '*No*, darling. If you run after him he will think he has you like *that*.' She made a fist in the area of his groin. 'And then he will demand even more money, for our whole holiday in the Philippines. He will come back tomorrow, don't worry, and then you bargain, darling – you will probably have to pay something to get my passport, but you must pay *nothing* more.' She pointed a finger at his nose: 'Play cool. How can we afford this holiday if you must pay crazy money? I refuse!'

How can *we* afford it? Hargreave grinned despite himself, and took her in his arms and kissed her fragrant neck. She was right: he must not appear a supplicant to Vladimir – give it another day. He grinned wider. Here he was, being threatened by the Russian Mafia – and he was happy. Yes, Vladimir would certainly be back, and he would handle the negotiations without Olga and gladly pay for last week – under heavy protest – in exchange for her passport. And this time next week they would be in the Philippines.

So meanwhile relax and enjoy the weekend.

They were spending quite a lot of money, but the Philippines would be cheap. Olga tried not to be extravagant, choosing the cheaper dishes on the menu, but he told her to have what she damn-well wanted. He was having the time of his life. He was a middle-aged man who had had his joie de vivre and virility restored by this gorgeous girl. And Olga was a girl whose knight in shining armour had arrived at last. She was radiantly happy.

And radiantly healthy. On Saturday she insisted they go to the resort's gymnasium to keep up his health-kick: they had done little more than make love, eat and drink for three days.

Hargreave was a little embarrassed: he did not want to show himself up as unfit and undignified. Thank God he had recovered his tan. Olga wore a golden leotard against her honeyed skin and she almost looked naked.

'You should wear that to bed sometimes,' Hargreave suggested.

'I will if you like, darling.'

And she was so fit; she knew how to use all the machines correctly. Hargreave watched, then copied her. She pretended not to notice his discomfort, until she just had to intervene. 'Darling, excuse me but you're doing that wrong, you'll strain yourself. Do it like this.'

Hargreave got off the machine and she demonstrated. 'See? That works these muscles.' She pointed.

'How do you know all this?'

'We had to learn everything the diplomats want to do. You're doing very well but you must be careful not to strain yourself by using too many weights. Take one weight off.'

He saw the funny side of it. 'If you can lift that much weight, I can. You don't go to a gym like this in Macao, do you?'

'Yes, and every day I do my own exercises.'

She worked her way industriously around the circuit of daunting equipment, the sweat sheening on her, but she was hardly panting while Hargreave toiled along behind her, following her example, feeling shagged out.

'Afterwards I'll give you a good massage.'

'Did they teach you that at KGB school too?'

'Yes; proper, scientific massage.'

And improper, he thought. But he did not care: he was very impressed by her accomplishments. All *he* could do was fucking law, and a bit of tennis and sailing.

There was a sauna at the gym. After their workout they sat in it for ten minutes, draped in towels, sweating out all the booze they had drunk the day before, and he felt wonderful – fucked but wonderful. He just had to slide his hand over her slippery goldenness, he wanted to taste her, smell her. 'About that massage?'

'Here?' she grinned.

Horror. 'No, upstairs.'

'But we've only been in five minutes. So maybe I could do a little of something else, just to pass the time? Like this?' She peeled back his towel. 'My – you *are* fit!' She lowered her head and for an instant he felt the bliss of her warm mouth before he took a handful of her hair and pulled her up. 'Upstairs?'

'But how can I walk out with *this*?'

That day she gave him a 'proper' massage. She laid him out on the table on the balcony after their workout, smeared him in oil and got stuck in. Kneading him, pummelling him, bending him, wrenching him, twisting him. 'Tell me where it hurts . . .' It seemed to hurt all over, but it also felt very good. She knew the names of all the muscles and kept up a commentary on what she was doing. He evidently had muscles he'd never used. He was amazed at the strength in those golden hands with the red fingernails. They hurt him, but they also felt very sensuous. 'It's starting to hurt man's best friend,' he warned. She was wearing a towel wrapped around her breasts and he trailed the back of his hand over her thigh.

119

'Okay, now turn over.'

He rolled over creakily, on to his back.

'Yes, I see what you mean. That muscle is very inflamed.'

'Agony.'

'It needs treatment.' She contemplated it sadly. 'I think I better call the doctor. But perhaps I have time to do the pectorals first . . .'

She smothered his chest in oil and got to work on his pectoral muscles. He slid his hand up under her towel and fondled her smooth bottom, in an agony of anticipation. Then finally there was the glorious feel of her breasts sliding over his rampant loins, slowly slipping and sliding, and he groaned. 'Enjoy,' she whispered, 'just enjoy . . .'

'Tennis, squash, golf, horse riding, skiing. Snooker. Ping-pong. Even lawn croquet – we had to learn them all properly so we could play when we were amongst the diplomatic people. And we had to understand baseball and football and cricket so we could talk about it.'

'You can play all those sports?'

'You can teach any healthy person any sport if you make them do it over and over again for eight hours a day and shout a lot. And our instructors were all professional teachers. But I was never very good at golf – so boring – and that was regarded as very important. I hope you don't like golf, darling?'

'No. A nice walk spoilt, as Winston Churchill said.'

'Good, so we'll play tennis, much better exercise.'

So it was gym before breakfast, tennis afterwards, before they allowed themselves their first drink. They hired the rackets from the hotel and he bought her a tennis dress from the boutique: white, it looked ravishing against her golden tan. She was damn good. Hargreave was very proficient at tennis yet he had a hard job beating her, and it was years since she had played. She did so with frowning concentration, her hair pulled severely back, her headband touching her eyebrows, shifting tensely from foot to foot as she prepared for his devastating service. Hargreave had had professional coaching and he could see that she had been well trained. And her energy and competitive spirit seemed boundless. She always wanted one more set so she could beat him just once.

'No, I'm going to quit while I'm ahead, it's my beer-time. I thought the KGB told you the object of the game was just to show a lot of knickers and then fraternize with the enemy in the clubhouse?'

'But I want to impress you.'

'You've impressed the daylights out of me.'

He felt very proud of her. As they re-entered the hotel and she crossed the marbled foyer to the reception desk to pick up their key, he watched her, her lovely young legs so golden against the white of her short tennis dress, her buttocks swinging jauntily, the spring in her healthy step; he could see all eyes on her, the bellhops' and the passing guests', and he thought: 'She's so beautiful, no matter how hot and sweaty . . .' He felt good and healthy, he was happy with what he was doing, and he loved life.

On Sunday she wanted to cycle around the island after tennis, to explore. Hargreave certainly did not, but he wanted to please her. The hotel rented bicycles: there was a row of gleaming, state-of-the-art mountain bikes.

'Haven't you got any nice, suburban bikes with only one gear?'

'You don't like mountain bikes, sir?' the attendant said.

Olga was convulsed in giggles.

He was given detailed instruction on the gears but he still could not get the hang of changing them and he just left the machine in a middle gear. He was relieved to find how fit he was: his health-kick had paid off, he was keeping up with her with comparative ease. And it was great fun whizzing down the hills beside her, the wind in their hair, even if he did have to toil up the slope beyond.

'Darling, you must put it into low gear for the hills. Like this.' She flicked the levers for him.

'How do you know that's low gear?'

'Look at the cogs.'

'They look the same to me. Incomprehensible.'·

'But the chain is now on the biggest one at the back.'

'Ah. But when you're riding along, how do you move the levers without crashing into the oncoming traffic, thus causing widespread alarm and despondency?'

'Just with your thumbs. Like this.' She manoeuvred them.

'Ah. But how do you know what gear you're now in? Without looking down and falling off?'

'You can feel. Now the chain is on the little cog, see? That's top gear.'

'How do you know all this crap?'

'It's common sense.'

'Ah, so that's the problem . . .'

They had a good time. They cycled all the way round Coloane and Taipa islands: he never improved with the gears but he enjoyed it because she was loving it, tendrils of blonde hair sticking to her neck and forehead; she loved giving everything her best shot. And sitting

121

beside the road on a hilltop overlooking the sea and the China mainland he could almost taste the sweet womanly scent of her and he just wanted to topple her on to her back.

'I want to make love.'

She stood up with a happy smile and held her hand out to him. They left the bicycles beside the road and went off into the subtropical foliage, grinning, and Hargreave felt as excited as a teenager.

Afterwards, lying on their backs, looking up at the China sky, she said, 'Know what I would love to do one day? Go to Holland in the springtime on a bicycle and see the tulips, ride around all those canals. And camp at nights and cook our own food over a real fire. Wouldn't that be lovely?'

It was a pretty thought – and Holland was *flat* country. 'Well, we can do that one day.'

But it was time he stopped playing it cool with Vladimir and confronted the bastard – Olga's method had not worked. If he had to pay, he had to pay.

That Sunday evening, without telling Olga, he went downstairs while she was dressing for dinner and called the Tranquillity Nite-Club. But Vladimir was not there. He then telephoned the number on the visiting card that Vladimir had given him: there was no reply. He called the night-club again and left a message, instructing Vladimir to contact him immediately.

15

Vladimir did not contact him that evening. Nor did he do so on Monday. Hargreave telephoned the night-club again, but once more Vladimir was not there. He tried his other number: no reply. Hargreave regretted following Olga's advice: perhaps the bastard had left town with her passport. Playing it cool had back-fired – *he* was getting nervous now, not Vladimir. He wanted to get going to the Philippines: this hotel was discreet, but sooner or later they would bump into somebody from Hong Kong he knew – and it was expensive, though that was a secondary consideration.

Then came an unpleasant surprise: that Monday he paid the hotel bill up to date, by cheque, to keep some track of what he was spending. On Tuesday the manager deferentially called him aside and told him that the cheque had not been honoured.

'Good heavens!'

How could this be? This was a mistake. Hargreave telephoned the manager of the Honkong & Shanghai Bank from the reception office.

'Derek, what's happening? You've just bounced a cheque of mine.'

'Have we?' Derek Morrison said. He called up Hargreave's account on the computer screen. 'So we have; I'm sorry, but you are over your overdraft limit, Al.'

'But there should be no overdraft! I've got about twenty thousand US dollars in my deposit account, even if my current account is a bit flat.'

'You *had* . . .' Derek mused, studying his computer. 'But there've been some heavy credit-card payments. And I see Elizabeth withdrew the rest last week.'

'*Jesus.*' Of course – he'd forgotten that Liz had signing powers on his deposit account as well, it had all been arranged so long ago.

'And my current account is in the red by how much?'

'Almost,' Derek said apologetically, 'six thousand.'

Oh God. 'Derek, cancel Liz's signing powers on all my accounts.'

'Yes?' Derek said doubtfully. 'If you say so.'

'So she's still in town?'

Derek sounded surprised at the question. 'Sure, saw her in passing on Friday, Where are you?'

'Out of town. On holiday.'

'Still in Macao?'

Lord. 'How did you know?'

'A seagull told me. At the yacht club.'

So he'd been seen. 'Well, keep that to yourself. And will you please cover that cheque until next week when my salary's paid in?'

'Sure.'

'That'll put me back in the black. But I'd like a bigger overdraft facility please, as a backup.'

'How much?'

'Ten thousand? US.'

'Okay,' Derek Morrison said. He added: 'I hope you're having a hell of a good time, Al.'

'I am. But keep that to yourself as well, please.'

He was angry with Elizabeth as he walked back to the gymnasium – she didn't need that twenty-odd thousand, she had enough in the housekeeping account; she had done it to wave a big stick at him. Well, he thought, to hell with you, Liz. First you shoot me, then you desert me, then you sue me – you'd better make that twenty thousand last a long time. Like until the divorce. Because that's what we're getting pretty damn quick, even if I've got to sue for it myself.

'What was it, darling?' Olga was knocking hell out of the exercycle.

'Just some office work.' He slung off his dressing-gown and got stuck into a weight-lifting machine, working off his anger.

But, after the initial resentment, he did not care about the money. It was only money and he earned plenty of the stuff. So, big deal, Liz had taken twenty thousand dollars but she was entitled to some security: he had recently blown plenty on Olga and himself, hadn't he? – and Liz had seen the credit-card slips. That must have been infuriating for her. It was understandable. So he was down about thirty thousand dollars? His salary would make that up in a couple of months: well, three months if you're talking about savings, because next month he had the girls' university fees, and their Blue Shield health cover. And his yacht insurance was coming up for renewal, and the house policies on London and San Francisco and Seattle, and all those niggling mortgages – so maybe it was four months. But what the hell, it was only money, and how can money compare with the happiness that girl beating the hell out of that exercycle gives me? I just wish Liz would find happiness too.

But today he had to make contact with Vladimir come hell or high water: living was much cheaper in the Philippines, and he didn't like the fact that it was known in Hong Kong where he was. If Vladimir did not show up today he would go to the Tranquillity tonight and find the bastard.

And then, late that afternoon, Vladimir appeared.

It was at sunset, in the hour after a long siesta, when Olga was upstairs going through that lengthy female business of dressing for dinner. Hargreave was sitting downstairs at the bar having his first whisky of the day before telephoning Vladimir, when a voice said behind him:

'Mr Hargreave, you owe me a lot of money.'

Hargreave gave an inward sigh of relief, but he played it cool. He turned slowly, looked grimly at the pimp with the greased-back hair, and steeled himself to bargain hard. Whereas yesterday he would have gladly paid the bastard to get that passport, today he had the reality of Derek Morrison and Elizabeth to consider.

'I thought Olga explained that no more would be payable. I sent you that cheque the week before last in full and final settlement. And I want her passport, please.'

'Her passport?' Vladimir smiled. 'She is going nowhere, sir. Olga has a contract with us, and she cannot end it just when she wants to, that is the law.'

Hargreave took a breath. 'Mr Vladimir,' he said, 'I am a lawyer, and you can take it from me that such contracts are unenforceable because they are *contra bonos mores*.' He smiled unkindly. 'You wouldn't know about that, but it means "contrary to good morals". Olga is no longer your prostitute, Mr Vladimir. She is my girlfriend.'

Vladimir smiled. 'Yes, I know you are a lawyer, Mr Hargreave, a very important lawyer. And very important lawyers do not like their reputations ruined?'

'Jesus.' Hargreave wanted to punch the bastard. 'Come here.' He slid off the barstool and strode across the room to the corner. He sat down at a table where nobody could overhear. Vladimir followed him politely, and sat. Hargreave resisted holding a finger up at the bastard's nose. 'So you're threatening to blackmail me?'

Vladimir held up his palms. 'Please, Mr Hargreave, such language!'

'Well, just get a few things straight, Vladimir. One: half of Hong Kong knows I'm here with Olga – including my wife. So I don't give a shit about your blackmail! In fact not only is my wife aware of this but our marriage is over. So fuck you and your blackmail, *Mister* Vladimir!' He glared. 'And secondly, blackmail is a *crime*, even in Macao! And not only am I an important lawyer but I have many contacts in the Macao police and all I have to do is walk over to that telephone –' he pointed at the bar – 'and they will be here in five minutes to arrest you, and give Olga her passport back. And when you eventually come out of jail they'll kick your arse all the way back to Moscow!'

Vladimir smiled. 'I don't think so, Mr Hargreave, I also have many friends in the police here, and in the Russian police. And if you do not pay, Olga will have to pay, and not only with money.'

Hargreave blanched inwardly, the threat to her appalled him. And that was it – *she was never going back to Russia*. Before he could muster a response Vladimir said, 'You owe us twenty-six thousand dollars, Mr Hargreave. Please pay now. Then maybe we can discuss Olga's passport.'

Hargreave snorted, shocked: 'Jesus! How do you figure *that*?'

'Olga costs five hundred dollars a day, bar-levy, another five hundred for her services. You sent me a cheque for the first weekend of her visit to Hong Kong, but not for the next week. That is seven days. This time you have had her for six days. Thirteen in total, thirteen thousand dollars. Plus interest at one hundred per cent, makes twenty-six thousand.'

Hargreave almost wanted to laugh. 'A hundred per cent?!' His eyes narrowed. '*Oh, you can fuck off, you fucking con-man!*' He stood up theatrically.

Vladimir said quietly, 'It is our rule, unless you make prior arrangements. Ask Olga.'

Hargreave stared down at him. *Olga knew?* Christ, was this bastard saying Olga had set him up? No – he did not believe it! Before he could reply Vladimir continued: 'However, in your case, because you have been a good customer, we will forget about the hundred per cent interest. Just give me the thirteen thousand and we will call it quits, as the Americans say. And Olga will get her passport.'

Hargreave glared, and again he wanted to laugh. So it *was* just a con-job! Thank God! So play it cool and you'll get the passport for seven.

'You can go to hell, Vladimir. I've paid you last time in full and final settlement! Bring me her passport immediately or I call the police.' He turned to stride away.

'You can run but Olga cannot, Mr Hargreave. If you don't pay, Olga will, dearly.'

Hargreave stopped, shocked again. He stared at Vladimir, sick in his guts at the threat. He sat down again and pointed at the bar.

'See that telephone? I can pick it up and call my friends in the Hong Kong police and they will call their friends in the Macao police, and they will be here in five minutes to take you away. But I tell you what, Mr Vladimir.' He held a trembling finger at his nose: 'I'll forget you uttered that threat against Olga, provided *you* make prior arrangements with *me*! And my arrangement is this.' He snatched his cheque book out of his pocket, wrote out a cheque in the sum of three thousand dollars, and held it out.

Vladimir looked at it. 'What is this?'

'It's six days since Olga joined me here. Six days of bar-levy at five hundred a night is three thousand! I refuse to pay for Olga herself, because she is now my girl. And I refuse to pay for that week in Hong Kong, because she was on holiday. Take it or leave it but give me her passport and get the hell out of here!'

Vladimir smiled. 'I reject it.'

'Very well!' Hargreave snatched back the cheque and ripped it in half. He wrote out a new one furiously, his hand shaking. It was for one thousand five hundred dollars. He thrust it at Vladimir dramatically, and hissed, 'That's half of three thousand, Vladimir! And half of one thousand five hundred is seven hundred and fifty! Got that message? Now take it or leave it!'

Vladimir looked taken aback for the first time. 'I would like the first cheque, please,' he said.

Hargreave smiled triumphantly. 'Too fucking late, Vladimir! You had your chance and you blew it! Now give me her passport. Or –' he pointed again at the bar – 'I'll use that telephone.'

Vladimir put the cheque in his pocket. 'I do not have her passport with me.'

'Then go and get it!'

'It is in a bank safety box.'

Hargreave did not believe that. 'Well you better have that passport here, at this hotel, by ten o'clock tomorrow morning, or I am not only stopping payment on that cheque, but I'm calling the police as well. *Got* that?'

He glared, then stood up and strode off furiously. He walked out through the French windows, on to the terrace. People were sitting at candle-lit tables. He strode to a dark corner and leant on the balustrade.

He was still shaking, but, God, he was pleased with himself. He had won! Tomorrow he would have her passport, he was sure, and he had saved a lot of money, and shown the bastard he wasn't a pushover. The lying crook, trying to cast suspicion on Olga – *Jesus*. He understood

127

criminals, he'd been dealing with them all his life; Vladimir knew he had no credibility now and would give him a wide berth from here on. If her passport wasn't here by ten o'clock he really would call in the police.

He walked shakily back to the bar. He was gratified to see that Mr Fucking Vladimir had disappeared. Yes – he didn't think he'd have any more trouble. He ordered a double whisky and took a big gulp.

Lord, Olga really didn't know about that hundred per cent interest, did she? Of course not – it was just a try-on, part of the threat to make him pay up gratefully when the bastard offered to waive the interest.

He looked at his wristwatch; where was she? She was taking a long time. Suddenly panic gripped him – Vladimir had gone up to the room! He banged down his glass and strode out of the bar, heading for the elevators. He hurried into the foyer – and stopped, in relief. His heart seemed to turn over.

Olga was emerging from the elevator, a vision of loveliness. Gold was the colour motif of the foyer, dust-gold marble floors, dust-gold walls, soft gold was the light shed by the chandeliers. And Olga was wearing a golden dress, her plunging neckline revealing her tan, her blonde hair piled on top of her head gracefully, her long legs ending in golden stiletto-heeled shoes. She was radiant.

'What's the matter, darling?'

'Nothing.' He smiled. 'You're so lovely, that's all. And when you're not with me I miss you . . .'

Later, lying in the big double bed, a hazy moon beaming through the window, she stroked his eyebrow and said, 'But something is worrying you, darling?'

He had not told her about Elizabeth emptying the bank account. It was her passport he was still worried about. He told her about Vladimir's visit.

She listened without interruption, looking at the ceiling. Then she said, 'You did well. But you should not have paid anything until you had the passport. Now he will ask for more.'

No, Hargreave was glad he had paid something. 'I made it very clear that it was in full and final settlement.'

'And if he asks for more money for me?'

He sighed grimly. Pay more, that's what, but only on delivery of her passport. 'We'll see. But as soon as we've got your passport, Max can sort out your misunderstanding with the immigration department, and we'll be out of here. And meanwhile, if Vladimir harasses me, I'll call the manager and get the hotel's security guards to throw him out.'

She snorted. 'The manager is frightened of the Mafia, darling, and so are the security guards.'

'Nonsense. The Westin Resort is part of a powerful international chain of hotels, they won't tolerate the Mafia harassing their clients. But if that doesn't work I'll call the bloody police.'

'The Macao police? The Mafia are who they get lots of *cumshaw* from.'

'Look, police work is something I know a great deal about, it's my job. I'm not worried about that, so you needn't be.' He said it with more conviction than he felt. But it was true – there *was* nothing to worry about that money couldn't fix, and money could always be raised.

She studied the moonlight coming through the window.

'Probably you are right. You are an important man in Hong Kong.' She turned to him solemnly. 'You are my knight in shining armour, as the English say.'

He loved her saying that, and he believed she really meant it. He did not believe Vladimir but now was the only time to ask. 'Did you know about the hundred per cent interest?'

She lay back angrily. 'No. I have never heard of it, because the customer always pays first. But if he asks for credit they probably say yes, then when he pays a week later they ask for a hundred per cent more. They are such *crooks*.'

Thank God. If she had known, as Vladimir claimed, it could have looked like a set-up – that would have devastated him. And he thought of Vladimir bending her finger and her kicking him: of course he believed her. 'But you sound worried. What about exactly?'

She sighed, then said, 'Vladimir can get the police to revoke my visa. Then I must leave you.' She looked at him. 'And that will break my heart.'

The thought of her visa being revoked panicked him. 'But why would they do that? They're demanding payment. If they get your visa revoked they can't claim you're working for them.'

'To make me work in Istanbul again? Or Russia?'

That possibility horrified him. 'We'll have your passport back tomorrow, Olga. Then if your visa is revoked you haven't got to go anywhere.'

She turned her head slowly and looked at him, her eyes moist. She smiled: 'Where? Where would I go, darling, after the Philippines?'

And oh God, this was it. This was the decision he would have had to make after they returned from the Philippines, this was the decision he had been making and remaking for a week, since that awful morning he had seen her with Judge Hackman. It was crystal-clear what he had to do, what he wanted to do.

'You're coming to Hong Kong, and living with me.' *There* – he had said it.

Her lovely eyes filled with tears. 'Oh darling, I've been waiting for weeks for you to say that.' She entwined her arms around him and held him tight. She sob-laughed against his neck: 'So you really are my knight in shining armour – I knew it the first time I saw you . . .'

She sat crosslegged on the bed, magnificently naked, the lamplight soft on her. 'No, I don't know where he keeps all our passports. Maybe in the Tranquillity, maybe in his apartment – or even in the bank. Maybe the other girls know, I will ask.'

'You're not going *near* the Tranquillity. How long would it take to get a new passport?'

She rubbed her forehead. 'My last one took only a week. But that is because the Mafia arranged it, with bribes.'

And the fucking Mafia could probably arrange for her to be denied another one. Anyway, it was a certainty it would take a long time in Russia. So that meant a forged one if Vladimir didn't show up with hers tomorrow and the cops couldn't help.

Oh, that's a lovely risk for the Director of Public Prosecutions, your career goes out the window if you're caught on that one. And disbarred from practising law for life – and that's after you come out of jail . . .

He said, thinking out loud, 'But if Vladimir gets your visa revoked, he's got to give you your passport in order to *leave* Macao.'

'No; when we came in the escort had all our passports, he showed them to the immigration men for us. We never touched them.'

Of course – a batch of slaves being imported. 'But when you leave Macao you'll go to the airport in Canton, to fly back to Russia. But *I* will be at the Macao bordergate with some of my influential friends. And I will demand that your passport be given back to you, and I will escort you back to Hong Kong.'

'And your friend Max can fix it with those Hong Kong immigration men to let me in? Even though I am a prostitute?'

Hargreave winced. 'You're not a prostitute any more, are you?'

'No! I've given all that up! No, I am a virgin now!' She grinned.

Hargreave smiled grimly. 'Oh, Max will arrange something.'

'*Wheeeee!*' She scrambled up on to her knees, then crouched on top of him. She waggled her loins across his joyfully and then smothered his face in kisses. 'And we live happily ever after? And sail your yacht around the world?' Then she said anxiously, 'But what about Elizabeth? And what will your friends say?'

Hargreave snorted: right now he did not give a damn about what the establishment thought. He smiled to himself. How he had changed – three months ago he had gone to ground, turned his face to the wall. Now he was going to let it be shouted from the rooftops.

'The only problem will be if Liz remains in Hong Kong and insists on staying in my government apartment. That means I'll have to find another place for you and me.'

'That will be expensive, yes?' she said anxiously. 'So can't we live on your lovely boat when it is fixed?'

Hargreave smiled. 'The Director of Public Prosecutions is expected to live to a certain standard.'

Olga understood. 'Okay, so it'll be expensive for a while. But I can work. I mean,' she added hastily, 'as an interpreter, for example. And I can type, and work a computer, they taught us at KGB school. I can work in an office, I'm not stupid. And I have money – nearly forty thousand dollars saved.'

Hargreave grinned. The Director of Public Prosecutions living on immoral savings of a prostitute? The press would love that. 'You keep it.' He added: 'I hope it's safe. Where is it?'

'In the bank, in Moscow.'

'In your name?'

'Yes. Well about half is, the other half the boss keeps for me until my contract is finished, but it is mine, I know how much it is, they write it in my paybook.'

Hargreave sighed inwardly. He didn't like her chances of seeing that money, but he didn't want to alarm her.

'I know what you're thinking,' she continued. 'If I run away with you they will steal my money. But I did finish my contract, the week after I first met you! I only extended my visa, and I paid for that, not them. I *did* finish my contract, darling. They know that if they steal my money no other girls will work for them.'

'No? So who will they work for?'

'For another Mafia. There are many. The girls will not trust my Mafia if they steal my money.'

Her Mafia. She could kiss that money goodbye. But what the hell – it was ridiculous that he was worried about her immoral earnings, he didn't even like to think about it.

'But darling,' Olga said, 'I am worried about your money. Will you have to pay Elizabeth very much?'

131

The two houses in America for starters; and, no doubt, a hefty monthly allowance. But he would be able to keep the London house and the mutual fund account – there must be a hundred thousand dollars in that by now. 'I'm afraid so. But I'll still have enough.'

'Do you have a pension?'

'Yes, but I wouldn't trust a pension to be paid after the Communists take over, so I bought houses as well. But Liz will get at least half of them.'

'I know you don't want to be a lawyer any more, but it is such a good job. And you will need to work, to live?'

'Depending on how we live, and where. But not for a while: first we're going to take a long, long holiday.' He took her in his arms. 'Now, let's stop worrying about money and talk about the things we're going to do.'

They were going to have a lovely time. In addition to the holiday he was taking now, his annual leave was coming up soon and they would have six whole weeks to do what they liked. Two weeks ago he had planned to take her sailing, but now he wanted to show her the world: the Hong Kong Government paid his air-fare back to England, so he only had to pay hers, and for a little extra he could make their tickets valid for around the world. 'Around the world . . .' Olga breathed.

Thailand was going to be the first stop, to see the temples and klongs and Thai dancing – 'They didn't teach us *that* at KGB school, darling!' – then they were going down to the Gulf of Siam to lie in the sun on the palm-fringed beach; then on to India to see the Taj Mahal – 'Oh, so romantic, and we can have a ride on an elephant!'

And then it was going to be Africa, the Serengeti in Tanzania and the Kruger Park in South Africa and the Zambesi Valley in Zimbabwe – 'I've never seen a wild animal in my life except in a zoo, if I could I would free them all!' – they were going to sleep in real tents and cook over open fires at night and listen to the lions roar. She flung herself back, her arms outstretched: '*Lions!* Is this really going to happen to me?'

Then they would fly on to London and see some shows and Big Ben and the Houses of Parliament and the Changing of the Guard and ride on the top of an omnibus. Then it was going to be a quick stop in New York – 'We have to see the Statue of Liberty, darling, and the Empire State Building!'

'And have a long boozy brunch at Fridays Bar.'

'Friday is always our day!'

And then it was going to be the Caribbean. Oh, the Caribbean. The sea so clean and blue, the beaches so white, the coral reefs, and the sumptuous hotels and the lovely rum punches – 'I have only dreamt about such things' – and they would charter a boat, swim off the reefs amongst all the wonderful tropical fish, and lie in the sun and have barbecues on the beach and in the sunset they would get into the dinghy and ride over to the hotel to dine and dance with the Beautiful People.

'But we'll be the most beautiful of all, darling, with our boat anchored out there!'

Yes, they were going to love it.

'You asked me what work I'll do after 1997? Well, what I'd really love to do is buy a big yacht and operate her as a charter-boat in the Caribbean. Taking nice rich American tourists out around the islands and make some money doing what I really love to do. Sail around the Virgins, and up to Puerto Rico and down to St Lucia and Guadeloupe and Martinique and Grenada and Barbados, and across to Venezuela and the Antilles. And to Cuba when Mr Castro collapses. Make a living doing what I really love doing.'

'Oh, how wonderful. Have we got enough money to buy such a boat in 1997?'

Hell, yes. Even if the divorce did take him to the cleaners. A boat like that would cost two hundred thousand dollars, second-hand, but he would sell his yacht *Elizabeth* for about a hundred thousand, and his mutual funds would cover the balance. Or he could sell the London house. And there were still almost eighteen months of salary before 30 June 1997 when the Comrades kicked the chair out from under his arse; he could save a good bit in that time if he and Olga lived quietly for a change. 'Yes, if we're careful.'

'We will save money, my darling!'

That's what he was going to do – not fucking law any more. And Hargreave knew loud and clear at last that he wanted to do all this with this lovely girl for the rest of his life. He was grateful that Liz had brought the problems of their marriage to a head – he just wanted her to be happy, as happy as he was. Life was fun.

Tomorrow Olga would have her passport back, and by the weekend they would be in the Philippines and have even more fun.

16

But Olga did not get her passport back the next day.

At ten o'clock they were waiting in their room for Vladimir. At ten-fifteen Hargreave telephoned him – no reply. He tried every fifteen minutes without success. At eleven o'clock he called his bank and stopped payment on the cheque. Now he was very worried, and so was Olga. '*Bastard.*' Hargreave waited another half an hour, pacing angrily up and down the room. '*Bastard . . .*' At half past eleven he telephoned Max, told him the story and asked him to get the Macao police on to the problem.

'Calm down and think about this before you leap in, Al,' Max urged. 'Give this Vladimir guy a bit more time. It looks like he's trying to stretch your nerves to make you cough up more money, but he'll at least want that cheque you cancelled revalidated, won't he, so he'll be back in touch with you very soon, don't worry. Whether you pay him any more is up to you – depends on how much he asks for, of course – but it seems to me it may be worth it to get shot of the problem rather than lay an official complaint with the police and open a can of worms – court and all that. Then there's the possibility of reprisals against your girl. And official repercussions – prostitution is technically illegal in Macao, remember. So if we can get that passport quietly, let's do that, even if it costs a bit more. I suggest you give him until the end of the week, Al.'

Oh Jesus, more delay, more suspense. 'Can't you get one of your Portuguese lawyer pals to get the police to recover the passport unofficially?'

'Exactly; that's preferable to laying an official charge – we'll use the old-boy network, my legal friends over there can certainly arrange for a little pressure on this jerk Vladimir. So don't panic yet, Al. If he doesn't show up by Friday night, come and see me on Monday and we'll figure out something.'

'We want to go to the Philippines. I'll give Vladimir till Thursday night, and come to you on Friday. We must get going.'

'No, give him more time, it's Tuesday already. Anyway, I'm in court all day Friday.'

'Can I come on Sunday? That's election day and I want to cast my vote, kill two birds with one stone.'

'Okay, I'll be working in my office anyway. Come even if you've got the passport because you want me to appeal to our immigration department, don't you? Bring Olga's identity card and work-permit as well. I'll also need an affidavit from her, you had better draft it, I'll have it typed and she can swear it before a Macao notary – you know what to say, how she's a bona fide singer, et cetera. Now relax, Vladimir will show up as soon as he finds out his cheque has been cancelled.'

Hargreave was somewhat reassured by Max's advice but it was hard to relax, waiting for Vladimir. And Vladimir did not show up. But Jake McAdam did.

He came over on the afternoon hydrofoil, telephoned from the reception desk and invited Hargreave for a drink.

'And Al? Can we be alone, in the first instance?'

They met in the bar downstairs while Olga was dressing for dinner. Jake said:

'No, it's not common knowledge as far as I'm aware, but it didn't take much imagination finding you. All I did was telephone all the hotels in Macao asking for Mr Hargreave. Liz knows you're somewhere in Macao, but she's not talking about it – that's why I'm here. Okay, I understand how you feel towards the marriage – but hell, Al, this isn't you.'

'What isn't me?' Hargreave demanded.

McAdam sighed. 'Look, I don't give a damn, but you're the Director of Public Prosecutions. You're next in line to be Attorney General, or you can become a Supreme Court judge any time you crook your finger.' He looked at him. 'And here you are –' he waved his hand – 'shacked up with a . . .' He left the sentence unfinished.

'She is not,' Hargreave said, 'a prostitute. She is a singer.'

'Okay,' Jake said, 'but a singer at the Tranquillity? It's a nice night-club, I agree, I've spent a few unwise dollars there myself, but at the Tranquillity a singer means one thing, Al.'

'Bullshit. Even the Tranquillity engages professional overseas singers, like the other night-clubs and big hotels.' He looked at Jake sternly. 'Anyway, she is not – repeat *not* – a prostitute any more.'

'You mean you've taken her off the game?'

'Yes.'

McAdam took a deep breath. He glanced around the bar. 'Okay, I think I understand. You . . . you've fallen in love with her.' He waved

135

a hand. 'I've fallen in love a few times myself over the years, and not all of them were entirely suitable –' He held up his palms. 'I understand what you're going through, Olga's a lovely girl, one of the loveliest I've ever seen. And when you two came on to my boat a fortnight ago, you couldn't keep your eyes off each other. Great, enjoy it. But Al – she worked for the Russian Mafia, mate. Do those bastards ever let go? And how do you know?' He put his hand on Hargreave's arm. 'You love her, but how do you know you haven't been set up?'

This made Hargreave angry, but he controlled it. 'Olga loves me.'

McAdam nodded sagely. 'I believe you.' He grinned. 'You're a lovable sort of bloke, Al. But how do you know her handlers are not setting you up for blackmail, unbeknownst to her? You're the DPP, one of the most powerful government officers in Hong Kong.'

'I'm impervious to blackmail because I'm not hiding anything any more. Next week Olga and I are flying to the Philippines for a holiday and when that's over – assuming we still feel the same way about each other – when we return she's going to live with me in Hong Kong, openly. I don't care what people suspect she was. And I don't care about my career. I've had enough. So the worst any blackmailer can do to me is make me put up with a bit of Hong Kong gossip for eighteen months.'

McAdam sighed. 'Okay, but where're you and Olga going to live during those eighteen months? And will you be able to afford to retire in 1997? Because I've got some significant news; I'm sorry.' He looked at Hargreave sympathetically. 'I'm here because Liz asked me to come, she's afraid you won't listen to her.' He breathed deeply. 'She's mad as hell about Olga – and she's not leaving Hong Kong, Al. She's staying put in your apartment as your legal wife until you come back to her. And she begs you to come back.' He paused. 'That's the message she asked me to deliver.'

Hargreave stared at him, his heart sinking. 'Oh, Lord.'

'And,' McAdam said, 'the divorce will be costly, of course. Where are you and Olga going to live if Liz is in your apartment? Can you afford to rent another place with our crazy prices?' He shook his head. 'I wouldn't bank on being able to retire in 1997, old mate. Think carefully what you're doing, Al. And remember: Olga *is* only twenty-three – and you're forty-six. Okay . . .' He sat back. 'I've said enough. I've done my duty to Liz, and you.'

'Are you suggesting,' Hargreave said, 'that I go back to Liz?'

McAdam sighed. 'Who the hell am I to judge? I married the same wrong woman *twice*. But, for what my opinion is worth, it appears to me you and Liz aren't good for each other any more, though I'm very fond of her. I gather it's been tricky between you for some years. All I'm suggesting is you remember Olga's age, and . . . her background. I'm suggesting you go'n have a civilized talk with Liz in the hopes of parting amicably.' He added: 'But there's little chance of that as long as Olga's in the picture, not only young and beautiful but . . . a Russian.'

'Say it: whore.'

'I mean Russian, an opportunist as Liz sees it. Please –' McAdam held up his palms – 'I'm not arguing, I just want what's best for all of you.'

Hargreave sighed. 'And thanks, Jake.' He glared across the room. 'Oh God. How can I afford to rent another apartment in that crazy town?'

McAdam raised his eyebrows, and said nothing. Hargreave shook his head. 'And there's another fucking problem. We're only staying in this hotel at the moment because we've got no choice.' He told McAdam about Olga's passport and reported Max's advice. He continued bitterly: 'If we don't get it back for any reason, maybe Max can get her admitted to Hong Kong as a distressed person, pending her getting a new passport. But if the worst comes to the worst I may have to get her a forged passport. Yes – I know the risks. But how do I do it?'

McAdam stared at him. 'Jesus. You're going to bring her into Hong Kong on a forged passport?'

'No. If necessary I'll get us a cheap apartment here in Macao and I'll commute to work every day. No, it's for emergency purposes only, if she has to get out of Macao in a hurry, for her safety – this bastard Vladimir has threatened her. If that comes to pass she's got to get somewhere safe, like Thailand, until we've sorted her problem out.' He sighed tensely. 'So I'd be awfully grateful if you made some discreet enquiries about how to get her a forged passport? Obviously I daren't ask.'

'Jesus . . . I shouldn't do it either, I'm a respectable politician now, not just an ex-cop.' He sighed. 'Yeah, Macao is a counterfeiting centre, a forged Portuguese or British passport will be no problem, I'm sure. Don't know about a Russian one.'

'Thanks, pal,' Hargreave said, with relief. 'It probably won't become necessary, we'll know this week.'

McAdam looked at him soberly. 'Hell, Al, I'm worried about you fucking around with the Mafia like this. Are you sure she's worth it?'

Hargreave abruptly changed the subject. 'How's the electioneering going?'

McAdam was relieved to change the subject too. 'I'm tired now. Sick of making speeches, canvassing, arguing, cajoling, pressing the flesh, kissing babies.'

'What are your chances?'

'Mine personally? None. I'm fighting a rather pro-China constituency. Don't really care, I've done my duty. The polls predict that Martin Lee's Democrats will win convincingly, they'll probably dominate the new Legco – that's good enough for me; I'll go'n work for them as a researcher or speech-writer or whatever. There'll be plenty to do because they intend to re-fight all the old battles they've lost with the government so far about enforcing our Bill of Rights, the Court of Final Appeal, freedom of information, et cetera – all of which China will fiercely object to as subversive activity. So we'll have plenty of conflict with Britain, who'll drag her feet for fear of upsetting China and the so-called "smooth transition".' He snorted disgustedly. 'Christ, isn't it marvellous? Britain actually hopes the Democrats *don't* win a majority lest we rock the boat with China.' He looked at Hargreave in wonder. 'Isn't the two-face double-speak amazing? And *China*'s double-speak? Have you read the Hong Kong newspapers while you've been here?'

Hargreave shook his head.

'Christ, it's mind-boggling. China vows to sweep Legco aside, fiercely threatens all us democrats as subversives – but then she gives the pro-China candidates all kinds of election money and this week she actually took *eight* full-page advertisements in *eight* newspapers for three days exhorting the electorate to vote for the pro-China candidates, for ass-kissers who can "forge a dialogue with China" – despite vowing to destroy Legco!' He shook his head. 'Christ, the double-speak is terrifying. What hope is there for Hong Kong with masters like that?'

Hargreave sighed. 'The only hope is guys like Martin Lee and you standing up to China – that the democrats make such a strong showing that China is forced to include at least some of you guys in the new administration.'

'That's the only faint hope,' McAdam agreed. He added: 'And officials like you who stay at your posts and fearlessly apply the Rule of Law.' He sighed bitterly. 'But why in Christ's name are we reduced to "hoping" – our rights are supposed to be guaranteed!'

Hargreave sighed. 'And how're the people taking it, what's the mood?'

McAdam shook his head wearily. 'Amongst the Chinese? Feelings are running pretty high. They worry about their livelihoods, about their savings. But I also detect a lot of fatalism, a 'What can we do?' attitude. Quite a lot are putting a brave face on it – and of course amongst some of them "face" means a kind of patriotic pride that Big Brother China is coming to town even if they're shit-scared of him. Fear, a lot of fear, particularly amongst white-collar Chinese who can't emigrate. They'll bend with the wind, of course, probably wave flags and cheer like mad when China comes marching in, but they're very worried. A great many will vote for the pro-China candidates for this fatalistic reason, possibly in the expectation that China will find out who voted for who – as China may well do, despite the secret ballot, simply by using informers, paying people to split on their neighbours.'

Just then Hargreave heard high heels clicking across the gold marble, and he turned. There was Olga, coming towards them, smiling, radiant.

Both men stood up. McAdam muttered as they watched her approach: 'Okay, I see what you mean, you're a lucky man . . .'

17

Yes, he was a lucky man and yes, she was worth it. He was very relieved that she could get a forged passport if absolutely necessary, but in all probability it would not be – Max had sounded very confident that his Macao buddies would recover hers without official fuss. The Portuguese knew how to do things unofficially, unlike the frightfully pukkah British. Anyway, Vladimir would surely show up tomorrow or the next day and re-open negotiations. There was nothing Hargreave could do about it till Sunday, so he might as well relax, as Max had advised.

They did manage to enjoy it while they waited. They worked out in the gym every morning, played tennis, had boozy lunches and long sensual siestas but they did not leave the hotel lest they miss Vladimir. But he did not show up. By Friday Hargreave was a worried man again. And then, that midday, Superintendent Bernie Champion called.

'I know you're on leave but I've got to see you. I've just got back from Russia. We've made an arrest in the uranium case! I'm coming across on the next hydrofoil.'

Hargreave had asked Olga for privacy and she had gone off to the gymnasium before Champion arrived. They sat on the balcony outside the bedroom, overlooking the sea. Champion had smudges of tiredness under his eyes but he was brimming with self-satisfaction. He took a swallow of beer and grinned. 'Good to see you looking so well, pal. I hear she's a stunner. Sorry to disturb you but I couldn't go through your deputy and explain the case all over again.'

'How did you know I was here?'

'Jake told me. Nobody at your office knew so I phoned your apartment on the off-chance and was flabbergasted to find myself talking to Liz. She referred me to Jake.'

Good that nobody in the office knew. 'And what have you heard about us?'

Champion grinned again. 'Jake only said you seemed to be having the time of your life – in confidence of course. Good, go for it, man, who gives a damn who she is as long as she's making you happy.'

Who she is? 'She's a singer, Champ, that's who she is. And how was Liz?'

'Fine. A bit frosty perhaps, but she was calm. Keeping a low profile, she said. What's the story, how come she's back?'

'Didn't Jake tell you?'

'Only that reconciliation looked unlikely.'

'A bit late for that.'

'Yes, none of my business, but bullet scars are pretty permanent mementos.' He smiled. 'So, be happy. Though this,' he waved a hand at the hotel, 'must be costing you an arm and a leg.'

'Yes. So don't let's waste it. Now, who have you arrested?'

Champion looked at him smugly. 'Ivan Gregovich himself! The boss man, remember him?'

Hargreave did not, but he raised his eyebrows to appear impressed. 'It's a long time since I looked at the file; give me the facts.'

Champion hunched forward, opened the file and pulled out a big envelope.

'In here's a copy of my new covering report, plus a new statement from me, and one from that Russian policeman, Colonel Simonski. Read them after I've gone. Now, remember the German police arrested a guy called Wessels in Munich, arriving from Russia, carrying eight grams of uranium? Under interrogation he suddenly died of a heart attack. The German police suspected Wessels was working for or with the Russian Mafia. The eight grams was only a tiny sample to show to potential customers – tons of the stuff would be available at the price of sixty thousand US dollars a kilo. You need about four kilos to make one nuclear bomb, so the purchaser would have to be rich. This guy, Wessels, was headed for Hong Kong, so it was probably a Triad society who wanted the stuff, to sell on to somebody like North Korea or maybe Taiwan. And that's how the Hong Kong Police got involved – the Germans asked for our help.'

Hargreave nodded. 'And you came up with nothing.'

'Nothing. We made all kinds of clever enquiries through our contacts, but no information was forthcoming.'

'So the Germans tried a sting operation.'

'Yes, their undercover agents put the word out in the underworld in Munich and Moscow that they had a customer in Hong Kong interested in buying a large quantity of uranium.'

'And again there were no bites.'

'And again nothing was forthcoming – the German police think that

141

the untimely death of Mr Wessels gave the business a bad name temporarily.'

'And that's the stage we'd reached last time you consulted me and asked me to recommend funny money. I hope you spent it wisely.'

Champion smiled. 'I sure did. I am now something of an expert on Russian crime in general and the Mafia in particular – and on Russian politics. It's all in my report –' he tapped the envelope – 'it's a masterpiece. There's also a long official report by Colonel Simonski, which I had translated into English, which is essential background knowledge for prosecuting counsel, though we can't lead the evidence at the trial. Anyway, to cut a long story short, we first set up our own sting operation in Hong Kong. We put out the word through our undercover agents amongst the Triads that we had access to uranium for sale. Huge profits available. And – we got a bite.'

'You did? Who from?'

'We're not sure, because the contact was made from a public telephone, and anyway there're so many layers between the talkers and the boss-man it's impossible to prove – but we believe it was the 14K. And that doubtless means Terence Chang himself, if they're spending that kind of money.'

Hargreave dearly wanted to catch Terence Chang. 'Yes, but to prove it?'

'Exactly. Anyway, this man speaking from the public telephone says his boss wants his chemist to see a sample of the merchandise. Of course, we couldn't supply a sample, so our sting operation collapsed. After you recommended the money, I flew to Vladivostok and then on to Moscow to do some sleuthing with the help of the Russian police. Long story, it's all in the file.' He patted it lovingly. 'Suffice to say many of the Russian cops are crooked as hell. Crime is terrible over there, everybody's at it, the politicians, the cops, the bureaucrats. Anyway, we've got two honest cops on our payroll. One is this guy Colonel Simonski. Hell of a nice chap, about fifty. In fact, remember he was fired from his top job in the Organized Crime Squad because of his report about corruption in the bureaucracy?' Hargreave nodded. Champion continued: 'He is now desk-bound, doing a dull administrative job, but he's kept his ear to the ground and it's all thanks to him that we've broken this case.'

'Is he bitter about being pushed out? Has he got an axe to grind?'

'He's angry as hell, but it wouldn't affect his reliability as an investigator. Anyway, Simonski works in Moscow. The other guy is Captain Kerensky, about thirty-five – he works in Vladivostok. Kerensky wasn't involved in this arrest but his statement gives you good general background information.' Champion took a swig of beer with relish. 'Briefly, the story Simonski and Kerensky have to tell is this.

'Since the collapse of the old Soviet Union the massive military-industrial complex which produced weapons has been thrown off the rails. Like the army itself, which has lost all its privileges. Because of roaring inflation, military pensions are almost worthless. The armaments industry has got vast stockpiles of weapons they don't need and the managers are having huge difficulties converting their factories to other products, and paying workers. So there's a massive black market in stolen weapons – army officers and bureaucrats are selling arms to the Mafia who are smuggling them out to Third World countries. *Jane's Defence Weekly* describes it as "the biggest and most dangerous arms bazaar in history".'

Champion paused for effect, on his hobby-horse now. He took a mouthful of beer, then continued.

'In addition, there are thirty *thousand* nuclear weapons in Russia. That's a huge worry for the world – imagine it some bureaucrat sold some to people like Saddam or Gadhafi! But even more worrying is the problem of the vast stockpiles of fissile radio-active material used in the manufacture of nuclear warheads – uranium and the like, which is much easier to smuggle than a whole big missile. And –' he tapped the file – 'it is now *clear* that a *nuclear* Mafia exists.'

Champion opened the file and traced his finger down a page.

'There are one hundred and eighty-nine sites in the former Soviet Union where nuclear material is produced, counting mines, factories, and nuclear power plants, plus dozens of research institutes where it is handled. How good is the security surrounding these places?' He looked at Hargreave with big eyes. 'Well, Al, in 1993 alone police in Europe made three hundred seizures of radio-active materials being offered for sale! Did you know that?'

Lord. 'No.'

'Nor did I till I started my investigations.' From his briefcase he produced a book called *Comrade Criminal*. 'This is by a reporter called Stephen Handelman, published by Yale University Press. Read it – it's a real eye-opener. Anyway, three *hundred* seizures in Europe in 1993 – and most of it came from the former Soviet Union and Eastern bloc countries. Of *course*,' Champion sat back, 'the Russian Atomic Energy Ministry – MINATOM – said none of *their* stock was missing. But then came the case of Mr Wessels being arrested at Munich airport.'

Hargreave nodded. Champion continued:

'After *that* Russia finally admitted over fifty thefts of radio-active materials had taken place! *Fifty!* And no wonder – the military-industrial complex in chaos, and bankrupt! These nuclear materials could be stolen by countless people – Christ, there are over a hundred and ten thousand nuclear employees in over twenty "nuclear cities" devoted exclusively to nuclear production – all lowly paid. And the inspectors from the State Atomic Energy Inspectorate complain that when they arrive at a site to check on the inventories the bureaucrats blandly refuse to open their doors to "unauthorized personnel"!' Champion looked at him: 'The bureaucrats just thumb their noses at the law, because they are the repositories of power now, along with their Mafia partners. The whole country is *lawless*! Jesus, it's frightening, Al.'

Hargreave nodded. Even allowing for some exaggeration on Champion's part, fresh from his exciting investigations in Russia, he was a very experienced cop and the picture he painted was very worrying indeed.

'And look at the effect it is having on Russian politics,' Champion continued. 'Gorbachev couldn't control the country once he let the genie out of the bottle and now Yeltsin can't either. So their new experiment in democracy is collapsing – the Mafia have taken the place of the police as law enforcers! And so there is a right-wing backlash: ordinary people are frightened, they've seen no benefit from democracy so they yearn for the old days of the Communist police state where criminals were at least underground.' He waved a hand. 'So this so-called New Communist Party is on the rise. And who will be their biggest allies? The army, who want their old power and privileges back! We could be back in the Cold War all over again.' Champion looked at Hargreave, big-eyed. 'The army is a political time-bomb in Russia, Al – that's why Yeltsin doesn't dare clamp down on the corruption, he's got nothing to offer to keep them on his side and he knows they'll rise up against him if he cracks down on them. So they and their bureaucratic henchmen can thumb their noses at his Atomic Energy inspectors.'

Hargreave rubbed his chin. So Champion was now an expert on Russian internal affairs? But, yes, it was a real and worrisome prospect. 'Bad news for the new Russia.'

Champion tapped the file: 'Bad news for the rest of the world too! Because what happens when this nuclear material gets in the hands of mad dictators and they build bombs to annihilate their adversaries?' He glared: 'World War Three, Al!'

Hargreave sighed. 'Okay, but let's get to the facts of our case.'

Champion leant forward: 'That *is* part of the facts of our case, Al – possibly the end of the world! Christ, imagine if one of these terrorist organizations like those Palestinian bastards who blew up the World Trade Centre in New York – the Islamic Jihad – imagine if they got their hands on a nuclear arsenal. Imagine if some of these tinpot countries in the Middle East or Africa started throwing atom bombs at us – or at each other. It could kill the whole world. That's the background story Kerensky and Simonski give us in their new statements. Al –' Champion paused impressively – 'this is a case of international importance.'

'Yes, it's very important, Bernie. So what happened?'

Champion sat back, and smiled. '*We*,' he said proudly, 'have arrested one of the biggest, baddest ganglords in this nuclear Mafia! Namely Mr Ivan Gregovich.' He tapped the file again. 'There's an update on his criminal profile in my new covering report.'

'Yes, but what's *happened*?'

Champion took a big swig of beer, relishing his triumph. 'When I was in Russia we spread the word in the Moscow underworld that my undercover boys in Hong Kong had a customer called Lawrence for eight kilos of uranium – Lawrence being one of my boys, of course. Finally I flew back to Hong Kong a week ago and hardly had I landed before "Lawrence" receives a contact from somewhere in Russia – don't know where – from somebody saying they've got uranium for sale and they'll be in touch. We get all excited and wait – but nothing happens for days. Then Simonski telephones to say he hears that a shipment is arriving by air in Hong Kong from Moscow – and that Ivan Gregovich *himself* may be accompanying it!' Champion grinned maliciously. 'Then, day before yesterday, Simonski telephones me from Moscow airport and says he's just seen Gregovich checking in on the Aeroflot flight to Hong Kong, and one of his flunkies has handed over a suitcase to a man called Kozkov who checked on to the flight with it.' Champion smiled. 'So obviously Gregovich is going to accompany the flight and relieve Kozkov of the suitcase once it's safely in Hong Kong. Then contact our "Lawrence".' He grinned. 'And so Simonski jumps on the same plane.'

Hargreave was staring at him. Jesus Christ, he thought. 'Go on.'

'*Well*,' Champion said happily, 'so we rush around like blue-arsed flies. Stake out our airport and meet the plane. Simonski is first off. He joins me and surreptitiously points out Kozkov and Gregovich. Kozkov gets the suitcase from the luggage carousel, enters the customs hall and we arrest him. Gregovich is following Kozkov closely but pretending to have nothing to do with him. We challenge Gregovich – and he tries

145

to make a run for it, but we grab him. *And* –' Champion held up his finger – 'we found the key to the suitcase on him!' He sat back, smugly. 'We sent the suitcase and contents to be analysed, and we took Grego and Kozkov-baby to the police station. And,' he grinned, 'after a while Gregovich was singing like a canary. A confession.' He added, straight-faced: 'Entirely voluntary, of course.'

Hargreave was staring at him. 'Jesus Christ . . .' he said.

'*Yeah*,' Champ agreed happily.

Hargreave sat back. 'Do you mean to tell me that you permitted eight kilos of radio-active uranium to be landed in Hong Kong?' He stared, then he exploded. '*Christ*, if the plane had crashed you could have contaminated thousands of square kilometres and killed thousands of people with radiation! And Hong Kong airport is one of the most dangerous in the world! You could have killed us all!'

Champion stared at him, astonished by the rebuke. Then he sat up straight and said indignantly, 'I didn't *permit* anything! The Russian police, Simonski, *he* permitted the stuff to leave Russia!' He glared at Hargreave, astonished. 'What did you expect me to do – fly to Moscow on my magic carpet and arrest Gregovich myself before take-off?' He tapped his broad chest. '*I* can't order the Russian Police to do anything!'

Hargreave was amazed. The guy's so pleased with himself, he thought, he doesn't see this. He leant forward: 'But *you* acted as the agent provocateur, Bernie! *You* put the word out in the Russian under-world that your boys had a customer for uranium! So you encouraged the shipment, you're morally responsible for its importation! And you'd have been to blame if there'd been a disaster!' He glared. 'I *told* you when we discussed this case last that we didn't want nuclear material flying into Hong Kong!'

Champion was still incredulous at the rebuke. 'It was packed in a lead-lined suitcase for Christ's sake!'

'*Jesus*.' Hargreave shook his head. 'And if the plane had crashed and that suitcase split open!' He waved a hand, bemused. 'Why didn't you consult me – I'd have forbidden it, and told you to tell Simonski to arrest Gregovich at Moscow airport! Why didn't you do that?'

Champion glared. 'I did,' he said angrily, '*try* to consult you. I tele-phoned you immediately but was told you were on –' he waved a disparaging hand at the hotel – 'on leave.'

'So why didn't you consult one of my deputies?'

Champion leant forward angrily. 'Because only *you* know the case and I didn't have time to explain it all to them – I've been working flat out and the Aeroflot plane was about to take off! *Jesus,*' he fumed, 'I pull off the arrest of the decade and this is what I get?'

'The plane wasn't going to take off immediately Gregovich checked in! You should have told Simonski to arrest him and seize the suitcase!'

Champion cried indignantly, 'Arrest Gregovich on what charge? Simonski hadn't seen him *do* anything except watch the suitcase being handed over from a distance!'

Hargreave sighed angrily. He looked at the sea.

'Hell, you took a chance! The jury are going to be angry with us about this – especially as we've all just seen the VJ Day celebrations on television, the horrific images of Hiroshima.'

Champion glowered: 'Then they'll be angry with Gregovich as well!'

'And we've just had that international outcry about those stupid French nuclear explosions in the Pacific. Is Simonski still in town? I want to talk to him about this!'

Champion said sullenly, 'No, he's rushed back to Moscow, to follow up information.'

'And where is this uranium now?'

'In a lead-lined box in a vault in military HQ.'

Hargreave shook his head. 'Does the press know anything about this?'

'No. This is top-secret, not even the Governor knows.'

Hargreave snorted. 'Well, keep it from the press or you'll have an outcry.' He sighed again. 'Okay, so you've got the merchandise, now what're you going to do? Try to catch Terence Chang with it?'

'*That,*' Champion said, 'is why I'm here consulting you when I should be in bed, I haven't slept in thirty-six hours.' He glared. '*Subject* to your advice, I intend putting out the word to the Triads that the stuff is now available. I'll try to get a message direct to dear Terence, and see who comes forward to take the bait.'

'I don't like your chances,' Hargreave muttered, 'now that you've arrested Gregovich – news like that travels fast.' He considered a moment. 'So did the courier – Kozkov – did he know he was carrying uranium for Gregovich?'

'No. He knew he was carrying contraband, but he didn't know what or for whom, he didn't even know Gregovich. I believe him, because that's how these smuggling jobs are done. And we were very persuasive when we interrogated him. He confessed immediately. He only knew that he would meet "Lawrence" at Hong Kong airport. Gregovich doubtless had backup men awaiting his arrival, local Mafia hoods, but he denies it, and we didn't identify anybody.'

'So, as Kozkov didn't know Gregovich, we should try them separately and then use Kozkov as a Crown witness in the Gregovich case. Will Kozkov cooperate?'

'Yes.'

'But as Kozkov didn't know he was carrying the suitcase for Grego-vich, the only evidence we have against Gregovich is his own con-fession, and the fact he had the key. Plus the little Simonski saw at Moscow airport.'

'There's the fact he tried to run when we accosted him. Plus the fact – I forgot to mention this – that the suitcase had a combination lock, as well as a key, and Gregovich knew the combination. He finally told us in his confession. That's how we managed to open it without smash-ing the lock.'

Hargreave said testily, 'That's *very* important evidence.'

'Sorry, I'm tired. The suitcase was made in Russia; Simonski has contacted the factory who say that one in every ten suitcases has the same key-lock, but only two in umpteen thousand of the combination-locks are the same. So Gregovich knowing the combination's number is conclusive proof.'

'And the confession will stand up in court?'

Champion said with a dead-pan face: 'His confession was voluntary.'

Hargreave sighed inwardly. 'You said you were "very persuasive" with Kozkov.'

Champion looked taken aback for an instant. 'Did I? I'm sorry, I haven't slept.'

'Yes, you did.'

Champion waved a weary hand. 'Oh, what I meant was we realized he was just the dumb courier, and that we wanted him as a witness for us even if he can't finger Gregovich as Mr Big – so we told him it would be best if he told us the truth, that he'd get a lighter sentence, et cetera. And he's a drug addict – we promised to get him medical attention. He immediately spilt what beans he knew, and I believed him.' Champion looked at Hargreave grimly: 'That's all I meant by "very persuasive".'

'How long did it take to make Kozkov spill the beans?'

'A minute or two.'

'Who was present?'

'Myself and Simonski, then a few minutes later in came Inspector Sullivan and a Russian interpreter. Then Simonski and I left, to interro-gate Gregovich in my office, leaving Sullivan to get any further facts from Kozkov. *But*, to anticipate your next question, when we interro-gated Gregovich we were *not* "persuasive" in any shape or form, there

148

was absolutely *no* duress or undue influence, we played it by the book, by the Judges' Rules, we wanted to be sure that his statement stood up in court.'

Hargreave concealed a mirthless smile. He hardly believed that. He doubted that a tough cookie like Champion would play it by the book with a bad bastard like Gregovich. But Champion's assurance was good enough at this stage: it was the defence lawyer's job to raise a doubt about the voluntariness. 'Did you caution him? And tell him his right to have a lawyer present?'

'Yes.'

Hargreave doubted that too. 'And he declined?'

'Yes. Protesting his innocence – "Why do I need a lawyer?" – Russian crooks are not accustomed to nice lawyers.'

'And how long did you interrogate him before he confessed?'

'It's in the Investigation Diary. About six hours.'

Long time. 'Non-stop?'

'Yes. Except for breaks for coffee and sandwiches and so forth.'

'Did you tape-record the interrogation?'

'No.'

'No? Why not?'

'Because there was no need. Simonski and I made lots of notes.'

Surprising, not to use a tape-recorder during a long interrogation. 'Who was present?'

'Just me and Simonski. No interpreter, both Gregovich and Simonski speak excellent English.'

'Were you present all the time?'

Champion said irritably, '*Yes*. Well, except to go and have a pee a couple of times.'

Hargreave was suddenly aware of Olga. She was standing in the balcony doorway in her gym suit, smiling. 'Hi – sorry, I've just come to get my bikini.' She immediately disappeared back into the bedroom.

Champion turned and looked at the empty doorway. He swung back to Hargreave. 'That the lucky girl?'

'Yes.' Hargreave wondered how long she'd been in the room, how much she had heard. He took a deep draught of beer while he waited for Olga to leave. He heard her call 'Bye . . .' and the door close after her.

Champion was grinning at him. 'Don't worry, I won't tell a soul.'

Hargreave smirked. 'Okay, where were we? You were with Simonski and Gregovich the whole time during interrogation except for occasional visits to the toilet?'

149

'Correct.'

'Now, the point is: could Simonski have threatened Gregovich, brought duress to bear upon him during your absence?' He added: 'I'm just trying to find out what we're going to be up against at the trial.'

'The answer is *no*,' Champion said irritably. 'I had impressed the Judges' Rules upon Simonski, how confessions have to be voluntary under English law. And Simonski is a good, honest cop. He wouldn't use third-degree stuff.'

Hargreave took a breath to control his own irritation. 'So what other evidence can Simonski give, apart from what he saw at Moscow airport?'

Champion dragged his hands down his face.

'He can tell the court about the Russian nuclear sites he's investigated, the anxiety about theft from those sites, about the security problems, how the personnel haven't been paid their salaries. He can tell the jury how quantities of nuclear material have gone missing over the last few years and the hundreds of cases in Western Europe of it being smuggled –'

Hargreave interrupted: 'That's all hearsay, Champ – the court can't listen to hearsay! That's like telling the jury in Al Capone's trial that there've been a lot of murders lately by unknown murderers.'

'*Je-zuz!*' Champion glared at Hargreave. 'Go'n teach your grandmother to suck eggs. Do you imagine I'm so unacquainted with the Law of Evidence that I don't realize that Simonski and I are tied hand and foot? Do you realize how infuriating it is, how toweringly unjust it is that I know, and Simonski knows, and you know how all this theft of nuclear material and corruption is going on in Russia, yet we cannot – by law – tell the jury about it, *despite* its obvious relevance to our case? Do you take me for a *fool*?'

Hargreave closed his eyes, and said quietly, 'Very well. Did Gregovich tell you where he got the uranium?'

'Not exactly – he pretended he didn't know the source his flunkies dealt with. But of course he knows. Simonski is following that up now.'

Hargreave thought: Well, if Gregovich withheld that important information it tends to indicate he was not being bullied, that he was in control of himself.

'So you want my advice on a sting operation now, to try to nail Terence Chang? Sure, put the word out in the underworld that you've got the merchandise, and see if anybody bites. But –' he held up a finger – 'remember the law about agents provocateurs. When you meet your man, don't encourage him to commit a crime, let *him* do the soliciting as far as possible. This is not much different from a plainclothes policeman inciting a suspected drug-dealer to sell him heroin.'

Champion glared. 'Of course. All I want to know is, can I cut a small chunk off this uranium – *under* controlled conditions, of course, *sir* – and offer it to the Triad's chemist for analysis? Remember, Terence Chang – *if* he was the gentleman involved – wanted his chemist to test the merchandise, and we didn't have a sample to hook him? Well, we've got eight kilos of the stuff now. Is it okay to show him a small slice?'

Hargreave looked at him in amazement. 'Christ, you can't go round Hong Kong offering chunks of radio-active uranium like birthday cake! The stuff's lethal! The answer is definitely no.' He glanced at his watch. 'Is there anything else?'

Champion seethed. 'In a hurry, are we? I wish,' he said, 'that you'd stop speaking as if I was a rookie – "like birthday cake"! I said "*under* properly controlled conditions". However –'

Hargreave sighed: 'I'm sorry, Champ.'

'However, yes there are one or two other points I'd like to consult you on – *sir*. The first concerns the courier, Kozkov. I respectfully suggest that we separate his trial from Gregovich's immediately and try him as soon as possible in front of a magistrate on a simple smuggling charge so that we can use him as a witness against Gregovich.'

Hargreave nodded. 'Yes, I agree.'

'Good, we agree about something. So would you kindly write that instruction in the Investigation Diary?'

Hargreave reached for the file, wrote the instruction and signed it.

'Thank you,' Champion said. 'We'll do that on Monday – he'll plead guilty. Now, as regards Gregovich's trial, do you wish to start with committal proceedings in the magistrates' court or go by way of direct indictment to the Supreme Court?' He added: 'I'd prefer direct indictment.'

'Why?'

'Because it's quicker. Strike while the iron's hot. Gregovich has confessed and the sooner we get him to court the better, before he changes his mind and alleges duress.'

Hargreave would also have preferred direct indictment: committal proceedings – where the evidence was first heard by a magistrate who then, if satisfied, referred it on to the Supreme Court for trial – increased the workload. But it had the merit of testing the witnesses before the trial, hearing what questions the defendant asks in cross-examination. 'I think we should start with committal proceedings.'

'Why?' Champion demanded.

'Because,' Hargreave said, 'it would be helpful if we knew what the defence is going to be in the Supreme Court – with luck, Gregovich may show his hand. And our case depends largely on his confession – let's see if he challenges it, and what he alleges happened.' He left out, And let's see how well you and Simonski stand up to cross-examination on this point.

'Okay,' Champion said tensely. 'But nothing untoward happened during the interrogation.' He tapped the Investigation Diary. 'Your instruction, please.'

Hargreave wrote: *Proceed by way of committal against Gregovich as soon as possible using Kozkov as Crown witness*. He said: 'I'll give this case to Neil Findlay to prosecute, he's very good.' He wrote that instruction also.

Champion said stiffly, 'There's no harm in Findlay doing the committal proceedings, but I was hoping you would prosecute the trial in Supreme Court.'

Hargreave sat back with a pained expression. 'Why me, Bernie? I'll be very busy when I get back to chambers. It's not usual for the DPP to go into court.'

'Because,' Champion said, 'this is a case of international importance. Black market nuclear weapon material, for Christ sake. *Time* and *Newsweek*, the international press are going to cover the trial. So I think it's a case where the DPP himself should go into court with a crack of thunder, like you did in that big heroin case, to show the crooks how seriously we take this matter – show the *world*. And Gregovich is doubtless going to hire the best defence counsel.' He added, grudgingly, 'I want you because you're the best.'

Hargreave smiled. 'Flattery will get you nowhere.'

Champion glared: 'Supposing Gregovich hires a QC? Or Shitlips Lipschitz – can Findlay cope with guys like that?'

'Findlay can cope with anybody. But if you want a QC I'll send Dusty Millar in with Findlay. If Lipschitz is defending I definitely won't do it; I can't stand that little thug.'

'Please, Al.' Champion spread his hands. 'This is my biggest case ever. After all these years of faithful service you owe it to me. Dusty Millar isn't nearly as good as you, he's such a mournful sonofabitch he turns any jury right off. But you've got flair.' He added grudgingly, 'Charm.' He added further: 'Though I've had difficulty spotting it today.'

Hargreave smiled. 'I said I'm sorry.'

'When are you going back to work?'

Hargreave sighed. 'I've taken four weeks' leave but it's almost half gone. Bernie, I'll see what my workload is like, but I promise nothing.'

'Jesus!' Champion smacked the table. 'You just don't take this case seriously enough, do you? You're too wrapped up in this . . .' He was going to say whore but changed it. 'This holiday. Okay, my old pal is too busy!' He stood up. 'Thanks for the advice and encouragement – *sir*.' He pointed at the envelope of photocopied statements. 'Simonski's statement may refresh your memory of the various Russian Mafias, and how our Mr Gregovich is one of the *very* big bad wheels. But in case you have any lingering doubts about the voluntariness of our dear man's confession and whether he deserves your worthy anxieties, look at this.' He pulled a photograph from the file and tossed it on the table.

Hargreave found himself looking at a handsome man of about forty-five, with a fleshy, lecherous mouth and a smile showing perfect white teeth. The eyes were cold and hooded above that perfect smile, piercing, and the bushy eyebrows were raised into arches; on his chin he wore a pointed beard. The whole effect was one of evil – it was a Mephisto-phelean face.

'Yes,' Hargreave said; and again the question crossed his mind how this man had volunteered a confession. 'Bernie, you've done a great job. Please sit down and have another drink.'

'No, more sleeplessness beckons imperatively!' He thrust the photograph back in the file and turned for the doorway, then he looked back. 'And talking about *sleep*, I believe your charming young lady is of Russian extraction? I wish you every happiness. But do be careful. You never know where she's *been*.' He turned and strode away. The bedroom door banged behind him.

18

Champion had said that Gregovich probably had muscle-men waiting at Hong Kong airport to assist him with 'Lawrence': that worried Hargreave. But surely Moscow Mafia-men dealing in uranium had nothing to do with prostitutes in Macao despite Champion's snide parting remark? International terrorism had no more connection with the Heavenly Tranquillity Nite-Club than it did with an ordinary Wanchai girlie-bar controlled by the Triads. Of course not. Nonetheless he found an opening over dinner to ask, 'Ever heard of a guy called Ivan Gregovich?'

'Yes,' Olga said. 'He is a big gangster in Moscow.'

Hargreave felt himself flinch. 'But you don't know him personally?'

'No. But ask any of the girls, he is a Mafia boss. Everybody knows about him.'

'Is he involved in prostitution?'

'All the Mafia gangs are involved in prostitution, I think.'

Oh Lord. 'But you never worked for Ivan Gregovich?'

'I don't know. I was controlled by a man called Sergei, he arranged everything.'

'Sergei? But was he a boss or just one of a gang?'

'Just a gangster.'

'Did Sergei work for Gregovich?'

She shook her head. 'I don't know, darling – remember I was away for nearly three years while all the gangster trouble was going on in Moscow, I only found out I was working for a gang when I arrived in Istanbul. And when I returned to Moscow there were so many gangs and I tried to run away to Estonia, remember? That is when I bought my gun, remember? But the Estonians deported me and my gang caught me again, and made me work in the Metropole Hotel? That's when I heard about Ivan Gregovich, and other gang bosses.' She shrugged. 'But I just obeyed Sergei, he was enough to make me sick.'

It made Hargreave feel sick too: *Gangs, whores, hotels, guns* . . . 'And your gun – where is it now?'

She took a sip of wine and pointed at her handbag, on the corner of the table. 'In there.'

Hargreave was astonished; then he grinned despite himself. The Director of Public Prosecutions lunching with his girl who is armed with an unlicensed, smuggled pistol in her handbag on the table. 'Why are you walking around with it here?'

'When we came to this hotel you told me to bring everything that was valuable. I must keep it somewhere safe.'

Hargreave reached for the bag, and opened it. Tucked amongst her lipstick and female paraphernalia was a little Browning pistol. He did not touch it.

'You're committing an offence walking around with an unlicensed firearm. We must get rid of this.'

'No way! When I go back to Russia that's my only protection.'

'You're not going back to Russia. Anyway, how would you get it on the aeroplane? And past customs?'

'Same way I got it here – in my suitcase. Or up my pussy, in a condom.'

Hargreave smiled, despite himself. 'I know nothing about that gun if it's found, okay? And please leave it in the room in future, hidden at the bottom of your case. As soon as we've got your passport we're throwing it in the sea, got that?'

'Very well, darling,' she smiled.

Also in the handbag were four identical photographs of her, obviously taken in a kiosk. He took one out. He wanted it in case he needed to get her a forged passport. 'Can I have this?'

'Of course. But you've got me right here, in the flesh.'

He slipped it into his pocket. He rubbed his chin. 'And Vladimir? Has he ever worked for Ivan Gregovich?'

'No, I don't think so, but that pig would work for the Devil.' She frowned. 'Why do you ask? Is that what your meeting was about?'

Hargreave shook his head emphatically. 'No. Just curiosity. As you say, he's a famous name.'

And after another bottle of wine he convinced himself that his anxiety was just curiosity, there *was* no connection between Olga Romalova and the notorious Ivan Gregovich who was now languishing in a cell in Hong Kong, there was no reason to think his relationship with Olga would prejudice his work on the uranium case. And next week – if Vladimir didn't show up tomorrow – Max would get her passport back easily, then appeal to the immigration department on her behalf.

He was tempted to telephone Vladimir again, but that would be unwise – that would open the door to more extortion. And it would be *most* unwise, as Director of Public Prosecutions, to be bargaining with one Russian hood when his department was about to prosecute another Russian hood, even assuming there was no connection between the two bastards. No, leave it all to Max – don't try to be your own legal adviser.

After a long siesta they went to the tennis courts and they both played brilliant games and attracted quite a crowd of guests: for the first time Olga beat him and she was so pleased with herself she did a row of cartwheels across the court after the final volley, showing flashes of scanty panties and golden limbs, leaped over the net and collapsed into his arms, laughing, '*I won!*' Everybody broke into appreciative applause, and the manager was so pleased with all the bonhomie he sent her a bottle of champagne.

They had a good time. And then, that Friday afternoon, while they were lying squashed up in the bubble bath, Vladimir telephoned.

'Good evening, Mr Hargreave. I must congratulate you on a spectacular game of tennis . . .'

Hargreave stood at the bedside telephone, a towel around his waist, his heart racing in relief.

'And Olga is such a pretty girl. So popular. And that gymnastic trick she did – *oh-la-la*. I understand your fascination with her.'

Hargreave tried to recover his composure. 'Why didn't you bring Olga's passport on Tuesday? I've stopped payment on that cheque you know!'

'It would be sad,' Vladimir said, 'to lose her.'

Hargreave felt his stomach contract. Before he could respond Vladimir continued: 'Mr Hargreave, this call is to advise you that your bill is now forty thousand dollars. We would like immediate payment, please.'

Hargreave blanched. Then anger took over. He did not bother to ask how Vladimir arrived at that outrageous figure. 'And Olga would like her passport immediately! It is a crime for anyone to withhold it from her!'

'Oh, a crime, yes you told me.'

Don't warn him about Max. '*You* have it, Vladimir, and if you don't return it right now, tonight, the matter will be handed over to the police at once.'

'Oh, the Macao police? I see, very serious. Mr Hargreave, I do not have Olga's passport but I think it can be found when you pay the forty thousand dollars you owe.'

Hargreave closed his eyes. Although he had been expecting that, it was like a blow. No way could he pay that. 'I don't owe you anything,

Vladimir. However, if you return the passport immediately I will give you another cheque to cover the one I cancelled.'

'Fifteen hundred dollars?' Vladimir chuckled. 'For such a beautiful girl?'

Hargreave was about to offer an additional fifteen hundred but Vladimir went on: 'Mr Hargreave, I warned you that you should make prior arrangements with us. Had you done so there would not be this worry about the passport. But because you are a *special* client, it is possible that I can persuade my superiors to cancel the hundred per cent interest and accept only twenty thousand, and even give the passport as well.'

Hargreave smiled shakily. He was winning. But, yes, he was tempted to accept and get shot of the problem – and he would do so if he had to. But twenty thousand was a helluva lot of money and Max would get it back for nothing. 'Go to hell! The most I will do is pay the original three thousand. Take it or leave it, but if that passport is not delivered to me in this room by ten o'clock tonight you'll be hearing from the police!' He banged down the telephone.

He stood there, eyes closed. He felt shaky, but somewhat elated. He had won that round, and if the worst came to the worst he knew he could get the passport for twenty thousand, or probably half that! Now leave it to Max! But, oh God, he wanted to get going to Hong Kong and get this sorted out. He returned to the bathroom.

'Who was it?' Olga said.

'Just some business in Hong Kong.' No point in worrying her.

He climbed back into the bubble bath beside her, reached for his glass and took a big swallow of whisky.

It would be sad, Vladimir said, to lose her . . .

'What?' Hargreave said.

'I said you look worried, darling.'

He shook his head. 'Not at all.' He took another big sip. 'I'm going to Hong Kong tomorrow, to vote in the elections and get Max to sort out your problem. While I'm away I don't want you to leave this hotel, under *any* circumstances. And if Vladimir comes here, you do not speak to him – you lock yourself in this room. And if necessary you call the manager.'

She was looking at him, blue eyes big. Then she laughed. 'Oh darling, I love you! Are you afraid of Vladimir kidnapping me?'

'I just don't want any trouble. Do you promise?'

She gave him a soapy kiss on the check.

'Yes, darling, I promise. And my gun in my hand?'

*   *   *

157

That night they did not go downstairs: they dined on the balcony outside their room to be on hand if Vladimir came. Besides, the hotel was full and though Hargreave had not seen anybody he knew it was best to keep a low profile on a busy Saturday night. But Vladimir did not arrive. After dinner Hargreave grimly drafted Olga's affidavit to give to Max to check and have typed. They went to bed at midnight, to the distant strains of dancing on the terrace below.

But Hargreave could not sleep, worrying about Vladimir and the uranium case. He lay in the dark, hearing Olga's gentle breathing, trying to convince himself there was no connection between the two. Finally he got up, pulled on a pair of shorts and went outside on to the moonlit balcony. He switched on the light, sat down in the hot China night to read the statements which Champion had left.

REGINA VS IVAN GREGOVICH: COVERING REPORT

GENERAL: The grave significance of this case can only be grasped if Crown Counsel has an understanding of the conditions extant in Russia today, and the impact this may have on the rest of the world.

With the collapse of the Soviet Union a power-vacuum was left behind. Because Russia had no traditional democratic infrastructure, and no capitalistic structures, this vacuum was filled by: (1) the same bureaucrats, or *nomenklatura*, who controlled the economic machinery of the Soviet Union, and who are now dividing up the spoils of Communism to their own advantage; (2) the old godfathers or *vory* of Russia's traditional underworld, who are exploiting the new chaotic conditions; (3) flashy new gangsters, or *avtoritety*, who are brutally seizing every criminal opportunity, often at war with each other and with the *vory*, and who are usually hand in glove with the corrupt bureaucrats – thus creating a new type of criminal power-baron in government.

Russia is awash in big-time corruption. In the words of President Yeltsin, it 'has become a Mafia power on a world scale'. The police are not only corrupt but inefficient because they were never trained to deal with 'capitalist' crime, so there is a nigh-total breakdown of law and order, and it is the gangsters themselves, particularly the *avtoritety*, who enforce their own law of the jungle and a semblance of cowed order amongst the populace.

One result of this chaos is that the genuine reformers in government circles have been pushed aside, and Russia's experiment in democracy is imperilled, if not doomed, like their experiment in capitalism, which is almost entirely in the hands of all-powerful 'capitalist bandits' – from agriculture and food distribution to ordinary retailing of all consumer goods, housing and real-estate development, transport, banking, insurance, mining, industry in general, in addition to their other activities of robbery, theft, extortion, prostitution, narcotics, gambling, smuggling – while the press is intimidated, judges are terrorized and the army paralysed. The ordinary man has no chance. Another result of this chaos is the right-wing political backlash of conservatives like the fascist Zhirinovsky and the New Communist Party who are calling for a reimposition of totalitarian government to rid the country of crime: they are finding great support amongst ordinary Russians who hanker for the days when they were poor but safe. In short, Russia has escaped from the dictatorship of the Communist Party only to be enslaved by another: the *avtoritety* ganglords are now the governing class . . .

There followed twelve closely-typed pages wherein Champion broke down Russian crime into subject areas, making sociological generalizations, all supported by numerous references to books and Simonski's original report that had cost him his job. Hargreave skipped it, and moved on to the next section.

PROFILE OF IVAN GREGOVICH. The history of the defendant Gregovich cannot be told at the trial, of course, but it is important that Crown Counsel understands the full evil of the man.

Aged forty-five now, Gregovich was born in Stalingrad and matriculated from high school top of his class, with a good athletic record. After completing his military service, he was recruited into the KGB. Assigned to Internal Security, he rose steadily through the ranks, serving in numerous Soviet cities: his duties were intelligence-gathering, generally being part of the 'sword and shield' of the Communist Party, enforcing its iron will. Reaching the rank of captain at age thirty he was transferred to External Security, being posted abroad in various diplomatic guises to London, Paris and Washington, where his duties were espionage. On the diplomatic social circuit he gained a reputation as a bon vivant, a dandy dresser, and something of a heart-throb with the ladies. He returned to Moscow with the rank of major in 1985. With the onset of President Gorbachev's *perestroika* he suddenly retired to go into 'business'.

Colonel Simonski has made a study of Gregovich's career, and attributes many political murders to him during his service, and countless incarcerations and tortures of dissidents: a great deal of inculpatory evidence has emerged from former KGB officers spilling the beans since the collapse of the Soviet Union. He was known to his colleagues, not renowned for their squeamishness, as 'The Knife' and 'The Electrician'. One of his favourite forms of torture of female dissidents, particularly pretty ones, was the insertion of a razor-sharp knife up their vaginas and toying with the handle whilst he interrogated them. Electrodes on the nipples was commonplace for him.

Perestroika, heralding an end to the Communist repression he cherished, opened a Pandora's box in which Gregovich consoled himself. With a vast network of contacts in government ministries, police and army, he first set up a 'security agency' consisting of ex-army and police thugs who offered 'protection' to newly-privatized businesses, extracting huge payments in exchange for non-violation, supplying bodyguards, and undertaking contract killings. Narcotics trade, smuggling of all kinds of consumer goods, marketing of stolen cars, and prostitution followed. Meanwhile he waged bloody gangland wars against rivals, establishing himself as *avtoritet* (meaning literally 'the authority') over large tracts of several major cities, including Moscow, until a summit of gangland leaders established 'law and order'. When Yeltsin became president, housing was privatized and tenants became owners of the dwellings they occupied, receiving a voucher as title-deed; similarly, industrial workers received share-vouchers: Gregovich (and his rivals) immediately made vast fortunes by buying up these vouchers from unsophisticated tenants and workers and thus became the legal owners of whole apartment blocks, housing estates, and large blocs of industry. In collaboration with corrupt bureaucrats (*nomenklatura*) he acquired even more control of industry, real estate, hotels, food distribution networks, mines and timber forests. Then, with the army bankrupt and demoralized, he collaborated with corrupt officers in the 'Red Army Bazaar', selling stolen weaponry to Third World countries, using his well-established smuggling routes.

For a full list of Gregovich's criminal activities, see Colonel Simonski's report, Annexure A, page 67 et seq. Those activities are now so complicated that much of the original criminality has blurred into his 'legitimate' businesses acquired with his ill-gotten fortune. A remarkable feature of the man is that despite his well-defined turfs, it is not known where he lives: he owns a number of dwellings, from seedy apartments to luxurious penthouses and dachas, but is never to be found in any of them. He travels a great deal around his fiefs and has many passports. He has never been arrested until now.

Colonel Simonski, during his service in the Organized Crime Squad, became convinced from snippets of evidence and hearsay that Ivan Gregovich was also one of the 'nuclear Mafia' bosses involved in the theft and smuggling of nuclear material to Third World countries – but he was never able to prove it. After his demotion Simonski lost track of much of Gregovich's activities but he managed to keep in touch with some of his old network of informers. It was a tip-off that sent Colonel Simonski suddenly rushing from his moribund desk to Moscow's airport to check out information that Ivan Gregovich was about to fly out of the country with a suitcase of uranium on 13 September 1995 . . .

Hargreave skimmed the facts about Gregovich's arrest at Hong Kong airport. Finally he came to Simonski's own statement, compiled by Champion. It began:

Antecedent history:
I am a citizen of the Russian Federation, having been born near Minsk in 1942. As a schoolboy I joined the Young Pioneers, and after matriculation from high school I did my military service. Thereafter I joined the Communist Party and enlisted in the police; in due course I was promoted to the rank of detective.

As a detective I had a high success-rate. However, crime in those days was of a comparatively simple nature because Russia was a police state and people were afraid of the authorities. Though it is true that the Russian populace had a bloody-minded attitude towards the government, which they regarded as corrupt and which they therefore cheated whenever possible – a favourite Russian saying was 'The government pretends to pay us, and we pretend to work' – they were essentially honest folk who would not steal from their neighbours. However, there was in those days a well-organized Russian underworld called the *Vorovskoi-mir* or the Thieves' World, and this subject deserves some attention.

Russia has a long history of bandit clans. The *vory*, or godfathers, who ruled these gangs were in many respects 'Robin Hoods' in that the target for their banditry was the government. The Bolsheviks

161

recruited these *vory* in their battles against the czars, and indeed Stalin was a sometime member of such a gang: but once Czar Nicholas had fallen Lenin turned his guns on the *vory*, and the new Communist government became the target of the Thieves' World. The *vory* thumbed their noses at the hated Communist Party and often ruled their criminal empires from prison.

As a detective I became very interested in these *vory* godfathers, but though I had numerous investigations against them I had little success; they were a tightly-closed book. Finally *perestroika* arrived (I now held the rank of major), and then came the collapse of the Soviet Union under President Yeltsin (I was then colonel) and chaos ensued. The *vory*'s traditional enemy, the Communist Party, had disappeared, so now they came out of the underworld to exploit Russia's spoils. Alongside them the bureaucrats exploited Russia's wealth, which they were supposed to privatize. Alongside both emerged the new type of Russian criminal, the *avtoritety*, Mafia who thumbed their noses at the old *vory*, waged war on them and moved in on the corrupt bureaucrats, the *nomenklatura*.

It was at this stage, in 1993, that I wrote a report to my superiors in the Ministry of Internal Affairs (MVD) summarizing my know-ledge of the *vory* godfathers, of the corrupt *nomenklatura* over decades of Communist Party rule, and my new-found knowledge of the *avtoritety* who were coming to dominate the criminal world in collaboration with the corrupt bureaucrats. In particular I wrote about the illegal arms trade in the (so-called) 'Red Army Bazaar', and about my anxieties that a Russian 'nuclear Mafia' exists.

Initially my report was well-received by the new Minister of Internal Affairs and he immediately promoted me to Lieutenant-General in charge of Special Operations within the Organized Crime Squad.

During my investigations I visited numerous sites where nuclear material was produced or stored. The difficulties of checking records against the physical weight of materials are enormous. However, it is noteworthy that most plants permit a small discrepancy between production and storage which they say is attributable to unavoid-able waste: this enables workers to consistently steal small quanti-ties without detection and thus build up a stockpile. It is also noteworthy that at many sites many workers, including managers and scientists, complained that the government had not paid their wages for months, and that roaring inflation had impoverished them.

Before I could come to grips with these problems my new position was suddenly abolished, I was demoted back to colonel, and transferred to administrative duties in Police Headquarters.

In my opinion I was demoted to non-active duties for two reasons. One: In Communist ideology (solidified over a seven-decade rule) Russia was supposed to be a socialist Utopia in which criminals did not flourish: therefore, although isolated pockets of criminality might exist, there could be no such thing as organized crime beyond that petty level; therefore a 'nuclear Mafia' could not exist; therefore I was heretical to suggest it did. Two: The corrupt bureaucracy pressured the ministry to get rid of me before I did any damage to their criminal business.

As a result I am now in administrative duties, handling such matters as pensions, leave applications, health entitlements: I have a large clerical staff but no practical police function. Nonetheless I have tried to keep contact with the network of informers I painstakingly built up over many years. One day an old contact in the West German police telephoned and advised me that Superintendent Bernard Champion of the Royal Hong Kong Police was desirous of coming to Moscow to try to investigate the background of the Russian 'nuclear Mafia'. I was pleased to be of service. I gave Superintendent Champion my report, a wealth of other information and we discussed strategies. As a result, I agreed to put the word out in the underworld that a customer existed in Hong Kong for weapons-grade uranium. Not long thereafter I received a telephone call, on 13 September 1995, from an informer who advised me that a shipment of uranium was about to leave for Hong Kong in the hands of a renowned *avtoritet* boss called Ivan Gregovich and as a result I rushed to Moscow's airport.

FACTS: Taking up an unobtrusive position I observed the people checking in at the Aeroflot counter for the flight to Hong Kong. I saw the man I now know as Nicolai Kozkov, who was frequently looking at his watch, and scanning faces. He had one small piece of luggage.

About fifteen minutes later I saw the defendant, Ivan Gregovich, arrive in the concourse: he was well-known to me though I had only met him once, about a year ago, when I questioned him about sundry matters in the Organized Crime Squad's offices.

Gregovich appeared to be unaccompanied, but a few paces behind him walked another man, not known to me, carrying a blue suitcase. When Gregovich was about twenty paces from Kozkov, he

163

stopped, and glanced backwards at the man behind him. This man proceeded to Kozkov, and appeared to identify himself. He then walked towards the toilet, which was about thirty paces away; after a few seconds Kozkov followed him. Gregovich observed them go. The man disappeared into the toilet, followed by Kozkov. About two minutes later Kozkov emerged from the toilet, and now he was carrying his own luggage plus the blue suitcase. The other man then returned to stand near Gregovich but they did not appear to communicate. Kozkov then joined the people queuing for the Aeroflot flight to Hong Kong. I saw him check in the blue suitcase and receive a boarding pass. Gregovich appeared to be observing him.

Gregovich then checked in to the same flight, carrying hand-baggage only.

As soon as Gregovich had disappeared I went to the Aeroflot desk and bought a ticket on the flight to Hong Kong. I checked in, then immediately telephoned Superintendent Champion in Hong Kong and told him what was happening. I waited about three quarters of an hour, until boarding time, then cleared immigration control and got to the departure lounge. I was the last to board.

I did not see Gregovich or Kozkov during the flight and I did my best to be inconspicuous.

On arrival in Hong Kong the next morning I was the first off the aircraft. I was met by Superintendent Champion. Taking up a concealed position, I pointed out first Kozkov, then Gregovich: they did not appear to be travelling together. We then followed them to the baggage-reclaim area . . .

Hargreave skimmed the rest of the statement. He then turned to the last document, Gregovich's confession. It read:

I, Bernard Champion, Superintendent in the Royal Hong Kong Police, hereby certify that at 2.01 p.m. on 14 September 1995, I charged Ivan Gregovich as hereunder:

'Ivan Gregovich, you are charged with contravening . . . of the Importation of Dangerous Substances Ordinance . . . in that upon or about the 14 September 1995 and at or near Kai Tak airport you did wrongfully and unlawfully import into the Colony of Hong Kong eight-point-nine kilograms of uranium, this being a dangerous substance within the definition . . .

'You are hereby warned that you are not obliged to say anything in answer to this charge but that anything you do say will be taken down in writing and used in evidence.

'Do you understand the charge and the caution?'

Ivan Gregovich said: 'Yes.'

Ivan Gregovich then freely and voluntarily elected to make the following reply:

'I admit the charge. That is all I wish to say.'

Question: 'Do you wish to tell me the number of the combination lock of the suitcase in which the uranium was carried?'

Answer: 'The number is 7391.'

Question: 'Do you wish to tell me the source of this uranium?'

Answer: 'I do not know the source. I believe it came from somebody in Grozny, in Chechnya. I wish to have bail. That is all I wish to say.'

Signed: Ivan Gregovich

Signed: B. Champion

Witnessed by: O. Simonski

Time: 2.29 p.m.

Hargreave tossed the documents aside on the table and stared out over the moonlit sea.

Well, thank God there was nothing in all that to suggest any connection between this case and prostitution in Macao.

But there were several things that worried him about this case. Oh, it was good police work, particularly by poor old Colonel Simonski – Hargreave hoped he got his post back after this – and it was conscientious work by Champion. But there were aspects of their evidence he didn't quite credit.

Why would a tough Mafia boss like Gregovich, a brutal ex-KGB thug with many murders to his discredit, who was experienced in interrogation, confess unless he was pressured? It was highly improbable that he decided to make a clean breast simply because he felt the game was up.

And there was the confession itself: a one-liner; 'I admit the charge'. That had a ring of truculence about it, the bloody-minded statement of a man determined to say as little as possible to get the cops off his back. The other details in the confession had to be elicited by questions (itself of very questionable propriety) and the answer to the last one was probably a lie: surely Gregovich knew the source of the uranium. Telling a lie on such an important point is not the behaviour of a man cooperating freely with the cops. Yet Champion had said that Gregovich

165

was 'singing like a canary' after a while. He probably was, because he'd had enough third-degree – but when the pressure was off he sure said the minimum. And another thing: if he was singing like a canary, giving all kinds of vital information – which Simonski had now flown back to Moscow to follow up urgently – Champion would surely have tape-recorded the six-hour interrogation to make sure no detail was over-looked later. Why had Champion denied using a tape-recorder? Because he knew that Hargreave and the court would want to hear the tape if Gregovich alleged that he was pressured into making the confession? That tape would probably support Gregovich's claim of duress.

And then consider Simonski's likely attitude to the case. In Simonski you have an elderly policeman with a grievance who has been humili-ated by demotion by corrupt superiors for rocking their lucrative boat. Simonski knew all about Gregovich's villainy and quite rightly regards traffic in nuclear material as a terrible international danger. So when Champion shows up in Moscow with a bee in his bonnet about the same thing, they become instant soulmates – and they set up a sting operation. Out of the blue, the sting pays off, fingering none other than Simonski's old *bête noire*, Ivan Gregovich. So Simonski rushes to the airport, uses his *own* money to buy a ticket – he may never get it back from the police authorities – and follows the villain and the suitcase. *Ah*, but that suitcase is a potential death-trap. Does Simonski use his police authority to delay the aircraft, seize the treacherous suitcase? No, because he has insufficient evidence against Gregovich so far and wants to catch him red-handed in Hong Kong. So he telephones Cham-pion – and does Champion advise Simonski to stop the killer shipment? No, for the same reason. In short, Simonski and Champion have had a breakthrough on a crime of international importance and, though both knew the risks involved in that suitcase, both agreed to take the chance for the sake of making an effective arrest.

Hargreave smiled grimly. Now, are two hard-boiled senior cops, in this frame of mind, likely to be squeamish about applying a bit of third-degree to our blackguard Ivan Gregovich, whom they've just caught red-handed, to get him firstly to confess, secondly to tell them as much as possible about the nuclear Mafia? Answer: No. Even if Simonski turned out to be a dear old fuddy-duddy pussy-cat of a cop – who had no axe to grind and who didn't mind wasting his hard-earned money on an unauthorized jaunt to sunny Hong Kong – even if *he* was squeamish, Champion certainly was not. Bernie Champion, first-class cop though he was, wouldn't bat a fucking eyelash about a bit of third-degree.

Hargreave gave a sigh. Well, Champ and Simonski denied any duress and that was good enough for the Crown to go to trial – the decision was the judge's, not Hargreave's.

And thank God all this had nothing to do with Vladimir-the-Terrible.

Hargreave packed up the papers and tiptoed into the room. He put the documents in his suitcase, then crept noiselessly into bed. Olga was lying on her side, her back to him, and he snuggled up against her smooth soft nakedness, put his arm around her and cupped her breast. She gave a little murmur, and he was happy. Tomorrow Max would sort out her problem. In a moment he was asleep.

19

The hotel's limousine was waiting for him at the portico on Sunday morning. Hargreave said to Olga at the car door: 'And you're not to go anywhere.'

'Yes, darling.' She kissed him. 'Come back quickly, please.'

'Goodbye, darling,' he said. Olga clapped her hands together, bowed her head and laughed. Hargreave grinned: 'What's funny?' The Chinese bellhops were smiling benignly.

'You called me *darling* at last! Oh –' she kissed him again, hard – 'I love you!'

He whispered, blushing, 'And I love you.'

'Yes, I know now!' She gave him a shove and he climbed into the vehicle. '*Whoopee!*' she laughed through the window.

As the car reached the hotel gates he looked back and waved. She was smiling and waving. He held up a finger to remind her of her promise and she nodded vigorously, grinning.

Hargreave sat back in the air-conditioned limousine, holding that happy image of her in his mind as the car crossed the islands and the long bridge to the teeming Macao waterfront; he held it through the hot, crowded ferry terminal with its immigration formalities and the stink of diesel, held it across the blue, sultry, island-studded South China Sea and perhaps for the first time he realized that he really loved her, that he wasn't just besotted with her. And he was glad with all his heart about what he was doing. He held that image of her as he hurried with the crowds along the elevated walkways through towering central Hong Kong, to the polling station for his constituency.

It was early but there was a large crowd already and long queues for the polling booths. Hargreave's seemed the only white face present so far. Everybody was very well behaved. There was the usual election paraphernalia, the rosettes and the hats, the parties' colours and emblems and banners, the rival candidates and their last-minute sallies of charm: beaming, shaking hands, welcoming the voters to this first-ever fully democratic election in Hong Kong. The last election, in 1989, had been only partially democratic, the majority of the council members then being appointed by the government. But for all the importance of today's results, which would carry the colony through into the new era of oppressive Communist rule, there was less hoop-la than in 1989. In those days the massacre in Tiananmen Square was fresh in people's minds: today that horror had faded, despite China's latest vow to sweep aside the Legislative Council and her flagrant breach of the Joint Declaration and Basic Law. It seemed to Hargreave that today these Chinese voters were more mature, more earnest – perhaps more fatalistic.

He felt sorry for them: they were the poor bastards who would be facing the music while Britain folded her tents and stole off into the night congratulating herself on a 'smooth transition' – those smiling candidates over there would be facing jail as subversives while he was sailing his boat in the Caribbean. He looked at the people and he felt like a traitor, a member of the elite class which had not had the guts to stand up to China and insist, on pain of international vengeance, that she abide by the agreed terms.

It was sad, yet another awful indictment of British honour, of pusillanimous British appeasement and retreat for the sake of expediency: these people, this magnificent colony were expendable, like Africa had been. All Britain had to leave these people here today was the Rule of Law, and she had failed miserably to leave them even that. Hargreave had been too wrapped up in his own problems over the past few months to give much thought to the Chinese people at this crucial time, but standing amongst them on this historic, crucial day he felt very guilty. And, Lord, he loved this colony, even though he was heartily sick of the law and all the colonial social bullshit.

Hargreave queued for an hour before casting his vote for Martin Lee's United Democratic Party. Then he made his way across Central to the offices of Popodopolous & Grant, Solicitors.

'Here he is,' Max Popodopolous said as he answered the door in his shorts and sandals, 'the Seldom-Seen Man. The Tango-Dancer . . .'

Max had a typist working this Sunday: she was busy preparing the affidavit Hargreave had drawn up for Olga. Max said, his Portuguese eyes solemn:

'I must tell you that Elizabeth has been to see me.' He paused. 'On Friday. She consulted me as the family lawyer, so to speak. She has stopped divorce proceedings, and she wanted to know her position if you took it into your head to divorce *her* – because she intends to contest such an action, Al – tooth and nail. Of course I told her that I could not represent her against you because you're my good friend, I advised her to go'n consult Winters, Holmes & Wong. But I did gather she's hopping mad about this Russian lass – whilst she sat in that chair and wept. That she intends making sure Olga doesn't get any of your loot.'

'Liz wept?' That didn't sound like the Liz he had last heard, hurling his yoghurt, liver and vitamin pills out of the refrigerator.

'Oh yes. Buckets. She was very dignified, very reasonable, but very weepy. And I would be failing in my duty to you if I did not tell you that I think she loves you, Al.'

Hargreave snorted. 'She's just jealous. "Hell hath no fury like a woman scorned." And I didn't scorn *her* – she shot me.'

'Oh yes,' Max said, his Latin eyes liquid, 'I did manage to squeeze in a murmur about that, being the razor-brained lawyer I am. But it was an accident, Al. She says so, *you* say so. And I'm sure it was, Liz isn't the type to shoot anybody, let alone her nearest and dearest. It was bravado. Of course she was silly to point a gun, but it was only intended to shock you.'

'Then why did she wrestle with me for possession of the gun?'

Max frowned. 'Al, you're being illogical – and you a lawyer forsooth! If she never intended to shoot you, as you agree, why do you raise the wrestling incident in self-contradiction?' He looked at him. 'Obviously she did so only out of natural reaction, in the heat of the moment, because you were now attacking her.' He shook his head. 'If that is lingering in your mind as a sinister detail, forget it, Al. Illogical.'

'Okay, but you've never been shot. It evokes a certain Pavlovian distrust in the victim. If I pulled a gun on you in anger, then accidentally pulled the trigger and hit you, you would be very inclined to give me a wide berth thereafter, very disinclined to argue with me again – let alone share a dwelling with me.'

'Al,' Max sighed, 'any judge – or jury – hearing the facts of your case would be reminded of the many times they have felt like throwing crockery at their spouses – and kicking his or her arse right down the stairs. If not braining them.' He waved his hand. 'Al, even my dear old granny of eighty, who had never said boo to a goose in her life, one day attacked my poor old grandad, out of the blue, fiercely kicking his shins as he sat reading the newspaper. We asked her why. She just said she'd had enough of the old bastard after sixty years of marriage.'

'We're not talking about juries,' Hargreave said. 'I'm not prosecuting Liz. But if your wife shot you, would you feel comfortable living with her thereafter? If your granny had shot your grandad instead of kicking

170

him, no matter how accidentally, would you worry about his safety or not?'

Max sighed. 'But the real nub of this discussion is: Liz has stopped divorce proceedings, she's staying on in your apartment, hoping for a reconciliation. What are you going to do? Divorce *her*?'

Hargreave glared. 'If I have to, yes.' Then he sighed bitterly. 'But it won't come to that. She'll change her mind again, and divorce me. The marriage is worn out, Max, has been for some time, and Liz knows it.'

'I hope you're right. Because few things are messier, and more embarrassing, than a contested divorce. And as the facts presently stand, or *appear* – you reeking of adultery with your pretty Russian mistress, spending money on her like water, while on the other side of the court is your virtuous wife whose only sin was to accidentally discharge a firearm at you after you came home with lipstick on your face – on those facts I don't like your chances of winning a contested divorce, pal.'

'Are you suggesting I go back to Liz?' Hargreave asked.

'I'm simply saying that you're stuck with Elizabeth's decision. Don't contemplate trying to divorce her – she's got the winning hand. All you can do is wait for the prescribed number of years of separation, then go the automatic divorce route. Meanwhile, Elizabeth is going to be living in your apartment for the foreseeable future – where are you going to live with Olga, assuming I've got her admitted to Hong Kong? What's that going to cost? Meanwhile you'll also be supporting Liz financially. Al?' Max raised his eyebrows solemnly: 'Think carefully, my friend. And I suggest you go'n have a civilized talk soon with Liz, to try to agree on an amicable arrangement. Right . . .' He stood up to put an end to that subject, and went to the bookshelf. 'Now, about Olga's problem with the immigration department.'

He plucked a volume off the shelf and flicked through it, pulling his lower lip. 'Found it!' he said, pleased with himself. He read in silence, grunted, then passed the ordinance to Hargreave. 'The substance of it is that the Director of Immigration may admit a person who has hitherto been prohibited as an undesirable provided he's satisfied on a number of grounds specified. I think we can get Olga in, and if we fail we can apply to the courts for a review, I suppose. But that would be conspicuous. You want this done quietly, in your position.'

'But,' Hargreave said, 'surely if I vouch for her, as my personal responsibility, the director will knuckle under? Lord, every day we have hundreds of so-called refugees getting into Hong Kong by junk and swimming the Pearl River and those people are penniless, and maybe criminals too. Surely we can bully old Percy Wallace, pull rank on him?'

'Pull *rank*? Al, Al, you know better than that. What about the Independent Commission Against Corruption? Jesus, you try to pull rank on old Percy Wallace and he'd have you for breakfast, particularly over a Russian . . . singer. Al –' Max held up a hand – 'don't *you*, as Director of Public Prosecutions, go *near* old Percy. I'll think up a good sob-story to sweet-talk him. But –' he smiled at his friend – 'I'm sure I can help you get her passport in Macao.'

Hargreave smiled in relief. 'Thank you.'

'Though thereafter we've still got to get her admitted into Hong Kong. But, yes, I know all the lawyers in Macao and between them they know all the cops – even the honest ones, aha-ha-ha! And if the Mafia still withhold her passport, there are other procedures.' He smiled. 'So go in peace: your pretty friend's passport will be returned to her. If not tomorrow, the next day, I imagine.'

Hargreave sighed with relief. 'Thanks, Max.'

'But, Al?' Max looked at him with soulful solemnity. 'Do your old pal Twinkletoes Popodopolous who's envious as hell about your latest achievement with the tango a favour – and think *carefully*? She's absolutely gorgeous, I agree, but she's twenty-three years younger than you.' His expression was serious. 'Can you handle that, after the honeymoon? Even if you can do cartwheels nowadays.'

'Cartwheels?'

Max reached for a newspaper, opened it to the third page and passed it over the desk.

Hargreave stared. There were four photographs of Olga cartwheeling across the tennis court then leaping the net into his waiting arms. The headline read: GOOD SPORT IN MACAO.

'Lord . . .' Hargreave breathed.

'Exactly,' Max said. 'You can imagine how Liz feels? Breathing fire. So please take my advice and go'n talk her into an amicable settlement. And think what you're going to do with this girl once you've got her passport.'

What was he going to do with her? This weekend they would be in the Philippines for two more glorious weeks, and if he still felt like this she would live with him, and when the divorce was over he was going to marry her – that's what! And the whole Hong Kong establishment could go'n suck hindmost. And Max was going to get her passport back for the price of a beer – not twenty thousand dollars! And, after a few stiff whiskies in the Chinnery Bar, he *loved* those pictures of Olga in the *South China Morning Post*! Look at her – look at her gorgeous legs! Show me another woman as beautiful! One photo showed her falling into his arms – how happy he looked! Her ravishing smile . . . Hargreave bought a half-jack of whisky which he swigged on the way back to Macao on the afternoon hydrofoil, and he was grinning with anticipation of getting back to his lovely, exotic, laughing girl.

That is how Alistair Hargreave was feeling as he hastened off the hydrofoil in the mid-afternoon, impatiently jostled through immigration formalities, then hurried to the taxi-rank. 'Westin Resort, Elder Brother!' He was grinning all the way back across the long bridge to Taipa, across the islands – the Westin Resort almost looked like home now . . . He was laughing inside as he strode down the corridor to their room, unlocked the door and entered.

The room was empty. So was the balcony. Her clothes were hanging in the wardrobe. Only her handbag was missing.

He retraced his steps down to the foyer and went out on to the swimming pool terrace. He looked around. There were many people. He said to a waiter, 'Have you seen my wife?' *Wife* – that was a lovely word!

'No, sir.'

He went to the lounge. She was not there. He went to the bar – she was not there, nor in the gym. He went outside to the tennis courts. 'Have you seen my wife?' he asked the attendant.

'Not since this morning, sir.'

It was almost five o'clock and he had told Olga he would definitely be back on the mid-afternoon hydrofoil. He went to the reception desk. 'Have you seen Miss Romalova?'

'I only saw her this morning, sir, when you left,' the Chinese girl said. 'I'll ask in the office.'

She came back half a minute later. 'No, but perhaps she went into Macao with the hotel bus.'

Hargreave shook his head. 'She said she would not leave the hotel. But can you ask the driver?'

The receptionist picked up the telephone and spoke in Cantonese. Then: 'No, sir. Shall I have her paged?'

Panic suddenly gripped him – Vladimir had got her somehow! 'Yes, have her paged . . .' He turned and strode for the public telephones. His fingers fumbled with the coin. He dialled her apartment.

It rang and rang – the girls had already left for work. He dialled the Heavenly Tranquillity Nite-Club.

'Is Olga there, please?'

'Olga? No.'

'Let me speak to Yolanda!' He waited feverishly for her to come on the line. 'Yolanda, this is Alistair, Olga's friend. Have you seen her today?'

There was a pause. Then Yolanda said soberly, 'Mr Hargreave, Olga is deported. The police came with her to the apartment, she was crying.'

It was like a blow to the guts.

'*Deported?*' Hargreave stared at the wall, aghast. '*What time was this?*'

'Four o'clock, about then.'

An hour ago! 'Was Vladimir there?'

'Yes.'

'Is he with you now?'

'No.'

Hargreave slammed down the telephone and ran across the foyer to the manager's office. He burst in. 'Pedro!' He snatched up the telephone and thrust it at the astonished man. 'Phone the Commissioner of Police! Olga's being deported – she's been kidnapped from this hotel! Tell the Commissioner I'm on my way to the police station now to stop the deportation! Tell him I'm the Director of Public Prosecutions! I'm taking the limousine!'

'Kidnapped?' Pedro said. 'How do you know?'

'Because her clothes are still in my room!' He snatched up Pedro's cellular telephone from the desk. 'I'm borrowing this. Call me in the limousine.'

He ran across the foyer. The limousine was in its usual place. He thrust a twenty-pataca note at the driver. 'The main police station! Fast!'

They were speeding over the Taipa Bridge when the mobile rang. 'Hullo?' Hargreave barked.

It was Pedro. 'I'm afraid Olga is already on her way to the border.'

'Je-*zuz*!' Hargreave shouted. He barked at the driver, 'The Barrier Gate, not the police station.' To Pedro he rasped, 'But how can they deport her with a valid visa? Did you speak to the Commissioner himself?'

'To the deputy. He said there was nothing he could do because the visa was legally revoked on complaint from a member of the public, because Olga is . . . I'm sorry, but a prostitute.'

That was fucking Vladimir! 'And suddenly prostitution is illegal in Macao? Give me the Commissioner's telephone number!'

Pedro said, 'He speaks no English; you don't speak Portuguese, do you?'

'Then phone him again, tell him I'm on my way to the border! Tell him I accept full responsibility for her, tell him I'm going to marry her!'

As the limousine swung through Macao Hargreave feverishly dialled Max, but he was not in the office. He cursed and tried Jake McAdam, but he was not in either. Then the limousine was racing towards the ancient wall that bordered the Portuguese colony. Ahead were the immigration offices beside the ancient archway, the line of traffic. *'Stop!'* Hargreave scrambled out and started running.

He ran frantically up the line of vehicles. There was a long file of Chinese leading into the immigration building. He ran up the side of the queue, desperately dodging, and shoved his way into the hall. *'Olga!'* There were people everywhere but there was no tall blonde in that mass of faces. Hargreave turned and plunged back outside.

He ran down the side of the building to the gate, and stopped at the iron railing, gasping, sweating. People everywhere, officials, vehicles grinding through. Beyond the gate was China, the Special Economic Zone, buildings and factories everywhere, people and vehicles thronging. *'OLGA!'* he bellowed – *'OL-GA!'*

'Alistair!'

She was fifty yards away, inside China territory, anguish on her face. *'Alistair!'* she shrieked and she started towards him, stumbling and bumping into people – *'Alistair!'* – and two men grabbed her, seizing her arms, wrenching her backwards. Olga shrieked and struggled, blonde hair flying, and Hargreave bellowed and he leaped the barrier.

With a bellow of anguish Hargreave vaulted the traffic barrier and started running into China, shouting *'Leave her!'* Then a Chinese policeman was flinging his arms around him, shouting. Hargreave jabbed him in the ribs with his elbow, yelling *'OLGA!'* Fifty yards away Olga was shrieking over her shoulder as the two Chinese dragged her towards a car. Hargreave twisted free and plunged onwards, and another policeman seized him. *'Let me go, I've got a passport!'* He filled his lungs and roared *'OL-GA!'* She was being shoved headfirst into the vehicle. *'OL-GA!'* Hargreave roared again, and another Chinese policeman grabbed him.

Sixty yards away the car started forward. Olga looked back through the rear window, desperately shouting. Hargreave wrenched and strained, until a policeman's arm was thrown across his neck, heaving downwards, the hand gouging into his face, and he doubled over under the shocking embrace.

'Olga . . .' he gasped.

There, on the threshold of China, under the blazing sun, surrounded

175

by hundreds of astonished Chinese, crouched Alistair Hargreave, Director of Public Prosecutions, doubled over in an armlock, sobbing *'Olga . . .'* And his heart was breaking.

PART IV

20

The weeks that followed were very bad.

He spent that awful night at the Westin Resort, but he was unable to sleep: the empty room, the hotel cried *Olga* at him. With the dawn he was packing her clothes, her cosmetics and dresses and pretty underwear and shoes, and the feminine things broke his heart. All she had taken with her was her handbag: he could not find her gun and he hoped to God she still had it. In the early morning he was riding the hydrofoil back to Hong Kong with her belongings, with tears in his eyes. *Please God, keep her safe . . .*

Elizabeth was in his apartment so he had to stay with Jake McAdam, and it was distressing not having privacy for his anguish. But at least, thank God, there was no story in the Hong Kong newspapers about the incident at the Barrier Gate in Macau: immigration officials are often on the payroll of newspaper reporters to tip them off about dramatic events on the borders. Hargreave attributed this godsend to the fact that the elections were being held and for days thereafter the press was preoccupied with the results. In fact it was Vladimir who saved Hargreave's hide, buying the silence of the border officials – Vladimir wanted Alistair Hargreave alive and well in his chambers in Hong Kong.

And at least Elizabeth gave him breathing space: she knew he was back in town, but if she knew about Olga's deportation she did not capitalize on it. She telephoned him only once and said: 'I'm not pressuring you, Alistair, I think I understand what you're going through, but I want you to know that I'm not being a dog in the manger, I hate to think of you miserable and uncomfortable, you can come home any time you want. We can have separate bedrooms if you wish, you can come and go as you like. And I want you to know that I'm so very sorry I shot you – it was unintentional. I was silly to point a gun, but one does silly things in anger. I apologize. And if you hear any gossip about us, any character assassination, I promise it is not coming from me – I am keeping my mouth shut. All right, don't answer. Goodbye.' For the rest, Elizabeth conducted herself with dignity, going about her social life as best she could, as if her husband were temporarily out of the colony on business.

Jake McAdam also gave him breathing space: he knew Hargreave wanted to be left alone so he busied himself until late at night with his political interests – they only met briefly at breakfast. McAdam had been narrowly defeated by the pro-China candidate in the election and now he was throwing himself completely into working for Martin Lee. The United Democrats had done well, and, with the help of like-minded independents, would dominate the Legislative Council: China had again roundly condemned the elections as unfair and unreasonable – while congratulating the successful pro-China candidates and denouncing the Democrats as subversives. The United Democratic Party now intended to go full-throttle on shaming the Governor and Great Britain into enforcing the Joint Declaration against China. Hargreave was grateful that Jake's political working hours left him the apartment to himself, to stew in his anguish in privacy, and he was grudgingly grateful to Elizabeth for her dignified posture, and he didn't care if her friends were conducting a character assassination. All he frantically, feverishly worried about was Olga. He did not care if the whole of Hong Kong society called him a fool – he knew with all his anguished heart that he loved her. Perhaps the worst part was his powerlessness, and the desperate waiting, *waiting* for word from her. At times, after half a bottle of whisky as he paced about Jake's apartment, he convinced himself that there would certainly be word soon because the Mafia surely wanted their money. But lying sleepless in the dawn, hungover and exhausted, he only saw her as vanished for ever into the vastness of Russia, never to be heard of again, the heartbreaking, heartbroken victim of his foolishness in not paying for her freedom when it was demanded.

'*You fool!*'

Everything he did produced no results: he tried to contact Vladimir, leaving messages for him, but Vladimir did not respond. Hargreave asked Max to instruct his friends in Macao to pressure the police to dig up information, but that only produced the fact that Olga had been flown from Canton to Vladivostok. From Vladivostok, on the Pacific coast, she could have been flown anywhere – and Vladivostok is a seaport notorious for its whorehouses. Hargreave took Bernie Champion into his confidence and begged him to ask Simonski and Kerensky to investigate: but their combined efforts produced nothing. Every day Hargreave telephoned Yolanda at the Heavenly Tranquillity, but she had no news: she did not know where Vladimir was, hadn't seen him for days, nor could she unearth any old addresses for Olga. He asked Champion to ask Simonski to trace the aluminium factory in which she had worked in Yekaterinburg, to ask her former workmates for old addresses, but though Simonski did his best, telephoning all over Russia, nothing was forthcoming.

'For Christ's sake – *please* ask Simonski to use his influence with the underworld.'

'Unfortunately Simonski has no influence with the underworld. Nobody's talking since Gregovich's arrest – even the address he gave us in the file turns out to be fictitious, and nobody is telling us where he really lived. But what're you going to do if you find out her where-abouts?'

'Fly to Russia and start from there!'

'Jesus, Al,' Champion sighed. 'You're sailing very close to the wind, my friend – your department's prosecuting the Russian Mafia in my uranium case and here you are frantically trying to get hold of one of their girls.'

'Let *me* worry about my professional responsibilities! Olga has nothing to do with Gregovich, and anyway I've handed over the case to Findlay!'

'And that annoys the shit out of me – you should be prosecuting this case *personally*.'

McAdam asked his business associates in Moscow to make enquiries, but nothing emerged. 'They say Moscow is full of prostitutes and Mafia gangs.' Hargreave finally engaged a firm of detectives to find Vladimir in Macao, to scour the colony for any information at all about Olga; and the word came back that Vladimir had left for Russia.

'Where in Russia?'

'It's not known, sir.'

'For how long?' Hargreave was aghast that the bastard had disappeared – his only connection with Olga was Vladimir, he desperately wanted Vladimir back.

'They don't know, sir.'

'*Well find out!*'

Hargreave telephoned Champion and begged him to ask Simonski to trace Vladimir.

'Jesus,' Champion said. 'As if Simonski hasn't got enough to do.'

Then, the next day, Bernie Champion telephoned and said angrily, 'Simonski is dead. Murdered.'

Hargreave was aghast. Aghast for Simonski but more so for what this meant to him – he had lost his only contact with Russia, his only potential ally! '*Murdered?* Who by?'

'One guess,' Champion seethed. 'Mr Gregovich's nice friends, to stop Simonski testifying in our case. And, no doubt, for revenge. Gunned him down outside his police station in broad daylight. Kerensky was with him at the time. No arrest.'

It made Hargreave's frantic blood run cold. If the Mafia could do that to a cop, what could they do to Olga? 'But another cop must have taken over the case?'

'No, Simonski was just an administrative officer, our uranimum case was a job on the side. There's a friend of his in Organized Crime Squad called Sepov, I've just spoken to him on the phone. I didn't meet him while I was in Russia but Simonski mentioned him as an honest cop. However, he knows nothing about our case.' He seethed. 'So we've lost our only witness to the important fact that Gregovich was at Moscow airport observing the handover of the suitcase to Kozkov! All we've got now is Gregovich's confession, plus the key, and the combination lock.'

Hargreave didn't give a damn about the uranium case now. 'Please ask Sepov to make enquiries about Olga! And Vladimir.'

'I've already done that,' Champion sighed bitterly, 'but he was not optimistic; the Mafia don't talk. He says you could hire a detective but that would be very expensive and he says most of them are crooks too.'

'I'll do it if I have to!'

'Are you crazy? How do you know they won't just take your money and do nothing? They're probably hand in glove with the Mafia!'

And then, ten days after Olga's disappearance, Vladimir telephoned from Macao. Hargreave's heart leapt.

'Good afternoon, Mr Hargreave. Perhaps we should meet for a drink this evening in the Heavenly Tranquillity? There we can talk in security.'

Hargreave felt sick with tension as he disembarked in Macao, but he was determined not to show it, determined to bargain hard in buying Olga's freedom – but if he had to he was more than willing to pay the forty thousand dollars last demanded, desperate to get this agony over. It was a grim-faced Hargreave who walked into the garish night-club, fortified by several double whiskies, and went to Vladimir's corner table.

'Mr Hargreave, how nice to see you again.'

'Cut the crap, Vladimir, and tell me where Olga is!'

Vladimir smiled. 'Olga is fine – at the moment.'

At the moment. Jesus, he hated the bastard – and feared him. 'Where?'

Vladimir smiled and sat forward. 'What would you like to drink?'

'Nothing. *Talk*, Vladimir or –' he pointed at the door – 'I'm walking out. I've had enough of this nonsense!' He added: 'And I've very nearly had enough of Olga.'

Vladimir grinned. 'Very convincing, as you have just come all the way from Hong Kong.'

'I'm only here out of compassion for her as a friend!'

'And that's why you've been making enquiries about her in Moscow?'

That the bastard knew about his enquiries in Macao didn't surprise him – but in Moscow? Lord. 'Correct – friendship only. Well?'

Vladimir sat back. Hargreave tried to steel himself to portray dismissive indignation about the money the bastard would demand. He was astonished to hear Vladimir say, 'The case of Ivan Gregovich starts soon, I believe?'

Hargreave stared at him, his heart knocking. *Oh no, please God, he's not part of the uranium case.* 'So? What's that got to do with Olga?'

Vladimir said quietly, 'Ivan Gregovich and me, we are business friends.'

Oh no . . . Hargreave desperately tried to recover his scattered wits.

'Are you saying you're involved in the importation of nuclear materials? If so, thanks for telling me, I'll call the police now, the Macao government doesn't want radio-active material in the area either – they'll cooperate with the Hong Kong police on this one, I assure you!'

Vladimir smiled. 'Good acting, Mr Hargreave. Of course I am saying no such thing. But Mr Gregovich is a friend of mine, and I can tell you that he would like to have bail now, please.' He added with a faint smile, 'You give bail to Mr Gregovich, and Olga will get "bail".'

Hargreave stared at him: Oh Christ – this was it. This was the price of Olga's freedom – the Director of Public Prosecutions must prostitute *himself*, break his oath to administer justice by allowing bail to one of the world's worst villains, who will then disappear . . . He said incredulously, 'That's impossible.' He snorted, then waved a hand. 'Any fool knows that as soon as Ivan Gregovich has bail he will abscond. The police would be outraged – the public would be up in arms.'

Vladimir said quietly, 'You are superior to the police, Mr Hargreave, it is your decision, not theirs.'

'But . . .' Hargreave almost smiled. He waved a hand again. 'You don't understand. It would be madness for me to agree to bail in this case – and it would be regarded as madness by the police. No judge would grant bail if the application was opposed.'

'You know all the judges, Mr Hargreave, you can bribe him.'

183

Hargreave actually did smile, shakily. 'No, no, Vladimir. This is not Russia, we don't bribe our judges here.'

'But many of your judges are Chinese.'

'Yes, but they're British-trained. Vladimir, you don't understand, you're such a crook.'

Vladimir appeared unoffended. He said pensively: 'And you would lose your job if you agreed to bail?'

'Laughed out of town. Probably prosecuted myself for blatant corruption.' He shook his head, no, no, no. 'Bail is impossible. Anyway, I'm not handling the Gregovich case, I've handed it over to my deputy.' He feverishly tried to look angry. 'Is that what you've asked me to come over from Hong Kong for? If so, I'm going.' He made to stand up.

'Sit down, please.'

Hargreave sat down again willingly, hoping that now they were going to talk about money. Vladimir looked at him fixedly.

'You are not handling the case yourself? Why not?'

'Because,' Hargreave sighed theatrically, 'I'm far too busy.' He pretended to glance at his wristwatch.

'But you could take it over again?'

Hargreave tried to glare. 'But I'm not going to. I'm going to have nothing to do with the case, Vladimir, *nothing* to do with your attempted blackmail! Got that? And let me assure you that if you approach any of my staff I'll have you thrown in jail! Got *that*?'

Vladimir looked at him narrowly. Hargreave waited, praying the bastard was convinced, praying for him to turn to the subject of money. Instead Vladimir suddenly stood up. 'Very well. We will see.' He turned and started walking for the door.

Hargreave stared at him, then scrambled up, desperate to start negotiations. '*Vladimir!*'

Vladimir stopped, and looked back. Hargreave went up to him. He was shaking. 'I'll pay the twenty thousand. Immediately Olga is back here safe and sound – with her passport.'

Vladimir looked at him scornfully. 'Olga's bail is only worth twenty thousand?' He turned to walk away.

Jesus. Hargreave grabbed his arm fiercely. 'How much?'

Vladimir smiled at him. 'Violence again, Mr Hargreave? In public, too?'

Hargreave blinked, and released him.

'Who do you think stopped the Macao immigration officers from reporting your last violence to the newspapers, Mr Hargreave?'

Hargreave stared at him. 'You?'

Vladimir smiled. 'And why? Because, Mr Hargreave, you're going to pay much more than the forty thousand dollars you owe, and you have to be able to *earn* it.' He turned.

'Vladimir!' Hargreave bounded after him and grabbed his arm again. 'Tell me where Olga is!'

Vladimir looked at him disdainfully. 'In Russia.' He pulled his arm free.

Hargreave grabbed him again and held a trembling finger at his nose: 'It is a serious matter even in Russia to hold anybody against their will!'

Vladimir smiled. 'Yes. Very serious.' He turned and strode away.

'Vladimir!'

But Vladimir kept on walking.

And Hargreave wanted to bellow his outrage to the sky, break down and weep.

21

It was an awful time.

Two days later the committal proceedings began in the case of Regina versus Ivan Gregovich.

Committal proceedings are a preparatory examination: the prosecutor leads the Crown's evidence, the defendant is entitled to cross-examine the witnesses or to reserve his defence until his actual trial in the Supreme Court. It is an unwieldy process because the case is aired twice, but Hargreave had chosen to use it in order to test the reliability of his Russian witnesses, particularly Simonski, because he had an uneasy feeling that duress had been applied to extract Gregovich's confession. But now Simonski was dead, so the proceedings would largely be a regrettable waste of time: and today something further regrettable was going to happen – today Gregovich would make an application for bail and Hargreave dreaded that it would be alleged that he had discussed 'exchange of bail' in a Macao night-club while trying to negotiate the return of a Russian whore who was, indirectly, under Gregovich's control. Although Hargreave had flatly refused the deal, by the time the press got through with that allegation the incident would reek of unethical conduct by the Director of Public Prosecutions. Furthermore, today the Crown or the police would come in for much criticism for 'allowing' the importation of radio-active uranium into Hong Kong.

For these reasons Hargreave had ordered that the committal proceedings be held in Fanling, a town in the New Territories, in the hope that no pressman would be present. It was not to be. He had sent Neil Findlay to present the evidence: when the court adjourned for lunch, Findlay telephoned him.

'Well, the press are here in force, even the guys from *Time* and *Newsweek*. And guess who's shown up to represent Gregovich? Lipschitz.'

Hargreave groaned. Arnold Lipschitz, the nastiest, crookedest lawyer in town – Shitlips Lipschitz. It was doubtless he who had alerted the press.

'And what line of defence is he taking?'

'He's giving Champion a roasting in cross-examination for being an agent provocateur, for permitting uranium into the colony, et cetera – and the press are loving it. Headlines tomorrow, Al. He's trying to embarrass the Crown and whip up public indignation so our future jury will be angry with us in the Supreme Court.'

Hargreave sighed, but it was the bail application he was most worried about. 'What questions is he putting?'

'He's asked Champion if he got your permission to allow the uranium in. Answer: No, well not exactly. You and only you knew about the case, but you hadn't been told the stuff was coming. Question: But a sting operation could only be conducted by the Hong Kong Police on Hong Kong territory so the DPP *must* have known? Answer: Well, not exactly, I tried to consult him before the actual shipment left Russia but he wasn't available. Where was he? On holiday in Macao. Oh, on holiday with his wife? Of course I strongly objected to the irrelevance of whether you were with your wife or not but the press got the message, and he succeeded in creating the impression of Nero fiddling while Rome burned.'

Hargreave flinched. Findlay knew about Olga, as did most of Hong Kong society since those cartwheel pictures were published, so it hardly mattered about her existence emerging – it was the disclosure of her connection to Gregovich through Vladimir that he was worried about. 'Did he ask anything further on that point, about who I was with?'

'No.'

No – just enough to signal that he knew about Vladimir in the hope of intimidating Hargreave. He changed the subject: 'What's Lipschitz doing about that confession?'

Findlay sighed. 'Oh, he's announced that he's challenging the confession – but not now. He's keeping his cards close to his chest. Now he's only maintaining that Champion was determined to catch somebody – *any*body – so he grabbed poor Gregovich, an innocent tourist, then let Simonski beat a confession out of him with unspeakable brutalities.'

Hargreave snorted. 'So, he puts the blame on Simonski? At least he's revealed that much of his tactics at the trial. And Simonski is dead, unable to stand in the witness box to deny it. Crafty bastard – a judge will be more inclined to believe Russian brutality than ours.'

'But Champion has denied it, of course. And he was present throughout the interrogation. Never left the room.'

Hargreave frowned. 'Champion has said that, in the witness box?'

'Yes.'

187

Hargreave inwardly sighed. He knew that wasn't true – Champion had let it slip when he visited him in Macao that he had on occasion left the room to go to the toilet. So Champion was lying under oath on this point? Or had he made an innocent mistake in Macao? Anyway, this placed Hargreave in the unhappy position of suspecting that his own witness was not telling the truth, and if that was confirmed he would have to tell the court, and Lipschitz: the Crown does not conceal perjury. But there was no need to tell anybody yet, until he had questioned Champion again. Lord, this case was looking weaker and weaker. 'Well, keep me informed . . .'

It was the bail application he dreaded. Of course it was irrelevant that he had spoken to Vladimir in Macao about bail, therefore Findlay would object, but that bastard Lipschitz would manage to say just enough to let the cat out of the bag for the press before he was shut up. And there would be a stink – 'no smoke without fire'.

Hargreave tried to get on with other work, but he could not. *Olga, Olga, where are you?* It was a long day waiting for Findlay to telephone again at four o'clock.

'Well,' he said, 'Lipschitz reserved his defence while loudly proclaiming that he would prove in the Supreme Court that Gregovich was subjected to "ghastly duress in flagrant contempt of the Judges' Rules" quote unquote.' Findlay snorted. 'Lipschitz reserved his cross-examination of all our other witnesses, except our scientific expert, and he asked him only one question: "As this uranium is so dangerous, would it not be madness for anybody to permit it to be carried on a civilian aircraft?" Answer: "Yes." The press loved it.' Findlay sighed. 'So we didn't learn much, Al. Tomorrow Lipschitz is going to make an application for bail.' He added wearily, 'And he intends to call witnesses in support thereof. Don't worry, he won't get it. Okay, I'll let you go back to work, I'm going for a drink.'

Hargreave almost wished Gregovich *would* get bail, do a disappearing trick and let Olga go. Lipschitz knew there was not a hope in hell of bail at this stage, and if he intended calling Vladimir as a witness he knew perfectly well that the evidence was irrelevant – the little shit was only making the application to try to intimidate Hargreave with the prospect of professional embarrassment. In fact Lipschitz would probably have the gall to telephone him now to sound him out. Just then the telephone rang.

'Hullo, Al,' Arnold Lipschitz cried. 'How are you?'

'What can I do for you, Arnold?' Hargreave said. 'I'm very busy.'

'Sure, sorry to bother you – and Al, I'm sorry to hear about the trouble you've had, with the missus and all that. Is that gunshot wound okay now?'

Hargreave had his eyes closed. 'Fine. I repeat, I'm very busy.'

'Sure, Al,' Lipschitz smarmed. 'I'm applying for bail for Ivan Grego- vich tomorrow and I just wondered what your attitude will be – maybe we can come to an agreement and save me calling witnesses and all that jazz. What we offer is forty thousand US dollars cash as security – that's all Gregovich can afford but it's a goodly chunk of money, isn't it? We'll surrender his passport, of course, and he'll report to the police station twice a day. Now those conditions are fair. What do you say?'

Hargreave's heart was knocking. *Forty thousand dollars?* The same amount Vladimir had claimed for Olga. Oh, that was loaded with menace of blackmail.

'No deal, Arnold. Gregovich will disappear into China within five minutes with a forged passport. But you can try the story on the magi- strate.'

'But Al,' Lipschitz whined, 'who wants all that expensive hassle – the law presumes Gregovich to be innocent and he's therefore *entitled* to bail.'

'Not if it'll defeat the ends of justice, because he'll run away and won't face trial.'

Arnold Lipschitz sighed at the injustice. 'He *won't*, Al – he wants to clear his name. And he's outraged by his police torture, that he's being framed, outraged that he's being blamed for something so irresponsible as flying uranium halfway round the world – in fact the poor guy has got such a bee in his bonnet he blames *you* for permitting it! Al, see reason, my friend. I believe you were in a reasonable frame of mind a few days ago. Look – if you instruct your man Findlay not to oppose the application, it'll save me calling . . . hang on, let me find my note . . . ah, here it is – it'll save me having to call a guy called Vladimir as a witness. You remember him?'

Hargreave wanted to slam down the receiver in fury – and fear. But he was sure that Lipschitz was recording this conversation and it was dangerous denying he knew Vladimir. He tried to sound mystified. 'The only Vladimir I remember is in Macao, but he can't possibly give any relevant evidence about your expletive-deleted bail application.'

'That's him,' Lipschitz gushed, 'that's the guy, a pimp! He says you were agreeable to granting bail provided he helped you get a young lady out of Russia. In fact he says you offered him about forty thousand dollars for the job? You offered a sort of "bail exchange", you said you

189

would let Gregovich out on bail but he must get the young lady out of Russia.' He paused. 'Is that right, Al?'

Hargreave was shaking with anger. He felt white with fear, and had to take a deep breath to control his voice.

'No, that is not correct, Arnold. No such unthinkable deal was discussed with that jerk. But go ahead, Arnie – make your bail application, try to call him as witness and you know as well as I do that his evidence won't be heard by the court because it is totally irrelevant as to whether Mr Gregovich is likely to appear to stand his trial in the Supreme Court if he is granted bail, which is the only point at issue. And pending the court's predictable decision on that, Arnold, you can go to hell!'

He slammed down the telephone. He was so tense he wanted to vomit.

22

Hargreave hardly slept that night. He went drinking in a noisy Wanchai girlie-bar, surrounded by tourists, lest Jake McAdam came home early: he dreaded having to talk to his host with the new worry of Lipschitz on his mind. Mercifully McAdam was still out when he got back: he closeted himself in the spare bedroom, the lights off, staring out of the window at the harbour below, drinking whisky, steeling himself for the fact: All is lost.

All is lost. Tomorrow morning Lipschitz would do his dirty number, fail in getting bail for his despicable client but succeed in dragging Hargreave down: tomorrow the story would be all over town that the DPP has tried to make a deal with the Mafia over the bail, tomorrow afternoon the Attorney General would tell him, kindly but firmly, that the Legal Department could sustain no more scandal, that though Hargreave was doubtless innocent of any professional misconduct it would not be perceived that way by the gullible public, who will say there's no smoke without fire – so perhaps he should consider early retirement? All is lost, Hargreave told himself. But the feeling that gradually stole over him as the level in the whisky bottle dropped was angry recklessness. *He did not care any more.* God knows he hated having his honesty and his ethics impugned, God knows he now *needed* the job for a few more years to pay off Elizabeth and save some money, but he was sick of having his private life dragged around town. I'm innocent, and I do not care what people think any more, *all I care about is Olga* – tomorrow when the Attorney General sends for me I'll tell him to stick his job and I'm going to jump on a plane for Moscow and hire detectives to look for Olga. *Please God, help me to find Olga . . .*

When he woke up the next morning, at his lowest ebb, he no longer felt reckless; he was dreading the day. The front page headlines of the *South China Morning Post* read: CROWN 'RECKLESSLY' PERMITS IMPORTATION OF URANIUM. The opening paragraph stated: 'In a dramatic confrontation in the Fanling Magistrates' Court yesterday, defence counsel Arnold Lipschitz alleged that the Director of Public Prosecutions had connived in the "reckless and shameful" importation of eight kilograms of radio-active uranium – enough to make two nuclear bombs.' This was bad enough, but it was the fall-out from Lipschitz's bail application he dreaded. He got to work early, retreated to his chambers with instructions to his secretary that he was not to be disturbed by anybody except Findlay. He ordered coffee, put a big slug of whisky into it, and awaited the worst. At half past nine the telephone rang, and he closed his eyes as he picked it up. 'Yes?'

'Well,' Findlay said cheerfully from Fanling, 'it's all over. Lipschitz decided not to make a bail application after all. Obviously he knew he couldn't succeed. So the magistrate committed Gregovich for trial, in custody. I'll be back in chambers in a couple of hours.'

Hargreave stared across the room.

Oh, thank God . . . He was smiling weakly. The first good news in two weeks. He felt like getting drunk as he put the receiver down. So that little shit Lipschitz had just been trying to frighten him into agreeing to bail – well it hadn't worked, had it? But the ridiculous part of it was that he actually felt grateful to the little bastard for desisting in his dastardly attempt to embarrass him! He actually felt *grateful*!

Then the telephone rang again, and it was the little bastard himself. 'Morning, Al – heard the good news?'

Hargreave felt shaky. 'Cut the crap, Arnie, you would have been laughed out of court.'

'Would I? Al,' Lipschitz said, 'you owe me one.'

Hargreave's anger rose through his relief. He said slowly, 'I don't owe you a damn thing!'

'Al,' Lipschitz said quietly, 'I've only decided not to apply for bail *for the moment*. I may apply later – to a Supreme Court judge.'

Oh, he hated the little shit. 'Fine, Arnold!' He slammed down the telephone.

He slumped back. He'd had enough of this tension. He knew what Lipschitz was up to: when the furore about the uranium had died down in the press, he would stir up public emotion again by making a futile but noisy application for bail in the Supreme Court, in central Hong Kong, and sneak in the scurrilous allegations against him. Oh, he had had enough of this shit.

But, with the help of the whisky, Hargreave didn't care any more. All he had to worry about right now was Olga.

And then there was another piece of news: at twelve o'clock Elizabeth telephoned and announced that she had vacated the apartment. She said tensely:

'I don't want a long conversation, Alistair, I just want to tell you that

I'm getting right out of your hair – I'm leaving Hong Kong today. I can't stand the gossip over this . . . girl. However, I don't want an argument, I want us to part as peacefully as possible. I'll be in touch when I've settled down and maybe you'll have returned to your senses, but how we could ever live together again in Hong Kong and hold our heads up I don't know – it's one of the things I've got to think about. Otherwise, of course, it's divorce. Very well, I must go now, my taxi's waiting to take me to the airport.'

Hargreave was bemused. 'Elizabeth – where're you going?'

'To London. I've phoned the tenant and she's agreed to vacate our house at short notice, I'll be moving in next week.'

'But Liz – we need the rent to pay off the mortgages.'

'*We*,' Elizabeth said, 'do not need the rent – *you* might, after your expensive fling in Macao. For the moment I've got enough money – I'll let you know when I need some more.'

Oh God, money . . . 'Liz, please don't get rid of the tenant – you can find yourself a lovely apartment for half the price she pays us.'

'You should have thought of that before you turned your back on me.'

'Jesus – you left me!'

'Yes, and why? Because you've *changed*. Just tell me when last we made love. Now look at you – chasing some whore like a dog on heat! No, Alistair, I love that London house and it's going to be my home from now on. You're welcome to come and visit me in it, but don't imagine you're going to kick me out.'

'I haven't kicked you out of anywhere!'

'Only out of your life. Anyway, let's not argue. Goodbye, Alistair, and good luck.' She hung up.

Hargreave slumped, and held his face. Oh God, it was sad for a marriage to end like this – but thank God it was happening; thank God she had found the strength to go off and make a new life for herself – he wanted her to be happy . . . But why did she have to do it in his London house, the only property that made good money? He was haemorrhaging money. But even that didn't matter, surely he could sort out the London house with her later – what mattered now was that they were out of each other's hair. Thank God he had got his apartment back – no more camping in Jake's flat, that was an enormous relief. But it was sad to part from Liz with this hostility – he hadn't even had the chance to wish her luck, to somehow say the right things, tell her she was a good soul, to thank her for twenty-four years of partnership and two beautiful daughters. He picked up the telephone and dialled the apartment: it rang and rang. Finally he hung up. He imagined her being driven in the taxi, weeping, turning away from her life in Hong Kong, and he dropped his face in his hands and sobbed.

After a minute he straightened. It was all for the best. He would write her a nice letter. And she could have all the money she needed until she remarried, or whatever. Of course Liz would remarry – she was a very attractive woman who had a great deal to offer. Oh, he so wanted her to be happy . . .

But at lunchtime he drove to Jake McAdam's apartment to collect his things, then on to his apartment to re-establish himself, and when he walked in he did not feel that Elizabeth was such a good soul. It was a shock: the apartment was bare. Almost everything except the government's furniture had been stripped out of it: the carpets were missing, the floors naked, the covers Elizabeth had had made for the sofa and armchairs were gone, even the curtains, the windows gaping naked at him. The television set and video were still there, but the sound equipment had gone. Every ornament had been removed, every picture, the walls bare, every lampshade: the bookshelves that lined the living-room were empty except for one volume – *Stephenson's Book of Quotations*. His liquor was still in the bar in the corner, but there was only one glass. He walked down the corridor to their bedroom, his footsteps echoing: there was one pair of sheets, neatly folded on the end of the bed, one pillowslip, one blanket, one towel. No curtains. He walked back down the echoing corridor, looking into the two spare bedrooms: they were stripped bare. He went to the kitchen: it was naked. The shelves and cupboards and refrigerator were all empty: on the table was one cup, one saucer, one knife, one fork, one spoon, one plate, one pot, one pan. And a note:

Dear Alistair

I have pensioned off Ah Moi – she said she didn't want to work as your servant any more. She'll be in touch with you about severance pay.

Love, Elizabeth

Hargreave sat down slowly at the kitchen table.

Oh God . . . the emptiness shrieked at him. So this is what happens when a marriage breaks up. This shell of a dwelling was what he had to show for a home after twenty-four years' service . . .

'*Bitch!*'

Then he took a deep breath. No, Elizabeth wasn't a bitch – she had only done what most women would do when a new woman threatens to take over her home. And wasn't she entitled to take with her all the things she had contributed to making the home? Even though he had paid for them, *she* had put the effort into making everything comfortable and pretty, she had chosen the carpets and had the curtains made, found the right crockery and cutlery and glasses and lampshades and pictures to go with everything – *she* had been the artist who made this home. Yes, she was entitled, morally. It was just the shock of coming home to the blunt evidence that a shell was all that remained now.

But it was a shell that would be filled up with Olga. When Olga came here she would fill this empty echoing place up again, with *her* choice, *her* things.

He stood up impulsively and fetched her suitcases from the hall. He carried them through to his bedroom, and began to unpack her belongings, to start filling the place with her right now.

He hung up her dresses, lingering over each one, tears in his eyes, remembering the occasion she had worn each. He put the soft fabric to his face – he could smell her scent, and it felt as if his heart would break. One by one he hung her dresses up, then he unpacked her underwear. Her panties and brassières, her suspender-belts and stockings. Feeling them, looking at them, lovingly folding them and placing them on the shelves. Then her shoes: her stylish stilettos, her espadrilles, her kinky boots, her gym shoes: he laid them in a neat row at the bottom of the wardrobe. Then her cosmetics: he took them to the dressing-table and slowly laid them out, one by one; her lipsticks, her face creams, her body-lotions. Her hairbrushes and combs and hairpins, her mother-of-pearl hand-mirror; her perfumes, her nail files and bottles of nail polish. They looked lovely sitting there on the dressing-table, as if she had used them that very morning. Heartbreakingly lovely.

He went into the naked bathroom, and put her toothbrush in the little rack, and her toothpaste. He hung up her shower cap, her bathrobe and towels. He placed her sponge, her backbrush, her nail-brush, her bath salts, her shampoos and hair conditioners neatly along the edge of the bath.

There. *It looked like her bathroom now* . . . His eyes were filled with tears.

He returned to the bedroom and looked around. He was filling it up with her. He turned to her suitcases. There were two nightdresses. He had never seen either. One was an old flannel garment that would reach to her feet – she must have worn that in Russia. He hung it up. The other was a short, filmy, frilly affair, blue and transparent, it would barely cover her bottom: with tears in his eyes he made up the bed, and placed it under the solitary pillow.

At the bottom of the second suitcase was a jumble of books, music cassettes and a photograph album. He took out the first book: it was a big Russian–English dictionary, well-thumbed. The next was a Russian –Portuguese dictionary, almost new. An old hardback novel: *A Many Splendoured Thing* by Han Suyin. An old paperback: *Doctor Zhivago*. There was *Teach Yourself Animal Husbandry*, *Spanish For Beginners*, *Foreign Mud*, *Red Star Over China*, *The Boxer Rebellion*, *The Sino-Japanese War*, *Taipan*, *The Gulag Archipelago*, *Comparative Religion*, *Man Kind?*, *The Travels of Marco Polo*. Several books written in Russian.

Hargreave laid the books out on the bed, one by one, his eyes burning. Each had her name neatly printed inside, both in the Russian alphabet and in English. Oh, he loved this girl – how many books had he read in a foreign language? None: the only foreign language he spoke was schoolboy French. And *look* at her wide interests . . .

He picked up the photograph album, but he could hardly bear to look at it. It was new but many of the photographs were old, faded, taken with a cheap camera on poor film. Olga, aged about three, with a mass of blonde curls, riding on a big man's shoulders, laughing all over her baby face – was that her father carrying her? Olga, holding a tall woman's hand in a chicken run – her mother: she looked a nice, worn, weary person in a shapeless, shabby dress. Olga in a faded class photograph, standing at the back because she was as tall as the boys, her hair in plaits, grinning at the camera. Olga cuddling a dog in a backyard, a goose in the background. Olga in a gymnastic team photo-graph, sitting in the middle of the front row – oh, look at her lovely strong body, look at that smile! Olga in a swimming-team photograph, her bosom bursting from a swimsuit too big for the rest of her. *Oh my poor darling*. Olga driving a tractor, hoeing a field, her hair in a scarf, Olga giving an unhappy-looking pig an injection while a man in a white coat looked on. Olga cradling a new-born calf. Olga in a veterinary surgery, holding two test-tubes up to the light for examination. Olga sitting on a lawn with a group of laughing women her own age, clus-tered round a birthday cake while a Turkish waiter filled her glass with champagne – oh God, was this taken in Istanbul? A glorious colour photograph, perhaps taken by a professional, of Olga doing a belly-dance, her beautiful body visible under the filmy garments . . .

Hargreave could not bear to look at any more right now – he thrust the album aside, to weep over later.

He picked up the first music cassette. There were over twenty; some

196

of them bore manufacturers' labels: modern American lyrics, love songs, he recognized a few of the titles.

Three cassettes had *Olga* written on them: were these recordings of her singing? Oh, he had to listen to these – but Elizabeth had taken the sound equipment. Then he noticed a tape-recorder in the corner of the suitcase: he examined it, switched it on – but the batteries were flat. *Buy some batteries today, tonight you listen to your love singing* . . .

Under the tape-recorder was a video-cassette. He picked it up, and his pulse tripped: a little white label read *Olga*.

Hargreave got up and hurried down the corridor to the living-room. He went to the television set, inserted the cassette into the video-player, switched on the machine and hit the play-button. He retreated into the centre of the bare floor. There was a flickering of lights, and then Olga burst on to the screen. And Hargreave's heart seemed to turn over.

Suddenly there was a burst of applause as the Tranquillity Nite-Club filled the screen; then there was Olga walking towards the stage, her back to the camera. She was wearing her blue silk dress that was now hanging in his wardrobe, her blonde hair cascading down her bare back, her buttocks sliding seductively under the shiny silk as she walked. Then she turned to face the camera, smiling widely; and her beauty took Hargreave's breath away. She was ridiculously beautiful. Then the band behind her struck up; she took the microphone in her hand, and began to sing 'Slow Boat to China'.

And, oh, she had a lovely voice, a silken, sultry voice!

Hargreave stood in the middle of the uncarpeted floor, staring at the woman he loved, her voice filling the room, his broken heart bursting with pride, the tears running silently down his face.

And then, that very afternoon, when he got back to his chambers, a letter arrived from Olga.

Hargreave stared at the envelope, his heart knocking with joy. It was addressed to him as 'The Director, Supreme Court, Hong Kong'. It was postmarked in Moscow.

He tore it open, his hands trembling. A photograph of her fell out – it had the imprint of her lipstick on it. The letter was written on a page torn from a notebook, and there was an address at the top! And a telephone number!

My darling Alistair
    I must hurry writing this because my friend will post it for me. I love you and miss you so dreadfully. I am always crying. They

are trying to make me work and I hate it so much because I love you. They have stolen my money. Please come to fetch me. Please make a plan immediately, I am waiting for you every day. I love you.

Yours faithfully,

Olga

Hargreave wanted to whoop for joy. Oh, he loved her. And he loved her innocence – her rounded schoolgirl handwriting, her stilted written English, her formal 'Yours faithfully' she had been taught at school. And her photograph, that fresh young beauty.

He wanted to snatch up the telephone and call her immediately, but restrained himself. He could not use the taxpayers' money, but equally important the call might be intercepted by her Mafia minders. *Oh my darling* – he imagined her in a bleak apartment, a captive being made to sell her beautiful body, and he wanted to bellow in outrage. *I'll get you out of there, I promise.* He snatched up the telephone and dialled Jake McAdam at his office.

'Jake, it's Al. I've had a letter! And remember that passport problem we discussed in Macao? I do need it!'

There was a silence. He heard Jake sigh. 'Well, I'm very pleased for you. But are you sure about the . . . document?' He paused. 'It's a risk. If you come unstuck the shit'll really hit the fan and you're in enough of that stuff as it is.'

'Quite sure!'

'And what about a picture?'

'Got one!'

'Okay,' McAdam sighed. 'Write out – *type* out – all her particulars and put everything in an envelope, together with a thousand dollars – in cash, not a cheque. Decide whether you want Portuguese or British. Leave the envelope under your car tonight – somebody will pick it up later. Needless to say I'll be having nothing further to do with this, and I wish you weren't.' He paused again. 'Right, nuff said, you should find the document under your car tomorrow night.'

'Many thanks. And Jake – Liz has left Hong Kong and I've moved back into my apartment. Thanks very much for putting me up.'

'Well, I suppose it's for the best . . .'

Hargreave felt limp with relief. And bursting with happiness. Shitlips Lipschitz could do his worst! He snatched up the telephone again and dialled his tame travel agents.

'Maggie,' he said happily, 'I want a Russian visa chop-chop and a return air-ticket to Moscow on the next available flight. Also, a one-way ticket from Moscow, to . . .' He stopped, considering.

'To where, Alistair?'

He hadn't thought this through. He couldn't bring Olga back to Hong Kong until Max had successfully appealed against the immigration department's ruling, and he certainly wasn't going to risk sending her back to Macao. He made a snap decision: 'To the Philippines, Manila. And make my ticket Hong Kong–Moscow–Manila too, then Manila–Hong Kong. Open-dated.'

'And in whose name is this second ticket?'

'Olga Romalova.' It was the loveliest name in the world.

Maggie sighed. 'Oh, Al. Is this the girl we've heard about? I'm so happy for you. It's so . . . romantic. And you've had such an awful time of late.'

Hargreave grinned. 'Well, I'm having a wonderful time today, Maggie – but this is all confidential of course.'

'Of course. Is she as beautiful as they say?'

'Even more so.'

'So romantic,' Maggie said again. 'And you're such a helluva nice guy, Al, I don't believe any of these things I hear.' She sniffed. 'Right, the Russian visa will be ready in two days; there's an Aeroflot flight the next day. Russian law says I've got to book you into a hotel so I recommend the Intourist Hotel, near Red Square.'

Oh, Hargreave was in love with the world! He paced across his office, punching his palm, trying to remember what else he had to think about.

He telephoned Max and invited him for a drink.

They met in the Captain's Bar of the Mandarin Hotel, and sat at a corner table. Max listened to the story, then he said, 'The less I know about the forged passport the better – and I hereby formally advise you, as your friend, and as one lawyer to another, not to do it. Having said that, I'll say this: don't try to bring her into Hong Kong, or England, on a forged British passport because the chances of detection are increased. Get her a Portuguese one – we're a dozy bunch and half our computers don't work.' He looked at him sternly. 'I wish you'd stop smiling. Don't forget I gave you the above advice. And I'll deny this conversation ever took place. Okay?'

'Okay.' Hargreave grinned.

'Secondly, we don't start any appeal against the immigration department's prohibition of Olga until the Gregovich case is finally over. You don't want any more embarrassment from Lipschitz, do you?'

'No. But that trial is weeks away, I can't bear to wait that long to get her here.'

'You have to. You're not thinking with your head, Al, you're thinking with your . . .' He left it unfinished. 'And thirdly, what plan have you made for Moscow? So, you've got her address at last – big deal. What're you going to do? Knock on her door, punch her Mafia guard on the nose, then take her downstairs to a waiting taxi to drive to the airport? Al, her letter implies that she doesn't have freedom of movement. That suggests you're going to encounter resistance to your knight-in-shining-armour number. You're going to need some help.'

'If so I've got a contact, a cop called Sepov, a friend of Simonski's. But I can't organize anything until I've seen the lie of the land – until I've seen how much help I need.'

'The Russian police? Do you think the Mafia will let you go to the police?'

'They won't stop me leaving her apartment alone. They want the money, remember.'

Max sighed. 'Al,' he said, 'has it occurred to you that this could be a set-up?' He held up the letter. 'How do you know Olga wrote this? Or maybe she wrote it under duress because the Mafia *want* you to come to Moscow so they can put the screws on you.'

'They've *already* set me up, trying to get me to agree to Gregovich's bail. But now they know the case is out of my hands, that it's going to trial and nothing can stop that, so all they can screw me for is money. And,' he took a grim breath, 'I'll pay it. No more fucking around. If I'd paid last time none of this would have happened.'

Max looked at him solemnly. 'Maybe they'll want much more money now.'

'I won't know anything till I get there, will I? But if they want more money, I'll pay that too, if I have to.'

Max sighed. 'Jesus, you're smiling.' Then: 'Okay, telephone me from Moscow collect if you're in trouble.' He snorted. 'Remember that a lawyer who has himself for a client . . . So, good luck, God speed, God bless you. You're going to need all that.'

PART V

23

Hargreave was tense but happy as he filed aboard Aeroflot's flight for Moscow two days later, with Olga's forged Portuguese passport, some traveller's cheques, his credit-cards and cheque book with which, by arrangement with his bank manager, he could draw cash in Moscow against the security of his mutual funds. And, by God, he liked the pretty, smiling stewardesses. *See what nice people these Russians really are?'* The Boeing 747 was shiny, new and clean, not the antiquated machine he had expected. And it was half empty – he claimed a whole row of seats for himself so he could lie down to sleep later to be fresh for Olga: he had been unable to sleep last night because of his excitement. He had brought a bottle of wine and a bottle of whisky, expecting the crew would serve only vodka, but as soon as the aircraft lifted into the sky over China the pretty hostesses brought plenty of everything.

The Russian passengers started to do some serious drinking, and so did Hargreave. He was feeling wonderful when he lay down after lunch and fell asleep, thinking of his beautiful Olga.

He was woken hours later by a stewardess asking him to fasten his seatbelt for landing.

Through the window was his first glimpse of Russia. Down there were forests, farms, winding roads, then scattered apartment blocks amongst plots and suburban houses. There were not many vehicles. Somewhere ahead over there was his Olga. Then they were descending. When the aircraft touched down safely the Russians burst into good-natured applause, and so did Hargreave. He was feeling good after his long sleep.

Moscow's Sheremetyevo airport did not have many aircraft parked on the apron, and all of them seemed to be Aeroflot's. And this was the capital city of the world's largest nation? The grey airport building was small by international standards, drab and depressing. Hargreave was tingling with impatience as he queued at immigration control. It was very slow, and he encountered his first unsmiling Russian official, who looked at his visa as if Hargreave had made it himself. He felt panic

as he realized that Olga's forged passport had no Russian stamps in it
– *how was she supposed to have entered the country?* At the customs control
his luggage was thoroughly searched by another unsmiling Russian and
his money was grimly counted and checked against his declaration
form.

He emerged into the drab arrivals hall feeling very tense. There were
many faces. He looked around for a moneychanger and a car-rental
desk, and was immediately accosted by unsmiling taxi-drivers. But there
was one smiling face.

'Mr Hargreave?'

Hargreave was astonished. 'Yes?'

He was looking at a young man with a soft, pleasant face. 'My name
is Sergei. I must take you to Olga.'

Hargreave's heart leapt and then sank. His mind fumbled: was this
good or bad? 'How did you know I was arriving?'

'Come with me, please.'

Lord – so the Mafia had friends in Aeroflot? He said firmly, 'I want
to go to my hotel. I want to take a shower first.'

'Okay, I take you in my car.'

No. You don't get into a Mafia car as soon as you arrive, you could
end up in the lake. 'I'll take a taxi, thank you.'

Sergei disarmed him by saying, 'Okay, fifty dollars only.' He picked
up Hargreave's bag and led the way.

Hargreave followed, his mind grappling with this. Was this guy being
nice? Hargreave desperately wanted him to be nice. They came to the
taxi rank and Sergei opened the door of the leading vehicle. It was an
old blue Lada. 'Please,' Sergei said.

Hargreave got in. 'Intourist Hotel, please,' he said to the driver. Sergei
climbed in beside him and spoke to the driver in Russian. 'Intourist
Hotel, please,' Hargreave repeated loudly.

'Yes,' Sergei said.

The taxi pulled out of the rank, drove a hundred yards and stopped.
Hargreave was startled. Sergei looked through the rear window. A car
immediately fell in behind them and the taxi started again. 'That is my
car,' Sergei said. 'Do not be afraid. We do not want trouble.'

Not afraid? Hargreave took a deep breath to control his shakiness.

And, no, he was not really afraid, now he was over the unnerving
surprise: he had to meet the Mafia some time. They didn't want trouble,
they just wanted their money; all that was going to happen now was
bargaining about how much. He said: 'So Olga knows I'm coming?'

'No.' Sergei pulled a cellular telephone from his pocket, dialled and spoke a few words in Russian. He put the telephone away and turned to Hargreave with a smile. 'No, so it will be a good surprise for Olga.'

Hargreave felt relieved. This seemed a nice kid. 'What do you have to do with Olga?'

'I look after her for my boss.'

Hargreave was very pleased this nice kid was the one looking after her. 'And who's your boss?'

'You will meet him.'

Hargreave sat back and let the old vehicle take him through the bleak Moscow outskirts. He knew from brochures which his travel agent had sent him that there were all kinds of old palaces and parks and sports stadiums for the tourist to marvel at on the way into the city but it all passed him by unnoticed. He stared ahead, trying to keep calm. The journey seemed to take an eternity, through countryside with a scattering of new advertising billboards, then there was a sprinkling of drab accommodation. Then they were entering the historic city, apartment blocks and commercial buildings everywhere. Hargreave glimpsed the famous Bolshoi Theatre flashing past, a McDonald's hamburger joint across the road. The taxi suddenly parked abruptly beside other vehicles cluttered outside the towering Intourist Hotel.

Sergei carried Hargreave's bag into the foyer. It smelt dusty; a maid was vacuum-cleaning the old red carpet. There was a long reception desk. Around the foyer were tourist agencies, shops, newsagents, moneychangers, a small casino – they were reassuring. Hargreave said to Sergei:

'Please tell your boss I will meet him here in the foyer in half an hour. *With* Olga.'

Sergei said apologetically, 'I have orders. But I will try.' He took out his cellular telephone again.

Hargreave went to the reception desk, produced the hotel voucher his travel agent had provided and checked in, glancing back at Sergei. He was talking earnestly. Then he came over.

'I am sorry. The boss says you come with me.'

'Is that so? Well call him back and tell him I insist. I will meet you down here after my shower.' He picked up his bag and walked towards the elevators.

Sergei followed him. 'I'm sorry, I must go with you.'

'Jesus!'

They rode up to the fourteenth floor in silence. The elevator's walls were lined with photographs of restaurants and bars in the hotel, all promising exotic food, drink and striptease. There seemed to be a bar on almost every floor. Hargreave breathed deeply to control his nerves. They walked in silence down the long corridor to room 1404. He slid his key-card into the door handle, then turned to Sergei.

'Please wait here. And telephone the boss again.'

He closed the door behind him with a firm click and leant back against it. His hands were shaking.

It was a small but adequate room, built in the heyday of Communism. There was a narrow double-bed, a Formica desk, a telephone, a television set offering cable pornography, a small tiled bathroom. The windows overlooked the rooftops of the Kremlin five hundred yards away. Hargreave pulled Olga's passport from his pocket and cast about for a hiding-place. He stuffed it deep under the mattress for the time being. Christ, maybe he should have left this all at reception for safekeeping? Then he decided that the safest place was on him. He unzipped his bag, stripped and hurried into the bathroom.

Ten minutes later he was ready. He looked at himself in the mirror. Tense – but okay, huh? Pity he'd lost most of his tan. He unstoppered the whisky bottle and took two big swallows. *Now calm down. You've got to be calm and tough for these bastards.* He took a deep breath and opened the door.

Another man was beside Sergei now. He was older and tougher-looking.

'Who're you?' Hargreave demanded.

Sergei said, 'My boss says sorry, you must come with me to Olga. This man drove my car here, he is Mikhail.'

Hargreave sighed theatrically. 'Very well.'

'Excuse me?' Mikhail said. 'I must search you.' Hargreave sighed again and raised his hands.

Mikhail frisked him, evidently looking for a gun. 'Thank you, sir.'

Sir? That was somewhat reassuring. 'Let's go.'

He led the way purposefully back towards the elevators.

24

Through his tension he tried to concentrate on the route they were taking, for future need: but he was soon confused by the mass of traffic and the number of turns; then they were leaving central Moscow, entering sprawling residential areas and he gave up and concentrated on trying to keep calm. About twenty minutes later they came to a halt outside a tall apartment block.

Hargreave climbed out of the vehicle, and he felt a ripple of relief: this was evidently a good area of Moscow – over there was a small park, the street was clean and the buildings looked middle-class.

He followed Sergei into the apartment block, Mikhail behind him. There was a small foyer and an elevator – that was another good sign. They rode up to the sixth floor in silence. They walked down a corridor. Hargreave's heart was knocking.

Sergei unlocked a door, and stood back for him to enter first.

Hargreave walked inside tensely, past a small kitchen, into a modest living-room: he saw flowers in a vase, a television set, modern furniture. Impressionist prints on the wall, a Chinese carpet, a white bearskin rug before an electric fireplace. Several doors led off, all closed. A small balcony overlooked the park.

'Where's Olga?' he demanded.

Sergei took off his jacket, to reveal a pistol in a shoulder-holster. He smiled and put his finger to his lips. He knocked on a door.

Hargreave heard Olga say, 'Da?'

'*Olga!*' Hargreave strode for the door and flung it open.

Olga was lying on the bed in a cheongsam, a book in her hands. She stared at him, eyes wide: then a joyous smile broke across her lovely face. She flung the book aside. '*Alistair!*'

She scrambled up off the bed and ran across the room, arms wide. They clutched each other. He plunged his mouth on to hers – the blissful scent of her again, the glorious feel of her in his arms.

'I've come to take you home –'

She clapped a hand over his mouth and pushed the door closed on

Sergei: she clutched him tight again, kissing him, then she dropped her head on his shoulder and burst into racking sobs.

Hargreave clasped her, his heart overflowing, kissing her tearful face, whispering, *'It's all right. I'm here, I'm here – I've got a passport for you.'*

Then she shuffled backwards across the room, pulling him with her. She collapsed on to the bed, pulling him down on top of her, and she wrapped her legs around him. They clutched each other, kissing through her sobs, his face wet with her tears: then she slipped her hand over his mouth and whispered, 'Have you got a gun?'

Gun? He hadn't come here to use a gun – he'd come to negotiate. He shook his head.

'My gun is under the mattress,' she whispered. 'Take it.'

The door opened and Vladimir walked in. 'Oh, I'm sorry,' he smiled.

Hargreave rolled on to his side, his heart pounding.

'You!' Olga shrieked, and she snatched up her book and hurled it at him. It bounced off the doorframe.

'Come in here immediately, please, Mr Hargreave,' Vladimir said. He stood there, waiting.

'I really do apologize,' Vladimir smiled as he followed Hargreave into the living-room. Mikhail slipped into Olga's room as they left it, to guard her.

Vladimir sat down in an armchair. He waved at another seat. Hargreave remained standing grimly. 'What will you have to drink?' Vladimir asked. 'Scotch? Vodka? We have everything.'

'Nothing,' Hargreave snapped – though Christ knew he needed a drink. 'I've come to settle our disagreement and take Olga away with me.'

'Please, Russians are hospitable. Sergei, pour Mr Hargreave a Scotch, then give me the same so he sees it is not doped.'

Sergei quickly obeyed. Vladimir said conversationally, 'So you fell for our little trick. Olga's letter.'

Hargreave's heart lurched. *So it was a set-up!* Before he could respond Vladimir continued.

'Oh, *Olga* didn't trick you – she loves you. No, we instructed her to write the letter, to encourage you to visit us in Moscow. But I must warn you that the address on the letter is not a real one. However, the telephone number is – it is the number of my cellular phone, for when you want to contact us about our future relationship. But in case you get any ideas of trying to trace this apartment, forget it – the phone is registered to a fictitious person and address.'

Our future relationship? 'Vladimir, I'm going to cut through this bull-shit. I've come here to pay twenty thousand dollars you claim I owe you. Cash. But only at the airport, with Olga, and her passport!'

Vladimir did not take his eyes off him as he accepted his glass of whisky from Sergei. He sipped, put his glass down carefully, then said, 'Of course you are, Mr Hargreave. You should have done this in Macao. But the money is the least of your problems now, sir.' He smiled. 'What I want to deal with now is the problem of Ivan Gregovich.'

Hargreave stared at him, his ears ringing. *Oh no . . .* With a huge effort he tried to look puzzled.

'What's Gregovich got to do with *this*? You know he can't get bail!' He tried to simulate anger. 'That's what this set-up is about? Well, you're barking up the wrong fucking tree, Vladimir!'

Vladimir sat back. He put his fingertips together.

'As I told you in Macao, Ivan Gregovich and I are business associates.' He held up a palm earnestly. 'Naturally I had nothing to do with any uranium – and neither did Ivan, of course. *But*, we share certain other businesses. For example, he looks after the import–export business, and I look after the girls.' He smiled.

Hargreave stared at him. *So Olga really did work for Gregovich.* His heart was racing. 'So? I knew long ago you dealt in girls.'

Vladimir took a sip from his glass, smiling in amusement.

'Mr Hargreave – we understand that bail may be difficult, though our lawyer says we must try again in the Supreme Court. But, Mr Hargreave, we do not understand why you have handed the case over to young Mr Findlay.' He frowned, then sat forward earnestly. 'We would like you to take the case back, and prosecute it in the Supreme Court yourself, please.'

Hargreave felt himself blanch. *Oh God no, not this . . .* He said huskily, 'Why?' He knew very well why.

'Because,' Vladimir said reasonably, 'of Olga. Her safe return to you.' He smiled. 'Mr Findlay is an enthusiastic young lawyer with a big case. He wants to win. But you are an old, wise, experienced lawyer. And so you surely know that Mr Gregovich's confession was made under torture – why would an experienced man like Mr Gregovich, who was also a senior policeman, why else would he confess to such a serious crime? And that confession is the only evidence against poor Mr Gregovich.'

Hargreave felt himself turn pale. He said: '*And* the key to the suitcase found in his pocket. And he knew the combination lock's number, Simonski saw him at Moscow airport when his companion handed over the suitcase to Kozkov.'

Vladimir waved a hand dismissively. 'Simonski is dead, I believe? And it would be such a simple matter for a nasty policeman like Simonski or Champion to slip a key into poor Mr Gregovich's pocket when he was arrested.' He leant forward: 'Mr Hargreave, we want you to prosecute this case *personally* to ensure that the so-called confession of Mr Gregovich is not allowed as evidence in the case, so the jury does not see it. To ensure that *justice* is done . . .' He let that hang, then ended, 'And if justice is done and Mr Gregovich is acquitted, your beautiful Olga Romalova will be sent back to you.'

Hargreave stared at him. He was being blackmailed to fuck up the Crown's case in exchange for Olga's freedom . . .

'Vladimir, you don't understand the law. It is not for the prosecutor to decide whether or not a confession was freely made, that is for the judge to decide. The prosecutor's job is to present to the judge – while the jury is out of the courtroom – the evidence surrounding the confession provided by the police. The police evidence is that Gregovich's confession *was* freely made. So it will now be Mr Lipschitz's task to prove that the police are lying. If Mr Lipschitz succeeds in raising a reasonable doubt in the judge's mind about the matter, then the confession will not be admitted as evidence and will *not* be shown to the jury.'

'But if *you*, the prosecutor, do not believe the police are telling the truth?'

'Vladimir, it is not my job to believe or disbelieve the police – that is the judge's job. I must not usurp the function of the judge, my job is to present the police evidence as given to me.'

'But if you *know* the police are lying?'

Hargreave sighed impatiently. 'Of course, if I *know* they are lying because they tell me so, then I cannot present their untruthful evidence because that would not be justice; but if I only *suspect* they may be lying I must still present their evidence and let the judge decide.'

'But you do know they are lying.'

'I do not. If *you* know they are lying because you have evidence to that effect, tell Mr Lipschitz and you can give that evidence to the judge.'

Vladimir sat back. He said slowly, 'Mr Hargreave, you will prosecute the case personally and that confession will not be used.'

'Mr Findlay will prosecute.' Hargreave tried to sound confident. 'The admissibility of the confession is for the judge to decide, not Mr Findlay, not me.'

Vladimir leant forward again. 'Mr Hargreave, why do you think

Gregovich did not apply for bail last week? I'll tell you – because it would have been so embarrassing for you if the magistrate was told that you tried to make a bail-exchange deal with me, exchanging Mr Gregovich for Olga, that you could not have prosecuted the case personally thereafter – that is what Mr Lipschitz says. And we *want* you to prosecute personally, Mr Hargreave.' He sat back. 'And that is final. In fact, so final we have reserved your flight back to Hong Kong tonight.'

Jesus. So this is what Lipschitz meant when he said 'You owe me one.'

'I offered to make no such deal! So Lipschitz knows I'm here now and that you're telling me this, does he?' He would have the little bastard's guts for garters! Get him disbarred for life!

Vladimir ignored the question. 'And, apart from the confession business, there are many other ways a lawyer can make his case fail, Mr Hargreave. And we insist you use them.'

Hargreave stared at him. He was not going to do any such thing! But maybe he could pull a trick of his own over the bastards. He tried to choose his words carefully.

'And Olga will be safely in Hong Kong while this is going on?' Once Olga was safe, he reasoned, the Mafia could do their worst for all he cared.

Vladimir smiled. 'Olga will be delivered to Hong Kong the day *after* Mr Gregovich is acquitted.'

Hargreave snorted. He said shakily, 'I refuse. And that is the end of that discussion. Now, for the last time, I offer you the twenty thousand dollars you claim I owe.'

Vladimir sat up straight. 'Oh – impossible! But you haven't seen this.' He snapped his fingers at Sergei.

Sergei went to the video-player on top of the television set and pushed a button. There was a flicker, then the bedroom next-door sprang on to the screen. Then there were the images of Alistair Hargreave collapsing on top of Olga on the bed, her cheongsam bunched at her waist, her legs wrapped around him.

Hargreave blanched – it was very undignified. But then fury rose.

'You don't frighten me with that, Mr Fucking Vladimir – the whole of Hong Kong knows I love Olga, I'm not ashamed of her! Show it, for all I care, but you'll be thrown in jail for blackmail!'

'Only if they catch me.' Vladimir smiled. He snapped his fingers again and Sergei went to a tape-recorder and pulled out a cassette. Vladimir took it and held it up. 'Everything today has been recorded. On this tape you have agreed to my terms provided Olga is safely in Hong Kong when you prosecute the case.'

Hargreave almost wanted to laugh. 'I agreed to no such thing – play it back and you'll hear I asked a *rhetorical* question about Olga being there! But that tape *really* proves Gregovich's guilt! I'll stand in the witness box myself and testify about it!' He leant forward and glared. 'What you want is impossible and I refuse.'

'Impossible?' Vladimir snapped his fingers again. 'Bring Olga in!'

Hargreave started. 'You leave Olga out of this!'

Sergei went to the door, and disappeared inside.

A moment later Olga emerged. Mikhail was holding a long strap. Olga looked both angry and nervous. Her hands were manacled.

'*Jesus!*' Hargreave was outraged. 'Take those handcuffs off her!'

Olga blurted to him, 'I promise I did not know about the video!'

'*Take those handcuffs off her!*'

Vladimir stood up. 'Sorry – she's a fighter, you know. And there are more handcuffs for you, Mr Hargreave, if you don't behave.'

Then he swiped at Olga. In one casual movement his arm flew out and he struck her angry face: there was the shocking sound of the blow and she reeled backwards, stunned. Hargreave bellowed and Sergei seized him. 'Take it easy,' Sergei whispered.

Olga crashed against the wall, then her shocked eyes flashed and her leg lashed out and her manacled fists rose like clubs: Vladimir jumped aside and his fist crashed into her stomach. Hargreave bellowed and wrenched, Olga gasped and Vladimir shoved her into a chair. She collapsed, her hands clutching herself, head thrown back, gasping in agony. Vladimir barked an order and Mikhail slung the strap around her and lashed her to the chair.

Hargreave yelled, '*Okay, forty thousand!*'

Vladimir snatched a roll of adhesive tape from his pocket and swiped a length of it across Olga's gasping mouth.

'*You bastard!*' Hargreave roared.

Vladimir cut off another strip of tape and advanced on Hargreave. Sergei grabbed his hair and Vladimir slapped the tape over his mouth. Mikhail was taping Olga's ankles and wrists to the chair. Hargreave struggled and twisted, gasping into his gag, his eyes wild.

'We own this apartment block,' Vladimir said, 'so nobody will come to your help. Now please watch.'

He took a barber's razor from his pocket, and held it up for Hargreave's inspection. Bulging-eyed, Hargreave watched. Vladimir picked up a sheet of paper. He held it between finger and thumb, then ran it over the razor. It sliced in two instantly. 'Very sharp, Mr Hargreave.' Then he turned to Olga. She was wild-eyed, wrenching against her bonds.

'Now keep still, my dear . . .'

Vladimir brought the razor slowly down to her bosom, then his other hand grabbed her neckline and ripped. The dress tore apart, exposing both breasts. Olga's eyes were terrified, Hargreave was shouting into his gag. Vladimir slowly brought the razor down on to her skin. He looked back at Hargreave enquiringly, then he stroked the blade up and down her breast, like a barber sharpening his instrument.

'Impossible, Mr Hargreave?' he asked softly.

Hargreave wrenched at his captor, gargling into his gag. Vladimir teased Olga's nipple with the sharp edge and leered. 'One flick and off comes the pretty little tip. There is so much blood . . .'

Wild-eyed, Hargreave tried to control his horror. *They aren't going to mutilate her, she's the hostage.*

Vladimir lifted her breast with his free hand: 'This is how we treat our girls who try to double-cross us, Mr Hargreave. See the line where the breast joins the chest? We start there – and we cut the breast *off*. As a lesson to all the other girls who think they are clever, like Olga. Like this . . .'

He brought the blade down, then he carefully ran it across her skin, and Olga screamed behind her gag. A thin line of blood appeared, and Hargreave wrenched and bellowed into his gag. Vladimir held the blade up to the light and examined it. A little line of blood was running slowly down Olga's chest.

'Of course,' Vladimir said academically, 'when we cut the whole breast off, there is a hell of a mess – and the ladies make such a noise. They do not like to lose a breast, they are very vain.'

Olga's eyes were screwed up, her head slumped, the sweat sheening on her. Hargreave's chest was heaving, his eyes bulging as he rasped into his gag. Vladimir frowned. 'I think Mr Hargreave is trying to say something? Take the tape off.'

Sergei peeled it off. Hargreave whispered, '*A hundred thousand dollars* . . .'

Vladimir strode to him impatiently, snatched the tape from Sergei and slapped it back on Hargreave's mouth. He turned and paced back to Olga.

'That,' he continued, 'is how we treat ladies who double-cross us. We find we do not have much trouble from the other girls after that. *But* –' he held up a finger – 'Olga's case is a little different. She has been so troublesome, despite so many warnings. But she is also very valuable because she is so beautiful. And men do not like to fuck a woman with only one breast – the popular number is two. So, if you don't agree to our terms, what we have decided is this.'

He snapped his fingers again and Mikhail hurried into the kitchen. He came back holding a surgical syringe. Vladimir took it and held it up.

'In this is heroin. What we will do, now, is give her this injection. That will make her feel very happy. And then, tomorrow, we will give her another injection. And the next day another one. That will be enough to turn her into an addict. Like all addicts, she will not be troublesome any more, provided we give her more heroin every day, and she will work for us with great enthusiasm.' He smiled. 'She will work for us for several years, making us a lot of money. Then, when she is worn out, we will cut off her breast, show it to the other girls, and then send it to you.' He smiled. 'Maybe you can stuff it, or make a nice purse out of it, Mr Hargreave. So now –' he held up his finger again – 'we give Olga injection number one.'

Mikhail grabbed her bound arm, and Olga bucked in the chair, her eyes wild, her knees trying to kick, and Hargreave bellowed into his gag, wrenching his captor's grip. Vladimir pinched up the vein on Olga's wrist. He brought the needle down to it, and carefully slid it into her skin. Then he looked back at the frantic Hargreave with a smile, his thumb poised on the plunger.

'Mr Hargreave is trying to say something again. Take the tape off.'

Sergei tore the tape off Hargreave's contorted mouth.

Hargreave slumped, chest heaving, his heart pounding, terrified, sick in his guts. He opened his mouth and tried to speak but nothing came. Vladimir put his hand to his ear. 'I beg your pardon?'

Hargreave took a deep juddery breath. 'I agree . . .' he whispered.

'Excuse me?' Vladimir frowned, syringe held impatiently.

'*I agree.*'

'To everything?' Vladimir enquired.

'Yes.' And oh God, he meant it.

Vladimir straightened, and smiled with satisfaction. 'And,' he said, 'you will pay a hundred thousand dollars as well . . .'

25

The long flight back to Hong Kong was nightmarish. Hargreave's mind was in turmoil reliving the horrific scenes, his nerves screaming, his heart breaking. He could not eat and when, finally, nervous and physical exhaustion were crushing him he could not sleep. He sat in the long dark cabin of the humming aircraft drinking his bottle of whisky, every fibre tense, turning over and over in his fevered mind the images: the shocking spectacle of Vladimir ripping the dress off her, the dreadful razor stroking her nipple, her wild eyes, the terrible line of blood under her breast, the terrifying syringe sliding into her vein. It was unreal, and yet it was screamingly real. He tried to push the images aside and think constructively but he could not: he tried to tell himself that she was safe for the time being, she was the hostage and they wouldn't do anything to her to make him break his deal – *she is safe for the moment – stop thinking about that and formulate a plan . . .*

But he could not. *Plan? The* only plan was to do as he was ordered, to prosecute the case in such a way that Gregovich was acquitted. What other safe plan was there – safe for *her?* Storm the building and get her out? He didn't even know the address. Report the matter to the Moscow police and hope they're honest, that nobody is in the Mafia's pay and tips off Vladimir? Hope the police put together a crack team who will find the apartment and shoot it out efficiently with Vladimir's thugs? Hope to God that Olga is not shot in the crossfire, that Vladimir does not win the gun-battle and shoot Olga in revenge . . . Oh no, no, he could not even bear to contemplate that plan. And how could he trust the Russian police? Half of them were in the Mafia's pocket. Sepov, Simonski's friend? Kerensky? Who would Sepov get to help him – would those people be trustworthy? And Kerensky was in Vladivostok, six thousand miles from Moscow. Oh no . . . Report the matter to the British Embassy in Moscow? Why should the British Ambassador concern himself with a Russian prostitute? He would tell Hargreave to report to the police or, worse, do so himself and the Mafia would hear about it. And if he reported it to any British authorities it would be *official* and he would effectively disqualify himself from prosecuting the case. No, no way could he involve the British authorities.

Hargreave rubbed his furrowed brow and tried to think. *Think.* Somehow find out the address where Olga was being held, then hire a squad of mercenaries to storm the building and get her out? Yes, and how long does that take to organize? Gregovich's trial in the Supreme Court begins in two weeks. He didn't care what it cost to hire mercenaries but those guys might fuck it up too and Olga might get shot in the crossfire. There must be no violence, nothing to imperil her . . .

Hargreave took a deep fevered breath in the unreality of the long dark aircraft, and tried to think of another solution.

But there was none: the only safe way was Vladimir's. And, oh God, he would do it willingly to spare Olga that razor, that heroin needle, and he did not care any more that he would be breaking his oath to administer justice, trampling his pristine professional record into the gutter. Oh of course he cared, with all his lawyer's heart he wanted to end his career with honour, with a clear conscience of never having abused his high office – he cared bitterly, angrily, furiously, but he would do what he had to in order to save Olga. Is there a man who can say: Do your barbaric worst, beat my loved one, cut her breast off, turn her into a heroin addict but nonetheless I shall remain steadfast to my duty, I shall turn my back on her rather than break my oath? No, Hargreave did not believe any real man could do that. Every man has his price and Alistair Hargreave had just discovered his.

He took a trembling slug of whisky, and screwed his eyes up to force all that out of his mind. Now grasp the nettle and think how you can carry off this dastardly business, how you keep your nefarious bargain.

He held his face and tried to concentrate.

The Crown case was weaker now that Simonski was murdered. Now there were only two pieces of evidence against Gregovich: his confession and the suitcase locks. If the confession were thrown out, were the key and the fact that he knew the combination lock's number enough to convict him?

Yes, in principle. But if the confession were thrown out it meant that the court had found that Champion was lying, or at least unreliable, when he testified that the confession was voluntary: and if he was lying on that important matter, could he not also be lying when he said he found the key on Gregovich? Might he not have planted it on him? Or Simonski might have done it during the scuffle to arrest him. And Simonski was dead, unable to deny such an allegation. Kozkov would deny he had a key, but Kozkov was himself a crook. Champion admitted

216

he had been 'persuasive' with him – might he not have been 'persuaded' to deny he had the key, to put all the guilt on Gregovich? Lipschitz would certainly argue that way at the trial.

So much for the key. But Gregovich also knew the numbers for the combination lock. However, he only divulged those numbers when he made the confession, and if the confession was thrown out his knowledge of those numbers went out the window too – that only left the *inference* that Gregovich supplied the numbers which enabled the police to open the suitcase. But was that inference *irresistible*? No, Kozkov might have told the police the number, might have been 'persuaded' to deny he knew it, to shift all the guilt to Gregovich.

Hargreave took a deep tense breath.

No, without the confession and without Simonski's evidence that he saw Gregovich watch the suitcase being handed over to Kozkov in Moscow, the key and the combination lock in themselves were possibly not enough to convict Gregovich.

Hargreave massaged his anguished brow and tried to force the image of that razor out of his mind: the aircraft was flying east and outside the windows the sun was rising. His whisky-laden body was crying out for sleep but his turmoiled mind would not permit it

So, to fulfil his bargain he would have to see to it that Gregovich's confession was thrown out. And how did he achieve that? Champion's evidence was that the confession was voluntarily made, and it was Hargreave's duty to present that evidence at the trial. Lipschitz had placed his challenge on record without revealing any of the allegations he would make in the Supreme Court, in order to leave the Crown in the dark. Par for the course. In the Supreme Court Lipschitz would get stuck into Champion to try to prove him a liar, trying at least to raise a reasonable doubt that Simonski *may* have applied duress, if only because a tough bastard like Gregovich would not have made a confession otherwise. Simonski was dead and could not deny the allegation: that gave Lipschitz a flying start. But what if Lipschitz should fail?

What if Lipschitz failed . . . He was a very smart, crooked lawyer, but if he failed and that confession was admitted in evidence Gregovich would be convicted, and Olga Romalova would have her breast cut off. Oh God . . . So the question was: What could Hargreave do to ensure that Lipschitz did not fail?

Oh God, he hated this.

Hargreave stared at the sunrise over Russia, and suddenly he knew how to help Lipschitz win: Champion *was* lying. Hargreave, personally, would not blame him one scrap if he knocked the living shit out of

Gregovich after seeing what Vladimir did to Olga. But the point was how was Lipschitz going to find a chink in Champion's armour of denial? And Hargreave knew where that chink was: it was in his claim that he was in Simonski's presence the whole time during the interrogation. Hargreave was almost positive that, in Macao, Champion had admitted that he had left the room sometimes to visit the toilet. Yet during the committal proceedings Champion had denied this, thus denying Simonski had ever had the opportunity to apply duress to Gregovich.

Surely this was a lie. Firstly, it contradicted what Champion said in Macao – Hargreave was almost sure of that fact. Secondly, consider the probabilities: it was highly probable that Champion left the room once or twice during the lengthy interrogation to go to the toilet. Thirdly, it was highly probable that having put so much effort and expense into catching the biggest Mafia blackguard unhung, Champion and Simonski would not be squeamish about applying some pressure to extract a confession from him.

Hargreave sighed tensely. Okay, but was he sure about what Champion said in Macao? He tried to reconstruct the scene, to remember the sequence of the discussion: but no, he could not be absolutely sure – he was only *almost* sure. He had not wanted to be bothered with the case, and Olga had suddenly appeared in the balcony doorway. But that was enough to justify his telling Arnie Shitlips Lipschitz that Champion, his own witness, might be lying on the point, thus giving Lipschitz ammunition to discredit him. That would be enough to raise a doubt about the voluntariness of the confession and get it thrown out of court.

But what if Champion, an experienced witness, credibly insisted that Mr Hargreave was mistaken in his recollection of what was said in Macao – and the judge believed him?

If the judge believed Champion, then Olga would have her breast cut off . . . No, he could not risk the judge believing Champion. So Alistair Hargreave would have to tell a lie himself, and say he was absolutely *positive* about what was said in Macao.

Hargreave dragged his hands down his exhausted face: Alistair Hargreave QC telling a lie, perverting the course of justice, destroying the Crown case against Gregovich, one of the most evil men in the world . . . It was horrific, but, yes, he would do it to save Olga from that syringe, from that razor, he would do anything to prevent that.

He stared out of the window. It was the middle of the night in Moscow where Olga was asleep, but here over Asia the sun was coming up, brilliant red and gold; it was beautiful, but Hargreave did not register it. All he saw was the dust and ashes of his professional ethics.

But what if the confession was nonetheless admitted in evidence, despite all this? It would only be his word against Champion's. What if the judge decided that Mr Hargreave was genuinely mistaken in his recollection? And then the thought occurred to him: it need not be only his word against Champion's – *it could be Olga's word as well* . . .

And his heart leapt. Why hadn't he thought of this before? Olga could be a witness in this case! And if she were a witness she would have to come to Hong Kong!

Of course! Olga had suddenly appeared in the balcony doorway in Macao whilst Hargreave and Champion were discussing this very point! Perhaps she had heard what Champion said about going to the toilet! But even if she hadn't, she could be *told* to say that she had! What was a bit of subornation of perjury to save her life? *Of course* . . . And once she was in Hong Kong as a witness she was safe! And the additional beauty of this was that he could not possibly continue to prosecute the case personally once his own lover became a witness for the defence! It would be impossible, how could the DPP be expected to cross-examine *her*? Even Gregovich and Vladimir would understand that, after Lipschitz had explained it to them.

Hargreave slumped back in his seat. Relief flooding over him. Oh God, this was a terrible thing for any lawyer to do, let alone the Director of Public Prosecutions, and maybe it was the whisky talking but he suddenly felt happy – he had solved the crisis! Killed two birds with one stone! If this worked he would get Olga out of Moscow *and* beat those Mafia bastards at their own terrible game! Then the thought occurred to him: there is another bonus – maybe Justice *would* be done! Because once Hargreave was removed from the case, Findlay could do his job as fearless prosecutor, tear into Olga and show her up as an unreliable witness! And the confession would be admitted and Grego-vich would be convicted!

Oh God . . .

Hargreave slumped back in his seat, elation coursing through him. It seemed the first time his nerves had let go for weeks. Olga was the key to this crisis – why hadn't he thought of this earlier? It all showed the truth of the adage that a lawyer who has himself for a client has a fool for a client – *and* a fool for a lawyer. He'd been unable to see the wood for the trees. Sure, he would have to suborn perjury, but it would be on the side of justice because clever young Findlay would show she was an unreliable witness! *What poetic justice! And Hargreave's conscience would be salved!*

Oh wonderful. Absolutely fucking wonderful! The only thing now was to sell the idea to Lipschitz – and surely Shitlips would go for it hook, line and sinker.

Hargreave slumped in his seat, eyes closed, an exhausted smile on his face. Out there a beautiful new day had begun. He poured himself another drink and looked at that morning, trying to think it through one more time. Then suddenly, with the relief, he was asleep.

26

He did not feel like that when the stewardess shook him awake, telling him to fasten his seatbelt for landing in Hong Kong: he felt terrible, hungover, unrested, jetlagged. And all his horrors came flooding back. What he had to do now, what he had decided a few hours ago, made every nerve in his lawyer's being cringe. The world seemed unreal as he passed through immigration and customs formalities and climbed into a taxi, his body stunned by whisky, his head aching. The teeming streets and roaring traffic seemed mad-making. He should go home and sleep before he made any more moves on the case, but he knew he could not rest.

He entered his bare apartment – it was screamingly unreal that the place he called home was an empty shell. His dirty plate was still in the sink, his rumpled bed with the only pair of sheets was as he'd left it three days ago – or was it four? His laundry unwashed. He would have to get a makee-cleanee *amah* for a couple of hours a day – he couldn't afford a full-time maid any longer. He showered, trying to scrub the ache out of his head, scrub out the dreadful images. His hand trembled as he shaved, and he cut himself. He felt no better when he was dressed. There was only one way to get rid of a hangover like this: he went to the messy kitchen and tore the top off a can of beer and upended it to his mouth.

He leaned against the kitchen cabinet, eyes closed, taking swallows from the can as if it were medicine, trying to think of the order in which he should do things. He wished he could consult Max, bring his clear legal brain to bear, but he could not: Max would be horrified that any lawyer, let alone the Director of Public Prosecutions, was about to suborn perjury. Max would tell him to go to the Attorney General as his nominal boss, tell him the whole story, including what he thought Champion said in Macao, and remove himself from the case entirely. Yes, clearly that was Hargreave's duty – but doing his duty meant death for Olga. So forget about having the comfort of another lawyer or anybody else to turn to for sympathetic advice – *You're on your own, Hargreave!* This is Olga and me against the Russian Mafia and the whole legal establishment and its code of ethics. So finish this beer and think how you're going to set about this now, then get down to chambers and start doing it.

Miss Ho, his principal secretary, was astonished to see him walk into chambers an hour later. 'Mr Hargreave, we thought you were on leave again . . .' The pile of files he had left behind three days ago was still on his desk.

'Give all those to Mr Millar and Mr Watkins to advise on. If they're too busy, distribute them down the corridor to other counsel.'

He ordered coffee, put a big shot of whisky into it, then telephoned Neil Findlay. 'Come and see me, please.'

'I'm in consultation at the moment, Alistair.'

'Tell him to wait and come immediately, please, and bring the uranium file.'

A minute later Neil Findlay entered his chambers with the file. 'I thought you were on leave again, Al?'

Findlay was a good-looking Australian with fair hair and blue eyes, twenty-nine, with a charming smile to go with a sharp brain and an excellent grasp of the law. He was incisive, the judges respected him, juries liked him, he had a quick wit and could raise a smile amongst them. He was married to a charming New Zealand girl, they had a new baby: everybody liked them. Findlay would have reached the top of the tree in the Hong Kong Legal Department if the colony were not being handed back to China in eighteen months. So young Findlay would return to Australia with his savings, go into private practice and one day become a QC and Supreme Court judge down-under.

'Sit down, Neil.' Hargreave took the file from the young man's hand, sighed and said, rehearsed: 'You've done a good job on this case so far, and I'm sure you could handle it by yourself, but because of its international importance I've decided I'd better prosecute it myself.'

Findlay looked astonished, then crestfallen. 'I see.'

Hargreave held up a placatory hand that trembled. 'With you as my junior counsel, of course – as a QC I've got to appear with a junior and you're my choice. You're one of my best counsel, if not *the* best.'

'Thank you,' Findlay said. But he was very disappointed that he was not going to do the case by himself, get all the kudos.

To sugar the pill Hargreave said, 'And if you do as well as I'm confident you will, there's a red bag in it.'

A red robe bag is a gift sent by a QC to his junior after the case to show his appreciation for a job well done. It is a kind of badge: other juniors have blue bags in which to carry their robes and books to court. Findlay smiled deferentially: 'Thank you, Al. But I already have a red bag.'

'Do you?' Yes, Hargreave remembered now. 'Who gave it to you?'

'Dusty Millar. For the body-in-the-refrigerator case.'

'Oh yes, I remember, I'm sorry. Anyway . . .' He paused. Should he say this now? 'Anyway, I can add that you're my next choice –' and this was true – 'for promotion to Senior Crown Counsel when the vacancy occurs the month after next.'

Findlay smiled. That promotion meant a substantial salary increase. 'Thank you, Al.'

'Well-deserved. However . . .' He rubbed his tired eyes. 'However, after all the hullabaloo in the press about this uranium I'd better front up in court and face the music. Now, tell me what we're up against. First, about Gregovich – what kind of impression is he going to make on the jury?'

Findlay's disappointment was almost in the past. 'He's a thoroughly *evil* swine, and looks the part. You've seen the photograph? Worse than that – those devilish eyebrows, that nasty little goatee beard – even the tops of his ears are almost pointed. Long black hair slicked back. And a hard, hard face with pearly-white false teeth.' He smiled: 'If I were on the jury I'd convict the bastard on sight.'

Hargreave sighed. 'Good.' He meant 'bad': he desperately hoped that Arnie Lipschitz would scrub Mr Gregovich up for the trial, give him a wholesome haircut, shave off that beard, trim those devil's eyebrows, give the swine a respectable grey suit. But certainly Shitlips would see to all that; he'd let his man appear in the committal proceeding looking like the Devil only to lull the Crown into a false sense of security. He said:

'But he didn't open his mouth during the committal proceedings?'

'No. Except to deny the charge.'

Hargreave shifted in his chair. 'Okay, so tell me about Lipschitz and Champion. Apart from placing his challenge to the confession on record, am I correct in thinking Lipschitz only cross-examined Champion on one point – namely whether or not he was present the whole time during the interrogation by him and Simonski?'

'Correct.'

'And was Champion an impressive witness on this point?'

'Oh yes,' Findlay said. 'You know Champion, he's an expert witness. Here . . .' Findlay reached across the desk, opened the file and pulled out the verbatim transcript of the committal proceedings. He flicked through the typescript and reached the appropriate pages.

'Champion is in the witness box having just testified that he recorded the voluntary confession from Gregovich.

'"Mr Lipschitz: Your Worship, the defence will strenuously challenge the admissibility of this so-called confession in the Supreme Court. However it is not our intention to enter into a *voir dire* at this stage. Nonetheless I have a few questions for this witness. Superintendent Champion, how long did the interrogation of the defendant last?

'"Mr Champion: According to my Investigation Diary it lasted about six hours.

'"Lipschitz: Continuously?

'"Champion: Yes. We had occasional rests for coffee, et cetera, but it was otherwise continuous.

'"And you were present throughout?

'"Yes.

'"Never left the room?

'"No.

'"Lipschitz: So if Mr Simonski had assaulted Mr Gregovich you would have seen it?

'"Champion: Yes, I would have seen it. And no such thing happened.

'"Lipschitz: No further questions, Your Worship."'

Hargreave rubbed his brow. Yes, Lipschitz had nailed Champion down for the Supreme Court. Of course Champion had left the room during those six hours, what a dumb-cop thing to have denied. 'So there's no indication of the type of duress that's going to be alleged at the trial. Okay.' Now was the time he should tell Findlay what he thought Champion had said in Macao, but he did not do so in case Findlay warned Champion. 'Right, thanks, Neil, go back to your consultation.'

Hargreave waited till the young man had withdrawn, then he poured another dash of whisky into his half-warm coffee. He pressed his fingertips to his eyelids. Oh God. Should he not wait until tomorrow, until he had had a night's sleep, given himself another chance to think this over? But no – 'If it were done, when 'tis done, then 'twere well it were done quickly . . .' – MacBeth urging himself to grasp the nettle and kill Duncan that very night. Do it now, when your blood is up. He reached for the telephone and called Arnold Lipschitz.

'Al!' Lipschitz said. 'To what do I owe the honour?'

'I'd like a brief chat with you about the Gregovich case, Arnold. Can you drop around to my chambers? I may be prosecuting the case personally, with Findlay as my junior, and I'd like to know how long you think it might take, et cetera.'

There was a moment's pause. It seemed to Hargreave he could almost hear a smile of satisfaction. So Lipschitz knew about the last few days, knew he'd been to Russia and what had happened there?

'Sure thing, Al. But how about lunch?' He added: 'I'm paying.'

Oh, you oily little bastard. 'Love to, but too busy.'

'How about two o'clock, in your chambers?'

How was he going to endure the day? 'See you then.'

It was an awful day. He could not concentrate on anything. He needed to sleep but he knew that if he went home he would not, he wanted to get drunk but he dared not. At lunchtime he locked his door, lay down on his carpet and tried to rest, but he could not. At five minutes before two he got up and poured another shot of whisky to prepare himself for the crime he was about to commit.

He closed his eyes and fiercely told himself: *Just think of Olga strapped in that chair, just think of that razor . . .*

Arnold Lipschitz was a small Jewish man with a wide Levantine smile, bushy black eyebrows and dark dancing eyes. Hargreave had heartily disliked him for twenty years as a sly, crooked, clever little lawyer who would break every ethical rule in the book if he could get away with it: today Hargreave loathed him because he was sure the bastard knew why he had decided to prosecute the case personally, knew what Vladimir had done in Moscow to procure his agreement. He sat opposite Hargreave at the desk with an innocent, expectant smile.

'Arnold,' Hargreave began, 'last week you said I owed you a favour because you didn't apply for bail – which you imagined would embarrass me. I want to make it crystal-clear that I don't consider I owe you a damn thing. I am about to tell you something only because I regard it as ethical that I do so.'

Arnold Lipschitz nodded earnestly. 'Very good, Al. Though I'd expect nothing less from a lawyer of your integrity.' He noticed the tremor in Hargreave's hand.

Hargreave indicated the uranium file. 'I've glanced at the committal proceedings and I notice that you allege misconduct, duress to your client by Simonski to make him confess; Superintendent Champion denies this is possible because he says he was present throughout the interrogation.'

'Terrible duress,' Lipschitz agreed solemnly. 'Simonski was a brutal, *brutal* cop, notorious throughout Moscow, I believe. And Champion is lying.'

Hargreave took a deep breath. 'Well, I happened to be on holiday in Macao with a young lady when Champion visited me to consult me on this case. And I feel duty-bound to tell you that I'm sure, or almost sure, that he told me that he left the room a couple of times to visit the toilet. Of course I cannot testify to that as I am the prosecuting counsel, but I am sure that my lady-friend also heard him. And doubtless you will want to call her as a witness for the defence on this point.' He closed his eyes and affected to rub them. His heart was racing.

Lipschitz looked at him. Then he said, eyes wide, 'Very correct of you to tell me, Al – very ethically correct. Thank you.' He took out his pen. 'And who is this young lady? And how do I contact her?'

It had worked! Shitlips had swallowed the hook! *Oh, you little shithouse, you know perfectly well who she is, Vladimir probably telephoned his achievements to you.*

'Her name is Olga Romalova. Russian. She was a prostitute, but by the time she was with me she had ceased that line of work. She is presently in Moscow, in the hands of that Mafia pimp called Vladimir, who is Gregovich's associate – you mentioned him last time we spoke.' He added: 'I should mention that she was once refused admission to Hong Kong because of her past, so you should subpoena her, and warn the immigration department that they can't stop her this time.'

Lipschitz put his hand on his heart: 'Gregovich associated with Mafia pimps? Come, come, Al . . .'

Hargreave ignored the facetious remark. 'Gregovich doubtless has a telephone number for her. I do have a number, but it's a cellular phone used by Vladimir. I don't know how reliable he is.' He handed over a slip of paper bearing the number Olga had supplied in her letter. 'So it's important that when it comes to contacting her . . .' He paused and took a deep breath. This was it; this was the crime of subornation of perjury. 'When you contact her, I should be the one to speak to her first about this. She will not be cooperative otherwise – she has no reason to feel helpful to your client.'

Lipschitz looked at him, and Hargreave could almost see his mind racing, figuring the percentages. Was this a trick? Prosecution counsel not only speaking to a defence witness, but a defence witness who was his lover? It was highly unethical, but it was not ethics that worried Arnie Lipschitz, it was being tricked.

'I would insist on being present when you speak to her on the telephone.'

If he was going to suborn perjury Hargreave didn't want a witness to the crime, especially one like Arnie Lipschitz. 'Okay, but remember she's my girl, I speak to her first.'

'And she's *my* witness,' Lipschitz said. His manner had changed abruptly, from smarm to steel. 'I will speak to her, thank you, without you being present.'

Hargreave felt panicky. 'She won't cooperate unless I've told her to!' Oh God, he could see that razor at her breast again as Vladimir persuaded her to cooperate.

Lipschitz said slowly, 'I'll explain that her evidence not only has your blessing but that you put me on to it. And that there's a nice little free trip to Hong Kong in it for her.'

Oh, that all-important trip to Hong Kong ... And maybe it was for the best if Lipschitz spoke to her; let him do his own dirty work, let him do the actual subornation of perjury, that would spare Hargreave some of the guilt – there was a certain poetic justice in that. But he was scared of Olga fucking it up if he hadn't spoken to her first. 'I had better be present at the outset just to introduce you to her.'

Lipschitz was looking at him, his eyes dancing. 'We'll see. Meanwhile, I forbid you to contact my witness, Al – I'll have your guts for garters in front of the Law Society if you do.' He glared, then went on: 'If this Olga is called as a defence witness, you can hardly prosecute the case, because she is your girl.'

Mentally Hargreave closed his eyes – of course not. But he wanted to cling to it now, to control it, to ensure Gregovich's acquittal. He nodded.

Lipschitz said, as if thinking aloud, 'But I'd *like* you to prosecute the case personally, Al. It's a long time since we did a trial together, we'd have a lot of fun ...' He paused, then added pensively: 'Of course, if Olga were a *surprise* defence witness, if you didn't *know* she was being called, you *could* prosecute the case personally, even if you had to hand over the actual cross-examination of her to Findlay and withdraw temporarily from the courtroom.'

Oh you bastard, so you do know about Vladimir's handiwork, you know you've got me by the balls, one day I'll have your guts for garters ...

Lipschitz suddenly stood up to leave and Hargreave felt panic again. 'Sit down, Arnie, we haven't finished yet.'

Lipschitz smiled at him coldly. 'What haven't we finished, Al? I'll let you know what I decide to do. In due course.'

'But surely you can confirm you're going to call her as a defence witness?' It was a plea. 'She's most important to your defence.'

Lipschitz grinned wolfishly. 'Maybe, Al.'

Maybe? 'But ... I'll have to introduce you. We ... you can come home with me right now and we'll phone from there.'

'I'll have to talk to my client about this.'

227

With a huge effort Hargreave managed to control himself. 'Please let me know as soon as possible.'

'Then she wouldn't be a *surprise* witness, would she?' He turned for the door. 'Goodbye, Al.'

Hargreave stared after him, sick in his guts. The door closed and he scrambled up and lurched into his private toilet, hung his head over the bowl and vomited.

He retched and retched, trying to rid himself of weeks of tension and horrors.

PART VI

27

The next ten days, leading up to the case of Regina versus Ivan Grego-vich, were very tough for Alistair Hargreave.

It seemed to take a week in itself just to get over his jetlag, though Ian Bradshaw prescribed him sleeping pills and tranquillizers. He went to bed early, exhausted by the nervous tension, fell asleep instantly as if his body had shut down on him in protest, but he always awoke long before dawn, staring into the darkness, his nerves crying out for more sleep, the images of Olga and that razor crowding in on him. And then came the guilt: no matter how much he shouted at himself that he was doing the only thing a man could, he could not suppress the shame of abusing his high office. Hargreave lay in the darkness, desperately trying to go back to sleep: then he gave up, showered and drove down the Peak to his chambers and tried to work.

There were many cases demanding his advice, and he had great difficulty concentrating. He had read the Gregovich file so many times he knew it backwards. His nerves cringed every time he caught sight of it. What he desperately needed and ached for was to hear from Arnold Lipschitz, telling him that Olga was coming to Hong Kong as a defence witness.

But Arnie Shitlips Lipschitz did not telephone. Hargreave finally con-tacted the registrar of the Supreme Court, asking if a subpoena had been issued for Olga Romalova, an order to appear as a witness: none had, Lipschitz had not applied for one. That made Hargreave feel pan-icked: but that did not mean that Lipschitz had not arranged verbally for Olga to appear – indeed this was more likely as Olga was supposed to be a surprise witness. Every time the telephone rang Hargreave's heart leapt – then it sank when he heard another voice. Twice in the week following their meeting he telephoned Lipschitz's chambers, but the man was never in – or so his receptionist said. He did not return the calls. Oh, Hargreave knew what the bastard was doing, taking delight in stretching his nerves. And after he had taken his tranquillizers he could handle it and even see Lipschitz's silence as a good sign – surely, if he had decided *not* to call Olga as a witness he would have dropped the bombshell by now and really reduced him to a juddering wreck begging to help.

Yes, after he had swallowed his first tranquillizer, Hargreave could reason like that and even close his mind to what he was doing. And on his second tranquillizer, at about noon, he even managed to turn the tables on Shitlips Lipschitz and Ivan Gregovich: once Olga was safely in Hong Kong to give her perjured evidence she would probably drop Ivan Gregovich right in the shit by denying (truthfully – that was the beauty of it) that she had heard Champion say a damn thing! And our illustrious Mr Shitlips Lipschitz would be apoplectic with fury, dancing from one foot to another in his inability to cross-examine and denounce his own witness as a liar . . . Mr Ivan Gregovich's confession would be admitted in evidence and the dear man would go down for twenty fucking years. *And the crowning beauty of all this was that Alistair Hargreave's conscience would be clear!*

That is how he felt during the early afternoon, but by five o'clock his nerves were stretched to breaking again. He went home and sat in the bleak, empty apartment drinking whisky, and this was his undoing: every night he promised himself he would have only two drinks, but the combination of whisky and drugs made him drunk quickly and the horrors of Moscow came crashing over him. He had another drink to thrust them aside, and then his subornation of perjury loomed large and terrible before him, shaming him; the thought of poetic justice did not assuage his guilt, and the only way he could handle it was to drink half the bottle. *Just remember that razor . . .* And then the thoughts came screaming up at him. *Supposing Lipschitz does not call Olga as a witness, suppose he suspects a trick, suppose Gregovich is convicted without Olga having been called to Hong Kong.* Hargreave wanted to bellow his fears to the night, snatch up the telephone and beg Lipschitz to call Olga as a witness, and all that mattered was Gregovich's acquittal.

He dared not try to telephone her himself: if he spoke to Olga at all Vladimir would surely be listening in, and doubtless tape-recording the conversation. Vladimir would smell a rat – and then Olga would surely not be coming to Hong Kong. The last thing he wanted was Vladimir having recorded evidence of Alistair Hargreave suborning perjury. No, he had to leave it all to Lipschitz, that was the only safe way. And then another terrible thought sprang at him: *If Olga doesn't come to Hong Kong and Gregovich is convicted you don't even have a plan to rescue her.*

He had no plan because he dared not make one: the only way to rescue Olga was to storm the apartment and shoot it out; he trusted nobody to do that and it would be fatal for Olga if Vladimir got wind of any such intention. Nor did he know where the apartment was. But he had to have a gun, at least, in Moscow. Thank God Olga still had hers, but he needed one of his own. How to get one? He dared not smuggle a firearm into Russia, that would blow the whole thing up in his face if he was caught. So he'd have to get one in Moscow. But how? He knew nobody there.

But Jake McAdam did, and Jake was a man of action. Besides, there would be the relief of talking about it to someone.

They met in McAdam's apartment the following day after work. But Hargreave could not tell him that Vladimir had forced him to agree to blow the Gregovich case: he did not want Jake's condemnation. Nor did he want to tell him of the connection between Olga and Gregovich. It was unfair to make Jake even the remotest of accomplices to perjury.

McAdam listened with concern to the expurgated story of his visit to Moscow. 'Jesus . . .' He got up and sloshed more whisky into Hargreave's glass. 'So what do you propose doing?'

'I'm going to pay them the hundred thousand dollars.' He took a deep breath. 'But I want a gun, Jake, just in case there's trouble.'

McAdam sighed. 'Jesus. A hundred thousand dollars.' But he did not comment further on what he thought of that. 'Yes, you sure need a gun. You'll need a battalion if there's trouble.' He sighed again. 'Yeah, I'm sure I can arrange for a gun in Moscow, the joint's bristling with them. But, Al? You're not a warrior, pal. You couldn't be efficient in a gunfight.'

'I did my national service in the army,' Hargreave said, 'I was on their marksmanship team.'

'Thirty years ago,' Jake said, 'with a rifle, not a pistol.'

'No, we competed with pistols too.'

'Al, you'll need help, pal, if there's trouble.'

'I daren't walk in with a bunch of guys – that'll *cause* trouble.'

'Not if there's enough of your guys.'

'Lord . . .' Hargreave rubbed his forehead. 'No. Can you imagine what it's like to see that razor at your woman's breast?' He shook his head. 'I'm not going to do anything to provoke trouble.'

McAdam thought a moment. 'But if you do need them? Of course, Moscow is full of gangs who offer so-called protection to businesses, but they're really just extortion rackets.' He got up, went to his study and returned with a booklet. 'This is called the *Moscow Directory*.' He flicked through it. 'A couple of detective agencies are listed. They'll organize a posse of muscle for you, I imagine.' He handed him the booklet. 'You can keep that.'

Hargreave took it. 'But do you think they'll be trustworthy? How do I know one of them won't tip off Vladimir?'

'I can ask my business associates in Moscow to recommend the most reliable bunch. But I guess nobody can vouch for the trustworthiness of musclemen. And you're right to worry about the police – *don't* involve them at this stage, many of them are crooked.'

'But the same applies to the detective agencies, perhaps?'

McAdam rubbed his face. Then said irritably, 'Jesus, Al, I don't want to get involved in a gunfight – not only do I have an aversion to dying prematurely, I'm a respectable businessman now, making a lot of money out of Russia.'

'Of course not,' Hargreave said earnestly. 'I wouldn't dream of asking you to. I'm only consulting you on how to get a gun.'

'Good.' McAdam sighed. He paced the floor. 'So, I arrange for your gun, you put it in your pocket, you go to meet the Mafia. Didn't you say they frisked you for weapons last time?'

'Yes, but this time I'll insist they meet me in my hotel, *with* Olga. This time I'll have the upper hand, because I've got the money in my pocket. They can't frisk me in a public place.'

McAdam snorted. 'No? They probably *own* the fucking hotel – or the management pays them protection money. But supposing they insist you go to them, like last time, and frisk you. Suddenly you're gunless again, and you've alerted them to your nasty nature.'

Hargreave considered this for a moment. 'So I need *two* guns.'

'Two guns?' Then McAdam grinned. 'Two-Gun Hargreave? The Fastest Gun in the East. That's how they'll ruefully remember you?' He burst into laughter.

Hargreave saw the funny side of it too. It was the first time he had laughed in weeks. Since Macao. And it was a relief to talk. He wiped his wrist across his eye and brought the discussion back to seriousness.

'So, if they find the first gun on me, the second one will be hidden somewhere. In my rented car. I'll reserve a car to be waiting for me at Moscow airport – perhaps you can arrange for the second gun to be concealed in that.'

McAdam nodded slowly. 'Yes, I suppose my associates can do that – they can rent the car for you, put a gun under the seat, leave the car keys at the Hertz desk at the airport. But how do you get that second gun into the apartment – where you'll need it – after they've relieved you of the first one?'

'At least I'll have it in the car as a getaway weapon.'

'A getaway?' McAdam shook his head. Alistair Hargreave, Q C, racing across Moscow making his getaway, shooting the shit out of pursuing Mafia vehicles? He dragged his hands down his face, thinking.

'The best trick is not to go to the apartment at all. You say they're making Olga work as a prostitute. Does she do outside calls – to hotels, for example?'

'I doubt it – they'd think she'd run away.'

'Not if she's guarded. I've seen girls arrive with guards in Moscow hotels, girls who've been sent for by guests. Happens all over the world. The guard is her driver, he's also there to protect her, make sure she gets her money.'

Lord – why hadn't he thought of this? 'Yes – she told me once that she used to do house-calls to the Metropole Hotel after she left Istanbul. Do you know the Metropole?'

McAdam nodded. 'One of the best in Moscow, I've stayed there a few times. Unfortunately too expensive for me usually.' He thought, then waved his finger at the telephone. 'We can call the Metropole right now, tell the concierge I'm calling from St Petersburg, staying at the Metropole next week, want to see my old flame Olga Romalova. And can he arrange it?' Then he snapped his fingers. 'And *you're* there, in the bedroom in the Metropole!' He chuckled: 'The dreaded Two-Gun Hargreave himself! And you overwhelm the guard! Sweep her into your arms and make your getaway down the fire escape.' He wiped the grin off his face. 'Sorry, Al. I'm serious, that may be the way to fly.'

Hargreave looked at him, thinking. 'But the concierge's response may be that Olga does not do hotel calls any more. So the next trick is to tell him I'm willing to go to *her*.' He spread his hands. 'The concierge arranges it, and off I go in a taxi. That way I find out the address! I cancel the visit at the last moment, return to my hotel and then hire some bodyguards! Then I telephone Vladimir and tell him to bring Olga to the hotel and collect the money. If Vladimir complies, well and good. On the other hand, if he insists I go to him, my bodyguards follow me. If I haven't emerged within five minutes, they come in and rescue us.' He looked at McAdam earnestly and took a tense breath. 'But that's exactly what I'm scared of. I'm terrified of Olga getting hurt in a shoot-out.'

'Sure, but you're talking sense now. You'll need help, my friend.'

Hargreave sighed. 'Yes, I will.'

'Olga getting hurt is better than her having her tit cut off. I know

235

my associates pay protection money to some gang of so-called karate experts. They're all crooks of course – but my friends seem satisfied with their deal. Perhaps they're the boys for you, at least they're known to us. I'll give my associates a discreet call tonight, if you like.'

'Many thanks, Jake,' Hargreave breathed.

'However, that's the worst scenario – it may be possible to get Olga to come to the Metropole Hotel. Your bodyguards get rid of Olga's thug for you, and you make a run for it.' He smiled. 'That way you save a hundred thousand dollars, pal. So?' He indicated the telephone again. 'Want me to phone the Metropole right now, find out if it's possible?'

Oh God. Hargreave wished he could tell Jake the whole truth – that all this might not be necessary, that Olga was probably coming to Hong Kong. 'No, not yet. It may alert the Mafia, especially if the concierge starts asking you awkward questions. When I go to Moscow I'll go to the Metropole and see what's possible. Then I'll hire the muscle, before I send for Olga.'

'That's right,' McAdam said. He felt very sorry for his friend. 'Oh, Al, the things I do for you . . . Look, I've got to go to Moscow soon anyway, I might as well go this week and make enquiries for you – I'm a better judge of muscle than you.'

Hargreave looked up gratefully. 'Many thanks, Jake.'

McAdam sighed. 'I admire your guts but you shouldn't be relying on your own judgement, Al. In fact you shouldn't be doing this at all, you're the DPP, for God's sake.'

Hargreave had to suppress a flash of anger – his nerves could not take criticism. 'So what do I do, leave Olga to her fate?'

'No . . .' McAdam shook his head. 'No, you love her, for Christ's sake. I'd do the same myself. Al,' he sighed, 'I'll do this for you, but I can't be there when you get into trouble. But as you say, most probably there'll be none, all the bastards want is your money.'

And Gregovich's acquittal. 'Of course, I wouldn't dream of asking you to be there.'

'Okay, so what date do you think you'll arrive?'

'The day after the Gregovich trial finishes. I'll have to fax the flight details to your friends. Signed . . . David Johnson.'

'David? Okay, Dave. But why the hell don't you leave the Gregovich trial to Findlay, and get your ass to Moscow with me?'

If only he could tell Jake the whole truth, his plan to get Olga to come to Hong Kong, that the guns were only a contingency plan. But he could not admit his guilt, his nerves could not stand the opprobrium.

236

'It's a case of international importance – and there's going to be a lot of criticism for allowing the importation of uranium. I must be there to face the music.'

McAdam sighed. He paced again. 'So you show up in Moscow, there's trouble, you grab Olga and dash to your rented car with your body-guards. Then what do you do?'

'Drive like hell for the airport.'

McAdam snorted. 'They'll chase you and overtake you – but even if they don't what happens when you get there? The Gunfight at the O K Airport? The aeroplane won't be waiting there especially for Two-Gun Hargreave and his pretty companion.' He shook his head. 'You *don't* drive to the international airport. You must drive to another airfield where a chartered aircraft is waiting for you.'

'You know of one?'

McAdam picked up the *Moscow Directory* again. 'Here we are: Stardust Air Services. Helicopters or fixed wing, competitive rates. American outfit. It'll cost you – but at least they'll be waiting for you, all night if necessary.'

It didn't matter what it cost. 'And fly where?'

'The hell out of Moscow, that's where. Helsinki, I should think. Look at an atlas. But, Al, if the Mafia are in pursuit you've got to shake them off, by changing cars to confuse them. That means a second rented car must be waiting for you somewhere. The best place to switch cars is a multi-storey car park – enter in one car, drive out in another.' He frowned. 'I've seen one somewhere in downtown Moscow. I'll find it. I'll fax you a map, showing where everything is, the airfield, the car park, et cetera.'

Hargreave pressed his face with his hands. 'I'm so grateful, Jake.' And, God, he hoped all this wasn't necessary.

McAdam put his hand on Hargreave's shoulder. 'You look like death.' He left out, 'I hope she's worth it.'

So he had some sort of plan, and he felt better. He would have two guns awaiting him in Moscow, and Olga probably still had hers: and he *would* hire muscle, after he'd seen the lie of the land. But in the cold light of day he doubted he would succeed in pulling off the Metro-pole Hotel trick and saving a hundred thousand dollars; he doubted the Mafia would send her out on hotel-calls even if she was guarded at the time – she was the hostage. They just might – she'd said they were making her work – but he had little hope.

For three days after McAdam left for Moscow Hargreave was feverish with worry lest Jake's enquiries reached Vladimir's ears. On the fourth day McAdam telephoned.

'Don't interrupt,' he said flatly, 'and don't mention any names, I want to make this brief because you never know with telephones. Here goes: the hardware samples you wanted have been arranged. Both are with my associate here. When you know your arrival dates, a rented vehicle will be waiting for you where you asked it to be and one sample will be in it.' He paused. 'As regards the other help, my associates recommended their employees and I went to check them out today. All these types are questionable, but allowing for that they looked all right to me. Young and fit, and their boss was impressive. Of course, I mentioned no names except my own. I'll leave a note for you with the hardware. Plus the details of the car park mentioned. Got that?'

Relief. 'Yes. Thank you.'

'As regards the aviation, I spoke to them on the telephone and they're eager for business. Any destination is no problem, provided you can afford it. Prices not too bad, considering the service you're getting. Right, that's it. Are you sure you don't want me to contact that hotel and find out the possibilities?'

Hargreave closed his eyes. 'Quite sure, thank you. Leave it to me. And Jake – I'm so grateful.'

'No *names*. Right, I'm off to London. It's over to you now. Good luck.'

Hargreave put down the telephone and held his face. *Thank God for Jake McAdam.*

He poured a big dash of whisky and took a gulp. To celebrate: if the worst came to the worst, if Olga didn't come to Hong Kong, he would have help in Moscow. And maybe he *could* get her sent to the Metropole and save a hundred thousand bucks!

Just please God Vladimir doesn't find Olga's gun . . . And that she doesn't do anything stupid with it, like try to shoot her own way out.

But above all, please God Arnie Lipschitz calls Olga to Hong Kong so Jake's good work is unnecessary.

Of course Lipschitz will. He's got to – Olga's evidence will be invaluable to Gregovich.

That night Hargreave drank half a bottle of whisky. He went to bed almost happy.

When he woke up, hungover, his relief had gone, and he was consumed with worry again. What if Vladimir heard of Jake's enquiries? Had Jake mentioned to the muscleman boss what kind of job it was? And today he had the very worrisome business of preparing to borrow a hundred thousand dollars, in case Olga did not come to Hong Kong. Indeed he had to borrow more – he had to be able to pay the musclemen in cash, and he had no idea how much that would be. Five thousand dollars for a night's work? Ten? And how much would the charter aircraft cost?

It was Friday; Gregovich's trial was starting on Monday, he could delay no longer – if Olga didn't come to Hong Kong he had to be on the next plane to Moscow with the cash in his pocket. He found his mutual-fund portfolio and the title deeds to his London house, and made an appointment with Derek Morrison of the Hongkong & Shanghai bank.

'Hell, Alistair,' the banker said, 'a hundred and fifty thousand is a lot of money. And you're already in the red with us, we paid your credit-card bill for the Westin Resort Hotel a week ago.'

Hargreave felt sick. Already overdrawn? 'My salary will cover that at the end of the month. I can pay this hundred and fifty thou off at the rate of nine or ten thousand a month. You'll have my mutual funds and title deed as security.'

Derek raised his eyebrows. 'I doubt you can pay off ten thousand dollars a month, Al. Anyway, what exactly do you need this money for?'

Hargreave steeled himself to perpetrate another crime. 'For divorce purposes. To try to buy off Elizabeth with a lump sum.'

Derek frowned. Then he consulted Hargreave's file.

'But you're married in community of property under Californian law, Al. She'll want a lot more than a hundred and fifty thousand.'

'It should be enough. She's already got the two Californian houses, I put them in her name.'

The manager looked at the mutual-fund portfolio, then punched buttons on his computer. Then he used his calculator.

'Alistair,' he said, 'your mutual funds are worth only eighty-two thousand dollars at the moment.'

Hargreave's heart sank. 'Lord ... I reckoned about a hundred thousand.'

Derek shook his head. 'There's been a world recession, mutual funds go down as well as up.'

'But they'll go up again?'

'In the long term. Meanwhile you'll be paying us substantial interest on the loan, Al.'

'But my London house will give you security for the balance.'

'I thought you said Elizabeth has gone to live in the London house.'

'She has, but I'm entitled to half at least – though I paid for all of it.'

'But,' Derek said, 'she's established occupancy rights, hasn't she? She can claim it as the matrimonial home in the divorce. Al,' he sighed, 'the Hongkong & Shanghai Bank is very reluctant to take as security property which will be the subject of a divorce action.'

Oh God. He had dreaded borrowing the money but he hadn't dreamt it would be refused him. 'So, what's my alternative?'

'Sell the mutual funds now, and take your eighty-two thou – though I wouldn't recommend that. Alternatively, try to sell the London house from under Liz – I'm saying this in confidence, please, because I like Liz. But real estate values are down too and you'll have to take a very disappointing price.'

'But houses take ages to sell. And Liz will take out injunctions to stop me.'

'Yes.'

Oh Lord. 'You've got to help me, Derek.' He added: 'And I've got the government pension when I retire.'

'Yes, but I'm loath to trust a Hong Kong pension after 1997. The *houses* are your real pension, Al. But Liz has got 'em. And –' He leafed through his file. 'And she owns your three life insurance policies.' He looked at him sympathetically. 'Alistair, you're in bad shape for a divorce.'

This advice his nerves couldn't stand. 'I earn a very good salary!'

'Yes, you do. But why the rush to buy Elizabeth off, Al?' He looked at him narrowly. 'This hasn't got anything to do with that beautiful Russian lass who does the tango, has it?'

Hargreave tried not to avert his eyes. And this was definitely it – the crime of obtaining money by false pretences. 'Not directly.' He blundered on: 'I want to marry her, yes. But I've got to settle with Elizabeth first.'

Derek was embarrassed. 'Don't mean to be offensive, but it's not to . . . to buy your girl out, is it? Out of her employment?'

Hargreave felt that his nerves could not stand these lies. But he *did* have the mutual funds and the London house to back up the loan! He forced himself to look his friend in the eye. 'Certainly not.'

Derek Morrison sat back. He sighed, then said, 'Okay, Alistair, I'll give you the loan. Just sign the documents and tell us how you want the dough, banker's draft, or whatever. But it's the last one, my friend. You're skating on thin ice now.'

Hargreave left the bank feeling limp with relief: he had the money and he had a contingency plan. Thank God for friends. He walked across

Queens Road to the Mandarin Hotel, went up to the quiet Chinnery Bar where none of his acquaintances were likely to find him at this time of the day. He drank a cold San Miguel down, down, to give his heart a kick-start, then he ordered a whisky. *He had the ransom, and he had a plan* . . . He ordered another whisky.

Then the guilt set in again: he had just obtained a loan of a hundred and fifty thousand US dollars by false pretences, for Christ's sake, he had just committed the crime of fraud on top of the crime of perjury. And he had to drink several whiskies to try to dull his nerves, to try to convince himself that Alistair Hargreave QC was not really a despicable bastard who broke his professional oaths, not a bastard like Arnie Lipschitz whom the whole profession despised – he had only done what any red-blooded man would do to save his girl from unspeakable atrocities – and what he had done might even result in poetic justice! As regards Derek's loan he really *did* have the assets to back it up even if he had bent the truth. But if he came unstuck he would end his career in shame, if not in jail, a pathetic figure of a public servant who had fallen among thieves 'over a whore' – that's how he would be remembered. And not only that – he was almost bankrupt. Between divorce and Vladimir he was almost technically bankrupt – what a terrible end to an illustrious, hard-won career. But he didn't care about the money, he would pay it back somehow: he just prayed that those guns wouldn't be necessary, that Gregovich's confession would be thrown out and that acquittal would follow . . .

And please God, make Arnie Lipschitz telephone and tell me Olga's coming to Hong Kong.

He was on his fifth whisky when he could stand the suspense no longer; he reached across the bar for the telephone and dialled Arnie Lipschitz's chambers. And, to his enormous relief, Lipschitz accepted his call.

'Yes, Al?'

Hargreave's guilty heart was knocking. He tried to speak confidently: 'Arnie, the trial starts on Monday; I'm going sailing for the weekend and it occurred to me that if you wanted me to speak to Olga Romalova, to introduce you to her, it better be done immediately.'

Lipschitz chuckled. 'Where are you, Al?'

Hargreave's heart leapt in hope. 'I'm having coffee in the Mandarin, if you'd care to join me? Then we'll go to my place and telephone.'

Arnie Lipschitz chuckled again. 'Coffee? Sounds like something stronger to me. No, I've already dealt with Olga Romalova, she is my witness and I don't want you talking to her at all before the trial,

241

thank you very much. So have a nice sail. See you in court, Al.'

The telephone clicked. Hargreave stared across the bar; then a smile spread across his exhausted face, and he wanted to whoop for joy.

So Olga was coming to Hong Kong! *I've already dealt with Olga, she is my witness.* Thank God! He wanted to shout it down the bar, wanted to buy everybody a drink. The crushing weight that had fallen off his shoulders – and the *money* saved – a hundred thousand plus!

Hargreave clutched his face and laughed into his hands. All that danger had melted away, all that money had been saved! He quaffed back his whisky and left, walking on air.

'Have a nice sail,' Lipschitz had said – and, by God, that was what he was going to do! Get out of those nerve-racking chambers, out of that empty apartment, get out of himself into the clean open sea and feel the wind in his hair and those surges of natural power purging him of all his horrors and tensions!

He strode across Statue Square towards the Supreme Court feeling a man again, a smile in his heart. He went into his chambers, picked up his copy of the Gregovich file, left a message for Findlay to meet him on Monday morning for a final pre-trial conference, told Miss Ho he was taking a powder for the weekend. He took the elevator to the basement, got into his car and drove through the teeming traffic to the yacht club, smiling all the way.

His boat was now repaired, and seeing her lying there at her mooring made him feel purged already. 'Hello, my beauty!' He could almost see and hear Olga clambering around her, exclaiming. He climbed aboard, unlocked the forward hatch, grabbed a bottle of whisky and started the engine. He went to the bows and unslipped her from the buoy. He went back to the wheel, put her into forward gear and swung out of the lanes.

He went chugging through the yacht basin, past the clubhouse, through the little harbour mouth, and out into the fairway. With a song in his heart. He was still in his suit, the wind blowing his hair and tie. He motored down the fairway, then he threw off the headsail sheet. There was a whirr as the sail unfolded, then billowed, and a lurch as it filled. The yacht went creaming between the ferries and junks, and Hargreave filled his lungs and threw his arms aloft and bellowed to the skies.

'*Olga Romalova is coming to Hong Kong!*'

That night he lay at anchor off Lamma Island.

He sprawled in the cockpit in shorts, finishing the bottle of whisky, staring up at the stars. Oh, he was happy. Some time next week Olga would be here, the nightmare finally over, next weekend she would be with him on this boat, she would be with him every day thereafter for the rest of his life. And because he wouldn't have to pay the ransom they would have enough money for him to quit in 1997 after all! And they would just sail this lovely boat away, heading for the Philippines, and from there through the Indonesian islands, up the Strait of Malacca, and from there to the Seychelles in the Indian Ocean, the whole of Africa beyond. Oh, they were going to have a lovely life . . .

And it was a wonderful bonus that his guilty conscience had been cleared by this: Arnie Lipschitz had done the dirty work and suborned Olga! Alistair Hargreave had not had to open his mouth beyond suggesting that Olga *might* have heard – which could even be true! And though he had certainly been less than truthful with Derek Morrison, he did not have to borrow the money now, so his conscience was clear on that one too! Everything had turned out beautifully! Yes, he had been lucky – this fool of a client had been lucky with his lawyer!

He slept deeply that night, with the torments of the last weeks thrown off him. Nor, after that first night, did he have another drink the whole weekend: he woke up that Saturday morning feeling wonderful, and he resolved to pull himself together. He had been drinking too much. He stuck to his resolve as he sent his boat creaming across the sea around the multitude of Hong Kong's islands, letting the sun and wind cleanse him, driving out the last vestiges of demons: it was wonderful to be alive! And even at this moment Olga may be flying to China!

In the late afternoon on Sunday he got back to the yacht club, his skin glowing from the sun and wind, his mind clear and rested. He drove to his gymnasium and worked out on the machines for the first time since he had left Macao, almost enjoying the effort. Then he had a long sauna. At the health bar he wolfed down a large rare steak sandwich on wholemeal bread, with a big salad. He felt good and exhausted as he drove up the Peak to his bare apartment, his body tingling with exercise and sun and good nourishment, his heart tingling with anticipation of Olga. He swallowed a sleeping pill to make sure of a good night's rest before the trial, and went to bed.

He lay there a moment, then he heaved himself up again. He knelt down and tried to concentrate: he offered up a rusty prayer of thanks to the Lord.

PART VII

28

The Supreme Court of Hong Kong is a dull, modern, towering block in the heart of the city, standing amongst the gleaming Bank of China, Citibank Corp, the Lippo Centre, the Regency Towers Hotel, Admiralty Towers, all trying to outdo each other in height and grandeur, all interlaced with ugly, sweeping, roaring, daunting flyovers and underpasses and walk-overs. The Supreme Court, in Hargreave's opinion, failed totally in the competition. Where was the imposing façade characteristic of halls of justice? It was outclassed even by the silly Lippo Centre with its corncob balconies. And within this new, soulless courthouse where banks of elevators served floor after floor of courtrooms like a department store, the decor was worse: where were the dark oak-panelled walls, the coats of arms? The courtrooms looked like giant saunas, the panelling pine-yellow, and the coat of arms traditionally placed above the judge's bench had been omitted because in 1997 the red flag of China would be nailed up there.

Hargreave was tense when he arrived early that Monday morning for his pre-trial conference with Findlay and Champion, and very excited: perhaps even today Olga was going to walk into his courtroom. He put on his butterfly collar and tied his white cravat. Then he paced around his chambers, trying to calm himself, trying to convince himself that now he was guiltless – Olga was not *his* witness, *he* had not spoken to her about her evidence, *he* would not be leading any perjury from her, that was up to Lipschitz, it was for the judge to decide whether she was a credible witness. It wouldn't be his fault if that long drink of water Judge Wilkins, who had been assigned to the case, was so scared of being reversed on appeal that he bent over backwards to believe defence witnesses. Then, at five minutes past eight, Findlay entered his chambers.

'Isn't it good news about Wilkins?'

'What about him?'

'The dear man's got flu and taken to his bed. I phoned you at home on Saturday and left a message on your answering machine. So good ole Harry Walters has been assigned as our judge, just the guy we want!'

Hargreave tried not to look perturbed, but his heart sank. Walters was a tough no-nonsense judge – the very opposite of Wilky Wilkins. The Honourable Mr Justice Walters had spent twenty years as prosecuting counsel before going up on the Supreme Court bench and if any judge was going to believe the police witnesses and let Gregovich's confession into evidence it was Walters J. Hargreave turned away to conceal his anxiety. But Olga was coming, Lipschitz had said so on Friday, he must stop panicking.

'Yes,' he said. 'Yes, that is good news.'

There was a knock on the door and Champion walked in, beaming. 'Hey – I hear we've got Judge Walters!'

'Yes,' Findlay grinned.

'Thank God. Milky-Wilky loves throwing out my confessions, thinks I'm a rough diamond. I'm less charitable – I think he's a prick. Anyway,' he rubbed his hands, 'what's the order of battle, boss?'

'Sit down, gentlemen.' They sat. Hargreave had difficulty concentrating. 'Anybody on the jury list that I should challenge?'

'No,' Champion said, 'the names all look harmless to me. Mostly Chinese, and quite a lot of women, but there're eleven whites, all male, all respectable businessmen. I don't think any of them is going to be sympathetic to a Russian gangster importing uranium to their colony.'

'Trouble is,' Findlay said, 'they mightn't be sympathetic to you either, for letting it happen. You can expect a roasting.'

'I'll handle it,' Champion said confidently, 'I didn't *permit* anything.'

'Don't get into an argument with Lipschitz.' Findlay warned, 'just tell it straight.'

'Sure, I know Shitlips of old.'

Hargreave sighed. 'Okay,' he said. 'Champion will be my first witness. Let's get the *voir dire* on the admissibility of the confession out of the way at the outset.' That meant Olga must arrive tomorrow at the latest. He could not bear to wait until later in the week for that to happen.

Findlay sat forward. 'I've been thinking about that, Al. Wouldn't it be better – to put the jury in the picture at the outset – to make Kozkov our first witness? Kozkov starts at the beginning of our story, he tells us how he received the suitcase at Moscow airport, without a key, brought it to Hong Kong, he got arrested. He sees Gregovich for the first time, also being arrested. The jury immediately has a picture of Gregovich's guilty involvement with the suitcase of uranium. Then we call Inspector Sullivan, who tells us how he hands over the suitcase to Professor Donovan at military HQ for examination. But the professor can't open it because he doesn't know the number of the combination lock – until Champion, much later, telephones and gives him the number. The jury knows Gregovich is in Champion's custody, so they *know* Gregovich must have told Champion the number – now the jury is convinced Gregovich is guilty. And so is the judge. Then we call Kerensky to tell us what he can about the black market in nuclear materials – that will really worry the jury. *Then*, we call Champion – and he tells us Gregovich eventually made a statement. Lipschitz objects because, he says, it was not made voluntarily. But the jury doesn't care – they're convinced he's guilty anyway. Then we send the jury out and hold the *voir dire* in front of the judge – even if the confession *is* thrown out the jury are still convinced he's guilty when they come back in to hear the defence evidence.'

Champion sat back. 'I absolutely agree – that's the most convincing order in which to present the Crown evidence, Al.'

Of course it was the most convincing sequence and that's why Hargreave wasn't going to do it – until Olga was safely in Hong Kong he had to do whatever he could to ensure Gregovich's acquittal. When Olga was here he could turn around and go all out for a conviction, but before that he dared not. So the sooner she got here the better, and that meant holding the *voir dire* over the confession straight away because that was the matter she would testify about.

'No, I want to clear the decks, then we know how strong we are. So, Champion is my first witness.'

Champion and Findlay both looked dissatisfied. Findlay said, 'But if the confession *is* thrown out –'

'It won't be,' Champion muttered.

'– but if it is, we've still got enough evidence for a conviction, so I think my suggestion is best.'

'Hell, yes,' Champion said. 'The key. The combination lock.'

Hargreave said, 'But I can guarantee you that Lipschitz's defence is going to be that Champion got the key from Koskov and planted it on Gregovich, that Kozkov knew the combination lock's number, told it to Simonski and Simonski forced Gregovich to mention it in the confession. So without the confession, our evidence will be pretty thin. I'd like to know as soon as possible how vulnerable we are.' He stood up, to end the conference. 'Very well, gentlemen, see you in court in half an hour. Go'n get togged-up,' he said to Findlay.

Findlay left the room, looking less than happy. Champion waited until the door closed, then he said, 'Al, Findlay's right about calling Kozkov first. Getting the jury on our side from the start.'

Hargreave's nerves twitched. 'No, Bernie, you're first. Or maybe I'll call Kerensky first, just to establish a bit of background, but then you'll be next.'

'This is *my* big case, Al,' Champion objected.

And mine. 'You wanted me to prosecute it personally. So don't argue with my decisions, please.'

Champion sighed and stood up. 'Sure. And I'm grateful, Al, I know you'll do a great job.'

'See you in court, Bernie.'

'But Al – how're things? I hear Liz has gone to London?'

'Yes. It's all over. Divorce, now.'

'Well, it's for the best, I think,' Champion said sympathetically. 'And the other girl, Al? No word from her?'

'No.'

'Well,' Champion said, 'maybe that's for the best too.' Champion slapped his big hand on his shoulder: 'So let's get drunk together when this case is over. Meanwhile . . .' he punched his palm: 'Let's get in there and give 'em hell!'

At five minutes to ten Findlay fetched him and they left for the court, in their wigs and gowns. They crossed the big atrium to the elevators and rode up to the seventh floor.

About fifty jurors were milling outside the courtroom. Most of them Chinese. Hargreave and Findlay entered Court Fourteen.

The public benches were filled. About a dozen members of his staff were there, to see their boss open the case, and there were a number of well-dressed colonial wives, come to see the infamous Al Hargreave. He recognized most of them. Elizabeth's friends. The two long press tables were fully occupied: he identified the correspondents for *Time*, *Newsweek*, the *Economic Review*, all habitués of the Foreign Correspondents' Club. The court registrar and shorthand-writer were at their seats below the judge's bench. Champion was waiting at the bar, two of his Chinese detectives sitting immediately behind him. Lipschitz and his instructing solicitors were clustered in conference further down. Hargreave had his first sight of Ivan Gregovich, the bastard who had caused all his misery. And the man made his blood run cold.

Gregovich was over six feet, strongly built, handsome in a hawkish way. His hair was black, his nose slightly hooked, his lips thin, his chin cleft, his neck broad. He exuded cunning and a lean, physical power. The eyes were pale blue, very alert and penetrating. The lids were heavy, the eyelashes thick. And the eyebrows: very black, vigorous, long, giving the face a daunting mien. Hargreave wondered again how

Champion and Simonski had made a tough bastard like this confess.

Findlay whispered, 'Nice-looking swine, isn't he?'

Hargreave went to his place at the bar, put his file down. 'Good morning, Arnold,' he said loudly. In his black gown and his white wig over his Levantine nose and beetling brow, Lipschitz always reminded Hargreave of a vulture. *Lord*, he hated the crooked little bastard.

'Morning,' Lipschitz scowled. He reverted to his conference with the solicitors.

'Vintage Shitlips charm,' Findlay muttered.

Hargreave sat, and Champion and Findlay took their seats on either side of him. Hargreave glanced at Gregovich again: he had shaved off the goatee beard and had a neat haircut, but that face was still devilish.

Champion muttered, 'Gregovich and Lipschitz make a fine-looking pair, don't they?

Findlay said softly: 'The jury will think they both should be in the dock.'

Hargreave pressed his fingertips to his eyelids. He had to keep reminding himself that this was a trial he was supposed to lose – but once Olga was here he could go for a conviction.

Then the registrar was telling everybody to get ready. Lipschitz asked Gregovich to get into the dock. The man sauntered into the big wooden box. Everybody sat down. The prospective jurors crowded in around the entrance. Silence fell.

There was a rap on the door, the registrar called 'Court . . .' and everybody stood.

The Honourable Mr Justice Walters entered in his red robes and wig. He was a big man in his mid-fifties, with a pleasant, florid face under bushy eyebrows. Hargreave liked him: he was one of his horse-racing friends. His pleasant manner belied a hard-boiled lawyer who didn't treat criminals gently. He walked to his high carved chair on the bench, and bowed to counsel. Counsel bowed to him. Then everybody sat again, except the registrar who intoned:

'Regina versus Ivan Gregovich.'

Hargreave found his heart knocking. He stood again. 'May it please your Lordship, I appear for Crown, with my learned friend Mr Findlay.' He sat. The judge gave him a pleasant smile and nodded. Lipschitz rose. 'May it please your Lordship, I appear for the defendant, instructed by Denison, Wu and Partners.' He sat, glowering.

The registrar picked up the indictment and said to the defendant, 'Please stand up. Are you Ivan Gregovich?'

'Yes, sir,' Gregovich said.

The registrar read the indictment. When he had finished he said, 'Do you understand the charge, Ivan Gregovich?'

'Yes, sir.'

'How plead you to the charge? Guilty or not guilty?'

'Not guilty, sir.'

The registrar lifted the box containing the names of all the jurors who had been summonsed, and shook it. Then he reached into it and pulled out a piece of paper with the first name on it. The process of jury-selection began.

The start of a jury trial tingles the nerves of most counsel, no matter how battle-hardened they may be.

When he was a young prosecution lawyer, Alistair Hargreave liked trials by jury because of the drama, the romance of the courtroom and this ancient procedure where ordinary, inexpert people sit in judgement on matters of life and death. As he became older he grew to detest jury trials: he resented that ordinary people should decide the case he had worked on expertly, people with no judicial experience, almost totally ignorant of the law, imbued with profound misconceptions and prejudices, most of them unable to present an articulate argument, let alone a logical one, ordinary people who can so often be misled. You can bullshit a jury whereas you can seldom bullshit a judge. Hargreave had no confidence in a jury's powers of concentration or memory; he had hardly ever seen a juror make a note of any evidence, he had *never* seen a juror even try to make a note of *all* the evidence. He doubted that when the law was explained to them they understood it properly, let alone remembered it. In short, he resented the hit-or-miss uncertainties inherent in jury trials: surely justice, of all things, should be reliable? Of course, defence lawyers loved the uncertainties: but a conscientious hard-working prosecution lawyer, whose duty it is to serve the law-abiding public, gets very angry when he sees justice aborted by bullshit.

But today Hargreave was grateful for the inherent uncertainties, for he wanted this evil bastard acquitted. Until Olga was in Hong Kong he had to do everything in his power to play it safe: he *wanted* there to be a miscarriage of justice. And now that the trial was beginning any thoughts of poetic justice went out the window. And yet, when the first juror was called and entered the jury box, his instincts as a prosecutor made him want to challenge him: he was a young Chinese who did not look very bright. Had this been an ordinary trial Hargreave would have challenged him, for who wants a young, dumb juror sitting

252

in judgement? But today was not a young, dumb juror best for Grego-vich? So Hargreave held his tongue: but immediately Champion nudged him, and Findlay whispered, 'Challenge him!'

Hargreave felt irritated. But he rose and said, 'May this juror stand by, my Lord?'

'Yes.'

As the bemused young man walked self-consciously out of the jury box again, Lipschitz leapt to his feet and started his usual tactics. '*Why*, my Lord?' he demanded. 'On what grounds can my learned friend possibly object to this juror?'

Hargreave sighed. 'My learned friend knows perfectly well the Crown is not required to supply reasons for a challenge.'

'I'm talking about *justice*, my Lord,' Lipschitz cried, his eyes big. 'My learned friend has no just grounds for getting rid of this gentleman! I defy Mr Hargreave to come clean and tell us what he's up to!'

Hargreave smiled, but inwardly he seethed – this was vintage Lip-schitz, creating the impression amongst the waiting jurors that the Crown was up to dirty tricks. Before he could respond the judge said, 'Sit down, Mr Lipschitz, Mr Hargreave is quite right.'

Lipschitz threw up his hands in theatrical despair and sat, scowling. But he had scored: now the waiting jurors probably suspected that not only Hargreave was up to something sinister but the judge as well. Hargreave's blood was rising, despite himself. The registrar called the next name.

And this juror Hargreave had to challenge: the man was an elderly Chinese, frail, with a nervous grin and a twitching eyelid. As he shuffled into the jury box, Hargreave said: 'Stand by, please.'

Lipschitz leapt to his feet again. 'My Lord! Is my learned friend trying to turn this into the O. J. Simpson trial? Never in all my years at the bar have I seen such astonishing discrimination by the Crown against Chinese!'

Jesus – now he was being branded a racist as well. Hargreave said:

'And never have I seen such misunderstanding of elementary law by learned counsel, my Lord. If I didn't know my learned friend better I would think he was trying to create the impression that I am a xenopho-bic persecutor. I would be most grateful if my Lord would explain the law on challenges to my learned friend.'

'Mr Lipschitz,' the judge said, 'you know the law, please sit down.'

'Justice, my Lord,' Lipschitz cried, 'must not only be done, it must be *seen* to be done, by the public and by the defendant! *That* is the overriding law, in my respectful submission, and my learned friend is today departing from it for reasons which worry me deeply. This poor man –' he pointed at Gregovich – 'is a stranger to our shores! From a country where justice is very rough, and he deserves – nay he has a legal *right* – to understand his own trial! And that cannot be the case if he is bemused, and mentally harassed, by incomprehensible and apparently persecutory manoeuvres by the Crown to pack the jury!'

Hargreave rose, goaded despite himself. 'My learned friend will please withdraw that remark.'

'Yes, Mr Lipschitz,' the judge said, 'you will withdraw that remark.'

Lipschitz turned smarmy. 'I said *apparent* manoeuvres, my Lord – and indeed that's how they appear to the defendant and public. However –' he held up his palms – 'for peace, I withdraw the remark. But I very much doubt that the defendant, and public, are reassured.'

Hargreave wanted to retort, but held his tongue – he had to lose this case.

'Mr Hargreave,' the judge said. 'For peace, would you like to explain to Mr Lipschitz why you challenged those two jurors?'

Hargreave stood up again.

'I'm indebted to my Lord for pouring oil on unnecessarily troubled waters. For the sake of peace and appearance I will explain in the hopes that my learned friend, his wealth of experience evidently having failed him, will cease his objections. My Lord, I challenged the first juror on account of his youthfulness. I challenged the second juror on account of his apparent frailty. Racism did not enter into it, and I resent the insinuation that it did. I am only a humble lawyer, my Lord, with a trifling twenty-five years' experience, but in my submission it is in the interests of justice that jurors are both mature and reasonably robust.'

The judge smiled. 'Thank you. So let us proceed.'

Lipschitz sighed injuredly, with a long-suffering glance at the waiting jurors.

The registrar called the next name: 'Trevor Arthur Davidson.'

A middle-aged white man emerged from the crowd of prospective jurors and walked into the jury box. Hargreave did not challenge him.

And then local legal history was made: the next six names to be called out all belonged to white males. One after the other the English names came out of the registrar's box, and they filed into the jury box.

And there sat a Hong Kong prosecutor's dream, a jury of seven stalwart white men, good and true, the Queen's English their mother tongue, all mature businessmen who would not be so easy to bullshit. '*Wow* . . .' Findlay breathed. '*Excellent*,' Champion whispered. Hargreave

254

could hardly believe his eyes: never had he seen this in Hong Kong, and under other circumstances he would have been delighted. But in this case he was alarmed – this was a convicting jury if ever he had seen one. Then, in a furious flurry, Lipschitz was on his feet.

'My *Lord*!' he cried.

'Are you addressing me, or the Almighty?' Walters J asked with a thin smile. 'Should I presume you have a challenge or two, Mr Lipschitz?'

'Indeed I have,' Lipschitz cried. His eyes were afire, his face creased in genuine, outraged incredulity. 'Oh indeed, *indeed*! What the Crown has achieved is truly astonishing! My learned friend has succeeded in flying in the face of justice by securing an all-white, all-male jury in this Chinese colony! In this city on the China coast that is bursting with Chinese people – and my learned friend has pulled an all-white jury of businessmen out of his hat! To pronounce judgement in this Hong Kong court on a humble Russian, at that! Oh –' Lipschitz gave a bow and an unctuous smile to the jurymen – 'I cast no aspersions on the *integrity* of these seven gentlemen! Unlike my learned friend, I do not complain of their immaturity or health. What I am saying is that this jury is unrepresentative of this Chinese colony! Both in race and gender! And therefore it is unjust –'

'Make your challenges, Mr Lipschitz! And provide reasons for each challenge.'

Arnold Lipschitz turned to the jury with an incredulous expression. 'The *Crown* does not have to provide reasons, but the defence does . . .'

'That is the law, Mr Lipschitz,' the judge snapped, 'and you know it! Now get on with it!'

'That is the law, my Lord, but in my respectful submission it is a bad, patently unjust law!'

'It has been the law for hundreds of years and the historical reason is probably that the Crown may have knowledge about a citizen's background, he may be known to the authorities as a type of person who may not serve the interests of justice. Now challenge the jurors, Mr Lipschitz, or sit down!'

Lipschitz said earnestly, 'I am indebted to my Lord, and I will do as bidden. But I wish to make it clear that I am challenging the justice of this archaic law which gives such a grossly unfair advantage to the Crown – and indeed I will bring the matter up before the Law Society. I am not challenging the integrity of these seven gentlemen.' He gave them a bleak smile, and sat down slowly with a long-suffering sigh.

'Jesus,' Hargreave whispered.

'What,' said Judge Walters, 'no challenges, after all that?'

255

Lipschitz rose piously, his eyes liquid with suffering: 'No, my Lord. My innocent but bemused client places his life in the hands of this jury.'

Hargreave could not let him get away with this. He rose. 'As my learned friend is obviously so distrustful of this jury, I offer, out of the goodness of my heart, to challenge two jurors for him, and let's see who else comes out of the hat! By the law of averages they are likely to be Chinese, and may even be of the fairer sex he seems to so lament the absence of!'

'No . . .' Lipschitz held up his hands in piety. 'No, my client does not wish to take advantage of anyone, not even the Crown. No matter how fair it would be to do so after what we've seen today.'

Findlay and Champion groaned. But Hargreave let it go: Gregovich could not complain that he had not made the offer. The judge said:

'Mr Registrar, please swear in the jury.'

And so Hargreave rose to open the case for the Crown.

'May it please my Lord, and gentlemen of the jury. I represent the Crown. It is my solemn duty to lay before you, fair and square, the evidence against the defendant. I repeat: fair and square. And let me emphasize at the outset – as I'm sure both my learned friend and my Lord will do when they address you – that it is for the Crown to prove the defendant's guilt beyond reasonable doubt, not for the defendant to prove his innocence. If, at the end of all the evidence, you have a reasonable doubt about his guilt, it is your duty to acquit him, for I will have failed to discharge the burden of proof that lies upon me. If, on the other hand, you have no reasonable doubt, it is your legal duty to convict him.

'Gentlemen, the evidence against the defendant is simple. He is charged with the unlawful importation into Hong Kong of a highly dangerous substance, namely uranium, the radio-active metal used in the manufacture of nuclear weapons. The international powers strictly control the movement, sale and use of uranium, lest it falls into wrong hands – terrorist organizations, or certain irresponsible governments.

'But where does the uranium in this case originate? Gentlemen, you will hear evidence that in Russia alone, the defendant's homeland, there are a hundred and eighty-nine places where nuclear material is mined, manufactured, and handled . . .' Hargreave proceeded to outline the facts. He concluded:

'There is one last point I should make before I start calling the witnesses: the Russian policeman who was also on the plane to Hong

Kong, Colonel Simonski, will not be called as a witness because he has since been killed, in Russia –'

'*Objection!*' In a flurry Lipschitz was on his feet, furious. 'My Lord, the Crown is insidiously planting the notion in the jury's mind that Simonski was murdered by . . .' He stopped.

'By whom?' Hargreave felt a flash of malicious satisfaction: it was the first time he had seen Shitlips Lipschitz shoot himself in the foot by putting the jury in mind of the very thing he wished to avoid. 'I made no such insinuation, my Lord. The fact is we will hear a great deal about Mr Simonski in the course of this trial, and I have to tell the jury that they will not be seeing him as a witness because he is now dead. He may have been killed in a car smash – and I'm quite sure that my Lord will instruct the jury to disregard any other possible deduction my learned friend complains of.'

'Will my Lord please do that right now?' Lipschitz demanded. 'And will my learned friend please watch his step?!'

The Honourable Mr Justice Walters said peevishly, 'Mr Lipschitz, I think Mr Hargreave knows his steps as well as anyone, and I don't consider he said anything inappropriate. But, yes, I will instruct the jury.' He turned to them. 'Gentlemen, do you get the point? Mr Simonski is dead: we don't know how he died. Maybe it was a heart attack. Disabuse your minds of any other possibilities.'

Lipschitz sat down, glowering. Hargreave warned himself: *You're supposed to lose this case, for Christ's sake.*

29

Kerensky was an honest Russian policeman and, like Simonski, an expert on the Russian Mafia. He knew which sites were sources of stolen nuclear materials. He knew the scientists and security personnel responsible for its safe-keeping, who had not been paid their miserable salaries for months; knew which of them were selling uranium to the Mafia. He knew the names of the men who were smuggling it out of Russia, and which terrorist organizations and dictators were the ultimate purchasers, and he had no doubt who had gunned down Oskar Simonski – the Mafia gangsters whom Ivan Gregovich controlled. But he could not testify about his vast knowledge in a British court because most of it was hearsay, what informants had told him during his many months of diligent investigation. Furthermore, Kerensky was stationed in Vladivostok, six thousand miles from Simonski in Moscow, and though they had collaborated closely it had mostly been by telephone and mail. Indeed, with Simonski dead, there was very little Kerensky could legally contribute to the case: but his evidence was needed to give the jury some idea of the background, and to establish Simonski's death. Because of his anxiety to get Gregovich acquitted, Hargreave would have preferred not to call Kerensky as a witness at all, to leave the jury without the background picture, but Findlay and Champion expected otherwise.

Now Kerensky stood in the witness box and took the oath, through a Russian interpreter, to tell the truth, the whole truth, and nothing but the truth. He was a big, pleasant-looking man of about thirty-five, in a shabby suit. Hargreave had never seen him before.

'Are you a captain in the Russian police, stationed in Vladivostok?'

The interpreter put the question in Russian. Kerensky said, 'Da,' and the interpreter said, 'Yes, my Lord.'

'Have you ever seen the defendant, Ivan Gregovich, before today?'

'No, but –'

'Thank you. Did you know Colonel Oskar Simonski?'

'Yes. He was in the police in Moscow. He and I were investigating cases of theft from Russian nuclear power plants and other sites where nuclear material was produced. We exchanged much information.'

'How often did you actually meet him?'

'Only once, for a few days. About five weeks ago I went to Moscow from Vladivostok, to discuss our work.'

'Where is he now?'

'Now? In the cemetery. Dead.'

'How do you know he's dead?'

'I saw him die, in the street, in Moscow. We were walking towards the police station after lunch when –'

Lipschitz rose indignantly to object but Hargreave forestalled him by saying to Kerensky, 'Stop there. Thank you. But tell us the date this happened.'

'On the seventh of October, 1995. Colonel Simonski had recently returned from Hong Kong. We were walking –'

'Thank you. Now, how many nuclear power stations were you personally investigating?'

'Two, in the Vladivostok region.'

'Did you visit any other nuclear sites in Russia?'

'Yes, I saw over twenty, and I've seen written reports.'

'Thank you. When you visited the two power stations in the Vladivostok region, did you see how the uranium, the by-product of the nuclear material, was stored?'

'Yes. It is stored in very strong vaults. Each vault has security guards, and the vaults are surrounded by high wire fences in a prohibited area of the station compound. Access to the vaults is very much controlled.'

'Did you get into the vaults and see the uranium?'

'Yes, I was escorted by the director and a guard. We all wore protective clothing. I saw the uranium was in the form of rods, standing upright in tanks. The rods are emplaced by a crane. Of course, there were records showing how many rods there were, the date they were placed in the vaults, and their weights.'

'What was the general attitude towards you by the personnel in charge of this nuclear material when you visited?' Hargreave expected Lipschitz to object, but he didn't.

'Most of them were cooperative, but in several places they were obstructive and refused me entry, even though I am a policeman.'

'Now, please describe what was involved when you, as a policeman, tried to check the inventories to determine whether there was any discrepancy between the nuclear stock on hand and the records of how much there should be in the sites you visited?'

'It is almost impossible to weigh all the nuclear material, and compare the result with the records,' Kerensky said. 'The discrepancies I found were possibly identifiable with what is called "leakage", waste in the manufacture or storage process. If a plant manager told me there was leakage, when in fact there was none, I would have little chance of finding out, unless I found a bucket of it hidden somewhere.'

'Now, in all your investigations of these sites, have you made an arrest?'

'Not yet. Insufficient evidence so far.'

'In your expert experience, what was the level of crime in Russia before *perestroika*?'

'There was crime, but we had it under control.'

'And since?'

'Now, crime is terrible. The police have lost control.'

Hargreave expected Lipschitz to object to his next question, but it was worth a try. 'Now, as a policeman, does the government pay your salary regularly?'

Lipschitz stood and said wearily, 'What's the *possible* relevance?'

He was right. But Hargreave had squeezed the thought into the jury's mind that government salaries weren't paid on time. 'I withdraw the question. But what can you tell us, Captain Kerensky, from your own experience, about inflation in Russia?'

Lipschitz cried, 'Objection – what's the earthly relevance? The defendant isn't charged with causing inflation, is he?'

True. Hargreave had chanced his arm but he'd got away with it, placed the background information before the jury. And made Lipschitz appear obstructive. 'I withdraw the question, my Lord. No further examination.' He sat.

Lipschitz rose indignantly. 'What's my learned friend up to, my Lord?' he complained. 'What's the relevance of this evidence? He has not even proved that a theft of uranium took place – and anyway the defendant is not charged with theft. So what is my learned friend up to?'

'As I understand it,' the judge said, 'the Crown has so far established that Mr Simonski is dead and therefore cannot give evidence, that nuclear material is stored under apparently tight security, that small amounts may go missing through leakage, that crime in Russia is out of control. Some of that evidence may be questionable but it seems harmless to me. If you challenge any of it, cross-examine this witness now. If not, let's get on with the case.'

Lipschitz sighed theatrically. 'I won't dignify the so-called evidence with questions, my Lord.' He sat, looking disgusted.

'Does the jury have any questions for the witness?' the judge asked.

The foreman, Mr Davidson, consulted with his fellow-jurors, then rose.

'My Lord, why are we not allowed to know how Mr Simonski died?'

Lipschitz snorted and Hargreave closed his eyes: under normal circumstances he would have been delighted by this development.

The judge replied, 'Because the manner of Mr Simonski's death has no connection to the defendant, Mr Gregovich. If the Crown could prove any connection I presume Mr Hargreave would do so, so you must assume that Simonski died fortuitously. And remember the defendant is charged with *smuggling*, not with being connected with Mr Simonski's death, and remember also that at the time Mr Simonski died, five weeks ago, the defendant was in custody in Hong Kong.' The judge turned to the witness. 'Thank you, Mr Kerensky, you may step down.'

Hargreave rose: 'I call Bernard Champion.'

Champion stood in the witness box and took the oath.

'Are you a superintendent in the Criminal Investigation Department of the Royal Hong Kong Police?' Hargreave asked.

'I am, my Lord.'

'Had you ever seen the previous witness, Mr Kerensky, before today?'

'No, my Lord, but I have dealt with him by telephone and fax.'

'Now, at seven a.m. on fourteenth of September, where were you?'

'I was in Kai Tak airport, near the immigration control barrier, awaiting the arrival of Aeroflot flight SU593 from Moscow. I had twenty-six other policemen assisting me, most of them in the adjoining customs hall.'

'How were you all dressed?'

'In plain clothes.'

'Who did you see arrive from that Aeroflot flight?'

'The first person I saw emerge from the flight was Colonel Simonski of the Russian police, also in plain clothes.'

'Did you know him personally before that day?'

'I had met him often in Moscow over the preceding months, where he and I collaborated closely in the investigation of certain cases. He immediately joined me, and we waited together in a partially concealed position behind a pillar near the immigration barrier.'

'Who else did you see arrive?'

'Amongst other passengers, I saw a Russian man whom I now know as Nicolai Kozkov. Some minutes later I saw the defendant arrive.' He pointed at Gregovich in the dock. 'He was carrying a small canvas hold-all.'

'Had you ever seen either of these men before?'

'No.'

'What happened then?'

'I observed both Kozkov and the defendant pass through immigration control – separately, not together. Simonski and I followed them to the baggage reclaim area. The luggage started arriving and I saw Kozkov claim a suitcase. I saw him compare the tag number with the counterfoil on his ticket. He proceeded with it through the Nothing-to-Declare gate into the customs hall, and I followed him. Mr Simonski remained behind, observing the defendant. I gave a signal to the senior customs officer present, Mr Poon, who then told Koskov to present his suitcase for inspection. Six of my men immediately closed in around him. Kozkov was agitated.'

'You can't tell us what he said. But did he open the case?'

'No. He was unable to produce the key. He was searched, by me, but no key was found.' He added: 'In fact I did not want the suitcase opened at that stage because –'

'Objection!' Lipschitz cried. 'We're about to get hearsay.'

Hargreave nodded. 'So what happened when Kozkov could not produce the key?'

'He immediately attempted to run away. He was arrested by Inspector Sullivan, and I seized the suitcase.'

'Is this it?' The court orderly held it up.

'It is. I hasten to add it is now empty, but for a lead lining.'

'I put that suitcase in as Exhibit One, my Lord,' Hargreave said. 'I'll describe it, for the record: it is a blue, metal-clad suitcase, with a police label attached to the handle. It has a conventional lock plus a combination lock.' He turned back to Champion. 'Meanwhile, where was the defendant, Gregovich?'

'At this moment the defendant entered the customs hall carrying only the same bag he had left the plane with. He was followed by Simonski and three of my men. I immediately signalled the customs officer, Mr Poon, to have him searched. He was escorted to the same table as Kozkov and stood a few paces away.'

'How did the defendant react to this?'

'He appeared shocked, my Lord. Nervous. His hands trembled. On my orders, Mr Poon did not search his bag because I wanted it done under the same circumstances as Kozkov's suitcase. But I searched the defendant's clothing and found a suitcase key in his pocket.'

'Is this it?' Hargreave held up a key with a label attached.

'It is.'

'I put that in as Exhibit Two. Have you tried to use this key?'

'Yes, I subsequently tested it on the blue suitcase, Exhibit One. It opened the lock. I will demonstrate if I may?' He took the key, inserted it and opened the suitcase. 'I should add that the defendant's bag was a hold-all, not a suitcase, and it had a zip without a lock.'

'So what happened, once you'd found the key?'

'I told the defendant and Kozkov that I was taking them to police headquarters for questioning – whereupon the defendant suddenly turned and ran, but after about three paces he was seized by myself and Simonski. I then told him his rights, that he need not answer questions but that anything he said would be used in evidence. I said all this in English, which he appeared to understand, but I asked Simonski to repeat it in Russian, which he appeared to do. I then ordered Inspector Sullivan to take Exhibits One, Two and Three to military headquarters in an armoured vehicle which I had waiting out-side. Simonski and I, accompanied by other policemen, went with the defendant and Kozkov in two vehicles to police headquarters, where Simonski and I proceeded to question them. First we questioned Koz-kov, *not* in the presence of the defendant. Then, after ten minutes, Inspector Sullivan arrived and Simonski and I went to question the defendant in my office.'

'After questioning him, did you formally charge the defendant with the unlawful importation of a dangerous substance, namely uranium?'

'I did. I read a pre-typed charge, and formally advised him of his right to remain silent, but that anything he said would be recorded and used in evidence. He was in his sound and sober senses. He freely and voluntarily elected to make a reply. I recorded it verbatim and read it back to him. He adhered to it and signed it.'

Hargreave turned to the bench: 'I tender this statement as evidence, my Lord.'

'Any objection, Mr Lipschitz?'

Lipschitz was on his feet. 'A thousand times yes, my Lord! It was obtained from the defendant by brutal torture!'

The judge sighed. 'Mr Lipschitz, it is customary in this court to be less theatrical.' He turned to the jury and explained. 'Gentlemen, I have to ask you to leave the court and wait in the jury room. We are about to hold a *voir dire*, which means a trial within the trial, so I can decide whether this statement is admissible in evidence. If I decide that the defendant made the statement voluntarily, it will be read to you. If not, you will not hear anything more about it. So, please leave the box now.'

The jury shuffled to their feet, filed out of the jury box and the orderly led them out of the courtroom.

And so the *voir dire* began, the most important trial of Alistair Hargreave's life. Olga Romalova's survival depended on this trial-within-a-trial. If the judge ruled that Gregovich's statement was made voluntarily, he would be convicted and Olga would have her breast cut off. So Hargreave desperately wanted the Crown to fail. But once Olga was in Hong Kong she was safe: so the whole crisis turned on whether or not Olga was coming as a witness. Lipschitz had indicated on Friday that she would. But was the little bastard lying? No way could Hargreave take a chance on that.

Hargreave rubbed his chin. 'My Lord, will my learned friend please supply particulars of his allegations.'

The jury gone, Lipschitz was all oily charm to his Lordship. 'My Lord, our primary allegations are against the deceased Colonel Simonski, of the *Russian* police.'

'And your secondary allegations, please?' Hargreave asked.

'Duress can take many subtle forms, my Lord,' said Lipschitz smoothly. 'There is the shock to an honest man of being arrested – being forcibly carted off to the police station. Can one imagine what a frightening experience that is to a blameless man? I assure my Lord that such subtleties will be revealed in my cross-examination.'

'Mr Hargreave,' the judge said, 'are you satisfied with those particulars?'

Hargreave sighed tensely. Under normal circumstances he would press for more specifics of the actual brutality to tie Lipschitz down to details, but he did not want to handicap him in this case. 'The Crown is long-suffering, my Lord.'

Lipschitz smiled. 'If the Crown is long-suffering, my Lord, it is doubtless because it is so accustomed to having such serious allegations made against its police force!'

His Lordship ignored the comment. 'Proceed, Mr Hargreave.'

Hargreave turned to Champion, who was still in the witness box.

'What time did you arrest the defendant and what time did you formally charge him?'

'I arrested him at the airport at seven-twenty-seven a.m. We started to interrogate him at Police Headquarters at eight-ten a.m. I charged him at two o'clock in the afternoon, almost six hours later.'

'From the time you arrested the defendant to the time you began interrogating him did you or anybody in your presence question the defendant? During the journey, for example.'

'No. Because we wanted to question him in a place where we could pay complete attention. But during the journey he repeated several times, in English: "This is crazy. Why are you doing this to me? I do not know that other man. I am one of you, I am a former policeman." Words to that effect. But none of us responded. I was sitting beside him in the backseat, on the other side of him.'

'So you arrived at police headquarters. Tell us what happened then.'

'We left Gregovich in the custody of other policemen in my office, whilst we proceeded to an interrogation room where Kozkov was waiting. Simonski and I questioned Kozkov for about ten minutes, then Inspector Sullivan arrived and Simonski and I then proceeded to my office, where we began questioning Gregovich at eight-ten a.m. We could not hear what was going on in Sullivan's room, but from time to time he did call me on the intercom to tell me what information he had.'

'Did both you and Mr Simonski question the defendant?'

'Yes. In English, which both the defendant and Simonski spoke perfectly. There were rare moments when Simonski said a sentence or two in Russian, which he thereafter translated to me, together with the defendant's reply. The defendant never challenged the accuracy.'

'Was this interrogation tape-recorded?'

'It was not.'

Hargreave didn't believe that. 'From the time of the arrest at the airport, to the time you charged the defendant, did you, Simonski or anybody else threaten the defendant, assault him in any way, or bring any form of duress to bear upon him?'

'Absolutely not, my Lord.'

'Did Simonski leave the room at any time, leaving you alone with the defendant?'

'Yes. Twice Mr Simonski went briefly to the toilet.'

And now for the all-important question: 'Did you ever leave the room, leaving Simonski alone with the defendant?'

Champion looked Hargreave in the eye. 'No. I was present throughout.'

Hargreave sighed inwardly. 'Did you go to the toilet yourself during this time?'

'No.'

'Did the defendant go to the toilet?'

'Yes, once. Both Simonski and I accompanied him, in case he should try to escape. But Simonski was in my sight the whole time.'

'Did the defendant ever complain to you or anybody else in your hearing of any duress?'

'He did not.'

'One last point, Mr Champion. According to the defendant's statement, you finished recording it at two-thirty in the afternoon. Did you, *before* that time, know the number of the combination lock on the suitcase, Exhibit One?'

'I did not. Only after the defendant made his statement was I able to telephone the number to military headquarters so they could open the suitcase.'

Hargreave turned to the judge. 'No further questions, my Lord.'

'Yes, Mr Lipschitz?' the judge said.

Arnold Lipschitz rose to his feet. 'Mr Champion, you must know, from Simonski, that the defendant used to be, until ten years ago, a major in the KGB, the Russian security police?'

'I do.'

'And you know, do you not, that the KGB have a reputation of being very tough policemen indeed?'

'I have heard that they had a bad reputation, yes. But I am not sure what you mean by "tough" – a rugby player may be tough on the field but burst into tears if caught stealing a lollipop. I have seen the toughest of criminals wilt under arrest and sing like a canary.'

'Kindly keep your answer to the point!' Lipschitz snapped.

'It *was* to the point,' Findlay said in a stage whisper.

'And I'll ask my learned friend's junior to keep his remarks to himself!' Lipschitz glowered at Findlay, then turned back to Champion. 'Now, Simonski and the defendant had known each other for over a year, had they not? Just yes or no, please.'

'I believe so, yes.'

'And Simonski had the reputation of being a ruthless policeman, had he not?'

Champion looked surprised. 'Nobody has confided that to me. My impression of him was that he was an honest, hard-working, efficient policeman who always behaved correctly.'

Lipschitz smiled. '*Really?* You know, of course, that he was dismissed from his job as a general in the Organized Crime Squad because of his brutality?'

Hargreave looked up. Champion was indignant. '*No.* Because he wrote a report saying there was widespread corruption amongst certain bureaucrats who were hand in glove with organized crime syndicates.'

Lipschitz gave his wide smile. 'Is that what he told you? He was probably too embarrassed to tell you the truth. However –'

'I've read his report!' Champion insisted.

'However, Simonski was in charge of a section of the police dealing with the so-called "nuclear Mafia", wasn't he? That's how you met him.'

'Yes. Except he had been removed from that post when I met him.'

'Yes, he'd been *demoted*. But he was glad to talk to you? He told you that the smuggling of nuclear material from Russia was widespread, and he felt frustrated that he could do nothing about it, because he'd been *demoted*. And he was bitter!'

'Bitter?' Champion said. 'I don't know. Hurt, I suppose.'

'Yes, hurt. And so he was delighted to help you, delighted to be back in business *un*officially.'

'Unofficially? Well, yes, the nuclear Mafia weren't his bailiwick any more, if that's what you mean.'

Lipschitz bunched the lapels of his gown. 'So you two became comrades-in-arms in this *un*official investigation, didn't you?'

Champion smiled. 'Yes, if you're speaking figuratively.'

'And literally!' Lipschitz sneered. 'When he came to Hong Kong you were both armed with pistols, were you not? Simonski even managed to fly on the plane with his pistol!'

'Yes, he told me he had a pistol.'

Lipschitz leaned forward and leered: 'It is a *crime* for anybody to bring a firearm into Hong Kong without a licence.' He paused. 'Why didn't you do something about it – take possession of it?'

Champion smiled. 'Yes, perhaps I should have. But I didn't because he was a fellow policeman, helping me in the investigation.'

Lipschitz's finger shot up. 'So *you* committed a crime – you made yourself an accessory after the fact.'

Champion nodded. 'Technically, yes, but I told him to leave any fireworks to me if possible – *if* trouble arose.'

'*If* possible. But you expected him to act like a policeman if there was trouble. Even if that help included using an unlawful gun.'

'Yes, I suppose so. But I was confident he would only use it as a last resort.'

Lipschitz looked at the judge, then sneered, 'You *suppose* so? Very well, Mr Champion, your reluctance to be frank speaks volumes.'

Hargreave stood up. 'I hesitate to interrupt my learned friend but, for the record, that is an unfair comment, my Lord. The record should state that the witness's demeanour is not one of reluctance, and he is answering forthrightly.'

'Yes. Continue,' the judge said.

Lipschitz glowered at Hargreave: then he began to unveil his big cannon. 'But a pistol was not the only weapon Simonski had, was it?' He paused. 'He also had a truncheon, didn't he?'

Champion looked mystified. 'Truncheon? Not that I saw.'

'Not that you *saw*? So Simonski *could* have had a truncheon on his person during the investigation without you seeing it?'

Champion turned to the judge. 'No, my Lord, he could not have had a truncheon on him, because we were in our shirtsleeves, we'd all taken our jackets off. That's when I saw Simonski's shoulder-holster for his pistol for the first time, yes, under his left armpit – as was mine. There was no truncheon hanging from Simonski's belt.' He turned back to Lipschitz and added, with a wisp of a smile: 'Unless it was down his trousers.'

'Don't you jest in this court!' Lipschitz snarled. 'This is not your police club!'

'I'm sorry, I was being serious. A truncheon would not fit into a man's pocket.'

Lipschitz said venomously, 'The truncheon was in *another* shoulder holster, slung under Simonski's right armpit.'

Champion shook his head. 'No. He had his jacket off. I would have seen a second holster.'

Lipschitz leant forward: 'You had air-conditioning, didn't you?'

'Yes?'

'Yes, and so Simonski had his jacket on! Because your air-conditioner was working full blast and it was chilly for him!'

Champion frowned, then said, 'No, I remember now that my air-conditioner was off, it had broken down the day before. So I had a fan on, and the window open. It was hot and we were all in our shirtsleeves.'

Lipschitz rocked back on his heels. '*Now* you conveniently remember the air-conditioner was off! How could you forget that detail?' he sneered. 'No air-conditioning in September – for *six* hours! It must have been sweltering! How could you forget?'

'You had distracted me,' Champion said, 'talking about this non-existent truncheon.'

'An experienced witness like you distracted? Oh come, come . . . And even though Simonski had his jacket on, the handle of the truncheon was visible, sticking out over his chest!'

'I saw no such thing,' Champion insisted doggedly. 'And Simonski had his jacket *off*.'

Lipschitz smiled. 'To relieve the sweltering heat? Which you forgot about?' He snorted. 'The defence evidence will be that Simonski had a weapon like *this*.' He opened his briefcase and dramatically produced a black truncheon. He held it up. 'This can be bought in many stores. Householders buy them to defend themselves against burglars. It can be used to hit people, like an ordinary truncheon. But inside it is a strong rechargeable battery, and on the tip, here, are two small metal nodules. On the handle is this little switch, here. Flick the switch and electrical sparks fly.' Lipschitz moved the switch and sparks crackled. He leered. 'Touch anybody with it and he gets an agonizing electric shock. Do the Hong Kong Police use such weapons, Mr Champion?'

Champion's face betrayed nothing. 'No.'

'No? Why not? Because of the pain? Because it is a pernicious, cruel weapon? Inhumane?'

'It may be considered so. Though if it's used to effect a difficult arrest it strikes me as less painful than a bullet wound.'

'Inhumane and therefore improper – *officially*. But don't some policemen nonetheless use such truncheons *unofficially*?'

'I don't know.'

Lipschitz looked incredulous, then cried, 'You don't know? You, an experienced senior policeman, don't *know*?' He shook his head. 'Oh come, come! Never heard of a policeman using one to assist his interrogation of a criminal? I suggest you're lying to us, Mr Champion.'

'I am not, Mr Lipschitz.'

Lipschitz gave his wide, vulture smile. Then he continued conversationally: 'You see, in the old days, if one wanted to give a prisoner an electrical shock, to loosen his tongue, one had to hook him up to two wires, connect them to the power-point, and tie the prisoner down so he did not wrench the wires off himself. Not so?'

'I suppose so,' Champion said stiffly.

'Never seen it done?' Lipschitz enquired.

'No.'

'*Really?* But you know the principle. How you wire the man up?'

'The principle, yes.'

'Then why did you just say you *suppose* so? Oh never mind, let's not waste time with more prevarications. Now, returning to this excellent bit of kit – all one would have to do is reach out, like this, and touch the suspect with it, and thereby give him a terrible shock. All over in a moment: no wires, no tying the suspect down, none of that tiresome hassle.'

'What's the question, please?' Hargreave said.

Lipschitz said: 'So let's turn back now to Mr Simonski, and his state of mind.' He paused. 'Simonski had been investigating the nuclear Mafia for many months before his demotion. And when you two policemen put your heads together he must have told you that he knew the defendant and had had at least one, shall we say "conversation" with him. Correct or not?'

'Correct.'

'And Simonski told you he had accused the defendant – wrongly of course – of being involved in the nuclear black market? Yes or no.'

'Yes.'

'Now Simonski felt very strongly about this nuclear black market. Did he not tell you that, in his conversation with the defendant in Russia, he had used one of these shocking truncheons on him?'

'He did not.'

Lipschitz's eyes widened in mock surprise. 'No? Did he not tell you that the Russian police habitually use these truncheons, with the result that confessions are usually quickly forthcoming?'

'He did not.'

Lipschitz smiled. 'Amazing . . . But Simonski *did* tell you that, in his conversation with the defendant, the defendant had denied any involvement with nuclear materials. Yes or no.'

'Yes.'

'But Simonski did not believe him?'

'Correct.'

'Nor do you.'

'Correct.'

'And before his demotion Simonski had had great frustrations, great difficulty tracing the places from which nuclear material was being stolen because officials at every nuclear site, and the Russian government itself, piously denied that any material was missing.'

'Correct.'

'And so you and Simonski hatched a plot. A "sting operation". You put the word out in the underworld that there was a customer for nuclear material called Lawrence, in Hong Kong. And you returned to Hong Kong to await developments. Then on the thirteenth of September, Simonski telephoned you to say he had a breakthrough, and he was delighted.'

'He was pleased, yes.'

'And so were you.'

'Yes.'

Lipschitz leant forward and leered: 'You were both so pleased that you were prepared to take the extraordinary risk of allowing the uranium to be flown ten thousand miles to Hong Kong in order to catch the culprits.'

Champion glanced at Hargreave. 'Well,' he said, 'Simonski actually made that decision. I was faced with a *fait accompli.*'

Lipschitz assumed surprise. 'Oh? Blame Mr Simonski, do you, the man who cannot now deny it! But did you try to dissuade Simonski, to make an effort to stop the shipment?'

'No, because –'

'No. Despite the extraordinarily dangerous nature of radio-active uranium – had the aircraft crashed, thousands of square miles could have been contaminated, killing countless people; is that not so?'

Champion seemed uncomfortable. 'There was no *time* to dissuade Simonski. He was at Moscow airport, the defendant and Kozkov had already checked in. At the stage he telephoned me, the aircraft was about to take off.'

'Oh, I see. Too bad,' Lipschitz observed with sarcasm. 'But had there been more time, you would have advised Simonski to stop the plane, arrest the defendant and Kozkov, and seize the suitcase?'

Champion appeared ill at ease. 'Yes,' he conceded.

Lipschitz nodded. 'Of course. But Simonski telephoned you from the airport *building*, not from the plane.'

'Yes,' Champion admitted.

'So there *was* time to stop the plane. Simonski could have run to the control tower and told them to stop it.'

'I have no police powers in Russia. I could not order Simonski to do anything.'

'*Aha!*' Lipschitz cried. 'But you have just told us that had there been more time you *would* have ordered Simonski to stop!'

Champion said, 'I agreed that I would have *advised* Simonski to stop – not "ordered". As it was I said something like "Christ, that's dangerous" – there was no time for more, I had to leap into action.'

'And you were prepared to take that mind-blowing risk because you were so pleased and now had to leap into action to catch the couriers. Do you know how many plane crashes there are a year?'

'No.'

'Haven't you heard that Aeroflot has a bad track record for crashes?'

'Yes, I have heard that, but that doesn't mean it's true.'

'Yet you took the risk because you were so pleased. And when you arrested Kozkov, and then the defendant, you felt you had caught them red-handed!'

'We *did* catch them red-handed.'

'You and Simonski felt triumphant!'

'We were pleased, yes.'

'Exactly. Your long hard work had paid off, now all you needed was a confession from both of them to really wrap the case up.'

'A confession would have been helpful, yes, but we had enough evidence without one.'

Lipschitz jabbed the air with his finger. 'And you wanted not only a confession, you hoped also to find out where this uranium was stolen from, so Simonski could go back to the source and arrest the corrupt bureaucrats!'

'We hoped for all that, yes. But I was not prepared to use any form of duress to get it, because that is against the law I am sworn to uphold.'

Lipschitz beamed. 'A commendable attitude, Mr Champion – if surprising after all the other laws you broke, like letting Simonski enter the colony with his gun, breaking international law by permitting uranium to be flown halfway around the world, breaking Hong Kong law on the same point, exposing thousands of people to the risk of death by radiation –'

'Objection,' Hargreave said, despite himself. 'This is argumentative. What is the question, and please get on with it.'

Lipschitz glared at Hargreave, then turned back to the witness. 'I was about to ask you, Mr Champion, before I was interrupted by my learned friend, whether, in view of your commendable attitude towards the law, you know what the law in Russia is about the voluntariness of confessions and the admissibility thereof? Yes or no!' he snapped.

Champion sighed. 'Russian law? No.'

'But you know the general attitude of the Russian police towards the voluntariness of confessions, don't you? *They* don't apply the English law of fair play about confessions, do they, the Judges' Rules?'

'I don't know. But I know Simonski's attitude, and that was that confessions must be voluntary.'

'You *think* you know, you mean?' Lipschitz took a deep, self-satisfied breath. 'Now, the interrogation itself lasted six hours. After how long did the defendant, this experienced KGB officer, start making his so-called admission?'

'After about three hours.'

'Three hours, my word! Up to that point he stoutly denied everything?'

'Yes. But we were questioning him about many other related points – people in Russia involved in the trade, and so forth.'

Lipschitz said, with narrow eyes: 'And you've told us that you did *not* tape-record this six-hour interrogation. Why not?'

'Both Simonski and I made all the notes we needed.'

Lipschitz looked astonished. 'But your questions covered a huge and vital area – where the uranium came from – Simonski was very interested in corrupt bureaucrats, and so on! Surely every tiny detail should have been recorded!'

'I didn't think it necessary – and I didn't want the distraction of changing tapes.' It sounded lame.

Lipschitz leered. 'I put it to you that you *did* tape-record the interrogation! But because it also recorded Simonski's threats, you deny the existence of the recording!'

'Not so,' Champion said doggedly.

Lipschitz sneered. 'So what brought on the defendant's sudden change of heart after three hours? Was it exhaustion?'

'No, he appeared in normal condition.'

'Normal? Despite his long flight and jetlag? Was it . . . hunger or thirst?'

'No, we had food and drink. If you ask me – which you do – I think he changed because he realized the game was up. The evidence against him was overwhelming. What Simonski saw in Moscow –'

'You can't tell us what Simonski said he saw!'

'Very well, sir, but Simonski told *him*, in my presence, what he saw. And we had the evidence of the key, plus his trying to run away, plus the fact that he waited at the luggage carousel although he had no luggage on it – he emerged with only his hand-carried bag. All impressive evidence.'

'Stop telling us what is impressive evidence, that's his Lordship's task to decide!'

'Very well,' Champion purred demurely, 'but you asked me and I'm answering as truthfully as I can.'

'Stop arguing! My Lord,' Lipschitz appealed, 'please instruct this witness to just answer my questions!'

Hargreave rose. 'I submit,' he said, 'that that is exactly what the witness is doing.'

'Mr Lipschitz,' the judge said, 'please continue.'

273

Lipschitz glowered. 'For the record I ask my Lord to note the witness's smug smile.' He turned to Champion. 'Now –'

'I'll note the *slight* smile,' the judge said, 'but not the smugness. Perhaps Mr Hargreave and Mr Findlay have the smug smile?' Everybody grinned, except Lipschitz.

Lipschitz glowered, then moved on to the area Hargreave was dreading. He stuck his thumbs in his gown and shucked it aggressively.

'Now, Mr Champion, you claim that you never left Simonski alone with the defendant during the interrogation.' He paused. 'Why not? Simonski went to the toilet twice. The defendant went once. Didn't you, during those six long, hot hours?'

Champion looked him in the eye. 'No.'

Lipschitz said in wonder, 'You must have a very strong bladder.'

Champion smiled. 'I have, sir.'

'*Very* strong, Mr Champion. And *very* convenient.' He frowned. 'How many times do you urinate in a working day?'

'I don't know, my Lord,' Champion smiled. 'But if the information is helpful, I recently flew from Miami to London without urinating, all of it during daylight. About six hours, the flight was.'

Everybody was grinning, except Lipschitz. 'Didn't you ever *want* to urinate, during the interrogation? When had you last urinated?'

'At the airport, I think,' Champion said. 'Yes, it must have been shortly before the Aeroflot flight landed, at about seven a.m.'

'What time did you get up that morning?'

'At four a.m. To get my team to the airport in plenty of time. I urinated then.'

'So a mere three hours later this remarkable bladder of yours advised you to urinate again?'

'It must have, I don't believe I would have done it otherwise.'

Laughter. Even Lipschitz smiled. 'Why?' he asked. 'Why did you find it necessary?'

'I don't rightly know. But I had drunk perhaps half a dozen cups of coffee.'

'And there was nervous excitement.'

'Yes, I suppose so.'

'And then you were interrogating the defendant in the hopes of getting a confession. Weren't you more excited?'

Champion said, 'I suppose I was, but I was determined to play the interrogation by the book.'

'But not excited enough to urinate for another six hours! Plus the hour since urinating at the airport before the defendant's arrival – seven hours!'

274

Champion smiled. 'It sounds a long time, but it caused me no discomfort that I recall, and indeed Mr Simonski and I had agreed that I would not leave him alone with the defendant in case there were accusations such as this – so that I was always present, because I was the official police officer.'

'Oh!' Lipschitz cried. '*Now* you tell us this detail!'

'Yes. You didn't ask me before.'

'Don't you dare fence with me! So you and Simonski had a *pact*? So you could testify as to his impeccable conduct?'

'So that I could testify as to the whole truth. The point is, Simonski had no police powers in Hong Kong, no legal right to interrogate the defendant unless I was present. I wanted everything to be done correctly and officially.'

'*Correctly?* Like Simonski's gun? So you never left Simonski alone with the defendant? We'll see.' He picked up his notes and studied them briefly, and Hargreave closed his eyes: now was surely the time Lipschitz would drop his bombshell that he knew differently, knew what Champion had told Hargreave in Macao, that Olga had overheard it . . . But Lipschitz said: 'Now, during this *impeccable* conduct by you two paragons of police virtue, steeped as you were in the Judges' Rules, and despite your excitement at having made, as you gleefully thought, a red-handed arrest – meanwhile the interrogation of Mr Kozkov by Inspector Sullivan was going on down the corridor, correct?'

For a moment Hargreave felt panic – wasn't he going to use Olga's evidence?

Champion said, 'Correct.'

'And Kozkov was the man you'd arrested actually *carrying* the uranium which you were so excited about. So surely you were interested in knowing what Kozkov was telling Inspector Sullivan, so you could use the information in questioning the defendant?'

'Indeed,' Champion agreed. 'But we had already questioned Kozkov, our case against him was cast-iron and our assessment was that he was just the dumb courier. The only point we were very interested in was who had instructed him to carry the suitcase to Hong Kong. And, of course, we already had what Mr Simonski saw at Moscow airport so –'

'Don't you *dare*,' Lipschitz cried, 'try to sneak inadmissible hearsay in by the back door like that!'

Hargreave rose: 'My learned friend has only himself to blame, *he* opened the door to hearsay, so can he please stop shouting at the witness?'

'I am not shouting, I am just flabbergasted at this attempt –'

'You opened the door to hearsay,' the judge said. 'Better close it, if you don't like it. Proceed.'

Lipschitz turned back to Champion. 'Inspector Sullivan was questioning Kozkov in an interrogation room which has a two-way mirror and a listening system. I put it to you that you did go into that room to hear what Kozkov was saying and that this was about three hours after your own interrogation began. You said you were going to the toilet.'

'Sullivan called me a few times, but I did not leave my office.'

'And on a second occasion you left the office, saying you were going to the toilet.'

'No.'

'And during both your absences Simonski pulled out his shocking truncheon and touched the defendant with it, giving him terrible pain.'

'I did not leave my office,' Champion insisted.

Now, Hargreave thought – now he's going to drop the bombshell and I'll be guilty of subornation of perjury. But Lipschitz continued:

'Why didn't you have an independent Russian interpreter present?'

Hargreave opened his eyes, his heart knocking. Champion replied: 'Because both Simonski and the defendant spoke good English, and Sullivan needed the interpreter.'

'But you have more than one Russian interpreter available! It seems very necessary to ensure Simonski was not saying anything threatening to the defendant! Simonski spoke a number of times in Russian, didn't he?'

'Yes. But the defendant's demeanour was not that of a man being threatened.'

'But Simonski could have slipped in a few words, such as "I have the truncheon". Yes or no?'

Champion sighed. 'I suppose so. But I consider it unlikely.'

Lipschitz sneered. 'Oh. Well, Mr Champion, what most people would consider unlikely is that you didn't go to the toilet in seven long hours!' (Hargreave closed his eyes again: this is it, here it comes.) 'Do you still adhere to that unlikely story?'

'Yes.'

Lipschitz leered at Hargreave. 'Well,' he said triumphantly, 'I put it to you that you are lying. Because when you visited my learned friend, Mr Hargreave, in Macao on the fifteenth of September, to consult him on this case, you told him that you *had* left the room a couple of times during the interrogation, to go to the toilet! Isn't that so?'

The judge looked at Hargreave, surprised. Findlay looked at him in astonishment: 'Jesus,' he whispered, 'is this true?' Hargreave nodded curtly. He forced himself to look at Champion. Findlay whispered, 'Why didn't you tell me?'

Champion was staring across the courtroom at Hargreave, astonished. Then anger flashed across his face for an instant. 'Did Mr Hargreave tell you that?'

'Yes! Very properly, as is his duty!'

Champion flashed Hargreave a look. He said grimly, 'Mr Hargreave is mistaken. His recollection is wrong. I said no such thing to him, because it wasn't true.'

Lipschitz smiled maliciously. 'You sat on the balcony of Mr Hargreave's hotel room and discussed this case. And Mr Hargreave asked whether you had been present throughout the interrogation, and you replied to this effect: "Yes, well, except when I went out for a pee".'

Champion said slowly, 'Mr Hargreave is *very* much mistaken.'

'Really?' Then Lipschitz delivered his punchline: 'No, Mr Champion.' He paused. 'Because your reply was clearly overheard by Mr Hargreave's lady-friend, Miss Olga Romalova!'

Findlay whispered, 'Jesus Christ . . .' But Hargreave's sick heart leapt. So Lipschitz definitely intended calling Olga as a witness. *Oh thank God* . . . There was an astonished silence. Champion stared, at a loss for words. Everybody was waiting. Hargreave sat there, massaging his eyelids: then he made himself look at the witness box. Champion was glaring at him; then he turned to Lipschitz.

'If that woman . . . If Olga Romalova says that, she is lying, because no such thing was said.'

Lipschitz gloated. 'And Mr Hargreave? Is he a liar, too?'

Champion looked at Hargreave. 'He is mistaken.'

Lipschitz smiled. 'Oh, Miss Romalova is a liar, but my learned friend is only mistaken? But she will corroborate him. Either both are liars or both are telling the truth. Which is it, Mr Champion? Is Mr Hargreave a liar?'

Champion took a deep, furious breath. 'The Director of Public Prosecutions, Mr Hargreave, is mistaken. Miss Romalova is lying, in an attempt to corroborate his mistake, because she is a . . . a prostitute, who wants a free ticket to Hong Kong.'

There was a hushed silence, and all eyes turned to Hargreave. He was staring sightlessly at nothing, sick in his guts: he had known it would come out, but not as badly as this. The answer hung, then Lipschitz said:

'Kindly don't be so presumptuous as to tell my Lord what is going

on in somebody's mind! You're not a thought-reader!' He turned triumphantly to the judge. 'No further questions, my Lord.'

Lipschitz sat down, satisfaction all over his vulturous face.

The judge cleared his throat, then said quietly, 'Any re-examination,
Mr Hargreave?'

Hargreave got to his feet, all eyes upon him. With all his sick heart
the wanted to say, 'In fairness to the witness I must make it clear that
I told Mr Lipschitz that I was only *almost* sure I heard him say that he
left the interrogation room to go to the toilet . . .' But he could not turn
back now.

'No re-examination, my Lord.' He took a deep breath. 'I call my next
and last witness on this *voir dire* issue, Inspector Sullivan – but I will
ask my learned friend Mr Findlay to lead his evidence.'

His Lordship hunched forward. He said diffidently, 'Mr Hargreave . . .
From Mr Lipschitz's cross-examination, it appears that you may be in
a difficult position if and when this Olga Romalova is called as a witness
for the defence.'

'To anticipate your Lordship's question,' Hargreave said, 'if and when
Olga Romalova is called as a defence witness, I will leave her to be
cross-examined by Mr Findlay. Indeed I will withdraw from the courtroom for the duration of her evidence.'

His Lordship fiddled with his pen. 'Yes. But were you aware, when
this case began this morning, that Olga Romalova would be called as a
defence witness? Because, if so, it seems to me that you should have
withdrawn from the case then.'

Hargreave looked good old Harry Walters in the eye. And it was
almost the truth – he was not *definitely* aware: 'No, my Lord, I was not.'
He prayed Arnie Lipschitz didn't let him down.

'So,' his Lordship said, 'she is – or will be – a surprise witness?'

'Precisely, my Lord.'

The judge sat back in his high, carved chair.

'Very well,' he said, 'call Inspector Sullivan. Thank you,' he said to
Champion, 'you may stand down.'

30

Champion strode across the courtroom. He did not return to his seat beside Hargreave, but shot him a hate-filled glance, made for the exit and disappeared.

Hargreave slumped in his chair, sick with the lie he had just told the judge – a lie which Lipschitz knew to be such – but his heart swelled with happiness because Lipschitz had just said loud and clear that Olga was going to be called. She *must* be in Hong Kong right now, or at least in Macao. It was through a haze of conflicting emotions that he heard Inspector Sullivan take the oath. Then Findlay was examining him.

'Are you an inspector in the Criminal Investigation Department, assisting Superintendent Champion in this case?'

'I am, my Lord.'

'On fourteenth of September did you question Nicolai Kozkov in an interrogation room in police headquarters?'

'Yes.'

'During the course of your interrogation did you summon Mr Champion from his office to your room, or to the adjoining observation room, to listen to what Kozkov was saying?'

'No. But I reported to him by telephone intercom two or three times.'

'Superintendent Champion's evidence is that he interrogated the defendant from about eight-ten until about two p.m. that afternoon. Did you, between those times, see Mr Champion in the corridor, in the toilet, or anywhere else?'

'No.'

'Thank you. No further questions, my Lord.' Findlay sat down.

Lipschitz rose to cross-examine, with a bored expression on his face. 'Of course, Mr Champion *could* have been in the adjoining observation room without you knowing?'

'Correct. One cannot see outwards through the one-way mirror.'

'And he could have gone to the toilet without you knowing. You're not his wet-nurse are you?'

'Correct,' Sullivan said, straight-faced.

'No further questions,' Lipschitz said, very bored. He sat wearily.

Findlay stood up. 'No re-examination, my Lord.' He consulted Hargreave, then said, 'I close the Crown case on this issue.'

His Lordship looked at the clock. 'Very well, we'll adjourn for lunch at this stage, and hear the defence this afternoon.'

Before the judge's door closed, Hargreave had slung his wig down on the bar and was striding out of the courtroom, his gown billowing and the vomit rising in his throat. He blundered down the corridor towards the elevators, dreading meeting Champion. Findlay called after him: 'Al!' He caught up at the elevator, but there were other people in it: they rode down in silence, Hargreave massaging his eyelids. He crossed the foyer towards his department and strode down the long corridor, through his secretary's office, into his chambers, Findlay behind him. Hargreave threw off his gown and slumped down behind his desk. He looked at Findlay.

'Well – out with it!'

Findlay closed the door. He ran his hand through his matted hair.

'Jesus, Al! Why didn't you tell me what Champion told you in Macao? That he did leave Simonski alone with Gregovich?' He frowned. 'I mean, I'm your junior, I need to know these things. Why was I taken by surprise?'

'Do you want a drink?'

Findlay looked taken by surprise again. 'No, thanks.'

Hargreave got up, went to his cabinet and sloshed a dash of whisky into a glass. 'Mud in your eye.' He took a gulp.

'Al, please answer me.'

Hargreave glared at him. He had not tasted the whisky. 'I did what I am ethically required to do. Champion is lying and so I told the defence counsel what I knew – it's not our job to connive at lies, Neil! We are required to tell the defence any earlier contradictory statement made by our witnesses, you know that.'

'Sure, if it's a *written*, official statement – but not a verbal remark that wasn't made with the full knowledge of the consequences. As Champion said, you may be mistaken, or he might not have meant exactly what you thought – you didn't give him a chance to reconsider and explain himself, like when recording a written statement.' Findlay looked at him. 'I think you were over-generous to the defence, Al, if you don't mind my saying so.'

'I *do* mind your saying so. I heard Champion loud and clear in Macao – there's no doubt about what he meant.' That wasn't quite true. 'And apparently Olga Romalova heard him too.'

'Well, I think you should have spoken to Champion and given him a chance to explain himself before dropping him in the shit like that. *And* dropping our case in the shit – this casts his whole evidence into doubt.'

'That,' Hargreave snapped, 'is precisely why I did not speak to him first. He would have tried to bullshit me. It's for the judge to decide what's bullshit, not me.'

Findlay snorted. 'Well, you certainly should have warned me.'

Hargreave took a gulp of whisky. 'I didn't want you nagging me to speak to Champion first – I made my decision and intended to see my duty through.'

Findlay turned and paced across the room. 'Well, you sure did that – beyond the call of duty, in my humble view, Al.' He turned back. '*Did* you know that Olga Romalova is going to be called as a defence witness?'

Oh Jesus. 'No.' Strictly speaking that was true – he'd only *hoped*. 'She's in Russia, for Christ's sake, and I didn't know whether she'd overheard anything or not.' Also true.

Findlay said diffidently, 'Is she still your girl?'

Hargreave was about to tell him to mind his own bloody business – but it was his business. 'I don't know. She's in Russia now, I just told you.'

'Is she . . .' Findlay began hesitantly. 'I'm sorry, but I have to know this if I'm cross-examining her: is she still a prostitute as Champion alleges? And scared of the Mafia?'

'I don't know,' Hargreave said slowly. 'But I imagine she's terrified of the Mafia, yes. Ask her.'

Findlay hesitated, then said: 'Al, in view of this development, wouldn't it be best if you withdrew from the case altogether and let me handle it?'

Oh God yes, he should withdraw. And once Olga was safely here he would do so gratefully. 'We'll see.'

Findlay turned and paced again. 'Well,' he said, 'it depends on how I do with her under cross-examination. If she's a good witness, Gregovich's confession goes out the window. But apart from that, how do you think we've done so far in this *voir dire*?'

Hargreave was relieved to change the subject. 'All the allegations are made against Simonski, and without Simonski here to deny them, we're pretty thin. Lipschitz has scored a lot of points on the probabilities – Champion most likely *did* go to the toilet at least once in six hours. And personally I think Simonski may well have given the defendant a

nice little electric jolt when Champ's back was turned. Simonski probably *was* a tough cop.'

'And you think Champion knows?'

Hargreave snorted. 'He's a tough cop too. But that's for the judge to
decide, not us.' He took a swallow of whisky. 'Neil, I've got work to
do.'

Findlay glanced at the whisky. 'Can I order you a sandwich?'

'I'm not hungry, thanks.'

Findlay sounded put out. 'I'll be in my chambers if you want me.'

As soon as Findlay was gone Hargreave poured another dash of
whisky. No – he couldn't eat a thing. He paced, in a turmoil of guilt,
excitement and dread at what might happen that afternoon: dread that
Olga might not show up, dread that he would be exposed as a conspira-
tor to perjury. But none of that mattered as long as Olga was here.
Please please please God Olga is here . . .

There was a rap on his door. Hargreave opened it. Champion stood
there, glowering.

He strode in. '*You bastard!* Of all the underhand things to do!'

Hargreave quickly closed the door. 'I'm not going to discuss it.'

'Oh yes you are, you bastard! Why did you tell Lipschitz that I'd told
you I'd left the room?!'

'It was ethical to do so.' Hargreave moved to his desk.

'I didn't say it!'

'I think you did.'

'I *didn't*!'

'Fine, you've denied it under oath in the witness box!'

'But now there's a doubt in the judge's mind! Because you told
Shitlips, to appease your exquisite professional conscience, that you
thought you remembered that *maybe* I had said in Macao that *perhaps*
I had left the room to have a pee!'

'Yes, and it was my duty to disclose it.'

Champion's face creased in fury. 'It was your duty to discuss it with
me first! And I would have laid your exquisite conscience to rest by
correcting your unreliable memory! You weren't even concentrating in
Macao, you were so wrapped up in that girl!'

'Okay, so now you've denied it under oath! You were an impressive
witness, as always. If there's a doubt in the judge's mind after he's
heard Gregovich's version, and after I've cross-examined him, so be it!
It's not my job to conceal evidence!'

'So *be* it?' Champion waved a hand in fury. 'So *be* it for you beautiful
lawyers and your holier-than-thou consciences while thugs rule the

282

streets? Rule the world!' He jabbed a big finger: 'Well it's not my job to let gangsters get away with mass murder! *International* mass murder!' He glared furiously. 'And now your whore is going to give evidence for the mass murderer and say I'm a liar!'

Hargreave gritted his teeth. 'Guard your tongue, Bernie.'

'You should have guarded yours!' Champion hissed. 'And your head! A *whore* – that's what she is – *she's* the liar, and you have lost your head over her! Did you know she was going to be called as a defence witness?'

'No.'

'Did she tell you she overheard me say that I'd left the room to have a piss?'

'No.'

'So why the *fuck* did you mention her at all to Lipschitz? Why didn't you let sleeping dogs lie? You discussed it with him, that crooked little shit, but not with *me*?' He glared, then sneered sarcastically, 'And of course you didn't *want* Olga to come to Hong Kong as a defence witness, oh no!'

Hargreave had to respond, for credibility. 'Are you imputing an improper motive to me in all this?'

Champion assumed exaggerated innocence. '*Heavens*, no, sir! Perish the thought!' He turned abruptly for the door, then stopped and jabbed his finger at Hargreave: 'I'm imputing that Olga Romalova is a liar! And I'm imputing that I will never trust you again! And *your* name –' he jabbed again – 'is going to be *mud* if this confession is thrown out!'

He strode out of the door, and slammed it.

Hargreave slumped back in an armchair. Oh God . . . He was so sick at heart he almost felt that he was right: he *was* right to have told Lipschitz . . . And it *would* have been wrong to warn Champion, to give him the chance to paint over the crack in his evidence – and he didn't give a damn what the whole police force thought – *he* was their legal adviser and if they didn't like his professional ethics they could go'n jump in the sea! He was a lawyer who applied the law that no matter what dirty tricks the criminals play the Crown does not play any!

And then the guilt reared its head. He had tricked Lipschitz into procuring perjury . . . God, he wanted another drink, to fortify him for the ordeals of this afternoon.

He heaved himself up out of his armchair, poured another whisky, went to his desk, slumped down and propped his forehead in his hand.

*   *   *

283

That lunch hour seemed unreal, as did the scenes with Champion and with Findlay. It seemed unreal that he was supposed to lose this case while every instinct made him want to win: unreal that Olga's life hung on the case, that at this moment she must be in Hong Kong and this afternoon she would be standing in the witness box. It was unreal that this afternoon everything might go terribly wrong and he could be exposed.

When Findlay fetched him to return to court he had drunk three whiskies and was feeling a little better. Was Olga going to be in the corridor outside Court Fourteen? They emerged from the elevator amongst the milling jurors and witnesses. His eyes darted. His heart sank: she's not here . . . He strode into court, eyes sweeping the crowded public gallery. Lipschitz was in huddled conference with his solicitors. Champion sat in his place at the bar, glowering. Hargreave said huskily: 'Good afternoon, Arnold!'

Lipschitz turned. 'Afternoon,' he smiled.

He *smiled*. Oh, thank God. Hargreave was bursting to ask him about Olga, but restrained himself. 'Let's go.' He signalled to the registrar.

He sat down. Champion glared at him furiously. Hargreave clenched his teeth. 'I *think*,' he whispered, 'that you and I better forget what was said at lunchtime.'

'*I* won't forget, chum.'

There was a rap on the judge's door. 'Silence in court,' the registrar called, and everybody stood.

The judge entered. He bowed, then sat. 'Yes, Mr Lipschitz?'

Lipschitz stood. He shucked his gown and intoned, 'May it please my Lord, I call my first witness on this *voir dire*.' He paused for effect. 'And that witness is . . .' He waved a hand like a showman: '*Alistair Cecil Hargreave, counsel for the prosecution . . .*'

There was a stunned silence. The pressmen started scribbling frantically. Hargreave stared at the judge; then at Lipschitz. He was so astonished that he was not alarmed.

'*Me*, my Lord?'

'Yes,' Lipschitz smiled, 'my learned friend, please.'

The judge looked amazed. The press were delighted. 'Jesus Christ . . .' Champion and Findlay whispered simultaneously.

'But,' the judge said, 'the defence cannot call prosecuting counsel as a witness, Mr Lipschitz!'

'With respect,' Lipschitz said blandly, 'I don't see why not, my Lord, if he is able to give relevant corroborative evidence. I know of no legal rule which prohibits it.'

284

'Well I *do*, my Lord!' Hargreave said. He rose angrily to his feet. 'First of all, anything that I can say about this confession would obviously be hearsay, and hearsay is not admissible – *I* wasn't present at the interrogation of the defendant! And secondly everything I know about this case is clearly privileged. Thirdly –'

'It can no longer be privileged,' Lipschitz purred, 'because he has already divulged it to me, my Lord. And I am not seeking the introduction of hearsay in an attempt to prove any fact, my Lord – I am simply leading evidence to disprove Mr Champion's credibility. Evidence to prove a previous inconsistent statement by a witness is not hearsay. I am simply going to prove that *this* witness –' he pointed dramatically – 'Mr Champion, told a different story on a vital point to *that* witness, Mr Hargreave. Such evidence is not hearsay and is admissible.'

'My Lord,' Hargreave said, 'the Crown is required to make known to the defence an earlier contradictory statement by a Crown witness. I have done that, even though that earlier statement by Mr Champion was only verbal, not written, and even though I am not completely confident of my recollection of the incident, nor did I ever discuss my recollection with Mr Champion. Indeed it is arguable that in those circumstances I would have been justified in keeping silent. However, I disclosed my disquiet to Mr Lipschitz, to make of it what he thought best. But for him to now try to call me, the prosecuting counsel, as a witness is so contrary to legal practice and procedure, so contrary to the principle of legal confidentiality and, I submit, so contrary to the ethics governing relationships between lawyers if not contrary to the Law of Evidence, as to be laughable! Indeed vexatious!'

'My Lord,' Lipschitz cried happily, 'I call Alistair Cecil Hargreave as my first witness!'

'He'll have to subpoena me first!' Hargreave promised. 'Next he'll be calling my Lord himself as a witness! If Mr Lipschitz can produce any precedent for his suggestion I'll be amazed to hear it! So, doubtless, would my Lord.' He waved a shaky hand. 'I respectfully submit that my Lord should cut through these theatrics and order Mr Lipschitz to get on with the case.'

'*Theatrics?*' Lipschitz cried. 'What a way for counsel to speak of his learned friend trying to achieve justice! My Lord, I formally apply –'

'Mr Lipschitz,' the judge sighed peevishly, 'have you any precedents to quote me for this remarkably unusual application? If not, your application is dismissed. You can take me on appeal, of course, but until then kindly proceed with your case.'

Lipschitz was suddenly all sycophantic charm again. 'As my Lord pleases. So I next call . . .' and he glanced at Hargreave with an oily smile, 'Olga Romalova!'

Hargreave slumped back in his chair, his sick heart knocking, relief flooding over him. *Oh thank God* . . . It did not matter what embarrassment he might now suffer! Nor did it matter if Gregovich was convicted! Now he could prosecute the case for all it was worth! Champion snorted: 'Jesus Christ . . .'

Hargreave turned to look at the court entrance. Lipschitz was watching the door expectantly. Everybody waited. The press were poised for the dramatic appearance of this girl who was known to be the mistress of the Director of Public Prosecutions. A minute passed.

'Yes, Mr Lipschitz, where is your witness?' enquired the judge.

'She should be in the building, my Lord. I'll ask my instructing solicitor to look.'

The solicitor hurried from the court. Hargreave slumped back and waited, his heart knocking deliciously. Champion snorted again. The judge drummed his fingers.

A minute later the solicitor returned, hurried across the courtroom and whispered to Lipschitz. Hargreave's heart sank. Lipschitz frowned, then stood up.

'I apologize, my Lord, my witness has not arrived yet. So, rather than delay the court, I will proceed with my next witness. I call the defendant, Ivan Gregovich.'

Hargreave stared at Lipschitz. The man's face was bland. Hargreave wanted to leap to his feet and demand reassurance, he felt frantic lest something had gone wrong, lest Olga had not arrived in Hong Kong. Oh God, until he was absolutely sure of that fact he did not dare be too hard in cross-examining Gregovich. He got to his feet.

'My Lord. Before we proceed can we establish whether Miss Olga Romalova, who is a surprise witness, will definitely be called? If so I will have to hand over to Mr Findlay to conduct that part of the case. Furthermore,' he added lamely, 'it would be good to know how long this *voir dire* will take.'

The judge nodded. 'Mr Lipschitz?'

'Oh, I intend calling her if she arrives, my Lord.'

'She may not?' Hargreave and the judge demanded in unison.

Lipschitz clasped his hands reassuringly. 'Oh, we expect her to arrive any moment.'

Hargreave subsided in shaky relief. The judge nodded. Lipschitz beckoned to Gregovich, and pointed at the witness box. Hargreave nudged Champion, who leant over truculently. Hargreave whispered:

'Post a policeman in the corridor to look out for Olga Romalova and to advise us immediately she shows up.'

Champion glared at him. 'You're very anxious to have that bitch corroborate what you *think* I told you, aren't you? Well, it'll be a lie!'

Hargreave closed his eyes. 'Please post a cop outside, Bernie. If she doesn't show up it drastically weakens the defence case.'

'And you don't get laid tonight, huh?'

Hargreave took a tense breath. 'And after she's testified, please assign two policemen to protect her.'

'It's not our job to babysit defence witnesses!'

'Please, Bernie!'

Champion seethed: 'Now I'm not only your fall-guy, I'm your fucking pimp!' He got up and strode for the entrance, beckoning angrily to his policemen.

Hargreave tried to concentrate. Gregovich was in the witness box, taking the oath. It was the first opportunity Hargreave had had to really look at him, and he had difficulty concentrating even on that. But, Lord, he was an evil-looking man. The judge was saying:

'. . . please understand that we are not concerned at this time with your guilt or innocence, Mr Gregovich. We are only concerned with whether you made your statement to the police voluntarily or not. Understand?'

Gregovich nodded politely.

'Mr Gregovich, what is your employment?' Lipschitz said.

'Now I am a businessman,' Gregovich replied. 'Before, until 1986, I was a major in the KGB, sir. Before that I was at school.'

'Now, in the KGB, was it part of your duties to interrogate people suspected of crimes against the Communist state?'

Gregovich said solemnly, 'Very many times, yes.'

'And how did you treat those people, Mr Gregovich? Please be frank with my Lord.'

Gregovich turned to the judge. 'Now I am ashamed to say it,' he said gravely, 'but sometimes we used torture, my Lord, I will not deny.'

'Why are you now ashamed?' Lipschitz cajoled.

Gregovich cast his eyes down. 'Because it is very cruel. And because it makes people say anything, so you do not always get the truth. You can even make people confess to killing Abraham Lincoln.'

'Yes,' Lipschitz said earnestly, 'I imagine one can. Now, what form of torture was most effective in your experience, Mr Gregovich?'

'Electrical shock, my Lord. It is agony. And it leaves no marks on the victim – just great fear inside.'

'Yes . . .' Lipschitz said, giving a little shudder. 'Now, did you know Colonel Simonski of the Russian police before the day of your arrest?'

'Yes. In Moscow.'

'How?' Lipschitz asked solicitously.

Gregovich said, with a touch of controlled anger, 'Last year, in 1994, he interviewed me. In the Moscow police station. In connection with uranium.'

'Did you know anything about uranium?' Lipschitz asked.

Gregovich shook his head. 'I had only heard that it was being stolen. In *Time* magazine I read it. I did not know by who, where or why.'

'So what happened when Simonski interviewed you?'

Gregovich turned to the judge solemnly. 'Colonel Simonski is a very ruthless policeman. He gave me electrical torture, sir.'

'How?'

'With a shock-truncheon, like you showed us this morning.'

'This one?' Lipschitz held it up. 'I put that in as defence Exhibit One, my Lord.' He turned back to Gregovich. 'How many times did he touch you with it?'

'You mean in Moscow?' Gregovich asked innocently. 'Or in Hong Kong?'

'In Moscow,' Lipschitz smiled.

Gregovich said angrily, 'Two times in about one hour!'

Lipschitz sighed sympathetically. 'And how did you feel?'

'Agony! And I was terrified of more shocks.'

'Yes. And did you confess?'

'No. Because I did not know what to say, and Simonski did not know what he wanted me to say because he did not know who was stealing uranium, or where! He only knew some was found by the German police on a German man who died in custody. So it was no use to him if I told lies under torture.' He sighed bitterly. 'So after about one hour he let me go.' He added: 'After that I was very frightened of Colonel Simonski.'

'*Oh sure,*' Champion whispered. Hargreave looked feverishly at the courtroom entrance for Olga. Lipschitz continued:

'After that terrifying experience, when next did you see him?'

Gregovich spread his hands. 'At Hong Kong airport when I was arrested. I was astonished to see him. I was . . .' he waved his hands, 'terrified.'

'Now, did you know Nicolai Kozkov before your arrest?'

Gregovich frowned bemusedly. 'Never *seen* him before, sir.'

'Please,' Lipschitz said unctuously, 'address your answers to my Lord.'

'I am very sorry, my Lord,' Gregovich said to the bench. His Lordship looked at him stonily.

'We have heard the circumstances of your arrest,' Lipschitz continued. 'Afterwards, we're told, you were taken straight to Hong Kong Central police station. Was anything said on that journey in the car?'

Gregovich said earnestly, 'I only remember Simonski saying softly in Russian: "Now we will have some more fun with the shock treatment". He was sitting beside me in the backseat.'

'Did you respond?'

'I was terrified, sir. I think I said, "I am innocent, sir", something like that.' He added: 'Mr Champion was sitting on the other side of me. I don't think he could hear Simonski.'

Lipschitz continued with satisfaction: 'Now, we're told you were kept in Mr Champion's office for the next six hours. 'Did you have water available?'

'Yes, there was always a big jug of water and coffee. We all had many cups.'

'Now,' Lipschitz said, 'did anybody leave the room during the six long hours, after so much liquid, to go to the toilet?'

'Yes. I was taken to the toilet once. Colonel Simonski went two or three times, I am not sure. Mr Champion went twice, I am sure of that.'

'Why are you so sure of that?'

'Because while he was away Simonski gave me electrical shocks with a truncheon. That is easy to remember.'

Everybody smiled, even Hargreave. Except Champion. Lipschitz glowed, like a showman. 'Pause there. When *Simonski* left the room to go to the toilet, how did Mr Champion treat you?'

Gregovich turned to the judge. 'Mr Champion is a gentleman. Yes, he said words like "We have caught you red-handed, Ivan, you may as well admit", but he never threatened me. I was very impressed by him, not like the Russian police who are bastards, everyone will tell you. So I was very surprised this morning to hear such a gentleman say he never left the room to go to the toilet. Very surprised, my Lord.'

'Yes . . .' Lipschitz said sympathetically, saddened by his fellow man. 'And how do you feel about Simonski?'

'Colonel Simonski,' Gregovich said solemnly, 'is a terrible man.' He added: 'As bad as the KGB.'

Lipschitz nodded earnestly. 'Now, as far as you could tell, did Mr Champion know that Simonski had a shock-truncheon?'

'I think so; Simonski kept it under his jacket, but the handle was sticking out.'

'Now the evidence from Mr Champion has been that for the first three hours you denied any knowledge of this uranium. Then, he says, you began to make admissions. Why? Why did you change?'

'Because Mr Champion went to the toilet.'

Everybody grinned, the press, the judge, even Hargreave. Lipschitz was delighted with his witness. 'Yes, but what happened when Mr Champion went to the toilet, apart from the irresistible probability that he relieved his bladder?'

Gregovich said earnestly, 'Suddenly Simonski pulls out his truncheon and he jabs me with it, like this!' He demonstrated a man thrusting a sword. 'And I cried out. It was agony, my Lord, and I almost fell off the chair. And Simonski said "Nice?" or "Good?" then he jabbed me again. And I fell off the chair in such agony.'

Lipschitz shook his head in sadness. 'And how long was Mr Champion away?'

'Who can say, in such pain? Maybe it was five minutes, maybe ten.'

Lipschitz nodded sympathetically. 'So Mr Champion came back. What happened then?'

'Simonski looked at me like this . . .' Gregovich narrowed his eyes. 'And then, my Lord, I began to say what they wanted me to say, because I was so terrified of more shocks from Simonski.'

'And what did they want you to say, as far as you understood?'

'That I knew about the uranium in the suitcase. They said I had the key to the suitcase. That I must know the number of the combination lock. All that. So I agreed. So would anybody agree if they gave you such shocks. Even the Queen of England.'

Lipschitz grinned. 'Was it true, what you admitted?'

'No! I knew what they wanted me to say, I am not stupid.'

'You said that Mr Champion left the room a second time,' Lipschitz continued. 'How long after the first time?'

'Maybe two or three hours.'

'And what happened this time?'

'By now they were asking questions about where the uranium came from. Names of people I did not know. When Champion was gone to the toilet Simonski touched me with the truncheon again. I screamed and fell over. He said, "Just admit these details and I won't do it again." I was very frightened. I said, "Yes, I will agree to anything." Mr Champion came back, and I said I will admit.'

Lipschitz shook his head sadly. 'One last question: did you sleep on the overnight flight from Moscow?'

'No. I was very tired when I reached Hong Kong.'

'No further questions.' Lipschitz sat down, solemnly smug.

Hargreave glanced at the entrance: he caught the eye of the Chinese policeman Champion had posted in the corridor, who shrugged. Hargreave rose.

'I'd be grateful for a brief adjournment before cross-examination, my Lord.'

'Very well. Court will adjourn for ten minutes.'

Hargreave hurried down the crowded corridor, his eyes darting. Champion followed him. 'No sign of her?' Hargreave breathed.

'Hope she got run over by a bus,' Champion growled.

Hargreave rode down in the elevator and strode to his chambers. He closed the door, went to his toilet and retched; but nothing came up. He shuddered, and held his face. Oh God, shouldn't he let Findlay do the cross-examination of Gregovich now? But no – don't give Vladimir any excuse to renege on the deal. But if Olga is here Vladimir doesn't matter . . . But is Olga here or is she still in Macao? Maybe Lipschitz will apply for an adjournment after my cross-examination – it's three o'clock already – then Olga will stay in Macao overnight and anything could happen if I've given Gregovich a hard time.

He breathed deeply, trying to calm himself. Now stop panicking, he told himself. Of course Olga is going to testify – they need Olga, so she must be here, or at least in Macao, of course she's not still in Russia. And if you give Gregovich a hard time in cross, they'll need Olga all the more – in fact the best way to ensure Olga testifies is to give Gregovich a rough ride. But oh God, if Olga doesn't come . . .

He went to his cabinet and upended the whisky bottle to his mouth, then shuddered at the burn. There was a knock on the door. He slapped the bottle back in the cabinet.

'Ten minutes nearly up, Al,' Findlay said.

'Has the witness Romalova appeared?'

'No. You all right? Want me to do the cross-examination?'

'No. Let's go.'

He started through his secretary's office. Findlay hurried after him. 'What do you think of Gregovich?'

'Clever bastard. Quite an impressive witness so far. And his evidence

291

has a ring of truth about it – very likely Simonski did give him a going-over in Moscow; Gregovich probably was shit-scared of him.'

Olga was not in the corridor outside the court. The Chinese policeman shrugged apologetically again. Hargreave went up to Lipschitz. 'Your witness hasn't arrived, Arnold?'

Lipschitz looked worried. 'Hope nothing has happened to her.'

Hargreave had to work at it to keep the tension out of his voice. 'But has she definitely arrived in Macao?'

'I believe she landed in Canton early this morning.'

'For Christ's sake! Yes or no?'

Lipschitz smiled. 'Do keep your hair on, Al.' He turned away.

Jesus. Hargreave strode furiously back to his chair and sat down beside Findlay. He nodded at the registrar.

'*Court . . .*' the registrar cried mournfully a few moments later, and in walked the judge.

Gregovich was back in the witness box. Hargreave glanced back at the court's entrance for Olga, then turned to Gregovich, who looked him in the eye with icy politeness.

'Mr Gregovich, September, when you arrived, is one of the hottest months in Hong Kong. Did you not feel the heat and humidity as soon as you arrived?'

Gregovich looked puzzled. 'Yes.'

'And so Mr Champion's office, where you went to immediately, had its window open, didn't it?'

'Yes. I remember the window was open.'

'And the overhead fan was on, because once the interrogation started the door was closed, yes?'

Gregovich frowned. 'The door was closed, yes. But I do not remember about the fan. Maybe it was on.'

Hargreave's prosecutor's blood was up, despite himself. *Remember Olga isn't here yet.* 'Now, you've demonstrated how Simonski produced the truncheon to give you a shock. Do it again.'

Gregovich slid his left hand under his right armpit, then withdrew it, and thrust.

Hargreave said, 'Simonski had his jacket on.' It wasn't a question.

'Yes, he was wearing his jacket.'

Hargreave looked amazed. '*What?* In Hong Kong? In September? In an office without air-conditioning? For six hours, with the door shut?'

Lipschitz leapt to his feet. 'What is the question?'

Gregovich said loudly: 'The office was air-conditioned, sir!'

Hargreave looked more amazed. '*What?* With the window open? Nobody has the air-conditioning on and the window open! The hot air coming in defeats the air-conditioner!'

'*What's the question*, my Lord?' Lipschitz snarled.

Hargreave ignored him. 'And nobody has the overhead fan on if the air-conditioning is on!'

'*What's the question?!*'

'Very well – *Do* they?' Hargreave snapped. 'That's the question!'

Gregovich shifted his feet. 'The air-conditioning was on. Now I remember, the window was closed. And the fan, it was not turning.'

Hargreave snorted. 'Oh, *now* you remember? A moment ago you distinctly told us you remembered the window was *open*.' He glared. 'I put it to you that the air-conditioning was *not* working, as Mr Champion said. And it was so hot you *all* had your jackets off.'

Gregovich's eyes shifted. 'No, Simonski had his jacket on.'

'You and Mr Champion were more sensible and took yours off. But Simonski definitely had his jacket on? Strange. Because Mr Champion said that he saw Simonski's gun in the shoulder-holster for the first time when he took his jacket off. What do you say to that?'

Gregovich shrugged nervously. 'He is mistaken.'

'Ah. I see. Now . . .' Hargreave changed tack abruptly: 'You've told us you didn't know anything about uranium when Simonski questioned you in Moscow last year. What did you know about uranium when you were arrested in Hong Kong, Mr Gregovich?'

'Nothing.' Gregovich glowered.

Hargreave waved a hand: 'So you didn't know anything about the details in your confession either?'

'No. Simonski told me what to say. I knew from their many questions what they wanted me to say.'

'So every detail in your statement was put into your mouth by Simonski and Champion? Including the detail that you did *not* know the source of this uranium, except that it came from somebody in the city of Grozny in Chechnya?'

'Yes.'

'They were torturing you into confessing but they advised you to say you did not know the source? Strange.' Hargreave changed tack. 'Were you offered a lawyer?' he enquired quietly.

'*No*, sir,' Gregovich said emphatically.

'So Mr Champion, the man you describe as a gentlemanly policeman, is a liar, is he?'

'Yes, he lied. On this point.'

'And when he says Simonski had his jacket off, he is also a liar?'

'Yes, he lied.'

'So everybody is lying against you! Even the gentleman. Poor Mr Gregovich!'

'*What's the question?*' Lipschitz cried again.

Hargreave could not curb his instinct. 'And that's why, at the airport, you tried to run away? Because you knew you were suddenly surrounded by all these awful liars you had never seen before?'

'I saw Mr Simonski there,' Gregovich said. 'I was afraid of him.'

'Oh. You, a totally innocent man, knowing absolutely *nothing* about uranium, suddenly presumed the Hong Kong police force had ganged up on you just because Mr Simonski happened to be in town?'

'I thought Simonski had told the Hong Kong police I was involved in uranium.'

Hargreave feigned surprise. 'But why? You've told us you didn't know Kozkov, who just happened, by appalling bad luck, to be carrying this unopened suitcase on the same wretched aeroplane you, by the greatest misfortune, were travelling on!'

'This is rhetoric!' Lipschitz cried.

Yes, it was rhetoric. *Watch it.* But he had to press the point. He said quietly, 'As you walked into the customs hall, all innocence, you didn't even know what Kozkov looked like. So what on earth possessed you to try to run away?'

'Because they planted Kozkov's key on me.'

Hargreave looked mystified. 'But you didn't *know* Kozkov, you say! The police didn't introduce you, did they? But because you saw Simonski you presumed that the Hong Kong police had ganged up on you in connection with this complete stranger, Kozkov, who unbeknown to you had just been found carrying something? You didn't even *know* it was uranium in that suitcase, according to your evidence! So what made you run away?'

Gregovich persisted doggedly; 'Simonski.'

'I *see*,' Hargreave sighed. 'Last question, Mr Gregovich.' And this was the question that would knock Gregovich's credibility dead. For that reason he hated to ask it until he knew Olga was safe, but he had to. 'You've told us that you knew nothing about uranium, nothing about Kozkov, nothing about the suitcase; you were only able to give the details contained in your statement because they told you what to say. Correct?'

'Correct.'

'Then *how*,' Hargreave asked, 'did you know the combination number of the suitcase lock, mentioned in your statement? Neither Champion nor Simonski could possibly have known that number.'

There was a silence. Then Gregovich said, 'Kozkov told them the number. Then they told me to put it in my statement.'

'Then please explain this: Mr Champion has told us that it was only *after* you finally made your statement that he was able to telephone military headquarters and give them the combination number – in the afternoon. Yet Kozkov admitted everything in the morning, as soon as he reached the police station. Can you explain that?'

Lipschitz leapt to his feet. 'How can Mr Gregovich be asked to explain police delays?'

Hargreave had made his point, and he had pushed Gregovich far enough – further than he should have. He sighed and wound up his cross-examination. 'I put it to you that you made your statement voluntarily because you were caught red-handed at the airport, with the key, and after some perfectly legitimate interrogation by the police you realized the game was up.'

Gregovich turned to the judge. 'No, my Lord. I made the statement only because I was tortured by Colonel Simonski.'

Hargreave sat down. He turned and looked towards the door for Olga. He didn't see her.

Lipschitz rose to his feet. 'No re-examination, my Lord.'

'Very well. Call your next witness, Mr Lipschitz.'

Hargreave closed his eyes, and held his breath.

'I call Miss Olga Romalova, my Lord,' Lipschitz said.

Hargreave's heart seemed to turn over. He massaged his eyelids with a trembling hand. He heard the solicitor hurrying across the court to the door to fetch her. Hargreave sat, staring at nothing. An agonizing half-minute passed. Then he heard footsteps re-entering the court. He turned.

Consternation entered his breast: *the solicitor was alone* . . . He hurried up to Lipschitz, and whispered to him. Lipschitz glanced at Hargreave with a wolfish smile, then turned to the bench.

'I regret to inform my Lord that the witness Olga Romalova has not yet arrived. I apologize profusely for the inconvenience. What I respectfully suggest, therefore, is that this *voir dire* be put to one side for the time being, and that the jury be recalled to allow my learned friend to continue with the rest of the Crown case. Thereafter, when Miss Romalova has been tracked down, we can send the jury away again and continue with the *voir dire*.'

Hargreave was getting to his feet angrily. 'Mr Hargreave,' his Lordship said, 'do you have any objection to that course?'

Indeed he did. He knew what Shitlips was up to – stringing out the suspense to unnerve him! 'Every objection, my Lord. It will confuse the jury to hear the case piecemeal, being shuttled in and out of the court, being allowed to hear one bit of evidence, then not the next, all because my learned friend can't produce his witness on time!'

'It's not my fault,' Lipschitz whined. 'If my learned friend would give evidence himself as to what Mr Champion said to him I would not have to call his friend Olga Romalova, thus wasting the taxpayers' money!'

Hargreave seethed at this, but the judge said testily, 'We've been through that, Mr Lipschitz!'

'What we want to know, my Lord,' Hargreave said angrily, 'is *why* any delay is necessary at all! Does he know whether she has even arrived in the Far East? If so, *what* is delaying her arrival at this court-room? In short, this court has the right to know why it is being so inconvenienced and why the taxpayers' money my learned friend sheds such crocodile tears over is being wasted!'

Lipschitz cried, 'I take the greatest exception –'

'Yes, I'm sure you do, Mr Lipschitz,' the judge said tartly, 'but what are the details about your witness?'

Lipschitz was all servility again, hands clasped. 'My Lord, I apologize, I was only informed that the witness would be flying from Moscow to Vladivostok, thence to Canton, thence proceeding overland to Macao, and from there to Hong Kong by hydrofoil. We can only presume that flights have been delayed, as flights are the world over. But I assure you my Lord that during the overnight adjournment my solicitors will get all these details.'

'And if the witness is not here by tomorrow?' the judge demanded, taking the words out of Hargreave's mouth.

Lipschitz smarmed: 'With great respect, my Lord, I cannot now com-mit myself. What is of paramount importance is that the right of this Russian defendant to call Russian witnesses all the way from Russia to China, on Russian and Chinese airlines, be sympathetically respected. And if that requires me to apply for a further adjournment, or indeed requires us to interrupt this *voir dire* and thus oblige my learned friend – to save the taxpayers' money – to proceed with the rest of his case pending Miss Romalova's appearance from halfway across the world, then so be it. Justice must not only be done, it must be *seen* to be done – that will be my respectful submission tomorrow in the unlikely event of Miss Romalova not being with us.' He rolled his eyes soulfully towards Hargreave.

Hargreave wanted to bellow *Where is she, you little shit?!* But he kept the anguish out of his voice. He said: 'The Crown is just as concerned with achieving justice as my learned friend. We will, of course, place no obstacle in the way of his calling any witness he chooses. All we ask is that he does his duty of ensuring they show up on time. If we have to adjourn now for the day, so be it. But I would be most grateful if my Lord reminds my learned friend of his duty in the strongest terms.' He sat, and propped his brow in his hand.

'Mr Lipschitz,' the judge said, 'please do not come to court tomorrow uninformed as to your witness's whereabouts. Court will adjourn until nine o'clock tomorrow morning.'

31

That night was very hard on Hargreave. He wanted to get drunk, to sit in a crowded bar and let the noise and booze purge the tension out of him, but he dared not: he had to be on the ball tomorrow. And he wanted to bellow his frustration and anger to the sky, grab Lipschitz by the throat and shake the bastard until his brains rattled – the little shithouse had staged this whole delay to unnerve him, to give him a sleepless night, playing upon his dreadful fear that Olga might not show up at all – the little shit had Olga tucked away in Macao and he would not produce her until he had wrung every drop of tension out of the suspense. Well, there was only one way to deal with those tactics and that was to stay calm and roll with the punches – and not having a hangover tomorrow. Then came the anguish of uncertainty: *did* Lipschitz intend to call Olga as a witness at all? Had Olga refused to testify? Perhaps he was telling the truth, perhaps he didn't know what had happened to her, perhaps Vladimir had refused to let her go; perhaps Vladimir had been gunned down in a gangland war, perhaps Olga was out of his physical control now . . .

He did not even have a drink. From the Supreme Court he went to the gym and tried to sweat out all the booze he had drunk during the day: he sat in the sauna, trying to close his mind to the uncertainties. When he could bear the heat no longer he went to the exercise machines, trying to squeeze the dreadful possibilities out of his head and heart; then he went back to the sauna and tried to sweat out some more. He was physically and mentally drained when he drove up the Peak in the sunset. He drank a pint of water while he cooked a big slab of liver. Then he took a sleeping pill and collapsed on his bed.

He lay in the air-conditioned dusk, waiting for the pill to take effect. Then, for the second time since this crisis began, he did something that he had not done for many years: he heaved himself up, knelt down at his bedside and tried to pray.

*   *   *

Maybe it was the prayer that did it, but Hargreave woke up at dawn feeling grimly calm, and rested. He got up before he could start thinking and had a cold shower, then ate a big bowl of wheatgerm and yoghurt. With the sunrise he was driving down the Peak, still calm: Lipschitz was going to call Olga as a witness, he had no doubt about that – so it was just a question of when. The bastard would surely try to spin the suspense out, so it was just a matter of keeping his cool. He went to the gym, the first person there, and morosely attacked the equipment. An hour later he was sitting in the Hong Kong Club working his way through a plate of steak and eggs as he tried to read yesterday's London newspapers. The front-page headline of the *South China Morning Post* cried: DRAMA IN NUCLEAR TRIAL. He did not read it. At a quarter to nine he strode across Queensway to the Supreme Court.

The corridors were almost empty at this hour because the other courts were not resuming work until ten o'clock, but in Court Fourteen the gallery was full when Hargreave entered. The jury were standing around, Gregovich was in the dock. Findlay and Champion were sitting at the bar, Lipschitz was in a huddle with his solicitors.

'Good morning,' Hargreave smiled bleakly at Findlay and Champion. 'Good morning, Arnold.'

Lipschitz ignored him.

Champion leaned forward and whispered, 'Al, I apologize for my outburst yesterday – I phoned you last night but got no reply.'

Thank God. 'That's okay, Bernie. Understandable.'

'You did a good job cross-examining Gregovich. You hammered him on that air-conditioning and the combination number.'

'Thanks.'

'I telephoned my pals in the Macao police last night,' Champion went on, 'to find out if they knew whether Olga Romalova had arrived yet. They called me back at midnight and said she hadn't.'

Hargreave's heart lurched. Oh God – *but surely she would arrive today.* And Champion shouldn't have done this! 'I hope you didn't say you wanted to speak to her? She's a *defence* witness.'

'No, of course not, I just wanted to know whether she's going to turn up and tell lies against me. My guess is she's not coming, I think she's just a Lipschitz smokescreen.'

There was a rap on the door and the registrar called 'Court'. Everybody stood.

The Honourable Mr Justice Walters strode in. He bowed to counsel and sat. 'Well, Mr Lipschitz, what have you got for us today?'

'My Lord, I have a most *serious* complaint,' Lipschitz said indignantly.

He paused dramatically. 'My Lord, I am informed that last night the Crown –' he pointed accusingly at Hargreave – 'attempted to contact my witness, Olga Romalova!' He leered significantly at the jury. 'What a travesty of ethics! It is utterly improper for the Crown to tamper with defence witnesses!'

Hargreave rose angrily. 'A less charitable soul than myself might think that Mr Lipschitz is making this spurious allegation in order to influence the jury, my Lord! The fact is that neither I nor the police have made any effort whatsoever to contact Miss Romalova. All the police have done is ask their counterparts in Macao to advise us when Miss Romalova enters Macao so that we know what further delays are in store for us. The police made this perfectly innocent enquiry on their own initiative, not at my request.' He ended angrily: 'So I'd like a retraction of the allegation of our "tampering".'

Lipschitz started to argue but the judge cut in. 'Are you satisfied with that response, Mr Lipschitz? If so, withdraw the allegation.'

Lipschitz rolled his eyes long-sufferingly at the jury. 'Satisfied, my Lord? If I am not, there is little I can do about it. I can only say it is unusual indeed for the Crown to take such an interest in a defence witness's whereabouts. But very well, I retract.'

The judge sighed. 'Satisfied with that, Mr Hargreave?'

Hargreave rose with a forced, weary smile. 'Not really, my Lord, but the Crown's shoulders are broad. So now can my learned friend tell us where his witness is?'

Lipschitz was suddenly all charm again. 'My Lord, apparently the delay occurred because Miss Romalova missed Aeroflot's direct flight from Moscow to Hong Kong on Sunday and had to fly to Vladivostok instead, yesterday, where she will have changed to China Airlines to Canton. My Lord, I am very relieved to tell you that even as I speak she should be landing in Canton, will be in Macao by noon, and should be here directly after the lunch adjournment.'

Hargreave slumped in his chair, relief flooding him. He kept a smile off his face. Oh thank God. Lipschitz was saying:

'. . . so I respectfully suggest my learned friend continues now with the rest of his case, leaving the *voir dire* to stand over until Miss Romalova arrives.'

'Mr Hargreave, do you have any objection to that course?'

Hargreave had no objection to any course now that he knew Olga was definitely on her way. Now he could go for broke on this case, do his utmost to get Gregovich convicted. 'Indeed I do, my Lord, but in the interest of the poor taxpayers' purse I will continue. I respectfully request my Lord to explain to the jury what's happening, and then I'll call Nikolai Kozkov . . .'

That morning seemed interminable. In suppressed excitement Hargreave led his witnesses through their paces in front of the jury.

Through an interpreter Kozkov testified that he had agreed with an unknown person in Moscow to carry a suitcase to Hong Kong for a fee of one thousand American dollars and deliver it, at the airport, to somebody who would identify himself as Lawrence. He had not known what was going to be in the suitcase, nor did he ask, though he presumed it was contraband of some kind. Following instructions he went to Moscow airport on 13 September where another unknown Russian male, in the toilet, handed him the suitcase, Exhibit One, a new passport, a return air-ticket to Hong Kong, and his money. He was not given any keys to the suitcase, nor was he told the number of the combination lock. On arrival in Hong Kong he retrieved the suitcase, then went to clear customs. There, to his alarm, he was challenged by Inspector Poon. When told to open the suitcase he was of course unable to do so, and tried to run away. But he was arrested by Mr Champion, who searched him but did not find any key. He subsequently saw the defendant being challenged, arrested and searched, and he saw a key. He had never seen the defendant Gregovich before this. He made a confession to the police, and at his subsequent trial before the magistrate he pleaded guilty to importing a contraband substance and was sentenced to one year's imprisonment.

Lipschitz rose to cross-examine.

'You're a criminal, aren't you, Mr Kozkov? You've been convicted several times in Russia of crimes of dishonesty, haven't you?'

'Yes.'

'And these days Moscow has many criminal gangs, hasn't it?'

'Yes.'

'And in the underworld you habituate you've heard the names of many criminals, yet you'd never heard of the defendant before, had you?'

'No.'

It was a harmless piece of cross-examination so far, which did no damage to the Crown case, but Lipschitz cast a smug leer at the jury as if he was scoring a major forensic triumph, as if the Crown had been concealing all this sinister detail from them. He went on:

'Mr Kozkov, you confessed to the police because you had been caught red-handed, didn't you? And Mr Champion –' he pointed ostentatiously – 'told you that you would get a lighter sentence if you confessed, didn't he?'

'Yes.'

'Yes. And Mr Champion told you that *he* believed you were just a dumb courier who did not realize you were carrying uranium, didn't he?'

'Yes.'

'Yes. And you were very relieved that he believed that. So you were very keen to cooperate with him, weren't you?'

'Yes.'

'And Mr Champion told you he believed that Mr Gregovich was the man who was importing the suitcase of uranium, didn't he?'

'Yes.'

'And so you told him the number of the combination lock, didn't you?'

Lipschitz had slipped the question in almost casually. Kozkov started to agree, then hesitated, looking puzzled. 'No, I did not know the number of the combination lock, sir.'

Hargreave, Findlay and Champion smiled.

'*You hesitated before saying No!*' Lipschitz thundered. He pointed accusingly. '*You're lying! You were about to say "Yes"!*'

Kozkov looked frightened at the sudden anger; he blinked rapidly. Then he spoke timidly to the interpreter, who translated:

'You were being so kind, sir, asking so many easy questions to which I said yes that I nearly made a mistake and said yes again.'

Beautiful. Hargreave smiled to himself.

'Oh, you nearly made a *mistake*?' Lipschitz leered. 'A mistake about such an important point? A point that should have been crystal clear in your mind!'

'Yes, sir, it was clear,' Kozkov said apologetically.

'A point that proved your guilt or innocence!'

'I *was* innocent, sir,' Kozkov said worriedly.

Lipschitz thundered, '*Then if it was crystal-clear and you were so innocent, why did you nearly make such a dreadful mistake?*'

Kozkov looked thoroughly alarmed. Hargreave rose and said, 'Will my learned friend please stop shouting at the witness, my Lord?' He added mildly, to enrage Lipschitz: 'Noise is no substitute for advocacy.'

It worked – Lipschitz exploded: 'When I need my learned friend's advice on advocacy I'll ask him! Who wouldn't get angry at such blatant lies and prevarication by a witness!' He glared around, wide-eyed. Then with an effort he controlled himself, turned back to Kozkov and stabbed

302

his finger at him: 'I'll tell you why you nearly made such a dreadful mistake! Because you *did* give Mr Champion the combination lock number!'

'No, sir. How could I do that? I did not know the number.'

'I will ask the questions! And you also had the key to the suitcase on you! Mr Champion found it in your pocket, then pretended to find it on Mr Gregovich.'

'*No,*' Kozkov pleaded. 'I did not have a key, sir.'

'No? We'll see . . . It was Mr Champion who searched you, wasn't it?'

'Yes.'

'Yes . . . And it was Mr Champion who searched Mr Gregovich moments later and "produced" –' Lipschitz made sneering quotation marks with his fingers – 'the key, wasn't it?'

'Yes.'

'Yes. And it was Mr Champion who told you he believed you were only the dumb courier. And it was Mr Champion's attitude you were so relieved about, Mr Champion who you wanted to cooperate with – wasn't it?'

'Yes.'

Lipschitz leant forward, eyes blazing: 'And you were so cooperative with nice Mr Champion that you agreed to say you had no key and that Mr Champion found it on poor Mr Gregovich!'

Kozkov shot a frantic look at Champion, then pleaded, 'No, sir . . .'

Champion groaned under his breath.

'Did you ask the unknown man who gave you the suitcase for the key, and the combination number?'

'No, sir.'

Lipschitz looked amazed. '*No?* Didn't you presume the suitcase was locked?'

'I didn't know, sir.'

'You didn't *know?* But you knew you were smuggling contraband! Contraband would not be in an *unlocked* suitcase, would it?'

'No. Yes, I presumed the suitcase was locked.'

'Oh, now you say you did presume! A moment ago you said you didn't!'

Kozkov looked thoroughly confused. 'I was muddled up. I thought the suitcase was locked.'

'Oh muddled up, were you? About this very important point of the suitcase lock! Why wasn't it crystal-clear in your mind if you had no key to the lock?'

Kozkov looked very unhappy. 'You muddled me, sir,' he mumbled.

'And me,' Hargreave said loudly. The jurymen grinned.

'I'll ask my learned friend to hold his tongue, my Lord!' Lipschitz cried furiously. 'He's said that to distract the jury from this witness's blatant lies!'

Hargreave half stood. 'I apologize, my Lord. But I *am* a bit muddled by the questions.' He sat down with a sober sigh. 'Carry on, Arnold,' he said in a stage-mutter, 'straighten us out.'

Lipschitz turned back on Kozkov angrily: 'If you presumed the suitcase was locked, why didn't you ask the man who gave it to you in Moscow about a key?'

Kozkov said simply, 'I did not think of it.'

'Oh, you did not think . . . And you were going to hand it over to a man called Lawrence in Hong Kong. What did you think you were going to say to Mr Lawrence when he asked you for a key, and the number of the lock?'

'I was going to say I knew nothing about a key, or the combination lock. I presumed he would know the numbers, and have a key.'

'Oh – so you *did* think about it!'

'No.'

'But you just told us you presumed he had a key and the combination numbers. So you must have thought about it!'

Kozkov looked thoroughly miserable. 'Yes, I thought about it.'

'But you've just told us you didn't! So if you thought about it, why didn't you ask the man who gave you the suitcase about the key and the combination? So you could tell Mr Lawrence?'

Kozkov sighed hopelessly. 'I don't know, sir. It was not my business.'

'But it *was* your business!' Lipschitz cried triumphantly. 'You were being paid to fly the suitcase ten thousand miles and risk going to jail for it!'

Kozkov nodded miserably. 'I think I did ask the man about the key and the number, but he said it was not my business.'

'Oh!' Lipschitz cried joyously: 'So you *did* ask. A moment ago you told us you didn't.' He leant forward, and sneered: 'Why didn't you remember that the first time I asked you?'

Kozkov shifted. 'I don't know, sir,' he mumbled. 'Maybe I am stupid.'

Thank God he said that, Hargreave thought. Lipschitz jabbed his finger and cried, 'No! You're a stupid *liar*! Caught out all over the place in your lies! I put it to you, *Mister* Kozkov – you, a convicted criminal, convicted both in Russia and Hong Kong – I put it to you that you *were* given the key and told the combination lock number, but you

304

cooperated with Mr Champion – you conspired with *nice* Mr Champion – to put the blame on Mr Gregovich, in exchange for a lighter sentence!'

Champion seethed under his breath. Kozkov mumbled, 'No, sir.'

Lipschitz rolled his eyes at the jury: 'But Mr Champion did tell you that Mr Gregovich was the real culprit, who deserved to be convicted?'

'Yes, sir.'

'*Thank* you, Mister Kozkov. No further questions, my Lord!' He sat down triumphantly.

There was silence. Then his Lordship said: 'Any re-examination, Mr Hargreave?'

How to patch this guy up in re-examination? Hargreave got to his feet. He said with affected weariness:

'Are you a drug addict? If so, what drug are you addicted to?'

Lipschitz leapt to his feet. 'How does this arise from my cross-examination, my Lord?!'

Hargreave sighed. 'The witness said he was muddled by my learned friend's questions. Arising out of that, I'm trying to find out why.'

'I'll allow the question,' his Lordship said. 'And if Mr Lipschitz wants to re-cross-examine on this point, he may.'

Lipschitz threw up his hands and sat, injuredly. The interpreter put the question to Kozkov, who replied, 'Heroin, my Lord.'

'And when you received the suitcase at Moscow airport,' Hargreave said, 'how were you feeling? – as regards your heroin addiction.'

'Fine.'

Everybody smiled. 'Meaning what?' Hargreave asked.

Kozkov said, 'I had recently had a fix.'

'I see. And when you have a fix, how does it make you feel?'

'Happy.'

'Is one thinking clearly?'

Kozkov considered, then said, 'Maybe you *can* think clearly, if you try, but you do not care, because you are happy.'

Hargreave nodded. 'Now since you arrived in Hong Kong, you've been in custody. Have you been receiving any help for your addiction?'

'Yes, the prison doctor is giving me medicine.'

'How do you feel at this moment?'

'Very nervous. And tired. I want my medicine.'

'You told my learned friend you felt muddled. How, if at all, did your physical condition contribute?'

'Objection!' Lipschitz said angrily. 'That's leading!'

'It's not,' Hargreave retorted. 'I said "How, if at all".'

'Yes,' his Lordship said. 'Answer the question, please.'

'I felt very nervous, sir,' Kozkov said. 'Confused by his questions.'

Hargreave sighed – all this was a two-edged sword. He ended, 'For the last time, Mr Kozkov: did you have the key to the suitcase, and know the combination lock number?'

'No, sir.'

'Thank you.' He sat down.

Lipschitz scrambled to his feet aggressively. 'Before landing in Hong Kong, when had you had your last fix?'

Kozkov thought. 'About three hours.'

'You gave yourself a fix in the plane's toilet, did you?'

'Yes, sir.'

'Did you have any more heroin available?'

'No. I intended to buy some more in Hong Kong.'

'So when Mr Champion questioned you at the police station, your fix was wearing off, wasn't it?'

'Yes.'

'And you were feeling very nervous? Because you'd been arrested and because of your addiction?'

'Yes.'

'Yes. And you told Mr Champion you were an addict.'

'Yes, he knew.'

'And you badly wanted another fix. And you asked Mr Champion to get you some heroin?'

'Yes, sir.'

'That was uppermost in your mind, wasn't it? Very important?'

'Yes, very important to me.'

'So you asked him right away – *before* the questioning started?'

Kozkov considered: 'Maybe it was during the questioning.'

'*Before* he asked you about the key and the combination number.'

'I don't remember, sir.' He added, 'He already knew I did not have a key because he found it on Mr Gregovich.'

'So *you* say! And Mr Champion said yes, he could get you a fix of heroin, didn't he?'

'*Jesus . . .*' Champion quietly seethed to Hargreave.

'You didn't, did you?' Hargreave whispered.

'*No,*' Champion hissed.

Kozkov said, 'Yes.'

'*Christ!*' Champion whispered furiously. Hargreave sighed.

Lipschitz's face lit up. He said gently: 'Provided you cooperated with him.'

'Yes,' Kozkov said.

306

Champion, Hargreave and Findlay groaned.

'And provided you told him the number of the combination lock?'

'Yes,' Kozkov said simply.

'So you *told* him the number!'

Kozkov frowned. 'No, I did not know the number. Even now I do not know the number. Now I am muddled again. Mr Champion said yes, he would take me to the doctor who would give me treatment for my addiction.'

Lipschitz cried angrily, 'Oh, now you are muddled again? Mr Champion said the doctor would give you some heroin, didn't he?'

Kozkov looked bemused. 'I did not know what the doctor would give me.'

'But Mr Champion said the doctor would give you a fix of heroin, didn't he?'

'I don't know, sir. He said the doctor would help me.'

'With *heroin*?'

Kozkov looked helpless. 'Maybe the medicine would have some heroin in it.'

Lipschitz pounced: 'You *expected* the medicine to contain heroin?'

'I hoped it would contain heroin, yes.'

'You hoped! Because Mr Champion said so!'

Kozkov sighed. 'Maybe he said that. I don't know.'

Lipschitz looked meaningfully at the jury. 'Thank you. "Maybe he said that",' he repeated for their benefit. He quit while he was ahead. 'No further questions necessary.' He sat down.

Necessary? Typical Lipschitz. Hargreave rose to his feet.

'My Lord, I submit I am entitled to re-examine again on this new evidence that's emerged in the second cross-examination.'

'Objection!' Lipschitz cried. 'My learned friend has already had his chance to re-examine! Now he wants a second one!'

His Lordship said mildly, 'You had a second cross-examination, Mr Lipschitz.'

'What's my learned friend up to now?' Lipschitz asked, turning to the jury.

'I am "up to" nothing, my Lord, and I resent my learned friend's innuendo, attempting thereby to prejudice the jury!'

'Objection!' Lipschitz rose again. 'How dare my learned friend imply –'

'That *you're* up to something?' Hargreave snapped.

'*Gentlemen* . . .' his Lordship sighed. 'Yes, you may re-examine, Mr Hargreave, confining yourself of course to the new matter.'

307

'Thank you, my Lord.' Hargreave turned to Kozkov: 'Mr Champion said he would take you to a doctor. According to your understanding at the time, was or was not that conditional on your cooperation?'

'Objection!' Lipschitz cried. 'That's leading!'

Hargreave groaned. His Lordship said, 'I don't think so, Mr Lipschitz, I would have asked the question myself if Mr Hargreave hadn't. Have you a better way of putting it?'

'The witness has already said that Champion offered to get him to a doctor *provided* he cooperated. What could be clearer than that?' He spread his hands and turned to the jury.

'You haven't answered my question, Mr Lipschitz. Anyway, let's see. Yes, Mr Hargreave, proceed.'

Hargreave repeated the question.

'I don't think it was a condition.' Kozkov said. 'Mr Champion is a nice man. He said, Yes, we will take you to a doctor, but first you must answer some questions.'

Lipschitz scrambled to his feet. '"But *first* you *must*", my Lord!' he cried triumphantly.

'Yes, that's what the witness said. Let Mr Hargreave continue.'

Glowering, Lipschitz sat down. Hargreave said: 'Did you or did you not understand from that that if you refused or failed to answer questions you would *not* be taken to a doctor?'

Kozkov looked bewildered. 'I don't know, sir, I did not think about that, I just wanted to see a doctor and get a fix.'

Lipschitz leapt to his feet and glared at Hargreave. 'You're stuck with that answer! No cross-examining your own witness!'

Hargreave sighed. Yes, he was probably stuck with that answer. So he had little to lose now, he might as well pursue it. 'Not necessarily, Arnold.' He turned to the witness: 'And what do you mean by "fix"?'

Kozkov looked mystified. 'Medicine, like I said, sir.'

The dangerous question had paid off. Hargreave went on quickly: 'You've told us, of course, that all this conversation was going on through a Russian interpreter. Did you understand any of the English Mr Champion spoke, before the interpreter translated?'

Kozkov shook his head. 'No, sir.'

'Does the English slang word "fix" mean anything to you?'

'Objection!' Lipschitz cried.

Hargreave rephrased the question. 'What does the English slang-word "fix" mean to you?'

The interpreter put the question in Russian, using the English word. Kozkov seemed puzzled. 'I don't know, sir.'

Thank God. 'No further questions, my Lord,' Hargreave said. 'But needless to say I will be calling the interpreter as a witness to tell us what Russian word he used for "fix", and its connotations in Russian.'

His Lordship nodded. 'Do the gentlemen of the jury have any questions?'

The foreman, Mr Davidson, consulted with his fellows, then stood up.

'What treatment did the doctor give the witness?'

The interpreter translated. 'Pills,' Kozkov said. 'I don't know the name. And some gas, I think it is called laughing gas.'

The judge said to Kozkov, 'Thank you, stand down.' He looked at the clock. 'Well, we'll take the tea adjournment now, for fifteen minutes.'

Hargreave strode into his chambers, on air. In four hours Olga would be here safe and sound! 'Coffee for three, please Miss Ho!'

Findlay and Champion followed him in, both looking serious. Inspector Sullivan had been instructed to summons the Russian interpreter who had assisted in the interrogation of Kozkov. Hargreave slung off his wig and sat.

Findlay said, 'What do you think, Al?'

'What do *you* think?' Hargreave replied. 'Bernie?'

Champion glowered. 'I did not, repeat *not*, induce Kozkov to cooperate by offering him heroin! The guy asked me for a fix and I simply said a doctor would treat him. He had already spilt the beans. And he did *not* know the combination lock's number.'

'I believe you; the problem is, does the jury?'

'Fucking juries,' Champion said.

'You did a good job patching Kozkov up in re-examination, Al,' Findlay said. 'It's clear from the guy's demeanour he wasn't induced, he's just dumb, the jury won't believe he knew the number.'

'But what about the appeal court? They won't see Kozkov's demeanour, just his contradictory answers in black and white. Will they think it's safe to convict on the word of a drug addict who's dying for a fix and who's just been told by the cops he'll get relief from his suffering after he's answered all the questions satisfactorily?'

'It wasn't like that,' Champion insisted.

'But the appeal court may see it like that. And Lipschitz is going to do his damnedest to make the jury see it like that.'

'Fucking juries,' Champion said. 'Why oh why did this business about him being a drug addict have to come up?'

'I avoided the subject in my examination-in-chief,' Hargreave said, 'but I expected Lipschitz to jump on it in his cross-examination. He didn't only because he had muddled up the guy so much it was best not to raise the heroin addiction as a possible explanation for his contradictory answers. So I *had* to raise it in re-examination, to patch him up.'

'You did a good job of it,' Findlay said.

'Fucking juries,' Champion said.

But Hargreave hardly cared about fucking juries. In a few hours Olga would be here, even now she was travelling through China to Macao, tonight she would be in his arms. Yes, he wanted to win this fucking case now.

Miss Ho brought the coffee in. 'Drink up,' Hargreave said, 'and let's get on with it.'

32

Hargreave began: 'I call Professor Derrick Donovan, my Lord.'

The professor entered the witness box. He was a tall, balding man with a sallow face. The registrar administered the oath.

'Are you the professor of nuclear physics at the University of Hong Kong?'

'I am, my Lord.'

'What are your academic qualifications, please?'

The professor reeled off half a dozen university degrees.

'With those qualifications do you understand all the principles involved in the manufacture of a nuclear weapon?'

'I do.'

Led by Hargreave, the professor briefly told the court the characteristics of a nuclear weapon and its components, what happened on detonation, the meaning of 'fall-out' and 'radio-activity', its lethal effect on living creatures.

'Very well,' Hargreave continued. 'Now, on the fourteenth of September this year you were requested by the Hong Kong Police to examine this –'

'Objection!' Lipschitz cried. 'My learned friend is asking a leading question!'

Hargreave smiled wearily. 'True. But I wasn't aware that my learned friend's defence challenged the nature of the substance we're dealing with in this trial. However –'

'You conduct your prosecution according to the Law of Evidence,' Lipschitz said for the jury's benefit – 'no more attempts at clever shortcuts!'

Hargreave grinned at the judge. 'If my learned friend considers my question clever, my Lord, he is very easily impressed. However, Professor Donovan, to satisfy my learned friend, please look at this suitcase, Exhibit One. Do you know anything about it?'

The professor smiled. 'Yes. On the fourteenth of September I examined this suitcase at the request of the Hong Kong Police.'

The jury smiled. Lipschitz crossed his arms across his chest, like a victor. Hargreave continued: 'Who delivered it to you, and where?'

'It arrived in an armoured police vehicle commanded by Inspector Sullivan. I received the suitcase in the military headquarters compound. I carried it personally into a special armaments room, which is designed for the testing of dangerous materials.'

'Did you receive anything else with the suitcase?'

'Yes. Inspector Sullivan handed me a key.'

'Is this the key, Exhibit Two?'

'It is.'

'What time was it that you received the suitcase?'

'At fifteen minutes past eight in the morning.'

'What did you do next?'

'I had donned the necessary protective clothing. I then tested the key, Exhibit Two, in the lock of the suitcase, and it opened the lock. However, I was unable to open the lid because, as you see, it also has a combination lock. I did not know the number.'

'How many digits are in the combination lock?'

'Four. So the correct number could be anything between four zeros and nine thousand, nine hundred and ninety-nine. As each digit can be in ten different positions in relation to the others, the chances of a stranger finding the right combination of numbers by trial and error are remote.'

'So, as you could not open the combination lock, what did you do?'

'I waited, until somebody could tell me the number. I read a novel.'

'And did somebody eventually provide the number?'

'Objection!' Lipschitz snarled. 'That's a leading question! *And* an invitation to hearsay!'

Hargreave sighed. 'Very well, my Lord. Professor, did you or did you not eventually manage to open the wretched suitcase? If so, how?'

'Yes,' the professor said. 'I was eventually provided with the number by Superintendent Champion on the telephone.'

'*Objection!*' Lipschitz thundered. 'My Lord, that is blatant hearsay! What's my learned friend up to now? He knows hearsay is inadmissible!'

'My Lord,' Hargreave said wearily, 'that answer by the professor is clearly *not* hearsay. He is telling us a fact, that he was able to open the suitcase because he was provided with the wherewithal, namely the number. He's telling us a *fact*, not what somebody said.'

'Yes, Mr Lipschitz,' his Lordship said wearily.

'My *Lord*,' Lipschitz protested, glancing at the jury for sympathy, 'with great respect I submit that it is sneaking hearsay in by the back door, and that's unlawful. The professor's answer clearly means, ''Mr

Champion told me the number was so-and-so"! And that's *hearsay*!'

'My Lord,' Hargreave said, 'the professor's answer amounts to no more than he was provided by Mr Champion with the metaphorical key to open the suitcase – he could have opened it with a sledgehammer, but as it happened he opened it with a series of numbers. That's a fact. That is *not* sneaking hearsay in the backdoor.'

'Mr Hargreave is quite right, Mr Lipschitz,' his Lordship said.

Lipschitz rolled his courageous, long-suffering eyes at the jury, sending the message, 'There is no justice . . .'

'Professor,' Hargreave said, 'you've told us you received the suitcase at 8.15 a.m. At what time did you receive a telephone call from Mr Champion, enabling you to open the suitcase?'

'Two-forty that afternoon. I then opened the lock, using numbers seven, nine, three, one, in that order.'

'And what did you find within? You may refer to any notes you made at the time.'

'The suitcase was packed with eighteen sealed glass jars. I took a photograph. I removed the jars and numbered them one to eighteen. The suitcase was lined in lead. I then opened the glass jars, one by one, took samples from each and subjected them to tests. I made notes and from these compiled a report. The results of my tests prove that the substance in the jars is eight-point-nine kilograms of weapons-grade enriched uranium.'

'Is this your report?' Hargreave handed a typewritten document to the orderly, who passed it to the witness.

'It is,' the professor said.

'I put that report in as Exhibit Four, my Lord. Are these the photographs you took?' He handed up an album.

The professor flicked through the pages. 'They are.'

'I put that in as Exhibit Five. Now please read your report to the court, referring where appropriate to the photographs.'

The professor did so. It took ten minutes.

'Now, tell us,' Hargreave resumed, 'what kind of nuclear weapon could be built with this quantity of enriched uranium?'

'There was enough uranium to build two nuclear warheads, each capable of destroying a substantial city such as Hong Kong and Kowloon combined. The subsequent fall-out would contaminate a very much larger area, depending on the winds.'

'Tell us, Professor: was the lead-lined suitcase, Exhibit One, a safe container in which to transport this uranium?'

'Barely. It was safe unless the suitcase were opened, or broke open.

313

Exhibit One is a strong suitcase, and the lead lining is expertly made, but an impact on it, such as would happen in a plane crash, or a car smash, could split it open. In that event radiation would have contaminated a large area.'

Hargreave nodded. 'Thank you, Professor.' He sat down.

Lipschitz sprang dramatically to his feet to cross-examine. 'If you had had the authority, would you have permitted this suitcase of uranium to fly halfway around the world?'

'I would certainly have forbidden it,' Professor Donovan said.

Lipschitz smiled at the jury, as if he had just caught the Crown out in another dirty trick. 'If a member of the Hong Kong police permitted the suitcase to be transported by airline from Moscow to Hong Kong, you would say he was acting *thoroughly* irresponsibly?'

'Unfortunately, yes.'

'Because if the airliner crashed on landing at Hong Kong's notoriously difficult airport, millions of people living in this jampacked colony could have died?'

'Or fallen dangerously ill, until treated.'

'In fact,' Lipschitz said, 'all of us present in this courtroom would not be here today if that had happened. So if *you* had been consulted, if *you* had been the law officer involved –' he pointed at Hargreave – 'you would have stopped this case at first base! You would have had the man carrying this suitcase arrested at Moscow airport, to avoid the terrible, unthinkable risk to the lives of millions of innocent people.'

'If I could have, yes.'

'Yes, *indeed* . . .' Lipschitz sighed loudly. He gave the jury a long righteous look, then sat down.

Hargreave smiled and shook his head. He stood up.

'I have no re-examination, my Lord. But I wish to place on record my objection to my learned friend's suggestion that I, the Crown, authorized the transportation of this uranium to Hong Kong. We will hear evidence that neither I nor any other Crown counsel authorized that – we were confronted with a *fait accompli* after the arrests described in this trial.'

Lipschitz said in a stage whisper for the jury to hear: 'Then I defy you to get into the witness box and say that under oath!'

'Mr Lipschitz!' the judge snapped. 'If you have something to say stand up and say it properly.'

Lipschitz got to his feet. 'I do apologize to my Lord.'

'My learned friend,' Hargreave said, 'was saying, for the jury's benefit, that I should get into the witness box to deny I had any previous knowledge about this uranium. My learned friend has tried that tactic before on my Lord, and he was laughed out of court. If my solemn assurance that I did not know about the transportation of this uranium is not good enough for my learned friend he can go to . . .' He paused. 'To the nearest police station and lay a complaint against me. Meanwhile, pending that unlikely event, can he please permit us to get on with our work?'

'Yes, proceed, Mr Hargreave.'

'My Lord, the Russian interpreter who assisted in the questioning of Kozkov is away on holiday, somewhere in Europe, and won't be returning for some time.'

Lipschitz was delighted – he had done well in cross-examining Kozkov, the word 'fix' had been used, and the interpreter might have upset the applecart by saying he had used the word 'treatment'. But he cried, 'The Crown should have realized the interpreter would be an important witness!'

'Well,' his Lordship said, 'we'll have to try to do without him.'

Hargreave said, 'I re-call Superintendent Bernard Champion, my Lord.'

33

'Mr Champion,' Hargreave said, 'you have previously told the jury that you recorded a statement from the defendant, but what happened thereafter was interrupted by the *voir dire*. Now, what time did you finish recording that statement?'

'At thirty minutes past two that afternoon.'

'What did you then do?'

'I telephoned military headquarters, spoke to Professor Donovan and gave him the numbers of the combination lock.'

Lipschitz sighed at the jury. Hargreave said to Champion: 'Had you known the number before that time?'

'No. I had asked Kozkov the number but he was unable to help me.'

'Now, during the time you and Simonski were questioning Kozkov, was anything requested by him?'

'Yes, he asked me for some heroin.'

'What word did he actually use, do you know, for heroin?'

'I simply understood he wanted heroin, from what the interpreter said.'

Lipschitz beamed and nodded at the jury as if the Crown had been concealing this hitherto. Hargreave said: 'When did he ask this? Before, during, or after the questioning?'

'During – about halfway through.'

'When he asked for heroin, had you yet asked him about the combination lock and what the number was?'

'Oh yes, that was one of the first questions I asked him because I wanted to tell it to Professor Donovan, who was waiting at military headquarters to start work on the suitcase.'

'What did you say to Kozkov after he asked for heroin?'

'I told him I could not give him heroin, but I would send him to a government doctor for treatment. I don't understand the treatment, but I know it involves drug-substitutes and I think I told him that much. I told him he'd be taken to a doctor after we'd questioned him. About five minutes later Inspector Sullivan took over the questioning. I don't know precisely when he was taken to a doctor.'

'Did you offer him any form of inducement to inculpate the defendant during the time you questioned him?'

'None. I simply wanted to get his story, the truth, as quickly as possible so I could begin questioning the defendant.'

'Very well. Now on what date and where did you first inform me of the transportation of the uranium to Hong Kong?'

'The day following the defendant's arrest, namely on fifteenth September, in the Westin Resort Hotel in Macao, where you were on holiday.'

'And when did *you* first learn about the transportation?'

'On the day before the arrest, at about eight o'clock in the evening. I was at home. I received a telephone call from Colonel Simonski at 4 p.m. Moscow time.'

'Did you have any power to stop the transportation of the uranium?'

'None. I have no authority over the Russian police.'

'Indeed did you believe you had *time* to stop the transportation?'

'No.'

Hargreave knew that was untrue: Simonski's statement revealed that he hid for about threequarters of an hour, *after* telephoning Champion, before boarding the aircraft. 'Why did you not inform me immediately?'

'Because,' Champion said, 'you were in Macao; I did not dare to telephone you with this sensitive information. I had a lot to do – organizing the cooperation of the military authorities and Professor Donovan, deploying my own men.' He added: 'I only had about two hours' sleep that night.'

'Thank you.' Hargreave sat down with an inward sigh. Now Lipschitz would tear into Champion.

Apart from the possibility of having the defendant's confession thrown out, Lipschitz's main hope of acquittal lay in making the jury so angry with the police for allowing the uranium into Hong Kong that they refused to convict out of sheer bloody-mindedness – as juries have been known to do. He rose portentously to cross-examine.

'Superintendent Champion, how long have you been in the police?'

'Thirty years, my Lord.'

'And as a senior officer, is the Commissioner of Police a personal friend of yours?'

Champion knew what was coming. 'He is.'

'And my learned friend, Mr Hargreave, the Director of Public Prosecutions, is he also a personal friend of yours?'

'He is.'

317

'Aha!' Lipschitz leered at the jury as if he had discovered a very sinister friendship. 'Now, you've been investigating cases of uranium smuggling for how long? About a year?'

'About that.'

'So you fully understood that uranium is a highly dangerous substance, capable of inflicting widespread, lingering, agonized, *horrible* death. You fully understood that if uranium got loose in Hong Kong, the most congested city in the world, *millions* of people could have suffered this. So why –' Lipschitz's finger shot up and his face creased in threatened fury – 'so how, in the name of all that's holy, did you have the unthinkable, nay the mind-blowing audacity and arrogance to permit this killer uranium to be flown into Hong Kong?'

'I did not permit it,' Champion answered grimly. 'I had no power over the Russian police to stop it.'

'Ah yes, so you've said.' Lipschitz nodded sarcastically. 'And you had no power to order the Aeroflot plane to turn back, or to land at some other airport far away? *But –*' Lipschitz's finger shot up again – 'the Director of Civil Aviation in Hong Kong has such power, to refuse to let the plane land?'

'Yes,' Champion said woodenly.

'Yes. And the Governor of Hong Kong certainly has the same power! And your friend the Commissioner of Police certainly had the ability to get straight on the telephone and warn the Governor and or the Director of Civil Aviation, didn't he? And so did you.'

'Yes,' Champion admitted.

'*Yes* . . .' Lipschitz growled with contempt. 'But you *didn't*!' He leered at the jury. 'But do tell me, when Colonel Simonski telephoned you from Moscow airport, did you *advise* him to seize the suitcase and keep it in Russia where it belonged?'

There was a pause: then Champion said quietly, 'I did. I said words to the effect: "Jesus Christ, that's dangerous – we can't have that!" But Simonski said the suitcase was already on the aircraft and he was about to rush on to it himself.'

Hargreave sighed grimly – Champion had not claimed in Macao that he'd said 'We can't have that!'.

Lipschitz glared at Champion. 'You call that *advice*? Did you add: "Get that suitcase off the plane!"?'

Champion said quietly: 'No, because he just gabbled the information and hung up.'

Hargreave sighed. So Champion was playing Lipschitz at his own game by putting the blame on the dead Simonski.

'Did you telephone back to Moscow airport to report this dangerous situation to the control tower?'

'No, I didn't know the number, it would have taken me a long time to find out and I had to spring into action.'

'But you knew the telephone number of Simonski's police station in Moscow! Did you phone them, to stop the aircraft?'

'No, because –'

'Because you didn't think of it, huh? A senior policeman learns that a potential atom bomb is about to fly to Hong Kong and he doesn't think of asking the Moscow police to stop it!'

'This case was Simonski's investigation,' Champion said, 'one he'd been working on for years. It was all highly secret and outside his normal duties. Simonski, knowing all the latest details of his detective work, which I did not, telephones me and reports this sudden breakthrough – which hopefully will bring very bad people to book. Now, if I were to go over his head, telephone Moscow police and tell them to stop Simonski, I could ruin everything. I might get hold of some dumb Russian copper – who may himself be corrupt – who rushes out to the airport like a bull in a china shop, the villains might escape – or open fire and kill many innocent people.' Champion shook his head. 'No way could I risk all that.'

Well said, Champ. Hargreave glanced at the jury. Lipschitz sneered: 'Sounds better to me than blowing Hong Kong to smithereens. So you made a quick decision: risk Moscow or risk Hong Kong. And you chose Hong Kong?'

Champion smiled faintly. 'The decisions were made for me. I had to spring into action.'

'Ah yes, a nuclear bomb was arriving in Hong Kong in ten hours, so it was time for some action! So did you telephone the Commissioner of Police and tell him what was about to happen? *No!* Did you telephone the Director of Civil Aviation direct? *No!* And you didn't telephone Mr Hargreave, your legal adviser, because the line was perhaps unsafe. But, did you send one of your thousands of policemen to Macao to warn him verbally? *No!*' Lipschitz threw his hands upwards and appealed to the gods. 'Why did you not? Why didn't you contact one of these important people so that the aircraft could be told to go back to Moscow with its treacherous cargo?' Lipschitz glared, then stabbed his finger. 'I'll tell you why – because you *wanted* that aircraft to come to Hong Kong, so that you could have the glory of arresting the smugglers of stolen uranium!'

Champion said calmly, 'The aircraft was coming whether I liked it or not: I wanted to arrest the smugglers involved, yes, to do my duty.'

'Don't fence with me! You couldn't arrest them unless the aircraft came to Hong Kong, could you? So you wanted that aircraft to come, didn't you? You said Simonski was excited on the telephone – he gabbled. And you were excited too, weren't you?'

'I was pleased that our hard work was bearing fruit at last, yes.' He shrugged. 'So I had to act decisively and quickly.'

'To arrest the villains! That's why you didn't report to anybody, that's what your decisiveness consisted of – you *decided* to let it come, despite the terrible risk!'

'I didn't consider there was any real risk.'

'You *didn't*?' Lipschitz cried. 'Then why, pray, did you say to Simonski: "Jesus Christ, that's dangerous"?'

'I meant in *principle* it was dangerous. But in practice I did not consider there was any real risk of the aircraft crashing.'

'Oh, you're an expert on the risks involved in aviation? So you know that Hong Kong is one of the most dangerous airports in the world? In fact only the year before last an airliner crashed into the harbour, didn't it?'

'Yes.'

'Yet knowing all this, you "decisively" refrained from advising anybody who could turn the aircraft back, because you knew perfectly well that that is what any sane person in authority would do!'

At the press tables the journalists were loving this, scribbling furiously. 'It was the only practical thing to do,' Champion said. 'If the aircraft had turned back to Moscow there may not have been any arrest, the smugglers may have escaped in the confusion, the evidence we have got today might have disappeared – the key, for example. Furthermore we hoped to find out why this uranium was being routed to Hong Kong – who was going to buy it here, for what purpose, to send on to whom, how, through which middle-men, which government or dictator or terrorist organization was ultimately getting it, et cetera. In other words we hoped the arrests would reveal the whole wicked network and thereby put a stop to this international danger.'

Well said, Hargreave thought – though this jury is angry with you. Lipschitz's face was alight with triumph. 'Aha! So you *did* want the aircraft to come to Hong Kong. Thank you!' Then his eyes narrowed and he hissed: 'So you chose to take the hideous risk of letting the aircraft keep coming, *coming* . . . closer . . . and *closer* . . . with its payload of death, risking the lives of millions of poor people out there –' Lipschitz waved his hand – 'frail old people, innocent children and babes at the breast, the lives of each one of us in this courtroom, the lives of the gentlemen of the jury and their wives and children – all through that long night you let it come, without telling anybody who would stop it, keeping your terrible secret to your egotistical self so that *you* could make the dramatic arrest!'

'Not so,' Champion said grimly. 'I only wanted to do my duty as an honest policeman.'

'And I put it to you, Superintendent Champion, that your "decisive" actions were so contemptibly irresponsible that it is *you* –' Lipschitz jabbed a finger – 'who should be in the dock!'

Champion shook his head. 'I can only say I disagree, Mr Lipschitz.'

'Oh, I'm sure you do,' Lipschitz sneered. Then, having softened Champion up, he moved on to his next strong point. 'And now let's turn to your good friend, Mr Kozkov –'

'He's not my friend,' Champion said, falling for the bait, 'he's just a witness.'

Lipschitz grinned maliciously. 'No? Because Mr Kozkov certainly has a high opinion of you – he thinks you're a *nice* policeman, because you relieved his suffering!'

Hargreave didn't like interrupting for fear of irritating the jury but he had to, to protect Champion. 'My Lord, what's the question? Can my learned friend please stop the rhetoric?'

'What's my learned friend afraid of, my Lord?' Lipschitz enquired. He turned quickly back to Champion before his Lordship gave him an earful. 'Have you no feelings of loyalty towards poor, broken-down Kozkov, who helped your investigation so much?'

'Loyalty? No,' Champion said. 'He only told the truth. And for throwing himself upon the mercy of the magistrate, he received a lighter sentence. And,' he added, 'he'll get a cure for his drug addiction, courtesy of Her Majesty, in the process.'

'No loyalty?' Lipschitz mused, deeply saddened by his fellow man's lack of the milk of human kindness these days. 'However, it was *you* who searched Mr Kozkov's clothing for the key. And immediately thereafter, Mr Gregovich having been accosted by your policemen, you searched him. Yes or no?'

'Yes – and I *found* the key – on Gregovich.'

Lipschitz turned a wide, disbelieving smile to the jury. 'So you *say* . . .' His voice rose. 'Because, if you admit you didn't find the key on Mr Gregovich, all the blame would have to be put on Kozkov, whom you considered to be only the dumb courier!' He snapped, 'Yes or no?'

With misgiving Hargreave interrupted: 'My Lord, my learned friend cannot demand yes or no answers to complex questions like that. My learned friend is bullying the witness.'

'What's my learned friend afraid of, my Lord?' Lipschitz appealed. 'Me bullying Mr Champion, six foot three and thirty years' experience as a policeman and professional witness – a man with the sheer nerve to allow an atom bomb to come flying into town?'

'Six foot two, Mr Lipschitz,' Champion said. 'No, I would still have detained Mr Gregovich, even if I had not found the key on him.'

Lipschitz was too smart to ask why lest Champion tell the jury what Simonski had seen at Moscow airport; he just shook his head in wonder and said, 'Yes, with all that excited determination abounding. Now, let's get back to your admirer, Mr Kozkov. As an experienced police officer, you could tell he was a drug addict, of course, from his appearance?'

'I usually can, yes, they look unhealthy, pinched, nervous, but at the airport he looked fit enough to me.'

'Because of your excitement, your determination to catch the big villain!'

'No, because I simply didn't notice anything untoward.'

'*No?*' Lipschitz thundered: 'And you an experienced police officer! We saw him in the witness box and he *still* looked patently like an addict, despite six weeks of medical treatment!'

'What's the question, please?'

'Oh –' Lipschitz waved a disgusted hand – 'I won't repeat it, your prevarications speak for themselves.'

Hargreave stood. 'My Lord, what *was* the question? My learned friend uses this annoying, unfair tactic of rolling two questions into one, smothering both in argument then pouring scorn on the witness when he seeks clarification. Thus confusing the witness and the jury. *And* me.'

'Unfair tactics?' Lipschitz cried.

'Please ask one question at a time, Mr Lipschitz,' his Lordship said. 'And cut out the rhetoric.'

Lipschitz looked conspiratorially at the jury. 'However, Mr Champion, by the time you saw Kozkov again at police headquarters, even *you* could see he was an addict, not so?'

'Correct.'

'But you didn't offer him treatment, relief, until he asked you for a fix, halfway through the interview, you've told us. Why not?' Lipschitz raised his voice. 'Have you no compassion for your fellow man? You could see he was suffering! And you've told us you considered him only the dumb courier!'

'Medical treatment would take time – I wanted to question him urgently.'

'*Exactly!*' Lipschitz cried. 'You wanted to question him while his resistance was low! While his nerves were screaming for heroin!'

'No,' Champion said, 'I just wanted to get his story, the truth, as quickly as possible so I could go to interrogate Gregovich.'

'Oh,' Lipschitz said, bunching his gown's lapels and turning to the jury. 'Oh, I see . . . And the truth as far as you were concerned, was that Gregovich was the real villain! Is that correct?'

Champion looked at Hargreave, then at his Lordship. 'Yes.'

'*Yes!*' Lipschitz cried. 'And for that reason you didn't offer him treatment right away – you asked a whole lot more questions instead! Despite the fact that you say he had already spilt all the beans! Why?' He glared. 'I'll tell you why! Because you wanted him to tell you the number of the lock – and eventually he did!'

'All untrue,' Champion sighed.

'Oh, you *would* say that, wouldn't you?' Lipschitz sneered. He turned to Hargreave. 'Your witness,' he said witheringly. He added in a stage mutter to the jury, 'What's left of him.' He sat down dramatically.

Hargreave glanced at the jury – they were looking solemn. He could have spared Champion some of that roasting by objecting more to mixed, argumentative questions but he had judged it best not to antagonize the jury by appearing obstructive. He rose to try to patch up Champion in re-examination.

'Mr Champion, let us understand your frame of mind when you made your decision about the uranium flight. Did you or did you not trust the Russian police to investigate this case properly?'

'Objection!' Lipschitz said. 'My learned friend is asking for hearsay.'

Hargreave smiled: now Lipschitz was appearing obstructive. He said: 'I'm not seeking to prove by hearsay whether the Russian police were efficient or not – I'm asking whether the witness, as a fact, trusted them or not.'

'That is not hearsay, Mr Lipschitz,' the judge said.

Lipschitz sat and looked at the jury for sympathy. Champion said: 'I trusted Colonel Simonski completely. I certainly did *not* trust the Russian police in general, as regards either their honesty or efficiency.'

'And as a matter of *fact*,' Hargreave continued, 'what was your state of mind as regards the aircraft returning to Moscow?'

'I was worried that the Russian police would bungle the case either through inefficiency, corruption, confusion, or all three, and allow the smugglers to escape arrest – and that thereby this international crisis of nuclear material getting into dangerous hands would continue unchecked.' He cleared his throat, then went on with a humility Hargreave knew was a sham. 'I was not concerned with any glory. I was just trying to do my job, as I thought best, for everybody, as an honest policeman. If I made the wrong decisions in the heat of the moment, faced with this crisis, I sincerely apologize. I did not intend to be reckless with anybody's life.'

Well said. 'And how urgent did Kozkov's need for medical treatment appear to be?'

'Not urgent.'

'Thank you,' Hargreave said. He sat down.

Champion walked out of the witness box, and came back to sit beside Hargreave. He whispered out of the corner of his mouth, 'Thanks for pulling me out of the shit, Al.'

'Any more witnesses, Mr Hargreave?'

Hargreave stood up. There was no point in calling Inspector Sullivan: Champion and Kozkov had corroborated each other about the key, and about the combination lock's number – there was no merit in allowing Lipschitz the opportunity to raise more confusion by cross-examining Sullivan on those points. He glanced at the clock: it was nearly half past twelve and even now Olga's hydrofoil was approaching Hong Kong!

'My Lord, the Crown case is now complete, apart from concluding the *voir dire*, which awaits the appearance of Miss Romalova. So I respectfully suggest that we now take an early lunch adjournment. But can Mr Lipschitz give us the latest bulletin on his witness's whereabouts?'

Hargreave sat down, his nerves deliciously aflutter. Perhaps Olga was outside the court entrance right now . . .

Lipschitz leapt to his feet indignantly. 'Why isn't the Crown calling Inspector Sullivan, my Lord?' He knew why and was asking the question in order to prejudice the jury. 'What's my learned friend hiding *now*?'

Hargreave sighed. 'Nothing, my Lord. If my learned friend wants to call Inspector Sullivan as a defence witness, he may do so.'

Lipschitz didn't want Sullivan corroborating Champion and Kozkov either but he cried, 'But I want to cross-examine him and show them all up as liars about the key and the combination lock! I challenge my learned friend to come clean and call Inspector Sullivan!'

'Mr Hargreave, as prosecutor and *dominus litus*, can call what wit-

324

nesses he needs,' the judge said testily. 'He's decided he does not need Inspector Sullivan. So be it. If you want him, you can call him but you won't be able to cross-examine your own witness. Now pending your decision on that, what's the information about Miss Romalova?'

Lipschitz cast an injured look at the jury. Then he gave a sycophantic smile to his Lordship, and said solemnly, 'Alas, my Lord, the defence has been struck by yet another disadvantage: it is not our fault, but the fact that vast distances are involved and the unfortunate defendant is thrown upon slender, fragile lines of communication, thus hampering his defence.' Hargreave was staring, aghast. *Oh no.* Lipschitz shot a glance at him, then looked demurely at his Lordship: 'My Lord, I regret to announce that I have just heard that, to the great handicap of the defendant, the witness Olga Romalova, despite our best efforts, and despite earlier misleading information to the contrary, has not been traced in Moscow.' He spread his hands. 'So, alas, we are forced to close our case on the *voir dire* without the benefit of her evidence.'

Hargreave was aghast. *Olga cannot be traced?* He wanted to bellow *'No! No you little bastard, you know exactly where she is!'* He found himself scrambling to his feet, his mind in a whirl, but no words coming out.

'Yes, Mr Hargreave?' the judge said.

Hargreave blinked. Horrified. 'My Lord . . .'

'Yes, Mr Hargreave?'

Hargreave looked desperately at Lipschitz. The man had his knuckles folded under his chin, looking at him expectantly with big brown soulful eyes, a wisp of a smile on his lips. And Hargreave wanted to bound across and grab him by his throat and shake him and pick him up and hurl him across the courtroom. He heard himself say huskily:

'My Lord, the Crown . . . the Crown certainly does not wish the defence to be at any disadvantage. I have no objection to granting my learned friend a further adjournment to enable him to trace his witness – an adjournment until tomorrow, or the next day. Or even until next week.'

Lipschitz smiled sadly at Hargreave as he slowly stood up. 'My Lord,' he said, 'alas, despite our best efforts the witness seems to have disappeared off the face of the earth.'

Hargreave stared at him. *Disappeared off the face of the earth?* The words struck terror in his breast. He wanted to shout, Lies – he knows perfectly well where she is – he's been lying all along to unnerve me and he's lying again now – he never had any intention of calling her as a witness and he's lying again now to terrify me!

'My Lord . . . My Lord,' he rasped, 'I wish to place on record my . . . *anger*. Anger that the Crown, and this court, and this jury, have been put through the inconvenience of hearing this case in bits and pieces, all because my learned friend was so –' he wanted to say mendacious, two-timing, devious, such-a-shit – 'All because my learned friend was so –' he shook his head – 'so *unlawyerly*.'

Lipschitz was getting to his feet indignantly: ' "Unlawyerly" – what does that mean?'

'Mr Hargreave,' his Lordship said. 'If you mean what I think you mean it is a very serious allegation to make, particularly in front of the jury!'

Hargreave wanted to shout, It means a hell of a lot more than that – it means he's a lying crooked twisted slimy cheating bastard who should be struck off the roll of lawyers! He said furiously:

'Yes it is a serious allegation and I make it again, my Lord! *Unlawyerly!* Meaning contrary to the ethics of legal practice!' His outrage swelled and he pointed to Lipschitz: 'I allege loud and clear that Mr Lipschitz deliberately misled this court! Misled my Lord, misled myself, and misled the jury into believing that he intended to call Olga Romalova as a defence witness and thereby persuaded me to break up my case into several parts – *whereas in fact the bastard had not the slightest intention of calling Olga Romalova!*'

'My *Lord* . . .' Lipschitz cried indignantly. Findlay and Champion were looking shocked.

'And he did so with the sole intention of discommoding me as prosecutor, stretching my nerves and tiring and confusing the jury! And he's lying now!'

'Mr *Hargreave* –' the judge began incredulously.

' – he is lying to the court, my Lord, in claiming that Olga Romalova has disappeared!'

'Mr Hargreave, you seem unwell!'

'Yes, I'm unwell, my Lord! I'm furiously sickened by the dirty tricks of Mr Lipschitz! Olga Romalova has not disappeared, my Lord – Mr Lipschitz knows her whereabouts because this man –' he pointed furiously at Gregovich – 'knows perfectly well where she is! She is being held by his thugs as a hostage in a Moscow apartment, being forced to work as a prostitute, threatened with mutilation and being turned into a heroin addict!'

'Mr Hargreave!' his Lordship snapped. 'Your saying this in front of the jury means I'll have to declare a mistrial!'

'As my Lord pleases! And I hope Mr Lipschitz is in the dock beside the defendant at the retrial! Meanwhile I'm handing over to Mr Findlay and I'm withdrawing from this case!'

'Mr Hargreave!'

'Thank you, my Lord!' Hargreave ripped off his wig and slung it on the bar. He turned and strode out of the courtroom, shaking, ashen.

Everybody was thunderstruck – then the pressmen began scribbling frantically.

Hargreave strode in a fury to his chambers, and threw off his robes. He snatched up the telephone, called his travel agent, told her to book him on British Airways' afternoon flight to Moscow, to reserve him a room at the Intourist Hotel. Then he telephoned Jake McAdam's business associates in Moscow to tell them David Johnson was coming.

Then he strode out of the building, heading for the Hongkong & Shanghai Bank to withdraw the hundred and fifty thousand dollars that the manager had agreed to lend him.

The telephone was ringing as Hargreave arrived at his apartment an hour later to pack a bag. He was going to ignore it, then he snatched it up in case it was McAdam calling him. It was Findlay.

'Well?'

'The Attorney General wants to see you, Al,' Findlay said soberly.

'Tell him to go to hell!' Hargreave rasped. 'Tell him I'm indisposed! Tell him I've had a nervous breakdown. What else?'

'Lipschitz is going to haul you in front of the disciplinary committee of the Law Society. The press loved that – they loved all of it. You'll be front-page news tomorrow.'

'Tell Lipschitz I'm looking forward to it! Tell him I'll have his guts for garters! What else?'

'Well,' Findlay said, 'the judge declared a mistrial, of course. The retrial is next week, in front of a new judge and jury.'

'Go for it! You're in charge! Crucify the swine! And crucify Lipschitz!'

'Except I doubt there will be a new trial, Al. Lipschitz made a song and dance about the towering injustice of it all, about his poor client languishing in jail midst alien corn, and what a shit you are – then he applied for bail. Successfully. I opposed it strenuously, but the judge was so mad at you he granted it.' He ended: 'Gregovich is loose, Al – he had to surrender his passport, of course, but my guess is by tomorrow he'll be in Russia.'

PART VIII

34

'. . . *by tomorrow he'll be in Russia.*' Those words struck terror in Hargreave's breast as the aircraft flew through that long night.

He had drunk half a bottle of whisky: he did not give a damn that he had lost his cool, blown the case and made an unseemly scene in court. He did not give a damn what the Attorney General or the Law Society said, nor that a guilty man would break bail and escape justice – what terrified him was that the murderous bastard was on his way to Moscow to wreak his vengeance on Olga because Hargreave had not kept his bargain to get him acquitted. That made his blood run cold. But his blood was also up now, boiling hot and icy-cold, and he did not care what he had to do to get Olga out of this! He did not care if he had to shoot their way out, or how many Russian thugs he had to kill to do it. First he would do his best to negotiate, he would pay the bastards their blood money, he would plead and cajole and promise and bluster and argue, promise them the earth, promise not to extradite Gregovich to face his trial in Hong Kong, promise them any bloody thing first – but when all the chips were down, when all else had failed, he would pull out a gun and shoot their way out of it.

He hoped to God that Olga still had that gun, that they hadn't found it.

Now calm down, he told himself, calm down and get the fighting blood back up. Of course Olga's got the gun, she'll have hidden it properly! Now drink this whisky and don't have any more, lie down and sleep, you've got to sleep, you've got to be on the ball tomorrow . . .

But he could not sleep. Around his waist under his shirt was a bulky moneybelt holding a hundred and fifty thousand American dollars. He lay down on four seats in the darkened cabin, a blanket wrapped around him, his eyes closed, his blood running hot and cold, his mind in a turmoil of fight and fear. And, it seemed, no sooner had he finally fallen into an exhausted sleep than the stewardess was shaking him, telling him to fasten his seatbelt for landing in dreaded Moscow.

*   *   *

It was a cold November morning. At the customs desk he had to declare how much currency he carried. He emerged into the drab concourse, carrying his small bag. He did not think that the Mafia would be waiting for him this time because he doubted they had contacts in British Airways, but he was wearing a hat and sunglasses in an effort at disguise. His eyes darted over the faces, but only taxi-drivers seemed to be interested in him. He looked around in the wan hope of seeing Jake McAdam – maybe Jake had come back from London and got the message Hargreave left with his business associates? He was not there. Hargreave went to the Hertz desk: yes, a vehicle had been rented for him by McAdam's associates, Kaleb Mistoff & Co. The receptionist passed over the keys and a city map. He found the car in the parking lot: it was a new Volkswagen Golf. He felt under the driver's seat. Yes – the gun was there. *Thank God for Jake McAdam.*

Suddenly the reality of what he was about to do came home to him: Alistair Hargreave, forty-six years old, who had not thrown a punch since he was in the boxing ring at Oxford – and then not very effectively – who had never fired a shot in anger in his life, who had never had to run for his life except on the rugby field – and then not all that fast – who had never got a speeding ticket, who did not like driving in foreign countries where they use the wrong side of the road, who knew all about criminal law but who had never had to deal with a criminal without the mighty resources of the government behind him – this Alistair Hargreave, jetlagged and hungover, was about to walk into the Russian underworld, into the den of the very bastard he had just been prosecuting, to negotiate with vicious hoodlums. And if that failed he was going to pull out a gun and shoot it out with them, then leap into a series of cars and race across Moscow to an airfield. *God, Jake was right, he would be mad to attempt this alone, he had to hire some muscle to do most of it for him.*

He studied the map feverishly and drove into the city. He recognized Tverskaya Street when he found himself in it, and finally pulled up outside the bleak Intourist Hotel amongst the same medley of battered taxis he remembered from last time. He walked into the same musty smell of old carpets and waited to be checked in by the same blowsy, unsmiling bureaucratic blonde who showed no sign of remembering him. Whilst she processed his passport he swept his eye over the foyer: there were many men lounging around who might have been observing him. He rode up in the elevator to the fifteenth floor. He dumped his bag, went to the telephone and dialled the office of McAdam's associates.

'My name is David Johnson, I'm a friend of Jake McAdam's. He's not there by any chance, is he?'

'Oh, Mr Johnson, Mr McAdam left for London some time ago, and I do not have a number for him. Have you got the car he ordered for you?'

'Yes, thank you.'

'He also left a parcel for you; shall I send it by messenger?'

That was the second gun. 'Yes, please. How long will it take?'

'In half an hour he can be at your hotel.'

He had to concentrate hard to think about what to do next. Jake had said he needed two cars: but there was a note containing advice in the gun package, he should wait for that. He had to find the multi-storey car park Jake had recommended. He had to check out the Metropole Hotel . . .

Hargreave sat on the bed; he breathed into his hands.

That left the charter aircraft to arrange. Jake's package probably had further advice on that too, but he had to occupy himself with something. He opened the brochure, *Moscow Directory*, which Jake had given him. There it was: Stardust Air Services.

He picked up the telephone and dialled. It rang a long time before a Russian voice barked: '*Da?*'

'May I talk to somebody about chartering an aircraft, please.'

The telephone was banged down, he heard shouting in Russian. Footsteps, more shouts. Finally: 'Yeah?'

'Do you speak English?'

An American voice said, 'Mother tongue, sir! Sorry, thought you were Fred. What can I do for you, Chuck Hunter speaking?'

Hargreave felt reassured by that American accent. 'I'm interested in chartering an aircraft to some point outside Russia where there's an international airport – or a port.' He added: 'Or maybe some point inside Russia from which I can catch an international flight.'

There was a pause. 'Certainly, sir. I can fly you to Timbuktu if you want. But *when* do you want this service, sir?'

'Well, I'm not sure, I don't think it'll be tonight but maybe –'

'I'm mighty relieved to hear that, because we need a bit of time to plan mystery flights. Fuel considerations, and so forth. Now, where is it you want to go, sir?'

Hargreave felt irritated by the man's tone. Then he had an idea. 'I'm not sure yet because this is a surprise for my wife. For my bride, actually, a honeymoon present. She's never been in a small aeroplane and she's mad keen to try it. So after our wedding I want to take her to your

333

airfield where your plane's waiting, with a bottle of champagne and a bunch of red roses, and I'd like you to fly us somewhere with an international airport. All I want to know now are your charges. Is it per mile, or per hour, or what?'

There was a pause. 'I apologize, I thought you were a joker. Sir, we charge three hundred US bucks an hour air-time, but for longer hauls, where we got to stop to refuel, it's more because of landing fees. So you decide where you wanna take your wife and I'll give you a price.'

Three hundred bucks an hour to get away from Gregovich sounded cheap to Hargreave. 'And will you fly any time of the day or night?'

'Yep. Provided you've given us time to file a flight plan.'

'How long does that take?'

'A telephone call to the control tower.'

'And if I'm not sure what time I'll be showing up at the airfield, will you nonetheless be standing by, day or night?'

'Sure. You book us and we'll be waiting, snow or shine, provided you pay ground-waiting time. A hundred bucks an hour.' He added: 'We'll need a deposit, the rest on boarding, sir.'

'Of course.' Hargreave massaged his eyelids, immensely relieved: this was easy. 'Well, I'll come back to you very soon.'

'Hey,' Chuck said, anxious to do business, 'give me your name and I'll give you my home number, in case you want to call me at night.'

Hargreave hesitated – did he want this man to know more about him yet? But he needed his goodwill. He noted down Chuck's home number, and gave his name as David Johnson. 'And what kind of champagne do you want, sir, we can lay that on for you. All part of the service. Not sure about the red roses, but we can surely find something similar.'

It seemed the first time Hargreave had smiled in a long while. 'Any kind of champagne is fine – and please add a bottle of Scotch. But not until I've made my decisions, of course.'

'Sure thing,' Chuck said. 'And is the lucky lady Russian?'

Hargreave grinned: 'The most beautiful one in the world.'

Chuck laughed. 'I know what you mean, I'm married to one myself! So may I suggest we add a bottle of vodka? They *love* the stuff, you can't have a Russian honeymoon without vodka.'

Hargreave thanked him and hung up feeling better. He had at least one problem solved, at least one friend in Russia.

He sat, trying to think what he could do next, how to use the time until the messenger arrived. He spread out the map of Moscow the

334

Hertz receptionist had given him: he needed to familiarize himself with the layout of the city.

And, Lord, it was confusing: the names were all in the Russian alphabet; only certain hotels and tourist sites were identified in English. He would have to get a better map. This was what he needed Jake for, to give him local knowledge. He feverishly got out the little tourist-guide his Hong Kong travel agent had given him, and cross-referred to the map. He identified the Intourist Hotel, Red Square nearby, the Kremlin. Tverskaya Street led out of the city to Moscow airport, didn't it? And, just a few blocks up the street, he identified the Bolshoi Theatre and the Metropole Hotel opposite it. The famous Metropole in which Olga used to operate.

He was beginning to get a picture. Next? Find a route from the city out to Chuck's airfield. And where the hell was that? He had not thought to ask him, he had been so tense. He telephoned him again, and spent the next ten minutes making a laborious note of daunting Russian street names as Chuck described the best route. Turn left here, turn right there, when you see that building on your right you've gone too far . . .

'But your girl will know the way, probably?' Chuck suggested.

'No, she's from Vladivostok.' He thanked Chuck and hung up. He transcribed his notes of the directions into proper English. Then he pored over the map again, marking in the route. He soon found himself running out of map, into *terra incognita*.

A much bigger map was needed, possibly a road-atlas – if such a thing existed: and he would have to drive the route, over and over, until he was thoroughly familiar with it. And then he had to work out some alternative, circuitous routes in case he was pursued.

He dragged his hands down his face.

All this depended on where he was starting from, and that depended on where Olga was. God, he wished Jake were there.

Now calm down, he told himself. Olga is somewhere in the western suburbs, in a middle-class apartment block with a small square opposite. You'll recognize it if you see it again. So if all else fails you can spend the next week driving around this city until you find that square.

And then you've got to hire some musclemen. Probably the karate gang that Jake's associates employ. Jake's note would have further information about that.

He sighed tensely. Right, so once you've got the lie of the land and you've hired your men, what's the plan? He got off the bed and began to pace, trying to think, but he was very tired.

There were two basic plans. Plan One: Jake's idea – check into the Metropole Hotel, speak to the concierge, pose as an old client of Olga's, slip him a hundred bucks and ask if he can arrange a one-night stand. Your musclemen are hiding in your bathroom. Your getaway car is parked outside. Olga arrives with her bodyguard, a minder. While the minder waits patiently in the corridor you and Olga climb out of the window, dash down the fire-escape to your car, and drive off at high speed to Chuck's airfield, with your bodyguards. You take off for Helsinki, or wherever, drinking Chuck's champagne, whisky and vodka. End of scenario. And that way you save the hundred thousand dollars.

Alternative scenario: there is no fire escape. So you call the minder inside, your musclemen hit him on the head, and you all walk out through the foyer, to your waiting car. You drive like hell to Chuck's airfield, as before.

Hargreave took a deep, tense breath.

That was the easy plan; and cheap – no ransom paid. But almost too good to be true. It was full of 'ifs'. What if Olga had two guards, not one? What if my bodyguards don't overwhelm them? What if a third minder is keeping watch downstairs? What if a gunfight starts in a crowded hotel foyer?

Next: assume that the concierge does not know Olga, or Olga is not allowed to leave the apartment for house-calls. That leaves Plan Two.

Plan Two: you simply telephone Vladimir on the mobile number he gave you and tell him where you're staying. You have your musclemen in your room, hiding. You tell Vladimir you've got the money, that his boys must bring Olga to you. They arrive with Olga, they leave with their loot, your musclemen escort Olga and you to Chuck's airfield, and see you safely on to the plane. End of story.

Oh, that was the best scenario: *Pay the money and Olga is free.* He would not need to use the guns, he would not need two cars, the multi-storey car park.

And was not this the most likely scenario? Why should it be more difficult? Vladimir and his Mafia would have everything they originally demanded: they would have the money; Gregovich is free, on bail. Hargreave had kept his bargain, more or less – he had prosecuted the case personally, and he had blown the case, albeit not in the way anybody had expected, but the result was the same – Gregovich was free with the opportunity of escaping.

Wasn't that the most likely way things would turn out? These Mafia thugs only wanted the money, and Gregovich free. So once they had both why should they refuse to let Olga go? Why expect anything worse to happen? Why go to all the anxiety of Plan One, why not just let the Mafia know you're in town, front up with the money, and take Olga away? Why should the Mafia not accept that, they're *criminals*, for Christ's sake, and you know all about the criminal mind . . .

Hargreave pressed his face with his hands. Just trust in the Lord?

Yes, but he *had* to prepare for contingencies, he had to expect the unexpected. Supposing they insisted that he go to the apartment, instead of bringing Olga to him? Should his musclemen escort him there openly, in a show of strength – or follow him secretly and burst in only if there was trouble? Which tactic was least dangerous, which most likely to succeed? If his bodyguards burst in unexpectedly wasn't there *more* likelihood of a shoot-out? And what if Vladimir not only out-gunned him but refused to hand over Olga, what if they demanded something more – Gregovich was only on bail, not acquitted.

So he had to be prepared to use his gun – and in that event he would need the escape plan, had to have Chuck's aircraft standing by, had to know the route to it like the back of his hand. And as he had to go to all that effort and expense, didn't it make sense to try Plan One first, luring them into sending Olga to the Metropole Hotel? Obviously it was safer to deal with the Mafia in the Metropole Hotel than in their apartment, and if his bodyguards dealt successfully with the minders he would not have to use his gun at all, and there would not be a chase. So of course he had to try the Metropole plan.

And it would be much, much cheaper, like a hundred thousand dollars cheaper. He would love to beat that Vladimir bastard at his own bloody game and save a hundred thousand borrowed dollars, but that was very much a secondary consideration: the main point was that it was *safer*.

Safer to screw the Mafia out of their ill-gotten loot than to pay up and forget it? How long would it take them to forget it? How long and far would they look for them, to wreak their revenge? How far did their tentacles extend?

Hargreave sat down on the bed again, trying to think it through.

If he escaped from Moscow without paying, he could never safely return to Hong Kong – he would be a sitting duck there. But fuck Hong Kong – the Attorney General had probably fired him by now. And Hong Kong was fucked anyway, going back to China, though it would have been very useful to earn another year's salary before it did so – the divorce was going to cost him plenty.

He stood up and began to pace again. Just then there was a knock on his door, and his heart lurched. 'Who is it?'

337

'Parcel for Mr Johnson.'

Hargreave tipped the messenger ten dollars. He ripped open the package. There was a shoebox: inside was a gun, a box of cartridges, a small canister and a map of central Moscow. The canister was labelled 'Mace' – it was the spray women carry in their handbags to squirt into the eyes of assailants. Good thinking, Jake! The map bore some marks in red ink. There was a typed note:

> Throw away hardware after use, in a river.
> 'Karate Club' is marked with red X off Arbat Street. Telephone 375861 evenings. Ask for Yakob, who is expecting David Johnson.
> Multi-storey car park marked with red O.
> Use Stardust, businesslike people.
> Destroy this note.

35

It was almost five o'clock, the rush hour, when Hargreave got back to his hotel in his rented car from a harrowing afternoon: he should have tried to sleep off his jetlag before driving around the city on the wrong side of the road – Moscow drivers were fucking maniacs. But, though worn out and tense, he felt he had achieved a lot.

He had acquired considerable local knowledge. He had found a book-shop which sold him a good road-map of Moscow and environs, and a good tourist map printed in both English and Russian. First he had driven to the multi-storey car park. It was near the centre of the city, but it appeared little-used. A boom barred the entrance until the driver took a card from an automatic dispenser. He watched a car enter and timed how long it took before the car's disappearance up the ramp. Twenty-some seconds. Lord, that was a long time when you're being chased: at sixty miles an hour a car travels half a mile in thirty seconds – that meant he would have to be at least a thousand yards ahead of his pursuers to get into the building safely if the chase was at sixty miles an hour.

Sixty miles an hour through Moscow's streets on the wrong side of the road?

Then he had driven into the building, and timed the process again. With a squealing of tyres he had reduced the entrance time to eighteen seconds. He proceeded upwards more cautiously. There was a one-way system upwards, another downwards. Plenty of parking space on all levels. He descended to the exit, driving as fast as he dared, his tyres squealing again, timing himself. He roared up to the boom, rocked to a halt, thrust his ticket and a Russian banknote to the pimply attendant in the kiosk. 'Keep the change! Open, big hurry!'

The attendant blinked at him. 'Huh?'

Hargreave sighed; he said slowly, 'Keep money. Big hurry.'

'Ah . . .' The attendant gave him his change and raised the boom.

Hargreave parked a little way down the street. He picked up his map, and figured out how to get from here to Chuck's airfield, the route he would be taking with Olga once they had shaken off their pursuers at this car park.

He was very relieved that it was not as difficult as he had feared. Although Muscovites seemed to have scant regard for the rules of the road, the streets were wide and he was able to hug the slow lane as he peered ahead for street names. He missed the first turn-off and had to return to the car park to start again: the second time he found it and, once off the main thoroughfares, the rest was fairly easy: his only difficulty was recognizing Russian street names. Finally he found himself driving down narrow country roads between scattered farm buildings and small pockets of grim industrial sites: finally he had seen the turn-off with a billboard proclaiming Stardust's services.

He came upon a high mesh-fence around a scattered array of huts and hangars. One had 'Stardust' painted reassuringly down its side. A light aircraft was visible on the apron. The gate was open and unguarded.

He had taken fifty-two minutes to get here. He looked at the milometer: the distance from the multi-storey car park was only twenty-six kilometres. He would have to improve one hell of a lot. He drove slowly back to the city, memorizing landmarks. From the car park he started back to the airfield again, trying to drive faster. Again he missed the first turn-off in the confusion of traffic, and had to start again. This time he got everything right: but he only reduced his time by six minutes.

Well, he would have to drive the route over and over until he reduced his time to twenty-five minutes maximum. He drove through the gate, and pulled up beside the Stardust hangar.

And that too was reassuring. Chuck Hunter, when he appeared from the depths of the hangar in overalls, exuded Yankee can-do confidence. He was a short, crew-cut American in his mid-forties with grey hair and a brisk manner – and, as Jake had said, what he wanted was business. He told Hargreave he also owned a successful air-charter business in Florida but he had married this gorgeous Russian chick he'd met on holiday so he had opened up here too. Only been operating here a year and the going was tough.

'Nobody in Russia has any money, I rely entirely on foreigners and they're not coming here much yet . . .' But, yessir, his struggles were going to be worth it because this country sure was wide open! Russia had stood still under Communism while the rest of the world took off: everything was under-developed, from agriculture to safety-pins. 'All you need is the savvy and you're in on the ground floor – fortunes to be made because nobody here knows their ass from their elbow when it comes to business. But you gotta have balls.'

'What about official corruption – I hear it's bad? And the Mafia?'

'*Corruption?* You never get anything done without back-handers – yet the government is crying out for investors! And the Mafia run the bloody country.'

Hargreave felt he had met not only a kindred spirit but a source of information. 'Do you have to pay protection to them?'

'Sure do. As soon as you open shop they walk in, offer their services, and if you decline they smash up the joint.'

'And the police can't protect you?'

'What police? Forget the police. Mafia in uniform.'

Hargreave shook his head. 'But there must be some honest ones.'

'Sure. But one's just been shot so the other guy's very busy.'

Hargreave smiled. 'And do the Mafia really give you some protection?'

'Sure. They keep the other Mafia off my back.'

Chuck was eager to show Hargreave his aircraft: two fixed-wing, one helicopter. 'All tuned up, tanked up and ready to go. I'm a qualified engineer as well as a pilot.' His other pilots were part-timers, formerly of the Russian air force. 'First-class flyers without two nickels to rub together, trained to fly supersonics and now they're lucky to get a couple of hours a week out of me doing tourist flips. So, when exactly are you getting married?'

'As soon as my girl arrives from Vladivostok, maybe as early as tomorrow night or the next day. What I'd like to do now is work out the best destination for our purposes, which I think is Helsinki, and leave you with a suitable cash deposit.'

Cash. That word was music in Chuck's ears. He took Hargreave into his kiosk and spread out an aviation chart of Europe. With dividers he measured the distance between Moscow and Helsinki. 'About seven hundred miles. Sir, we can do that in one hop, without refuelling. So we can probably pull the whole thing off in about five hours, depending on headwinds. Plus the trip back makes ten hours, plus landing fees in Helsinki, makes it about four thousand dollars, sir. But I'll work it out more precisely and call you.'

Four thousand dollars sounded very cheap. But Chuck in his enthusiasm said hastily, 'Of course for that distance I can do a special deal, ten per cent discount for cash – call it three-six.'

Which probably meant he could get it for three – but Hargreave was not going to argue. 'And the deposit?'

'Twenty per cent?' Chuck said hopefully. 'Call it seven hundred.'

Hargreave put his hand in his pocket and pulled out several thousand-dollar bills. He peeled off one, held on to it and said, 'And for that we can fly any time of the day or night?'

Chuck tore his eyes off the banknote. He pointed at his cellular phone on his desk, then at the conventional one. 'All you gotta do is call. Day or night. If I'm in bed it'll take only fifteen minutes to get here.'

Wonderful. 'And how long thereafter to get your aircraft out on to the runway and take off?'

'Fifteen minutes?'

That meant he had to be a long way ahead of the Mafia. 'Can you have the aircraft waiting *on* the runway?' He fingered the note.

Chuck looked at him. 'Yeah. *Near* the runway. Very few planes use this field. If I have a bit more warning.' He frowned. 'There's nothing illegal in this trip is there, Dave?'

Hargreave forced a solemn smile – and decided he had to take a risk.

'I assure you I am a very respectable businessman, Chuck. But I have not been entirely frank with you. The lady in question will *not* yet be my wife when we arrive. We will be eloping, and we may possibly have a jealous husband to contend with. And so the less time we spend hanging around this airfield waiting for the aircraft to taxi around and warm up the better.'

Chuck considered this; then his no-nonsense face broke into a smile.

'I thought maybe you were aimin' to rob a bank or somethin'.' He added: 'So you think this husband may be chasing you?'

'I doubt it,' Hargreave said. 'But I don't want any dramatic domestic scenes on the runway, tears, threats of suicide from the husband. My girl is already in a highly emotional state about the whole thing. That's why I'm not sure when she's arriving. She has to leave her child behind, you see. And her mother. All very fraught and complicated.'

Chuck winced in sympathy. 'But he's not a gangster is he, the husband? He's not going to pull a gun on us?'

Hargreave forced a smile. 'He is everything *except* a gangster. He is a liar, a cheat, a wife-beater, a pervert, a bully, a schizophrenic, a gambler, a drinker, probably a drug-addict. A gangster is about the only thing the bastard isn't. In fact, he's a gynaecologist.'

'Gynaecologist?' Chuck looked relieved.

'Failed,' Hargreave said with contempt. 'So he does abortions instead. But, anyway, he's insanely jealous of Olga – that's my girl. And I don't want this prick chasing us to this airfield, making a scene as she clambers into your aircraft. We can do without that.'

Chuck sat back in his chair. 'Christ, yes. So, you just give me an extra bit of warning and the aircraft will be warmed up and waiting.'

He had given Chuck a deposit of one thousand dollars, plus another five hundred to cover possible waiting-time, and bound him to confidentiality. He had driven back to Moscow feeling very relieved. Chuck was a kindred soul and he trusted the man – one very big problem solved. And another, too: seeing Chuck's cellular telephone had made him realize he needed one. When asked, Chuck had said, 'Christ, they practically give them away, go to AT&T, American Telephone and Telegraph, they'll sprain their wrist grabbing your credit card . . .' So he had found AT&T and walked out with a cellular telephone with which he could call Chuck's bedside. *That* was reassuring.

Then he had returned to the multi-storey car park and driven back to Chuck's airfield as fast as he could. He reduced the time to thirty-seven minutes – not good enough, but a big improvement.

And so Hargreave felt he had got somewhere on his first day in Moscow. He was very tired when he arrived back at his hotel. All he wanted to do was go upstairs to one of the numerous bars, swallow a few stiff drinks and collapse on his bed; but there were still two more things he could do today. He parked his car in a side-street, consulted his city map, then started trudging up Tverskaya Street to check out the Metropole Hotel.

It was only four or five blocks away. It was the rush hour, the street thronging with hurrying pedestrians. The men looked drab but the younger women seemed well-dressed and many were very pretty. Some were beautiful. And some of the prettiest ones, he noticed to his surprise, were well over six feet tall, statuesque, striding along. Hargreave was over six feet but he felt short against these handsome Amazons in their high heels, hurrying home from their miserably-paid jobs to their miserable apartments and miserable dinners, with nothing to look forward to for years and years. Probably for the rest of their pretty youthfulness, until Russia finally managed to heave herself up out of the ruins of Communism. God, the damage Communism had done to the world. The whole of the vast USSR in economic ruin and paralysis, the whole of Eastern Europe, because some rich, conceited undergraduate called Karl Marx thought he had a bright idea. Christ, what fools human beings are, to follow their upstart leaders . . .

Hargreave found himself on the edge of Karl Marx Square, and there was the twit himself, in bronze, seated pensively on a throne. Covered, Hargreave was grimly pleased to note, in pigeon shit. On the far end of the big square stood the imposing Bolshoi Theatre. On the adjoining side stood the Metropole Hotel.

He looked at it tensely. It was big, taking half the side of the square.

343

So this was where Olga used to operate. He trudged grimly towards it.

The entrance was at the end of the long building. There was a portico with steps leading up into a marbled lobby. To one side stood the big desk of the concierge and his flunkies, all dressed in livery. Beyond, a marbled foyer.

Hargreave walked slowly across the foyer. It was almost as big as a tennis court. Chandeliers hanging from the high ceiling. To the left, a long reception desk, a dozen staff busy: to the right a lounge area with leather armchairs. Beyond, a bank of ornate elevators, a sweeping staircase up to the accommodation. To the left of the elevators was a horseshoe bar; beyond, a large, gracious dining room.

Hargreave paused in the middle of the foyer. An expensive hotel, where expensive girls operate. And, oh Lord, he could imagine Olga walking across this foyer, looking marvellous, turning heads, making for a luxurious bedroom upstairs to perform expensive services. And he hated the thought of it. But all that was behind, all he wanted was her walking across this foyer heading upstairs to *his* bedroom.

But not tonight, not until he had checked everything out thoroughly; the emergency exits, where to park his car, the bodyguard situation; not until he had reduced his driving-time to Chuck's airfield. He walked wearily across to the horseshoe bar.

He ordered a beer. There were half a dozen people at the bar, all Americans, talking business. That was reassuring too: it seemed less likely that there would be a shoot-out in this gracious hotel patronized by these respectable American businessmen. He drank half of the beer, flooding his exhausted system with its balm. 'How much?' he said to the barman.

'Forty thousand roubles, sir.'

Lord, now much is that? A few years ago it would have been more than forty thousand US dollars. He did a mental calculation as he peeled off the notes: now it was about eight dollars. Thank the Lord for those American businessmen, only that sort of people could pull Russia out of this. He massaged his eyelids, then looked around the foyer.

There were half a dozen couples sitting in the armchairs. Then he spotted the first whore. She was sitting alone, with a cup of coffee, a good-looking girl, about twenty-five, well-groomed, in a two-piece suit. She caught his eye: he gave her a fleeting smile and looked away.

In the next few minutes he saw several girls who could be on the game, walking in alone, heading for armchairs. They were all well-dressed – maybe they weren't whores at all. Would a good hotel like the Metropole let whores trawl? He sipped his beer, watching. The foyer was getting busy. He looked back at the first girl. She raised an eyebrow at him. He smiled and shook his head briefly; so, the good old Metropole did tolerate a little discreet trawling.

The next job was to check out the rooms and the emergency exits. He drank back his beer, and walked to the long reception desk. 'I think I would like to make a reservation for tomorrow, or maybe the next night. Is it possible to see a room, please?'

'Certainly, sir,' the pretty girl said. Hargreave thought, *Everyone is so nice*. The girl rang a bell and one of the concierge's flunkies appeared with a smile.

Hargreave followed the young man into the gilded elevator. They rose to the third floor. Hargreave followed him down the carpeted corridor to room 307, the number in polished brass. The flunky opened the door and stood back.

It was a spacious room with a double bed, tastefully furnished, and the big windows overlooked Karl Marx Square. There was a tiled bathroom. He looked at the windows: they were metal-framed, double-glazed, and could not be opened – there was an air-conditioning unit instead. 'Where is the fire-escape?'

The young man led him back to the door and pointed down both ends of the corridor. There were small 'Exit' signs.

'Of course. Thank you. Very nice.'

They proceeded back to the elevator. On the ground floor Hargreave tipped him five dollars, for future goodwill. The man looked delighted.

Hargreave went back to the bar and ordered a whisky – sixty *thousand* roubles worth of whisky. The girl who had given him the eyebrow-treatment was gone. He asked the barman where the toilet was: beyond the elevators. He left his whisky, walked past the elevators, then turned up the sweeping staircase. He climbed to the upper levels.

The first floor was identical to the third. He walked down the corridor to the emergency exit sign. He passed through swing doors into a stairwell. He descended, turned the corner, saw the edge of the concierge's lobby and the big front entrance.

He retreated upstairs. Okay, so that was not the exit to use – it led to the front of the hotel, where any Mafia thugs awaiting Olga's reappearance would likely be hanging around. He walked down the corridor to the other exit.

More swing doors – he descended the stairwell to an area adjoining the kitchen. A short corridor led towards toilets and the main foyer.

There was a big double door, marked 'Emergency', locked with a horizontal bar. He looked over his shoulder, then raised the bar. The doors swung outwards, into an alleyway.

The alleyway led in two directions, one towards the hotel entrance, the other past the kitchens and around a corner. Hargreave ducked underneath the kitchens' windows and stopped at the corner. He peered around it. The alley led past garbage buckets, several doors, and opened on to Karl Marx Square. Good.

He hurried back into the hotel, heaved the doors closed behind him, and walked towards the foyer. Halfway were the toilets. He shoved open the door marked 'Gentlemen', went to the marble-topped washstands, turned on a tap, slumped his shoulders. He felt as if he had just stolen something. He looked at himself in the mirror.

God, he looked terrible.

Exhausted. There were lines on his face he did not remember, and the tinges of grey at his temples looked wider. Stubble prickled on his chin. Please God this is only jetlag, I don't really look like this. And Olga so young and beautiful – what does she see in me? Perhaps I'll look better in the morning after a proper night's sleep.

He splashed his face thoroughly, doused his hair, and combed it. *There* – that made the grey almost disappear. He realized he was ravenous and that he hadn't eaten since breakfast on the plane – that probably accounted for about five years of his beat-up appearance? This morning seemed like yesterday, and yesterday seemed days ago. For a moment he wondered what the legal fraternity were saying about him in Hong Kong – lawyers love a good fuck-up – but he thrust it out of his mind. He straightened his jacket and walked back into the big foyer.

He returned to his half-finished whisky, gulped it and ordered another. He made himself think about what he was going to say to the chief concierge now.

One of the Americans down the bar was speaking on his cellular telephone. Hargreave remembered his own new gadget. Maybe he should speak to the concierge by telephone, rather than show his face? He pulled his telephone from his pocket. How did it work? He switched it on and a red light glowed. He looked at his beermat: the number of the hotel was printed on it. He dialled.

'Metropole Hotel,' the voice said.

Hargreave hunched over his whisky. 'Good evening, I want to speak to my old friend your concierge, but can you remind of his name, please?'

'Henri, sir.'

'*Henri*,' Hargreave said. 'Of course. That's the man who has worked there for years, speaks good English?'

'Yes, sir.'

'Thank you, I will telephone him later.'

Well, the machine worked – and he knew something about the concierge. He took a big sip of whisky, thinking it through.

Should he telephone Henri, or talk to him face to face? Stay anonymous for the moment, or slip him a hundred-dollar bill? Yes, that was surely the best way: on the telephone Henri might deny all knowledge of prostitutes as a matter of principle. Front up to him, slip him a hundred, and it would be a different Henri.

Hargreave sat there, exhausted, trying to think it through for the last time before committing himself. Could this go wrong? If it worked, the worst of his troubles would be over: all they had to do then was escape unnoticed from this hotel. But speaking to Henri could backfire on him: if he did not know of Olga nothing was lost, but if Henri made enquiries in the underworld Vladimir could hear of it and then Hargreave might never find her. And Vladimir would send his heavies to sort him out.

Hargreave rubbed his brow. Forget about the heavies – he had to face them sometime. And he didn't know where Olga was anyway, so if Henri didn't produce her he would have to contact Vladimir and his heavies himself, so he had nothing to lose by speaking to Henri. He quaffed back his whisky, and stood up.

He walked across the foyer, his heart knocking, and descended into the lobby. There was the desk, the concierge and his minions behind it. Hargreave stopped in front of the elderly man and studied his face.

'Henri? Aren't you Henri?'

'Yes, sir?'

Hargreave smiled shakily. 'You probably don't remember me. May I have a word with you in private?'

'Yes, sir.' Henri deferentially led the way down a corridor towards a sign marked Conference Rooms. Hargreave slid a hundred-dollar bill from his pocket. He slipped it into Henri's hand and said in a confidential undertone:

'Henri, can you help me? About a year ago I stayed in this hotel, visiting from England, and I met a very beautiful girl called Olga. A call-girl. Now, I'm not staying at this hotel tonight, but I will be tomorrow night. And I would very much like to see Olga again.'

Henri glanced at the size of the banknote before slipping it into his pocket. 'Olga, sir? Of course call-girls, strictly speaking, are not permitted in this hotel, sir – but such things do happen sometimes. Olga?' he mused. 'It is quite a common Russian name.'

'A tall girl,' Hargreave said, 'only above five centimetres shorter than me. Blue eyes. Wide mouth, very good teeth. Very good figure. Long blonde hair, but maybe she sometimes wears it on top of her head. And I think . . . yes, I'm sure her surname is Romalova.' He repeated: 'Olga Romalova.'

Henri frowned. 'Of course many Russian girls are tall and blonde. Olga Romalova? The name sounds familiar, sir . . .'

Hargreave's heart leapt. 'Very beautiful. Very . . . *sportif*. Perhaps you haven't seen her for a year or so – unless recently – because she told me she was going to work in China, in Macao. But I'm sure she's come back to Moscow recently.'

'Of course,' Henri said piously, 'I do not normally have anything to do with such things, sir, but I can make some enquiries with people who usually know.'

Oh please God. 'Thank you very much, Henri. But please . . .' He pulled another hundred-dollar bill from his pocket and slipped it to him. 'It is most important that you don't mention me to anybody at this stage – I only want to know whether you can get hold of her. After you've told me that, we'll arrange a time for her to come here, my room number and so forth.' He added: 'I have a wife to worry about. So please don't mention me, an Englishman, or anybody who looks like me.'

'I understand, sir. And how do I contact you?'

'You can't – I'm staying with friends – with my wife, you see. So I'll telephone you here. When?'

'Tomorrow morning, any time after eight o'clock, sir. I'm on early shift.'

'Many thanks, Henri. And there's another hundred dollars in it for you if you find her. Plus any expenses . . .'

36

Hargreave left the Metropole feeling upbeat. Drained but upbeat: it looked like this idea of Jake's was going to work. He had achieved a lot today. But before he went back to his hotel he had to check out places to park his car, near this hotel.

He walked around the perimeter of Karl Marx Square, exhausted but feeling positive. Evidently Moscow had so few car-owners that parking was not a problem: there were plenty of spaces. Several side-streets abutted on to the square, mostly empty – almost seven o'clock on a Wednesday night.

Was it only Wednesday still? It seemed as if he had left Hong Kong days ago.

He was very tired, but there was still one job he had to do before collapsing into bed: check out the bodyguard situation. Jake's note indicated that he should telephone Yakob in the evening: if he did not do so tonight he would have to wait until this time tomorrow.

He trudged across the square and sat down on a public bench, under the gaze of the great man. He pulled out his cellular telephone, and Jake's note, then dialled the Karate Club.

A male voice barked in Russian. Hargreave said, 'May I speak to Yakob, please.'

The telephone banged down. He could hear grunts and thumps coming from the background. After a minute a voice rasped, 'Yes?'

'Good evening, Mr Yakob. My name is David Johnson. I believe you're expecting me to call?'

There was a moment's silence. Then: 'Yes?'

'I'd like to talk to you about a possible business deal. Can I meet you?'

'Yes.' Hargreave could almost hear the man sweating.

'Thank you. Where do I meet you?'

'Here.'

'When?'

'Two hours.' Yakob banged down the telephone.

Hargreave winced. He switched off his telephone and returned it to his pocket. Well, Yakob sounded somebody to be reckoned with – he imagined the man striding back to his karate students and hurling them about sweatily.

He heaved himself up. Two hours? He felt in no shape for this new tension, but it had to be tonight. Strike while the iron is hot.

He turned back into Tverskaya Street to trudge back to his hotel, to have a few drinks and something to eat whilst he waited for two hours. Lord, he was tired. Tired down to his bones with jetlag and weeks of tension. Was he in any shape to deal with Yakob, to negotiate prices, choose his words without revealing anything that could endanger Olga? Shouldn't he postpone the meeting to tomorrow night? Shouldn't he have just one more drink to dull his nerves and zonk out?

At that point of his indecision, halfway back to his hotel, he passed a big doorway with a colourful signboard outside an impressive building, proclaiming that the Highlife Club lay within. Music flooded out. It sounded jolly. It sounded a better place than most to have his drink and think about it. Maybe they even had a hamburger.

Inside was an atrium: a queue of Russians of both genders were waiting to pay an entrance fee of twenty dollars. They were well-dressed and well-behaved. It was interesting that young Russians could afford twenty dollars on a midweek night. Hargreave paid and descended through a stout door into a big Gothic vault.

Other vaults led off it. At the far end was a dance floor, where a few couples were shuffling to music. Hargreave was taken aback: this place was full of young people who looked like yuppies, middle-class management types, many of them pretty girls. It could have been an upmarket singles bar in Manhattan – and everybody was so animated.

He made his way to the crowded bar and secured a place between two clusters of girls. He ordered a whisky from the attentive barman, paid ten dollars for it, and looked around.

'I haven't seen you here before,' the nearest girl said. 'Are you a tourist?'

Hargreave smiled at her wearily. She was very pretty, about thirty. Was she on the game? Surely not. 'Yes.' He added, for something to say: 'Does everybody speak such fluent English in Russia?'

She grinned, revealing good teeth. 'In Moscow.'

What to say next? 'What work do you do to speak English so well?' 'I'm a secretary.'

A secretary. He wondered how much money she earned – drinks here cost ten dollars a throw. 'What kind of business are you in?'

'Architect's office. Really, I am nearly an architect too. One more year. But there is no money, so for this year I must work as a secretary.'

Well, good for her. 'Is there much building going on in Moscow?'

'No,' she said solemnly. 'Moscow needs much housing but nobody has money. So we are also a real-estate office. That needs people with money too. But it will come, my boss thinks.'

Were all Russians this friendly? Was it his big blue eyes? Yes, the money will come, he thought. Russia is wide open, people need houses like they need food – but when? As if she read his thought, she continued, 'But how long must we wait before people earn enough to buy houses, have a decent life like you in Western Europe?'

Hargreave nodded sympathetically. 'Will you have a drink?'

'Thank you. Vodka, please.' She added: 'My name is Tanya.'

'And I am David.' He was feeling less tired. He ordered her drink. 'And, how do Russian people like the changeover from Communism?'

'They are nervous. They don't understand. Before, the state took care of them and told them what to do, they paid small rents for small apartments, so now they are afraid to spend money on a nice apartment. They do not like responsibilities. So, how long must we wait before people change? Will it happen before I am an old lady?' She looked at him, her brown eyes big. 'I am nearly an architect, so I have a good job. But can you guess how much is my salary? Two hundred dollars a month. And I am lucky.'

Lord. And he earned over fifteen thousand dollars a month. 'Can you live on that?'

'No. I must share my small apartment with some girlfriends, but I still cannot live.' She looked at him with a twinkle in her eye: 'So, at night I work like this.'

Hargreave was taken aback – so it wasn't his big blue eyes. 'I see.'

'What do you see?' Tanya said with a touch of truculence. 'A nice Russian girl, speaking nice English, in a nice bar. But also a prostitute. Too bad. Must be, unless I want to be poor all my life.'

Hargreave was not embarrassed; just tired and unaccustomed to being solicited by architects. 'I understand.'

Tanya smiled. 'I charge a hundred dollars an hour.' She added: 'Or until you have finished with me. I like giving good service.'

Until you've finished with me. Lord, he wanted his Olga, wanted her out of this life. He glanced around; several girls locked eyes with him, all pretty and well-groomed. Tanya smiled: 'So? Shall we go, David?'

No, of course he wasn't going to 'go' with her. But wasn't this an opportunity to get some important local knowledge from an intelligent, friendly whore? He heard himself say, 'Tell me, do you work in hotels too?'

'Sure, no problem getting into your hotel with you, don't worry.'

Hargreave was waking up now. 'And tell me, are you controlled by anybody? Like the Mafia?'

'Yes, but don't worry about them, all they want is business.'

Of course – if only he had followed that advice in Macao. He hesitated, his tired mind trying to weigh the odds: was it safe to question this girl about Olga? Shouldn't he leave the subject alone and let Henri give him the answers? He took a tense breath and decided to strike while the iron was hot.

'Tanya? If I pay you a hundred dollars for an hour, will you come to my hotel room and talk to me in private? Where it is quiet.' He added, 'You see, I am a journalist, I'm writing a story about Moscow. And I need to know some things about your life . . .'

He went ahead of Tanya to his hotel, so that she was not seen entering with him. Five minutes later she knocked on his door, smiling.

'Do sit down.' Hargreave indicated the bed. He sat at the little desk. 'Is whisky all right?'

'Nothing, thank you. Can I mention the money?'

'Of course.' Hargreave pulled out a hundred-dollar bill.

Tanya put it in her purse. She indicated the bathroom. 'One minute.'

Hargreave poured himself a whisky; God, he hoped he was doing the right thing. But he had to have local knowledge and this was a pleasant girl, an architectural student. The bathroom door opened, and Tanya re-entered the room. She was naked.

'Okay,' she smiled.

Hargreave tried not to stare. 'I really did mean to talk.'

'Sure. Before or after?'

Hargreave was blushing through his tiredness. 'Before.' He was going to say 'Instead of' but didn't lest he hurt her feelings.

'Fine.' Tanya grinned impishly. 'Better that way, then maybe you want me for *another* hour. All night if you like! Okay.' She got on to the bed, sat crosslegged and looked at him expectantly.

Hargreave wished she would drape a towel over herself. He marshalled his thoughts.

'What's the name of the company, the architect you work for?'

Tanya opened her purse, extracted a visiting card and handed it to him. 'Why?'

It had the name and address of her firm on it, Russian on one side,

English on the other. *Architects and Estate Agents* – so, she was for real.

'Are your parents alive?' Hargreave asked.

'Yes, they live in Leningrad. My father is a teacher, my mother is also a secretary.'

'Do they know what you do at night?'

'No! They would kill me.'

Hargreave smiled. Good – nice family. He wanted her to come from a nice family. 'Does your boss know?'

'*No*. He would fire me.' She added: 'You won't tell him?'

'Of course not.' *Good*. Nice boss, reputable firm. 'How long have you been doing this?'

'Nearly two years.'

He didn't want to ask the next question but the lawyer in him demanded it. 'Do you like it?'

She smiled. 'Of course not, David. Except sometimes when I meet nice people like you. But once you start this business it is difficult to stop. Because of money. Now I have things I cannot have if I stop – my apartment, my savings, my clothes. The food I like. And you think, "It is better than staying at home every night without a husband, maybe tonight I will meet some nice, interesting man like David".'

Hargreave smiled. 'And if it is an ugly man?'

'Then I do not go with him. *I* choose, not him.'

He thought of Olga choosing her man, and felt a stab of black jealousy. 'So how long will you do it?'

'Until I can earn a good wage.' She pointed solemnly at his head. 'You earn a good wage with your brain. In Russia I cannot. Only with this.' She pointed at her pubic area. 'So I must do it until I have enough money.'

'And then?'

Tanya leant back against the wall and stretched her arms to the ceiling, her breasts lifting. 'Then I will travel! Now we are permitted to have passports. I want to see the world very much. *Then* I want to get married, and have children.' She dropped her arms and added earnestly: 'Of course, if I met a nice man I would stop this business immediately.' She smiled wanly. 'That is every Russian girl's dream.'

So far, Tanya impressed him as an honest witness – but be careful how much you tell her.

'You said in the bar that you were controlled by the Mafia. Would they just let you quit, if you suddenly wanted to get married?'

Tanya shrugged. 'If I do not owe them money. There are plenty more girls if I do not want to work.'

'And if you do owe them money and refuse to pay?'

'*Refuse?* They would force me to pay. If I *cannot* pay they will make me work until I have paid everything.'

'How would they force you to pay up?'

'First threaten me,' she said simply. 'Then they would beat me. Finally they would kill me. To teach the other girls.'

Oh God . . . 'But how do they actually control you, day-to-day?'

'They have my address, telephone, my office, on their computer – and a man is in charge of me. If I have a problem I speak to him, Boris. If I do not work for a week because I am sick Boris knows, he telephones me, I explain, he says okay or not-okay. Maybe he brings me to a doctor. If he thinks I am working privately and not paying my money, there's big trouble.'

'What kind of trouble?'

She smirked. 'I always pay, so Boris has never beaten me, I am sensible.' She went on: 'In Tverskaya Street I pay them every month for protection. And every time I go to the Highlife Club I pay twenty dollars, and every time I leave with a customer I pay twenty dollars. If I come back afterwards, another twenty dollars. Same with the hotels.'

'And how much do you pay them in addition, every month?'

'Fifty per cent. They can calculate, they know how many times I go in and out, the concierge and security men write it down.'

'So the concierges actually *work* for the Mafia?'

'Yes. Usually.'

Oh Lord – but he had known he was taking a calculated risk with Henri. 'But generally, how do the Mafia treat you?'

Tanya shrugged. 'If you pay, there is no trouble, they want business. And if a customer gives us trouble, they give us protection, they look after us like that.'

Yes, of course they only wanted business – pay up and there's no problem, refuse and you're in big trouble. God, what a fool he had been! Now it was costing him ten times what it would have done. *And* Ivan Gregovich would be safely behind bars now.

'This area in Tverskaya Street where we are now – does the same Mafia control the . . . Metropole Hotel for example?'

'Yes. Sometimes I go to the Metropole.'

Oh yes. Maybe he was on to something. 'So your man, Boris, he's in charge of all the girls I've seen tonight, and the girls in the Metropole?'

'He is one of the controllers. All working for the same boss.'

'And do you know the boss's name?' He tried to sound casual.

'No. We are not told. He is the *big* boss.'

'This computer your name is on – have you actually seen it, or do you just presume it exists?'

'I have seen it. Once I had to go to Boris's office and I saw it. He showed me on it, how much money I owed.'

If he could get his hands on that computer and find out where Olga actually was . . .

'And are there actual whorehouses, where girls are kept? So that customers can visit them there?'

'Very few, I think. Most girls like to go out and choose their customers.' She looked at him in surprise: 'You want to go to a whorehouse? When you can have me?'

Hargreave smiled bleakly. 'No. Just for my story. But the concierges of the hotels, I presume they know about the computers which people like Boris have?'

'Oh yes, I am sure.'

'And so, for example, if I come back in one year's time and I want to see you again, I could speak to the concierge of, say, the Metropole Hotel, and he would be able to trace you?'

'Probably, yes.'

Oh yes, this was going to work – Plan One was going to work, this time tomorrow Olga would be safely airborne with him. And a hundred thousand bucks saved!

Tanya continued, with a twinkle in her eye: 'I hope you come back and ask for me. Maybe even tomorrow.'

Hargreave smiled weakly. Maybe he should not ask the all-important question now that finding Olga through Henri seemed a certainty? But surely he should cover all possibilities whilst he had the chance? He hunched forward.

'Tanya, you say you sometimes go to the Metropole Hotel. Well, about a year ago I was there and I met a girl called Olga Romalova. Heard anything about her?'

Tanya looked at him, sadly. 'You want to fuck Olga?'

'Do you know her?'

'Many girls are called Olga. What does she look like?'

Hargreave described her.

Tanya shook her head. 'But I can ask my friends.'

Hargreave thrust his hand into his pocket and pulled out a hundred-dollar bill. 'Perhaps Boris has her details on his computer? Would it be all right for you to ask him?'

Tanya looked at the banknote. 'Why not? It is only business, more money for him.'

'But *please* don't tell him anything about me,' Hargreave said earnestly. 'Make it sound as if she's just an old friend of yours. Can you do that?'

Tanya looked at him, then shrugged. 'Sure, why not?'

'Promise? You'll do it discreetly?' He gave her the banknote.

Tanya took it sadly. 'Okay. But what can she do that I can't?' She indicated her sensuous body. 'I can do anything you want.'

Hargreave smiled. 'And, please call me on this number.' He pulled his telephone from his pocket, consulted the dial, took a piece of paper off the desk and scribbled down the number. 'All I want to know is how to get hold of her direct. Her address, her telephone number. Nothing more.'

Tanya took the note and put it in her purse. She sighed. 'Okay. But what can she give you that's so special?' She waved a hand. 'I'll do it as good as Olga, I promise.' She smiled. 'Or do you love her?'

'No. We just had a good time, Tanya.'

Tanya shook her pretty head. 'I think you love her.' She sat up straight, thrusting her breasts towards him. 'Have we finished talking now?'

'Yes.' Hargreave smiled. 'Thank you very much.'

'Okay,' Tanya said decisively. 'So let's make love.' She ferreted in her purse and produced a condom. 'Anything you want.'

Hargreave smiled and closed his eyes. 'Tanya –'

'Or just a blow job, if you like.' She smiled impishly. 'I want you to *remember* me if you don't find Olga!'

'Tanya, I'm sorry,' Hargreave said ruefully. 'Yes, you're right, I do love her. And I can't think of anybody but her.'

She looked at him sorrowfully, her head on one side. 'Yes, you love her.' She said again, dreamily: 'You love her.' She sighed. 'Okay, I'll try to find out.'

She rose from the bed in a lovely unfolding of young womanflesh and walked for the bathroom, to dress.

'I wish it would happen to me . . .' she said.

Hargreave took a taxi to Arbat Street, then found Yakob's Karate Club on foot, following McAdam's map.

The club was in the basement of an old apartment block in a sidestreet. The entrance was behind the building: Hargreave was surprised to find a big backyard filled with late-model Western cars and shiny motorcycles. He descended some steps and rang a bell beside a grey steel door with a spyhole in it. He heard thumps from within, waited, then rang again. Finally the spyhole darkened; then locks clanged and the door opened. He found himself looking at a machine pistol held by a young man in a white karate suit.

'I have an appointment with Mr Yakob.' By now Hargreave presumed that everybody in Russia spoke English.

The man motioned him inside with the pistol, and the door clanged shut behind. He led the way down a short passage, past a windowless office, into a large basement. It smelt of sweat. Thick canvas mats covered the floor, a dozen pairs of white-clad, mean-looking young men attacked each other. In their midst stood a big man, barking instructions. His barrel chest and bulging arms were covered in thick black curly hair, but his head was completely bald. The man pointed with the gun. 'Yakob is that teacher.'

Hargreave hovered on the edge of the martial activity, impressed by the skill and ferocity of the combatants. Now *this* was really reassuring – with guys like this on his side he would feel much more confident.

Yakob suddenly strode through his fighting men, jerked his head and walked towards the office. Hargreave followed him. Yakob closed the door, walked behind his desk and sat. Sweat gleamed on him. He motioned Hargreave to sit, looked at him unsmilingly, and said with a heavy accent: 'So you are Jake's friend. And you want protection. Who from?'

Hargreave sat forward, feeling nervous: he had dealt with criminals all his life but he had never solicited their services, never placed himself in their hands.

'I am a private detective from England. I have to do some negotiations on behalf of my clients with a certain Mafia boss in Moscow. There may be trouble. Violence. I want some bodyguards to accompany me to those negotiations. If there's violence they must get me out and rush me to a safe place which I will tell them about.'

Yakob's expression did not change. 'Which Mafia boss?'

'I'm afraid that's confidential at this stage. But of course I will tell you if we make a deal. I want to know how much you charge, please.'

Yakob said flatly, 'How do you know I am not a Mafia boss?'

Hargreave was sure he was. 'Jake recommended you.'

'I am the biggest Mafia boss in Russia. Didn't Jake tell you that I have over fifty karate schools, and my best students are my enforcers – I call them, they come. Anywhere, anytime. Didn't Jake tell you that I *rule* the Mafia?'

'No.' Lord, he thought, what better source for your enforcers than a string of karate schools across the country?

Yakob's unwavering eyes were opaque. 'The Mafia bosses would like to pay *me* protection – but I won't take their money because they are shit.' He spat the word again: '*Shit*. New gangsters with no morals, no respect, they rob everybody, even the *muzhik*, the ordinary guy who has nothing. There is no order in Russia because of those shits. Me? I only take protection money from rich businessmen, like Jake's friends, and the banks, and the big factories and the fat men in the government. But I give them good service. They sleep good in their beds, thank you to me. I leave the little guys, so they like me also. If they come to me, I give them protection, *free*. I call my boys, they go to work on the shit.'

Hargreave smiled; if this was true it was very good news. Thank God for Jake McAdam – with Yakob's guys and their karate there might not be any bloodshed at all. Maybe he should just hand the whole problem over to Yakob and wait for his boys to bring Olga to him safe and sound? He said: 'But your boys don't only use their karate, do they?'

'Karate, guns, knives, even bows and arrows, nice and quiet. I am a black-belt karate expert but I also use this.' He stretched his foot out and opened a big cupboard with his toe.

The inside was lined with a gleaming array of hardware: knives of all kinds, bayonets, swords, daggers, knuckle-dusters, garrottes, an awesome array of pistols, sub-machine-guns, even a crossbow. Each item was strapped to the woodwork and labelled.

'I was an instructor in the Russian army,' Yakob said. 'My boys know how to use everything. Can you do karate?'

'Not much need for that sort of thing in England. But I can box.'

Yakob snorted. 'Boxing?' He held up his little finger. 'With this I can kill Mike Tyson in ten seconds.'

Hargreave didn't doubt it. 'So what are your charges, please?'

For the first time Yakob gave a thin smile. 'If there's trouble, violence, will you fight too?'

'Of course.'

'How? With your boxing? Have you got a gun?'

Should he admit it? 'No. I couldn't bring mine on the plane.'

'You're lying,' Yakob said. 'Your friend Jake bought two guns from me. I think they were for you.'

Hargreave smirked. 'Yes. Yes, I have two guns.'

'Do you know how to use them?'

'Yes. I was in the army too.'

'Why did you lie? Because you don't trust me? If you don't trust me, get out.'

Hargreave took a tense, exhausted breath. 'Yes, I trust you.'

'Why? Because Jake said so?'

Jake had only said Yakob was the best of a bad bunch. 'Yes. But I am also an experienced judge of people.'

Yakob seemed to like that: he smiled thinly again. 'You were right to lie because we do not have a deal yet.' He looked at him. 'I will charge one thousand dollars per man for twelve hours' work. After that, fifty dollars an hour for each man. How many men do you want?'

That price seemed cheap to Hargreave. How many? Four? Six? How many guys can you crowd into a bathroom? Into his car?

'At least three. But I'll telephone you when I know my plans, all the details. Probably tomorrow.'

'We also will want to know your plans. My boys do not like being the Charge of the Light Brigade.' He tapped a cellular telephone on his desk. 'You got the number. You call me anytime, day or night. Yakob is like Mr Pinkerton, he does not sleep.'

Hargreave left the club feeling elated. Everything was going right. Now he had muscle! Yakob inspired confidence – Jake recommended him, Jake was a good judge of these things! Of course Yakob was a crook too, but even allowing for exaggeration he was the old-fashioned god-father-type, an honest crook who would keep his bargain, and he hated these new smash-and-grab *avtoritety* like Gregovich. Yakob was just the boy for this job. But he hoped he hadn't said too much to Tanya.

He trudged back to Arbat Street and eventually flagged a battered taxi. He got back to his hotel and rode up in the elevator to find something to eat. It was after ten o'clock, he had drunk too much and his nerves, already stretched tight, felt at snapping point – he still had not eaten since breakfast on the plane. He stopped at the third floor. The elevator foyer was sprinkled with girls who looked at him with interest. He gave them a brittle smile and entered the corridor. There was a row of seedy shops, and more girls. He found the Saint Lucia Bar. Green palm trees were painted on the walls. There were only half a dozen people inside, all girls, chatting. He sat down at a table and ordered the house special, a double hamburger. The girls smiled at him speculatively; two of them were talking on mobile telephones. Hargreave thought Moscow sure beat Hong Kong and Macao for girls, and those places are pretty damn good. And all these Moscow girls looked so respectable – maybe they *were* respectable, like Tanya.

And, oh, he wanted his beautiful Olga safely out of all this. Then the thought returned: Had he said too much to Tanya? Would he have said as much if he'd been clear-headed? Could she screw things up, asking

Boris for information? Was she as sensible as she looked? Shouldn't he have just left everything to Henri?

But no, surely he was right in having two irons in the fire – supposing Henri didn't come through, at least Tanya might come up with information. He'd done the right thing . . .

His hamburger arrived immediately, but he did not want to eat it with all eyes on him. He paid the ninety thousand roubles it cost, wrapped it in a paper napkin, and left. In the elevator he bit into it. It was dry and precooked and re-heated and almost tasteless, but he wolfed it down ravenously.

He got to his room, stripped off and collapsed into bed. In an instant he was asleep.

37

He awoke at about three a.m. His nerves cried for more sleep but his tense body was still functioning on Hong Kong time and he was wide awake. His first thought was: Today is it, today you try Plan One through Henri, tonight you'll be in Helsinki with Olga but if something goes wrong both of you could be dead ... He got up immediately to stop himself worrying, and showered. First hot, then cold, trying to knock out the jetlag. He strapped on his moneybelt, dressed and left his room to drive to Chuck's airfield again while the streets were empty, to improve his time.

The gloomy, musty foyer was silent: one security guard was asleep on a sofa, the other reading a magazine. Hargreave went out into the cold darkness. Tverskaya Street was silent. He walked around the corner, to the dark backstreet, to his rented car.

He drove back to the multi-storey car park, then drove as fast as he dared to the airfield. It was easy because the streets were empty; the journey took him thirty-six minutes – not good enough. But he had not missed any turnings in the dark. He returned to the car park and tried it again. Thirty-three minutes. An average of about fifty-five kilometres an hour, still not fast enough. The city was waking up when he drove it the third time: twenty-nine minutes. Well, at least he knew the way thoroughly.

It was nearly eight o'clock when he parked behind the hotel. The rush hour was on, pedestrians hurrying to work. He was ravenously hungry again, he had to have a big breakfast to fuel his nerve-racked system. As he was locking the car, his cellular telephone rang in his pocket. His pulse tripped. 'Hullo?'

'Good morning, David, did you sleep well?'

Tanya. His heart was knocking. He got back inside his car. 'Fine, thank you! Have you any news for me?'

Tanya chuckled. 'Not yet, lover-boy. I asked some of the girls last night after you left me so very cruelly, so maybe I will hear something today. And today I will phone Boris.' Then: 'Can I see you tonight? Will you come to the Highlife? Or maybe I come to your room?'

Was this for another hundred dollars? 'Maybe. You will phone me if you have information?'

He could almost hear her smile. 'Don't worry, David, I won't rape you, although I would like to do that. But I am really trying to help you find your Olga. You paid me, I am not a cheater.'

'I know, but with Boris – you'll be careful, won't you? No mention of me.' Perhaps he should tell her to leave Boris out of it?

'Don't worry.' Tanya sighed. 'So romantic . . .' Then she teased, '*But*, if you don't find Olga, maybe you can take me for your holiday?' She giggled.

Hargreave smiled weakly. 'Where are you now?'

'At my office. I have to go out soon but I can call you anytime because you gave me your mobile number, yes?'

'Yes.'

'And you will meet me tonight? At the Highlife?'

'I'll try,' Hargreave lied.

'Okay, David. Have a nice day.'

He slumped behind the steering-wheel. So he had been right to speak to her! Tanya really was working for her two hundred dollars. He trusted her – she really was a nice girl, and she would be discreet with this Boris bastard. If that paid off he would have a second string to his bow if Henri failed him; but surely Henri wouldn't fail him.

Hargreave looked at his wristwatch. It was after eight, the time Henri said he could call. He scrabbled in his pocket for the Metropole Hotel's card, dialled the number and asked for the concierge's desk.

'Henri?' Hargreave's heart was knocking. 'This is Mr Johnson. We spoke last night about my lady-friend, Olga?'

'Oh yes, sir.' Henri paused. 'Yes, I think your request should be possible, sir.'

Oh yes! Oh thank God! Everything is working out!

'Thank you very much, Henri,' Hargreave breathed. 'Have you actually spoken to –' he groped for a word other than 'pimp' – 'her controller?'

'Not directly, sir, but to somebody who will do so. Will you definitely be staying at the Metropole tonight, sir?'

'Yes – I'll make a reservation right away.'

'Very good, sir. If you will contact me when you have arrived. I am off duty at noon but I start again at four.'

'Many thanks indeed. But, Henri – is this definite?'

'I foresee no difficulties, sir.'

Hargreave thanked him and switched off. He held his face. Everything was going to be all right . . .

Now he had to phone Yakob and set up his bodyguards: arrange a meeting, explain the plan, get the boys in position at the Metropole in plenty of time. How many boys? Four? It sounded enough, but he would discuss it with Yakob. He looked at his watch. A bit early to phone, Yakob worked at night – call him after breakfast. But it wasn't too early for Chuck Hunter. He dialled the Stardust hangar.

'Chuck, this is David Johnson. It looks like all stations go for to-night!'

'Congratu*lations*! So the lady's hit town?'

'I think she's going to. So you'll be on standby, tanked up, warmed up and ready to go?'

'Sure thing!' Chuck beamed. 'And the scotch and the vodka and the flowers. What time you arriving?'

Hargreave's eyes burned. *Flowers.* 'Not sure yet, I'll call you back this afternoon. My guess is after dark. Can you be standing by from five o'clock?'

'Sure, I'll file a flight plan for five o'clock. But you can make it earlier or later, I'll be here, just give me fifteen minutes' warning.' He added: 'Are we – er – likely to have an unwelcome send-off? Like the jealous husband?'

Hargreave closed his eyes. 'Don't think so, but you'll be ready?'

'All heart, that's me . . .'

Hargreave thanked him and switched off his telephone. He felt fever-ishly happy; it was all happening. Now what did he have to do, apart from telephone Yakob? He dialled the Metropole Hotel again.

Yes, the receptionist said, they had a room for tonight. What name?

'David Johnson.' Then he remembered he would have to show his passport when he checked in – so he would say the reservation was made for him by David Johnson.

Now, as Henri had things under control, shouldn't he telephone Tanya again and tell her to cool it, not to speak to Boris? Yes, that was safest – two enquiries about Olga in one day might arouse suspicions. He dialled Tanya's office. A man answered, in Russian.

'May I speak to Tanya, please?'

'I'm sorry, Tanya is out of the office most of today,' the man said pleasantly, switching to English. 'I will take a message?'

Hargreave sighed. 'No, I'll call back, thank you.'

His hands were shaky, and he was so tense that he had forgotten his hunger; the thought of food made him feel sick, but he had to eat.

He locked the car and walked back to his hotel. Upstairs in the bleak dining room he made himself eat a big plate of porridge, three fried eggs and three Russian sausages. Once he started he felt better. But still so tense.

Please God everything keeps going right. Please God we don't have to shoot . . .

He finished breakfast, rode up in the elevator and walked back to his room to telephone Yakob. He unlocked his door, and walked inside.

His heart lurched as he saw a silhouette against the window.

'You fucking bastard!' Bernard Champion snarled softly.

Hargreave closed the door and slumped against it, his heart thumping. '*Jesus!* What are you doing here?'

'You *bastard*. Fucking up my case with your fucking outburst! Now Gregovich has done a runner, do you know that?'

Hargreave closed his eyes. 'Findlay warned me he might. I'm very sorry.'

'You're *sorry*?' Champion advanced from the window and stood in front of him, big and seething. '*Sorry?*'

'Yes!' Hargreave snapped. 'Very.' His nerves could not take this. 'And I repeat – what the hell are you doing here?'

Champion glared at him. 'Same as you! Looking for Olga Romalova, though for a somewhat different reason! I have *here*,' he tapped his jacket pocket angrily, 'a warrant of arrest for your friend Ivan Gregovich, issued by the Supreme Court of Hong Kong – the bastard did a runner within hours of getting bail, thanks to you! Jumped in a speedboat and in Macao before you could say uranium! From Canton he flew here yesterday on a false passport!' He glared, then sneered furiously: 'And that's where your precious Olga Romalova comes in! Because we don't know where he is, but I reckon Miss Romalova does – and that's where you come in, you bastard.' His eyes narrowed. 'Oh you *bastard*, fucking up my case by losing your temper all because your beloved Olga didn't show up to perjure herself!' He clenched his fist. 'We had him! You'd have got that confession admitted in evidence! And even if it had been thrown out that all-white jury would have convicted him on the evidence of the key alone! You'd done a *brilliant* job – then you go and fuck it up, so the judge declares a mistrial, and releases the bastard on bail!' He glared, then jabbed his finger: '*And* you knew all along your precious Olga was in Gregovich's clutches! Why didn't you tell me you were professionally compromised by that nasty little detail?'

'I only knew she was in *Vladimir's* clutches – the pimp's. Not Gregovich's.'

'No? Then why did you say in your disastrous outburst that she was Gregovich's captive?'

'Because it's fucking obvious she's *indirectly* in his clutches! Vladimir's got Olga, Gregovich arranges for her to come, so Vladimir and Gregovich are obviously Mafia partners!'

Champion looked at him witheringly. 'And obviously Gregovich is the fucking boss! And you told me you owe Vladimir money – so you really owe Gregovich money! *Charming* – prosecuting counsel owes the defendant money! Ransom for his girl!' He turned away in disgust. 'You should hear what the police think of you! And your staff. And the press – I brought yesterday's newspaper, hope it gives you a heart attack!' He snatched it off the desk and flung it on the bed.

The front-page headline read: DPP'S OUTBURST ABORTS NUCLEAR TRIAL.

Hargreave came from the door and sat down on the bed. He ignored the newspaper. 'You've got a warrant of arrest? That means you've got to execute it through the Russian police, and first go through extradition proceedings before a Russian court.'

'How very perspicacious of you.'

Hargreave waved an angry hand. 'But that'll take a week at least. And you said you don't trust the Russian police – half are Mafia them selves. So Gregovich is bound to hear about it and he'll disappear – *with* Olga probably. Then we'll never find her!' Hargreave stared. 'Christ, you can't do that – you can't show up here like a bull in a china shop and ruin everything!'

'*Me?*' Champion said incredulously. Then he pointed a finger: 'You're the bull in the china shop! My heart doesn't bleed for Olga Romalova. I don't give a shit about Olga, it's Gregovich I want! I have not arrived like a bull in a china shop! I am here entirely unofficially and incognito! And I do trust at least one Russian cop – Kerensky! He's arrived from Vladivostok to help me – also unofficially and incognito! And we've got Simonski's old friend Captain Sepov, he's going to help us.' He leant forward and hissed: 'And we're going to find Gregovich – through you and your precious Olga Romalova – and arrest the bastard on some holding charge before he hears about the extradition proceedings – before some dumb lawyer from your department shows up here to apply for extradition and alerts Gregovich!' He jabbed his finger again. '*You should be fucking grateful I'm here.* You bull in a fucking china shop!'

'You're here incognito? Bullshit. What airline did you fly in on this morning?'

'Aeroflot. What you expect me to do, charter a Lear jet?'

Hargreave slapped the bed. 'That means the Mafia *knows*. They've got pals everywhere. So you're not very incognito!' He pointed at the door: 'We can expect them through there any moment. You're very high on their shit-list!' He glared, furiously worried. 'I go to all this effort to remain undetected . . . How did you know where to find me?'

'Our mutual travel agent,' Champion snapped. 'Anyway, it wouldn't have taken long to find you – there're not many hotels in Moscow hosting Mr Fuck-up Hargreave.'

'Jesus – guard your tongue!'

'Guard *my* tongue? If you'd guarded your tongue in court Gregovich would be behind bars and I wouldn't be here!'

Hargreave took a deep breath to control his anger – and his nerves. 'And how did you get into my room?'

'Hired Bill Sikes, the burglar!' Champion snapped. He snorted. 'Kerensky gave me a pass-key-card, which any Mafia thug could get hold of – that's how safe you are, pal. Christ, you should be bloody grateful we're here, you're a babe in the woods, you're a dumb lawyer, not James Bond! And all you do is bitch about your cover!'

Hargreave dragged his hands down his face. Yes, now he was thinking straighter, he was relieved Champion was here – of course he was. But he also had Yakob now – he didn't really *need* Champion and he was worried sick about the police blundering around and alerting Gregovich. 'And where's Kerensky now?'

'With Sepov. We're meeting them shortly, I'm here to fetch you. Because you're going to cooperate with us, pal, whether you like it or not!' He turned and paced to the window.

'And what is your plan?'

'As they say in the classics, *we* will ask the questions.' He turned and glared. 'But at the moment, *you* are the plan. You're the guy Gregovich will be expecting to show up looking for the beautiful Olga Romalova, you're the guy he wants his pound of flesh from, so he'll come looking for you. And that's when we pounce on him.' He jerked his head at the door. 'So come on, we're going to meet Kerensky and Sepov.'

Hargreave remained seated. 'Why the hell don't they come to me if I'm so fucking important?' He held out a finger. 'Now let me make one thing clear, Bernie! Yes, I'm relieved that you guys have materialized out of thin air, and I'll cooperate with you if I approve of your plan – but this is *my* operation, to find Olga, not yours. And I will not cooperate with any plan that does not ensure Olga's safety – she must be the primary objective; getting Gregovich is just a bonus as far as I'm concerned. I'm as anxious as anybody to see him behind bars, but I'm much more concerned – *totally* concerned – with Olga. Got that?'

Champion scowled at him. 'You, Al,' he said, 'will do as you're told for once. You may be a shit-hot criminal lawyer but you know fuck-all about the physical business of catching fucking criminals! They've already *been* caught by the time they're brought to your august court-room, caught by guys like me who risked our skins, who've got a lot more experience in strong-arm stuff than you, even if you did box for Oxford a hundred years ago! Now stop trying to throw your weight around and get off your ass!'

Hargreave remained seated, thinking desperately. If Champion and Kerensky were hiding in his Metropole bedroom tonight he wouldn't need Yakob and his expensive boys. 'Olga,' he said grimly, 'is my *only* objective when the chips are down. Is that understood?'

Champion closed his eyes. 'Oh boy,' he groaned, 'is that understood loud and clear after your outburst in court? Now come on!'

Hargreave did not get up. 'Where are we going? Why don't Kerensky and Sepov come here?'

'Because,' Champion explained, 'as you so profoundly observed, the Mafia may come bursting through this door at any fucking minute looking for you! So we are going for a little drive in my rented car, to follow Kerensky and Sepov to a quiet lane, like they do in the movies, where we can't be seen or heard. We're not going to the police station because Kerensky does not want to be seen by Moscow cops who may be in the Mafia's pay. Nor do I. Nor do you.' He added nastily: 'Do you think you can remember all that, Rambo?'

Rambo? But Hargreave got up. 'How do we know we can trust this guy Sepov?'

'Because Simonski said so, and I trusted Simonski! And to anticipate your next question we *need* Sepov because he knows Moscow – Kerensky doesn't. Now I'm going to walk down to the foyer by the emergency staircase. You go down by elevator. Once outside, turn left, go down the lane and you'll see my rented car, a blue Ford. Get in and wait for me. I don't want us to be seen together in the foyer.'

The country lane was a few miles from Chuck's airfield. Hargreave and Champion sat in the backseat of Sepov's car. It did not look like an official police vehicle, but a portable police lamp lay on the dashboard, the magnetized type that can be placed on the roof when needed.

Andreovich Sepov was a stout, middle-aged man with wire-rim spectacles and a jolly smile. He spoke fluent but heavily accented English. He said in answer to Hargreave's question:

'I am in the fraud section of Organized Crime, I am not one of those tough homicide detectives – I am like a bookkeeper, Mr Hargreave. And I do not know anything about this uranium case except what Kerensky has now told me. Simonski was my good friend, but he told me nothing. But of course I know something about Gregovich – every policeman in Russia has heard of Ivan Gregovich. Maybe Mr Gregovich is not as rich as Mr Al Capone yet but we must give him time, we cannot catch up with America immediately. But that is all I know about him.'

Champion said, 'But you do definitely know he arrived in Moscow last night? From China?'

'Yes, I checked with my friend in the immigration department. But where he is nobody knows, maybe he lives like a bachelor with so many of his prostitutes to oblige him.' (For an instant Hargreave saw the swine rumbling on top of Olga and his blood surged in hate.) 'If you wish I can ask my colleagues for more information.'

'No,' Hargreave, Champion and Kerensky replied in unison. Hargreave added, 'And a man called Vladimir, who looks after the prostitution side of Gregovich's business; heard of him?'

'Vladimir is a common name. I can ask.'

'Not yet,' Champion said. He looked at Hargreave as if to say 'satisfied?'

Hargreave was worried that Sepov really did look like a bookkeeper – if he was involving the Russian cops he wanted a man who knew how to throw his weight around. 'Mr Sepov,' he said, 'we are very grateful for your assistance, but if it comes to raiding the apartment where Gregovich and Olga are, will you be with us, with a number of other policemen, or will we be on our own?'

Champion started to speak but Sepov said, 'I can get a number of my colleagues to come with us, but Kerensky said –'

'Not yet,' Champion interrupted. 'Don't talk to anybody yet.'

'*Correct*,' Hargreave said. 'No more outsiders at this stage, please. And I wish to make it clear how serious this is for my friend Olga –'

'I've told them how you feel, for Christ's sake,' Champion broke in irritably. 'Stop laying down the law, you're not in Hong Kong now, we're in these guys' hands! We need their help. Now, let's start by hearing what your plan is, what *you've* been up to in the last twenty-four hours in sunny Moscow. And maybe we'll start patching up your blunders.'

Blunders? Hargreave wanted to leap out of the car in high dudgeon, tell them to fuck off and find Gregovich without him.

He did not tell them about his last visit to Moscow – Champion would have exploded if he knew about that, he would suspect he had made a deal with Vladimir. Nor did he mention Jake McAdam. He told them briefly what had happened in Macao, about Vladimir's demands for payment and Olga's consequent deportation. He told them his plan to get Olga to the Metropole Hotel as a call-girl, about his conversation with Henri. He did not tell them about his meeting with Yakob: he only said that he had been considering hiring bodyguards. Nor did he mention his fortuitous meeting with Tanya, nor about chartering Chuck Hunter's aircraft – why tell that at this stage to this stranger, Sepov? He did not suspect the man of treachery but there was no need for them to know.

Champion listened in judicial silence, then said, 'And if it worked, if Olga came to the Metropole, and your bodyguards succeeded in over-powering her minder, what were you going to do?'

'I hadn't yet worked that out by the time you unlawfully entered my room. But perhaps you've got some bright ideas. In principle I was going to drive like hell, then jump on a plane to gay Paree.'

'Most security agencies are Mafia too,' Sepov said. 'Have you got a gun?'

He was about to say yes, to show he wasn't a complete prick, but he didn't want to explain how he got it. 'No.'

Kerensky asked, 'If Henri could *not* get Olga to the Metropole, what was your plan?'

'I was going to call Vladimir on his cellular phone,' Hargreave said grimly, 'tell him to bring Olga to me and collect his money.'

Champion stared at him incredulously. 'You know Vladimir's telephone number? *How?*'

God, he'd almost let the cat out of the bag about his last visit. 'After Vladimir had Olga deported from Macao he telephoned me from Moscow to demand the money. I refused, but he gave me the number of his mobile phone in case I changed my mind.'

'Why didn't you tell us this before?' Champion demanded. 'This makes things easier.'

'Because,' Hargreave said acidly, 'you've only just asked me my plan.' He added: 'It's only his cellular phone, you won't be able to trace his address from it, he assured me of that.'

'Correct,' Sepov said. 'Fictitious address.'

'And did you ever telephone him?' Champion demanded suspiciously.

'No.' That was the truth.

'Why fuckin' not? He's got your girl. I don't believe you!'

'Because I had decided to prosecute Gregovich myself! So it wouldn't do for me to be telephoning the Mafia, would it?'

Champion looked at him disbelievingly. He said slowly: 'Vladimir didn't put the screws on you about the Gregovich case, did he?'

Oh Jesus. 'No! What d'you take me for? And what's the meaning of this cross-examination? If you don't believe me I'll fuck off and you can find Gregovich by yourself! *I* don't want to see the bastard, *you* do – I only want Olga!'

Champion subsided, controlling his anger. Kerensky said: 'You've brought the money Vladimir wants?'

'How much?' Champion demanded.

He dared not tell them the real amount: he did not want their ridicule nor their suspicions aroused. 'Forty thousand US. I owed twenty, but Vladimir demanded a hundred per cent interest.'

Champion stared. '*Jesus.* Forty thousand bucks for a . . .' He was going to say 'whore'.

'And where is the money now?' Sepov asked. 'Somewhere safe I hope?'

'Of course.' It was in his moneybelt right now. 'In a bank.'

'But it won't be in the bank when Mr Vladimir arrives to collect it, will it?' Champion said derisively. 'Mr Vladimir won't want a cheque, will he? No, so it'll be *un*safely in your pocket? So Vladimir arrives with Olga, takes your money, shoots you dead and walks away. Free as the air, with your money, with Olga to whore for a few more years before he bumps her off too. Jesus, Al, can't you see what an asshole's plan that is?'

Hargreave said slowly and furiously, 'You better guard your tongue, Champ, or you can do your Gregovich thing without me. I will have my bodyguards with me when Vladimir brings Olga!'

'*If* he brings Olga!' Champion cried. 'And you can't trust your body-guards – can't you see you need us –'

'And you need me as the bait, you asshole!'

Champion closed his eyes in exasperation. Then he held up his hands. 'Yes,' he said, 'we need you. Shall we acknowledge that we both need each other? And I apologize for speaking hastily – okay? Now.' He looked at Hargreave seriously, trying to contain his anger. 'Al, your Metropole plan is theoretically not bad. *If* it works. If the Mafia are letting her out on house-calls, if your bodyguards are reliable and Olga's heavy minder doesn't overwhelm you, if you manage to jump in your car without them catching up with you. Fine – you get your girl and you save your money. But that's a lot of ifs, pal. And from our point of view –' he gestured around the car – 'it's no good, because it does not get us to Gregovich – the dear man is unlikely to escort Olga around town himself.' He sighed bitterly. 'So what I suggest, Al, is that we put our heads together and try to kill two birds with one stone: we'll get both your girl *and* Gregovich. And this is how we'll do it: we scrap your Metropole plan –'

'Why?' Hargreave demanded. 'You guys could be hiding in the room! When Olga arrives with the pimp we all jump on him – that'll be easy with four of us. You force him to tell you where Gregovich is. Meanwhile Olga and I escape. Perfect – I get Olga, you get Gregovich.'

Champion smiled thinly. 'But the pimp may not know where Gregovich is, Al – maybe Gregovich is holed up in some hideout –'

'That's your problem, not mine! You get the pimp, you find Gregovich.'

Champion ignored the interruption. 'We must use an adaptation of your second plan, Al – that is the only sure way to get Gregovich. Because Gregovich wants *you*, Al – you've got the money, and he doubtless wants a little chat with you –'

'You mean murder me?' Hargreave snapped. 'How about *you* as the bait? Gregovich would love to get his hands on you, you're the guy who arrested him.'

'But we won't let Gregovich murder you, Al,' Champion said. 'We'll be there with you. You phone Vladimir, tell him you'll only pay the money to Gregovich because he's the boss, you insist on a meeting with him. Gregovich sends his heavies to fetch you – we'll be hiding in the room next door and we'll follow you to Gregovich's place. Then we'll burst in and arrest the bastard on a holding charge, then lug him in front of a Russian judge for extradition proceedings.'

But the Metropole Hotel plan was safer. 'Supposing you can't follow me, supposing you guys get lost?'

'Al?' Champion spread his hand. 'Trust us – we're professionals. And what have you got to lose? Until we showed up this morning you were going to hire expensive bodyguards and probably end up going into the lion's den anyway to get Olga. What a risky business that was going to be! Can you trust your bodyguards? Sepov says they're all crooks. And look at the money we're saving you.'

Hargreave rubbed his forehead. Champion continued: 'So what we must do now is discuss all the details of the plan – where, when, how, what you're going to say on the telephone, how we're going to stake out the place Gregovich's hoods fetch you from.'

371

Hargreave considered the plan. 'So I arrive at Vladimir's pad – or Gregovich's. Suppose Olga's not there, suppose she's being kept in a dungeon elsewhere – it'll be too late then for me to try my Metropole trick.'

'I promise you, Al,' Champion said with a smile, 'that once either Gregovich or Vladimir is arrested we'll *persuade* them to tell us where Olga is.'

Yeah, like you persuaded Gregovich to confess. 'So you guys burst into Gregovich's pad. There's likely to be a shoot-out, and Olga gets shot in the crossfire, or Gregovich grabs her as a human shield.' He shook his head emphatically. 'No way am I going to risk that unnecessarily. That's why I devised the Metropole plan as my first option, because it's so much safer than going into the lion's den. We *must* try that first.'

'Al,' Champion sighed, 'we know how to handle a shoot-out. It's a small risk we've just got to take. And it's the least you can do to recapture Gregovich after the fuck-up you made at the trial.'

Hargreave snorted. 'Risking my girl's life unnecessarily is the least I can do, huh?' He jabbed his finger. 'Well, let me tell you the *most* that I'll do! You want me as the bait for Gregovich – okay, I'll be the bait, and risk getting myself shot. But only after Olga has safely escaped. That means we try the Metropole trick first. Olga arrives, we jump on the pimp, Olga escapes to some safe place. *Then* you use me to draw Gregovich out. How we achieve that is up to you smart cops to figure out. I suggest we order the pimp to lead us to Gregovich's lair, but if that doesn't work I'll telephone Vladimir as planned and arrange a rendezvous with Gregovich on the pretext of paying the money. They fetch me, you guys follow, you burst in and do your cop number.'

'But nobody will fall for that,' Champion objected. 'Why would you pay the money *after* the hostage has escaped?'

'They won't yet know Olga has escaped if we act fast – they'll think she's still humping some jerk in the Metropole Hotel.'

'And if we can't get hold of them that fast? If they find out that Olga's escaped and they've been tricked?'

Hargreave sighed angrily. 'Then I tell them I still want to pay the money as a kind of insurance, to ensure they leave me alone in future.'

The policemen smirked. Champion said, 'I doubt they'd fall for that unlikely story. Gregovich will do another disappearing trick, and we'll never get him.' He shook his head. 'Sorry, Al, but the only sensible plan is the one I've outlined. Now let's work out the details –'

'Let me make it abundantly clear, Champ,' Hargreave interrupted, 'that you are not calling the shots with me! I'm telling *you*, Champ, that I insist on trying the Metropole plan first. After that, you can do any fucking thing you want with me.'

There was silence in the car. Champion glowered at him. 'And let *me* make something abundantly clear, Al.' He paused. 'You're in Russia now, serious crimes have been committed by a certain Ivan Gregovich, these two gentlemen here are lawful Russian policemen who intend to arrest the man, and anything you do to obstruct them is an offence for which you can be clapped in irons. Have you got that, Mr Lawyer? You will "insist" on nothing!'

'Are you threatening me?'

'Take it any way you like, Al. But we don't think you'll be unco-operative for long, sitting impotently in a cell while Olga's in Gregovich's clutches.'

Jesus. 'So unless we do it your way, you arrest me on a trumped-up charge until I agree?' He looked angrily at Sepov for confirmation. The man looked away, embarrassed. Hargreave looked at Kerensky: he gave a wisp of a smile. 'So I'm a hostage too now!' He stared incredulously. 'Olga is Gregovich's hostage, and I'm your hostage! Beautiful!' And, oh God, he knew what he was going to do about this! His woman's life at stake and no bastard was going to tell him what to do, let alone threaten him! But there was no percentage in arguing about it, in telling them another damn thing! He sat back furiously. 'Okay, so you smart cops tell me what you *think* we're going to do!'

Champion said gently, 'Does that mean you agree to do it our way?'

'*Yes*, for Christ's sake! You don't have to lock me up! Now tell me how you propose using me! How? Where? When?'

Champion sighed tensely. 'Thanks, Al. So, now I suggest we all cool down and start using our heads instead of our tempers. Then, having made some decisions, we go back to town and scout out the land – decide where we're all going to be waiting, et cetera.'

'And *when*,' Hargreave demanded, 'are we going into fucking action?'

'Patience, Al,' Champion said. 'We know every minute counts for you. But it probably won't be today – for one thing, both Kerensky and I need to sleep off some jetlag. And before that we've got a lot to think about.'

38

The Ukraine Hotel towers up in tiers like a huge grey wedding cake. From its upper windows Hargreave could see the Moskva River, the Kremlin, the Intourist Hotel.

Early that afternoon he moved into a room on the ninth floor in accordance with Champion's plan. Sepov reserved a suite almost directly opposite so that he, Champion and Kerensky would be on hand, lying in wait when the Mafia came. This hotel had been chosen because it had been possible to arrange this juxtaposition of accommodation – Sepov knew the manager. As instructed, Hargreave drove to the hotel, left his car in the parking area, registered at the reception desk under his real name. Five minutes later Sepov checked into the suite. A few minutes after that Champion and Kerensky arrived in a taxi and climbed up to the ninth floor via the emergency staircase. Sepov had provided them all with radio-telephones and he had given Hargreave an electronic alarm device: when the Mafia came he would alert the others in the suite by pressing a button.

'All very professional,' Hargreave admitted grimly to Champion, 'but who's paying for all this expensive accommodation?'

'You are,' Champion said, 'out of that nice fat moneybelt of yours. Dry your eyes – your bodyguards would have cost you a fortune.' He held out his hand: 'Your car-keys, please.'

'Car-keys? What the hell for?'

'Because,' Champion said wearily, 'we're going to need it, to follow you once Vladimir sends his heavies to fetch you. You're not going to need it, are you? I haven't got a car because I've just handed mine back to the rental company and Sepov doesn't want to use his.'

Like hell Hargreave didn't need his car. 'Why not? Sepov used his car this morning.'

'That was an unmarked police car. And this is an *un*official operation, remember? With a foreign cop. Keys, please.'

'You want to use it now?'

'You sound like a father worrying about lending the family car to his son!' Champion complained irritably. 'I'm going to sleep off my jetlag now, *Dad*! Nobody's going to drive the fucking car until Mr Vladimir's boys come to fetch you. Then we'll follow you in it – so give me the keys!'

Hargreave slapped them in Champion's hand angrily. He had a spare set in his other pocket.

'And you're not armed, are you?' Champion asked. 'Leave any shooting to us, please!'

'Yes, I'll gladly leave any shooting to you, Sherlock. Just try to miss Olga – *and* me.'

Champion stomped off bad-temperedly, leaving Hargreave seething. It angered him that he had been threatened, that matters were taken out of his hands, that they were staying at the Ukraine instead of the Metropole where Henri was expecting him. But it was true that it was a great comfort to know that he had reliable allies across the corridor rather than Yakob's boys. But no way was he going to let them risk Olga's life in a shoot-out if he had the chance to get her safely out of the way first – *no way*!

His 'orders' were to stay in his room 'and rest', while Champion and Kerensky slept off their jetlag in the suite, leaving Sepov on watch: when they woke up, refreshed, Hargreave was to telephone Vladimir. He waited, pacing up and down his room, until four o'clock – until Champion and Kerensky must be asleep – feverishly turning his private plan over and over in his mind until his nerves were stretched to screaming.

Olga arrives, leaves the pimps outside in the corridor. You buzz Champion and the others, present them with a fait accompli, *tell them to sort out the pimps. You and Olga run for the airfield. You throw Olga on Chuck's aircraft and off she flies to Helsinki. You come back here and fulfil your bargain with Champion. On the other hand if Vladimir sends his heavies without Olga, you buzz Champ, Sepov and Kerensky, who burst out of the room, sort out the heavies, then force them to lead us to Olga and Gregovich . . .*

At four o'clock, the deadline he had set himself for action, he stood staring over Moscow, reviewing his decision one last time; then he poured a big dash of whisky into a glass and gulped it. He took his cellular telephone into the bathroom, closed the door and dialled the Metropole Hotel. He asked to be connected to Henri.

'Henri, this is David Johnson. We spoke this morning about Olga?'

'Ah yes, sir,' Henri said.

'Henri, I won't be staying at the Metropole after all. But I presume you could arrange for Olga to come to another hotel?'

'Yes, sir, no problem.'

Hargreave sighed in relief. 'So, I would like you to arrange for Olga to come as soon as possible to room nine one seven, the Ukraine Hotel. Please arrange it immediately. Then call me back, confirming that.'

'Yes, sir,' Henri said.

'How long will it be before she arrives, Henri?'

'I do not know where the young lady lives, sir. But I would think one hour. However, I will telephone you back. But, sir?'

'Yes?'

'Sir said he would pay a little extra for expenses?'

'Yes,' Hargreave said. 'How much?'

'Two hundred dollars, sir?'

'A pleasure, Henri.'

'Would sir be kind enough to give the money to my friend the concierge of the Ukraine? His name is Andre, he will probably be bringing the young lady to your room.'

This detail proved that Henri was genuine. 'Of course.'

'Thank you, sir. I will call you back soon.'

Hargreave slumped against the wall. His plan was going to work! And a hundred thousand dollars saved! Fuck you, Champion – Olga's going to be safe before you rush in with all guns blazing!

He went into the bedroom, poured another slug of whisky, swallowed it, then he returned to the bathroom and shakily called Chuck Hunter.

'Chuck, it's all stations go. My bride-to-be is arriving in about one hour. You'll be standing by at the airfield?'

Hargreave could imagine the dollar-signs in Chuck's eyes. 'Sure thing!'

'The engine warmed up? Parked right on the edge of the runway?'

'The props turning, if you like!'

Hargreave closed his eyes. He was about to say, 'And one other thing, my lady will probably be flying alone with you to Helsinki,' but this was no time for explaining himself. 'Okay, Chuck, see you soon.'

As he switched off, the telephone rang in his bedroom. He opened the bathroom door and picked it up. 'Hullo?'

'This is Henri, sir. I am happy to say that the young lady should be with you in about one hour.'

Hargreave wanted to whoop for joy. He thanked Henri profusely, hung up, and punched his palm.

'*Oh thank you, God . . .*'

* * *

It was a very long hour. He felt feverish, almost sick with relief. He desperately wanted a drink, to calm his nerves, but he dared not because he would soon be driving across Moscow at speed. He had another shower instead, letting the cold water beat down on his head to steady him up, frantically getting dressed again in case they arrived sooner. He combed his hair, his hand shaking, he brushed his teeth thoroughly and inspected his fingernails. He put on his jacket, checked his pistol, put it in his pocket. He checked Sepov's alarm-device, the little canister of Mace that Jake McAdam had given him, and put them into his other pocket. Then he remembered the moneybelt. He slung off his jacket again, ripped off his shirt and buckled the belt around his waist. He took out two hundred dollars for Henri's friend, the concierge. He counted off a hundred thousand dollars, put them back in his belt, the balance in his trouser pocket. He dressed again feverishly. He checked his pistol again.

Then there was nothing to do but pace up and down, fingering his gun and his bleeper, thanking God and trying to calm down.

It was almost exactly an hour later when the knock came on the door. Hargreave's heart lurched. He thrust his hand into his pocket and gripped the gun – then released it. *Don't pull the gun yet, this is supposed to be an ordinary callgirl situation* . . . He pulled out the can of Mace and held it at his side, concealed. He swallowed, went to the door, and opened it.

A thickset Russian man smiled. 'You sent for a lady, sir?'

'Yes . . .' Hargreave's eyes darted, his heart pounding. The man bounded into the room and seized him.

In one expert movement he slung an arm under his shoulder and around his neck in a half-nelson: in one irresistible jolt Hargreave found himself bent over, a hard hand about to snap his neck, the blood rushing to his face. The canister of Mace clattered to the floor. The man rasped in his ear: 'Vladimir wants to see you. If you come quietly, nobody will hurt you, nobody will hurt Olga. If you struggle, if you shout, I will kill you, like this.' He jerked down on his neck and Hargreave felt dreadful panic at the pressure. 'And my friend will push his knife in your back, like this . . .' He felt a sharp point against his ribs. 'And then Olga will also die, with the razor. First we will cut her tits off, then her throat. Slowly. Do you understand me, sir?'

Oh God, yes, Hargreave understood. *Champion*, he cried in his head, *Sepov!* He desperately groped for the alarm in his pocket. The man knocked his hand aside contemptuously. 'Any tricks and Olga is dead! So we are now going to walk out of this room to the stairs, like nice people. If you shout, you are dead and so is Olga.'

Then another man was frisking his pockets. He pulled out Hargreave's gun – snorts of derision. In his other pocket the alarm was found. Then the moneybelt was detected. He was wrenched upright, his shirt pulled out. The belt was unbuckled and unzipped. Exclamations. 'Ah, very good, sir!' The Russian stuffed the belt in his own pocket, then he shoved Hargreave towards the door. *'No trouble!'*

Hargreave was trembling as he tucked his shirt back into his trousers. He looked desperately for the canister of Mace but couldn't see it. He was pushed towards the door again. The second Russian opened it, peered out, then beckoned.

They walked fast down the corridor abreast, Hargreave in the middle, a knife pressing on his back. He prayed for the suite door to open. They passed it. *Sepov* . . . he prayed – he dared not shout it. They came to the emergency staircase, and began to descend.

Down and down the stairwell they clattered. Hargreave's heart was pounding, his legs trembling. Finally they came to the bottom; a corridor led to the gardens, through an emergency door. The Russian opened it.

A car was waiting, its engine running, a third man at the wheel. Hargreave was bundled into the backseat between his two captors. A hand shoved his head down between his knees, a blanket was thrown over him, and the car started to move.

39

The car raced across Moscow, turning left and right: under the blanket Hargreave desperately tried to memorize how many turns, in which direction, but he could not. After about fifteen minutes the car halted.

The blanket was removed; he clambered out, and glanced desperately around for a street name, but saw none. He could not see the square he remembered. Apartment blocks reared up on either side.

He was hurried towards the nearest, but it was not the building in which he'd last seen Olga – this entrance was bigger: he desperately tried to memorize features – there was no name. They entered a foyer and stopped at an elevator. Steel doors, postboxes on the wall, brown marble floor. The elevator doors opened, he was pushed inside. The blanket was thrown over his head again. His heart was pounding – but, surely, covering his head showed they intended to let him go? The elevator rose briefly, then stopped. No more than three floors? He was led outside, down a corridor. Stop. A door opening. He was pushed inside. The door closing. The blanket was pulled off his head.

He found himself in a large living-room with garish modern furniture. Dark corridors at each end – a big apartment, perhaps two knocked into one? A balcony overlooking treetops. Nobody was present but his two captors. Then a figure appeared in one of the corridors. Vladimir strolled into the room.

'Ah, Mr Hargreave, how nice to see you. But why didn't you tell us you were coming to Moscow, you have the number of my cellular phone?'

Hargreave's legs were trembling. He hated himself for wanting to ingratiate himself with the bastard.

'I had every intention of contacting you – I've brought the money. Where's Olga, please?'

Vladimir shook his head sadly. He sat down on a yellow vinyl sofa.

'No, Mr Hargreave, you tried to cheat us. You tried to hire Olga out to your hotel so you could run away with her without paying.'

Hargreave pointed at his captors: 'They have my money! And I kept my bargain about Gregovich's trial – he's run away, on bail. Now will you please keep *your* bargain and give me Olga!'

Vladimir raised his eyebrows at one of the thugs, who nodded and tossed the moneybelt on the table. Then another figure appeared in the passageway, and Hargreave's heart seemed to miss a beat.

It was Ivan Gregovich. He was dressed in slacks, a polo-neck sweater and a satin Chinese smoking jacket adorned with dragons. He was smiling.

'Mr Hargreave, I hardly recognize you without your wig. You know,' he said to Vladimir, 'the English really wear those wigs in court. So impressive. But Mr Hargreave does not look so impressive now, he looks worried.' He strolled across the room, sat down languidly in an armchair and crossed his legs elegantly. 'Maybe it is because he is not surrounded by his policemen, as in Hong Kong. Where are your bodyguards, Mr Champion and Mr Kerensky?'

So he knew they were in town but didn't know where? 'I have no idea.'

Gregovich said to Vladimir, 'Mr Hargreave has no idea where his bodyguards are. How careless. But in court he knows everything.'

'I kept my bargain in court!' Hargreave rasped. 'You're free! Now count the money and let me take Olga away!'

'Yes, count the money,' Gregovich said to the guards. One of them tipped out the cash and started counting. Gregovich went on: 'By the way, don't worry about the neighbours hearing us – I own the whole apartment block, I have very understanding tenants.' He smiled. 'No, you did not keep your bargain. You were trying your best to convict me. But then you lost your temper and said such awful things about me that the nice judge ordered a retrial.'

'I did not lose my temper! I *pretended* to do so in order to get you a retrial and bail!'

Gregovich shook his head. 'No, Mr Hargreave, you are not such a good actor. You were very angry with me and poor Mr Lipschitz, so you said too much – I am free only because you made a mistake.'

'You're *wrong*,' Hargreave blustered. 'Jesus, the case was going so much against you I *had* to blow the trial by pretending to lose my temper and saying what I did in front of the jury!'

'Not because you were angry about Olga?'

Hargreave spread his hands. 'Yes, I was angry about Olga not coming, because she was the one witness who could have confirmed your evidence that Champion was lying when he said he never left you alone with Simonski! Without Olga's evidence you were going to be convicted! And I was worried, because then you would say I had not kept my bargain, so you would refuse to release Olga! I *had* to do something to save you, so I pretended to lose my temper!' He glared at the man desperately, almost believing it himself. 'You and Lipschitz made a very big mistake in not letting Olga come to Hong Kong to testify! If you had you would be a free man now, acquitted!'

Gregovich smirked. 'And once she came to Hong Kong she would have denied she heard anything and even made it worse for me. And once she was safely in your arms, would you have paid the money you owe us?'

'Yes!' Hargreave cried, almost believing it. 'And *why*?' He jabbed a finger: 'Because I wanted to get rid of you guys, pay you off so you'd leave us alone! I didn't want you threatening us for the rest of our lives!'

'It is a pity that you did not think like that in Macao, Mr Hargreave,' Vladimir sneered. 'If you had, you would not be here today.'

Show contrition. 'I know. Don't I know it?'

Gregovich smiled benignly. 'You have learned a lesson, Mr Hargreave?'

Jesus. 'I have indeed,' he said. 'The hard way.'

Vladimir loved that – he gave a short guffaw. Gregovich smiled, eyes twinkling. 'And what is the lesson?'

They were enjoying humiliating him. He forced a sheepish grin: 'Don't fuck about with the Russian Mafia.'

Gregovich liked that. 'Yes . . . But anything else?'

'Pay up on demand,' Hargreave said grimly.

Gregovich nodded, then waved a hand. 'Of *course*. But anything else? What about . . . the lesson for our girls, for example?'

'Same lesson. Don't defy the bosses.' He added, hoping to please the bastard, 'Don't fall in love and buck the system.'

Gregovich jabbed his finger. '*Right*, Mr Hargreave! I knew you were a clever man.' He gave his Mephistophelean smile. '"Don't give trouble to the *boss*".' He spread his hands reasonably. 'Because imagine the difficulties, the . . . *chaos* in our business, if our girls thought that they can fall in love and just run away. Defy us and neglect their responsibilities. Business would be impossible, wouldn't it?'

Hargreave took a deep breath. 'Yes, of course.'

'Of course. Could *you*, Mr Hargreave,' Gregovich asked, 'run a business if your employees treated you like that?'

Oh Jesus, where was this heading? 'No.'

'*No*,' Gregovich agreed. 'And that is why we have to have discipline with these silly women – *discipline*.' He paused. 'And that is why,

Mr Hargreave, when a girl is naughty, we have to cut her tit off.'

The words were like a blow. Hargreave stared at the man, aghast. 'It was my fault, not Olga's!' he blurted. '*I* refused to pay you in Macao, not Olga! She is innocent! And now I am here with the money!'

Gregovich continued earnestly: 'We have found that if you cut a naughty girl's tit off, then send her back to her friends, the other girls give no more trouble after that. So that is our policy now.' He looked at him soulfully, a businessman seeking understanding from a difficult customer. 'Do I make myself clear, Mr Hargreave?'

Hargreave shouted, '*Olga is innocent. It's my fault. The money's here!*'

Gregovich continued, with a little frown: 'But there's one thing you said which interests me. You said that if Olga *had* come to Hong Kong you would have paid the money you owe in order to stop us threatening you for the rest of your life.' He smiled. 'That was smart thinking, Mr Hargreave. But tell me,' he raised a finger, 'when I do give Olga back to you – *if* I do – what do you propose doing?'

If . . . Hargreave's mind fumbled with the question. 'I'm going to retire. Hong Kong is almost finished. Olga and I will live somewhere quietly, like America or England.'

Gregovich's eyebrows went up. 'And not work? How can you afford that?'

Oh, not more money, please God. 'Yes, I'll have to work. I'll get a job in a small town as a lawyer, I suppose.'

Gregovich shook his head. 'A small-town lawyer, Mr Hargreave? What a waste – you are a *big-time* lawyer.' He looked at him soulfully. 'No, no, that would be a waste. *You*, Mr Hargreave,' he smiled at him, 'will go back to Hong Kong. And you will continue in your big-lawyer job for many years. Earning your big salary. And –' he paused again – 'you will also be working for me.'

Hargreave stared at Gregovich, aghast. Oh *no*. Oh no, not that . . .

Gregovich continued in a kindly tone. 'As Director of Public Prosecutions, Mr Hargreave – or even if you are demoted temporarily after your little outburst – as a senior government lawyer you'll also be working for *me*.' He frowned, then explained: 'You see, Mr Hargreave, in the years to come I am going to be doing a lot of business in Hong Kong. And *through* Hong Kong. Business to and from China, the whole Far East. Import–export business. And much of it is going to be –' he waggled his hand – 'sensitive. Products that the new Chinese government may be *difficult* about.' He smiled, wolfishly. 'And you, Mr Hargreave, are going to smooth over these little difficulties for me.'

Hargreave was appalled. Gregovich went on: 'Oh, I know what you're going to say, Mr Hargreave. That you are not Director of Public Prosecutions any more, that you have probably been fired, et cetera. But no, Mr Lipschitz tells me that you will only be temporarily replaced, because the government will decide that you had a nervous breakdown. You will quickly be well again and back in your job because you are so good at it. A senior government servant has a guaranteed position, Mr Lipschitz says. Not so?'

Agree, agree to anything just to get out of here! 'Yes, that's so.'

'But then you are going to tell me that even so you have no power over the customs officials, you cannot forbid them to search vessels and aircraft and containers, and you have no authority over *any* officials in China. Et cetera.' He sighed. 'Technically that may be true. But you *do* have power when something comes to court – you can refuse to prosecute, for example. Or you could . . . *spoil* the prosecution, like you promised to do in my case.' He shrugged. 'And in practice you have influence over the customs officials – because you hold a very important position. You can make friends with the senior customs officers, you can *persuade* them with little presents – which we will provide.' He waved his hand. 'The same with the police. They will all listen to you, because you are so high-up.' He smiled encouragingly. 'So you see, Mr Hargreave, you are going to be very useful to us in Hong Kong – we cannot permit you to become a small-town lawyer in England.' He raised his eyebrows: 'You understand?'

Hargreave felt sick. Agree, he thought – agree to any fucking thing to get out of here with Olga, then run like hell and never be seen again! 'Yes, I understand.'

'But do you agree?'

Yes, yes. 'I agree.'

Gregovich frowned: 'You seemed to hesitate, Mr Hargreave.'

Oh God please. 'No, I did not hesitate.'

Gregovich seemed deeply perturbed. 'But why did you *not* hesitate, Mr Hargreave? You are supposed to be an honourable man, how can you so readily agree?'

'Because I have no option.'

Gregovich slapped his knee. '*Good*, Mr Hargreave.' He turned to Vladimir: 'There speaks a sensible man!' Vladimir smiled and nodded. Gregovich turned back to Hargreave and held up a finger. 'The same sensible man who told me that if Olga had come to Hong Kong you would nonetheless have paid the money you owe me. Because you did not want to be troubled by me for the rest of your life!'

'Correct.'

'*Correct.*' Gregovich paused benignly. 'Because if you cheat me when you go back to Hong Kong, you *will* be troubled. You *will* be trying to run away from me for the rest of your life, Mr Hargreave.' Gregovich looked at him earnestly. 'And even if you manage to run away for a while, you will never be able to work as a lawyer, Mr Hargreave. No, never again, anywhere in the world, because I will denounce you to the Hong Kong authorities.' He paused, then went on brightly: 'Everything you've said has been tape-recorded. Everything you said to Vladimir last time – how you promised to spoil the case, everything you said today.' He smiled with mock sympathy. 'You will be – "struck off", I believe is the expression. You will never be able to earn a living again in your profession.'

Hargreave felt sick in his guts, but all that mattered was getting Olga out of here. 'I understand.'

Gregovich added, 'And very unpleasant things will happen to Olga.'

Surely to God he's not going to keep Olga as a hostage? Hargreave swallowed. 'Yes, I understand.'

Gregovich frowned. 'But I wonder if you're just saying it to humour me.' He sighed and nodded to one of the guards. The man turned and disappeared into the kitchen.

Hargreave heard a refrigerator door open and close. A moment later the man returned, carrying a plate with a domed silver cover. He stopped in front of Hargreave and looked at Gregovich for instructions. Gregovich nodded. The man lifted the cover with a flourish.

Hargreave stared at the plate. Then vomit surged up his throat, and he clutched his mouth. He lurched, his stomach heaving, he scrabbled in his pocket for a handkerchief, clutched it to his mouth. He slumped against the wall, gagging.

'*Oh Jesus . . .*'

On the plate, sitting in congealed blood, was a woman's breast.

'Take it away,' Gregovich said. The flunky turned back to the kitchen. Gregovich smiled. 'Relax, Mr Hargreave, that is not Olga's breast. Not yet. But do you see now what I mean about discipline?'

'*You fucking barbarian . . .*' Hargreave whispered.

Gregovich smiled again. 'As you wish. But that's what I mean by *discipline*.' He raised his eyebrows. 'In fact, guess whose breast that is, Mr Hargreave.'

Hargreave leaned against the wall, eyes closed.

'It belonged to a very pretty girl called Tanya.' Gregovitch smiled. 'You spoke to her last night in the Highlife Club, which we protect.'

Hargreave slowly raised his head, horrified. *Oh no . . .*

Gregovich continued quietly, 'She was going around to all our girls asking if they knew Olga Romalova, telling them that a handsome Englishman was in love with her – and asking about the Mafia. And this morning she telephoned her controller, asking him.' He shrugged. 'So, of course, we tried to ask Tanya some reasonable questions, about this Englishman and his Olga.' He shook his head wearily. 'But she told us lies, Mr Hargreave. She denied she knew your telephone number, but then we found she did know it. She was trying to protect you, I suppose. So,' Gregovich sighed regretfully, 'we had to discipline her. To teach our girls, not to help each other to escape.'

Hargreave's mind reeled red-black. He roared, *'She wasn't assisting Olga to escape! All Tanya did – '*

'Was try to find out where Olga was, so you and Mr Champion and Mr Kerensky could rescue her.'

'No such thing! Last night I didn't even know Champion was coming to Moscow!'

Gregovich looked pained at the noise. 'Like you don't know where they are now?' He waved a hand, dismissing the point. 'Anyway, we will have no more trouble with our girls for a while.' He smiled. 'Like we will have no trouble from you, Mr Hargreave, because the same will happen to Olga if you try to double-cross us when you get back to Hong Kong. Quite apart from what will happen to you.'

Hargreave swallowed his sickened outrage. What had they done to Henri? He slumped against the wall again and whispered 'Okay, you've impressed this upon me sufficiently. *Vividly.* Now can we please get this over and let Olga and me go home!'

Gregovich smiled. 'Not yet. We haven't heard from Mr Champion yet; I am very anxious to meet my friend Mr Champion and give him some of the nice medicine he gave me.'

'Champion is absolutely innocent!' Hargreave shouted. 'I've no idea where he is! And he didn't come to Moscow to help me rescue Olga – he came because he was so furious with me for blowing your trial! And he's proceeding directly to London to drown his sorrows!'

'Sure . . .' Gregovich said. 'And I admire loyalty – you will find me very grateful, very generous if you are loyal to me in Hong Kong. You will end up a rich man. Like we are very good to our girls – ask them. If they are loyal we treat them well, we protect them from trouble. Like Henri, the concierge at the Metropole. He was innocent, he just thought you were a tourist who wanted to screw a pretty whore called Olga again, but as soon as he learned the truth he cooperated and told us everything.' He spread his hands. 'So he's been rewarded. But silly people like Tanya? Poof . . .' He flicked a hand. 'No left tit.'

'You're free and I've paid the fucking money!' Hargreave rasped desperately. 'Champion is probably on a plane to London by now! So can we please leave?'

Gregovich said conversationally to Vladimir, 'Was it her left tit or her right?'

'Her left,' Vladimir said, 'I think.'

'Can we now leave!'

Gregovich smiled. 'Patience, please. I haven't finished telling you about your job in Hong Kong.' He pulled a cheroot out of his pocket, lit it carefully. 'The first thing you are going to do for me, Mr Hargreave, is drop the case against me. Completely. Finished! Finito!' He raised his eyebrows. 'As the boss you are going to say that because Mr Gregovich has disappeared there is no point in trying to extradite him from Russia – or South America or the Congo – because not only is it far too expensive, there is no injustice because the evidence was very weak.' He looked at him pleasantly. 'Correct?'

Hargreave closed his eyes. *Agree to every fucking thing.* 'Correct.'

'You can do that?'

'Yes, I can do that.'

'No problem?'

'No problem.'

'And if the police complain you can ignore them?'

'I can ignore them.'

'You have the power?'

'I have the power.'

'And you *will* use it?'

'I will use it.'

Gregovich sat back and blew smoke at the ceiling. 'Very good. Because Olga will suffer if you do not.'

'I've said I will do it! Now give me Olga and let us go!'

Gregovich puffed on his cheroot pensively. 'I wonder where Mr Champion is? I may be able to offer the good man a job working for me in Hong Kong. A top policeman is always very useful.'

'Good,' Hargreave rasped. 'So look for him in the pubs of London!'

'And Kerensky?' Gregovich mused. 'I wonder where he is? Unfortunately I doubt I can offer the man a job because he's one of those Russians who are so *honest*. The Asshole of Vladivostok, we call him. Would you believe his grandfather was a *White* Russian? One of those aristocrats?'

'You don't say.'

'I do say. And yet he still rose to be an officer. So,' he sighed, 'the man is useless to me. He must go.'

'Give me Olga!'

Gregovich looked at him. 'Oh, Olga. Pretty girl. Yes, Mr Hargreave, you'll get Olga, safe and sound. *In* due course, when you've proved to me that you are trustworthy, when you've returned to Hong Kong and the case of Regina versus Ivan Gregovich is finally dropped – the extradition proceedings cancelled, and so forth.'

Hargreave stared at him, a ringing in his ears. Then he wanted to roar and bound across the room and grab him by the throat and throttle him until his eyes bulged and his tongue stuck out and he finally writhed his last.

'But you made a deal!'

'And so,' Gregovich smiled, 'did you. And I will keep my side when you have kept yours.'

Hargreave's mind reeled in rage and panic. 'No. Now! You don't understand the legal process. There's a warrant out for your arrest – when you jumped bail Mr Findlay automatically applied for a warrant!' He waved a frantic hand. 'It exists. In black and white, in the name of the Queen of England, ordering your arrest!' He shook his head at Gregovich. 'I can't just walk back into Hong Kong tomorrow and cancel that order!'

Gregovich frowned, perturbed. 'But you told me that you could. "No problem", you said.'

Oh Jesus. Hargreave took an anguished breath, his mind fumbling. '*Yes*, I can do it! But you must realize that it will take *time*. This is a big case, there's a lot of public interest, the press is full of it especially after all the publicity about VJ Day, the atom bomb on Hiroshima, the horrors of nuclear war and so forth. And the police are furious, they're very anxious to get their hands on you –'

'You're saying,' Gregovich interrupted, 'that you cannot help me?'

'*No!*' Hargreave said desperately. 'I *can*. But it will take *time*. The extradition process has already started – *already* my department will have filed an application to the Russian courts.'

'And you can't stop that? You said you could. Did you lie to me?'

'No!' Hargreave lied desperately. 'I can do it! But you must disappear until public interest has died down – if I tried to stop it now there would be a public outcry!'

Gregovich smiled. 'So in the meantime you want me to let Olga go to Hong Kong with you? Then you will do it when the heat is off?'

387

'Yes!'

Gregovich put his hand in his pocket and pulled out a barber's razor. He opened it, and fingered the blade.

'So you lied to me when you said you had the power – like Tanya lied to me.'

'*No –*'

'*Then do it!*' Gregovich barked. 'You work for me! When you've done it, *when* I'm satisfied that you're trustworthy and won't tell any more lies, Olga will be sent to you!' He glared and snapped: 'Bring her in here!'

A man turned and strode down the corridor. Hargreave shouted at Gregovich, '*Don't you dare touch her!*' The other man grabbed his arm and twisted it behind his back.

Gregovich flicked the razor. He sneered: 'And when I do, you'll beg to be allowed to obey me!'

There was a muffled shout down the passage, then a door slammed. A few seconds later Olga appeared through the gloom. The guard was following, twisting her arm behind her back. Her blonde hair was awry. She was wearing a loose dress with big buttons down the front.

Hargreave stared, his heart pounding. 'Olga!' He started towards her but his guard wrenched his arm.

Olga walked tremulously into the room, and stopped two paces in front of him.

'Hullo, darling.' She smiled nervously. 'I am very sorry about this.'

'Olga – everything is going to be all right!' Hargreave moved towards her again but the guard held him back.

'Sure it is,' Gregovich said; '*if* you keep your bargain. Let them go,' he said to his men. 'Let the dear lovers embrace.'

The guards released them. Olga lurched into his arms, and they clutched each other, desperately, frantically holding each other tight. Oh God, he just had to agree to everything and run like hell to the nearest police station and bring them here – and then he felt the gun. It was pressing against his loins, it was hidden in Olga's panties, against her belly. His mind fumbled, and Gregovich said, 'Very touching. That's enough.'

The guards pulled them apart. They stood staring at each other, hearts racing, Olga's eyes frantically demanding *What shall I do?* Then Gregovich stood up. He strolled to her and put his hand on her hair.

'Pretty isn't she, Mr Hargreave? Beautiful. Take a good look at her, because it is the last time you'll see her intact, with two breasts, if you do not do as I order.' He stroked his thumb over the razor's edge. 'In fact –' his hand went to her neckline and undid the topmost buttons – 'have a *proper* look.' Olga closed her eyes. The razor went to the brassière and sliced the two cups apart. Her breasts stood naked.

'Leave her!' Hargreave rasped.

'Beautiful, aren't they?' Gregovich mused. 'Probably the best in Russia. Big, but perfectly proportioned and self-supporting.' He stroked them with the flat of his razor. 'Such a pity to spoil them.'

'I'll do what you say!'

Gregovich turned to him, tapping Olga's left breast absently with the razor. 'It is this one – the one over her heart – that we will first send to you in Hong Kong if you fail me.'

'I've said I'll do it!'

'Would you like to see the rest of her, her beautiful pussy?'

Olga's eyes widened in horror. '*No!*' Hargreave shouted. Just then there was a loud bang on the door.

'Ah,' Gregovich smiled, 'that'll be Mr Champion.'

A guard went to the door, his gun out. He looked through the spyhole, then opened up.

Champion stood there, bloodied. Sepov was behind him. The guard grabbed Champion by the collar and slung him into the apartment. Champion sprawled on the living-room floor. Hargreave stared. Sepov sauntered into the room, smiling, a gun in his hand. Sergei follow him.

'Why were you so long?' Gregovich demanded.

'Kerensky,' Sepov said apologetically. 'He got suspicious. I had to shoot him.'

'Where's the body?'

'In the trunk of Mr Hargreave's rented car,' Sepov replied. 'I didn't want blood in my police car.' He took the keys out of his pocket. 'Want me to dump it now?'

'No,' Gregovich said. 'Later – you'll have to wash the blood out of Mr Hargreave's car thoroughly; we don't want him to have any trouble if he's going to work for us in Hong Kong, do we? Mr Hargreave must appear respectable.'

40

Hargreave stared. 'You *bastard*!' he whispered at Sepov. Olga was wide-eyed. Hargreave made a lunge at Sepov but the guard wrenched him back.

'So, we have the truth at last,' Gregovich said. 'From the lips of learned prosecution counsel himself.' He snorted. 'Of course, I knew it anyway. But . . .' he wagged the razor at Hargreave admonishingly, 'You lied to me, you told me porky-pies, as the English say.' Champion was getting to his feet. '*Stay down!*' Gregovich roared, and kicked him.

Champion sprawled again, clutching his guts. He looked murderously up at Hargreave. 'Congratulations,' he rasped. '*Brilliant!*'

Sepov snickered: 'You were not very brilliant yourself.'

'No,' Gregovich agreed. 'The big Hong Kong policeman is out of his depth in Moscow. Like Mr Simonski. They imagine they can fight me – ridiculous, such arrogance. Like Mr Hargreave, like Mr Kerensky – but I'm sad you shot him so soon, I wanted to have a little chat with him first. Never mind, I will content myself with Mr Champion.' He turned to Sepov. 'Take Sergei downstairs and wait in your car until I telephone you.'

Gregovich went to the sideboard, opened a drawer, and took out a stun-truncheon. It was identical to the one Lipschitz had produced in court. He flicked a switch and sparks crackled between the two metal nodules. Hargreave stared.

'Useful weapon. Every policeman should have one.' Gregovich turned to Champion, and crouched beside him. 'You have one, don't you, Mr Champion?'

Champion looked at him murderously, but he was frightened. 'No.'

'No? But first tell me this – and I want *you* to pay attention, Mr Hargreave. You *did* leave me alone with Mr Simonski during your interrogation, didn't you?'

Champion's eyes darted from the truncheon to Hargreave, back to the truncheon. He swallowed. 'Yes.'

'*Yes*.' Gregovich smiled up at Hargreave. 'You see?' He turned back to Champion. 'How many times?'

'Twice,' Champion rasped.

'Exactly as I said in my evidence. Yes?' Gregovich appealed to Hargreave. 'And for how long each time?'

Champion said huskily, 'About five or ten minutes.'

Hargreave was staring. 'And tell Mr Hargreave,' Gregovich continued. 'Was your air-conditioning broken, or was it on?'

'It was working. On.'

'*Yes* . . . So did Simonski have his jacket on, or off?'

'On,' Champion admitted softly.

'Correct. So Simonski could have concealed his truncheon under his jacket, not so?'

Champion glanced at Hargreave, then said hoarsely, 'Yes.'

Gregovich turned on his haunches, and looked up at Hargreave. 'You see, I was telling the truth. Mr Champion was lying to the court, to get me convicted.'

Hargreave was looking at Champion grimly. Gregovich continued: 'And even though he had his jacket on, you knew Simonski had such a truncheon, didn't you?'

'Yes,' Champion admitted.

'And why did you leave us alone, Mr Champion?'

Champion licked his lips. 'To go to the toilet.'

Gregovich smiled. 'Of course you probably *did* go to the toilet, few people can go six hours without a piss, especially after all that coffee. But in fact you left the room in order to give Mr Simonski the opportunity to torture me with this –' he waved his truncheon – 'so that *you*, as a respected policeman, could deny any knowledge?' He leered, then his arm shot out and the truncheon touched Champion's chest. '*Not so!*'

'*Aaarh!*' Champion screamed, and he contorted. He clutched his chest, eyes screwed up, gasping. '*Oh Jesus, Jesus . . .*'

'Exactly,' Gregovich smiled. He looked up at Hargreave again. 'See the pain?' He turned back to Champion. 'That's why you left me alone with Simonski, isn't it?'

'*Yes*,' Champion groaned, eyes closed, gasping.

'Yes,' Gregovich said. 'And isn't it true that until then I was denying I knew about the suitcase of uranium? But after the first shock I said I did, and then you continued trying to find out the source. I denied knowledge of it, so after many more questions you left me alone with Simonski the second time?'

'Yes . . .'

'And when you came back I agreed to say whatever you wanted.'

'Yes,' Champion whispered.

391

Gregovich swivelled on his haunches and looked up at Hargreave with wide, innocent eyes. 'So you see, the confession was *not* made voluntarily, and therefore was not admissible as evidence. Mr Lipschitz was quite right.' He spread his hands: 'And without that confession, you had a weak case, didn't you?'

Hargreave took a trembling breath – anything to please the bastard. He nodded.

'Say it, Mr Hargreave.'

Hargreave swallowed. 'Our case was weakened, yes. But the key was found in your pocket. And you knew the combination of the lock.'

Gregovich smiled and stood up. 'Stay there,' he said to Champion conversationally. He paced across the room. 'Mr Hargreave, we are not deciding my guilt or innocence, I am simply proving to you a few facts that did not emerge at the trial. Proving to your lawyer's conscience that Mr Champion was a liar, to make it easier for you to justify dropping the charge against me.' He held up a finger. 'I mentioned the combination for the lock in the so-called confession, but as the confession itself was inadmissible because I was tortured, the fact that I gave the combination should not have been told to the jury. It prejudiced me.'

'The jury was *not* told that you knew the combination!' Hargreave said. 'The confession was not yet admitted in evidence when I fucked the case up. The jury was simply going to be invited to draw the *inference* that you told the police the number, because no policeman nor Kozkov knew it!'

'Exactly,' Gregovich agreed. 'And that was very unfair of you – that was getting inadmissible evidence in by the back door, as Mr Lipschitz said. He was *very* angry with you. And so was I, because you were breaking the bargain you made with Vladimir to get me acquitted.' He wagged the razor at Hargreave whilst he paced. 'Naughty, naughty . . . That alone is worth Olga's left tit.'

'Jesus!' Champion stared up at Hargreave. 'You made a deal with this bastard? So I was right when I asked you this morning!'

Hargreave rasped at Gregovich, 'You don't understand the Law of Evidence! A confession obtained by duress is *not* admissible, but subsequent evidence obtained as a result of that confession is admissible. *Listen to me,*' he shouted as Gregovich started to interrupt. 'If you, under torture, confess to the police that you stabbed your wife and that you buried her under the oak tree, with the knife, that confession is *not* admissible, and cannot be told to the jury because it was not made voluntarily! But the police *can* tell the jury that after speaking to you

392

they went to the oak tree, dug up the ground and found your wife's body, plus the knife with your fingerprints on it. From that evidence the jury may or may not infer that you told the police where to look. Whether that is the only inference that can reasonably be drawn is the jury's decision, not mine. And that's all I did!'

'And did it very well. But *so* unfair to a man presumed innocent until proved guilty. But let us talk about the key which Mr Champion –' he pointed with his truncheon – '*says* he found in my pocket.' Gregovich smiled: 'You found the key in *Kozkov*'s pocket didn't you, Mr Champion? And planted it on me.'

'*No*,' Champion gasped. 'The customs officials and Inspector Sullivan saw me search Kozkov's clothing and find nothing!'

'But you *did* find the key on Kozkov, and you concealed it from everybody and then planted it on me.'

'Jesus Christ . . .' Champion groaned. 'I'm not a crook like your pal Sepov – I don't try to convict innocent men. Can I get up now?'

'No. You look nice down there.' Gregovich leered at him. 'But we've just proved that you committed perjury about my so-called confession.' He smiled: 'You planted the key on me, didn't you?'

'*No*,' Champion glared.

'No?' Gregovich crouched down beside him with the truncheon. 'No?'

'*No*.'

'And Kozkov *did* know the number of the combination lock, didn't he? He pretended he didn't, but when you offered him heroin he told you. And then you eventually forced me to put it into my so-called confession?'

'No.'

'No?' Gregovich touched him with the truncheon. Champion screamed and contorted, clutching his arm, eyes screwed up. 'Didn't you?'

Champion lay gasping, glaring at Gregovich murderously. '*No* . . .'

'No?' Gregovich touched him again and Champion jerked and screamed. The Russians all laughed. '*Didn't* you?'

Champion lay fighting for air. '*Yes* . . .' he whispered, face contorted.

Gregovich stood up. 'You see, Mr Hargreave, I am innocent. Mr Simonski and Mr Champion were so convinced I was guilty that when they caught Kozkov with the suitcase they were sure *I* was the villain, so they cooked up the case against me. But what you have just seen will make it easy for you to stop all further action against me. It also shows how anybody can be made to talk.' He waved a hand. 'So you have no evidence against me – no confession, no key, no combination number. So,' he spread his hands reasonably, 'it would be most unjust, knowing what you know now, to hold a retrial.'

Champion glowered from the floor: 'And I also sank the Titanic.'

Gregovich turned to him. 'What?'

'If I planted the key on you I also sank the Titanic eighty-odd years ago. It wasn't an iceberg, it was me, with my snorkel. Single-handed in mid-Atlantic.'

Gregovich smiled. 'Wise guy? Trying to confuse poor Mr Hargreave . . .'

He suddenly bounded across the room and swung his leg to kick Champion in the guts. Champion twisted and lunged, caught the foot, wrenched and heaved. Gregovich went lurching backwards, Champion scrambled up and threw himself after him, and hit him in the guts. Gregovich crashed against the wall, Champion on top of him. The two guards scattered, pulling their guns out; Vladimir bounded off the sofa, the razor in his hand, and Hargreave hit him. Hit him with all his might on the head with his fist like a club, and Vladimir sprawled. Hargreave bounded wildly after him and kicked him in the stomach – and Champion screamed as Gregovich jabbed him with the truncheon again. Champion reeled across the room and crashed against the window, stunned, gasping. Hargreave roared and turned on Gregovich, and Vladimir grabbed his leg. Hargreave lurched and a shot rang out. There was a shattering of glass, blood flying: then Champion slid slowly down the window, shock in his eyes, a bullet hole in his chest. Gregovich was holding a smoking gun.

For a long shocked moment the tableau seemed to stand still: Gregovich panting, Champion slumping, blood smearing, two guards with their guns out, Vladimir crouched, razor in hand. Then Gregovich's face broke into a smile.

'Mr Hargreave,' he said, 'now you really *worry* me. I was just beginning to have such confidence in you – and you would be *so* useful to me in Hong Kong. But now, with Mr Champion dying and unable to testify against me, you have no case against me at all, do you? So I don't need you, do I, to stop those silly extradition proceedings?'

Hargreave panted desperately: '*Wrong* – you do need me! Inspector Sullivan saw Champion find the key in your pocket, and he will testify to that! And there's still the inference that you told the police the combination for the lock . . . *and* you tried to run away. So you need me to quash those extradition proceedings – and for all the future work you want me to do!'

Gregovich smiled, and shook his head in wonder. 'Now Mr Hargreave *really* wants to work for me. Such loyalty I cannot –'

Then a shot rang out, and Gregovich lurched, shocked. Then two more shots – *crack! crack!* One guard crashed against the wall, dying, the other sprawled.

And there stood Olga, her gun held in front of her with both hands. Gregovich, blood flooding from his shoulder, stared at her gun incredulously: for a long moment all seemed to stand still again, everybody staring astonished at the beautiful wild-eyed girl with the trembling pistol: then Vladimir leapt at her, and things happened very fast.

Vladimir sprang, his razor on high, Olga shrieked and stumbled backwards, Gregovich raised his gun at her, and Hargreave gave a roar and hurled himself at Gregovich. It was the frantic roar of a man wildly charging to the defence of his woman, a roar of terrified fury to draw the attack on to himself, to shock his terrible enemy, to make him swing his gun aside, the hate-filled suicidal roar of a maddened man charging to lay down his life; then there was another crack of gunfire as Olga swung wildly on Vladimir, as Hargreave hit Gregovich. Hit him with all his outraged weight, one arm outstretched for the gun, struck him in the chest so the man flew backwards. Gregovich crashed against the sideboard, Hargreave on top of him, and they sprawled. All Hargreave knew was that the hated man beneath had to be killed, the wild determination to kill kill kill before the monster killed his woman, all he knew was the contorted gasping face of the worst man in the world beneath him as he roared from the bottom of his hate-filled heart and smashed his forehead down on the hated face as they wrestled for the gun, bashing and battering the snarling face, the nose, the eyes. Gregovich sank his teeth into Hargreave's cheek and Hargreave roared and rammed his knee between Gregovich's legs with all his frantic might, and Gregovich screamed and Hargreave wrenched the gun free. He scrambled up wildly, reeling, blood streaming from his face, ready to blast Vladimir, and he stopped, aghast.

Olga's gun lay on the floor: she was on her knees, Vladimir crouched behind her, one hand clutching a bunch of her hair backwards, the other holding the razor to her throat. Blood flooded down his chest.

'Drop the gun or I cut her throat . . .'

Hargreave crouched there, horrified, his reeling mind trying to grasp this situation: then he held out his trembling hand, gasping, 'Okay, okay . . .' He reached down to place the gun on the carpet. Then he jerked it up again and fired.

It was a frantic impulse: he really did intend to put the gun down, he was ready to do anything to avoid that dreadful razor at Olga's throat. Then his mind snapped as he saw Vladimir's hated face clear above her shoulder, and he whipped the gun up again and fired wildly. It would have been a safe shot for a marksman, the range only three paces, but it was a dreadfully dangerous shot for a trembling, gasping, middle-aged lawyer who had never fired a gun in anger in his life, using a weapon he had never handled before – it was a treacherous shot. But no such considerations raced through Hargreave's terrified mind as he jerked the gun up and pulled the trigger – he did it with the same desperate outrage with which he had hurled himself at Gregovich moments before. The gun kicked in his hand, and the bullet did not hit Vladimir in the face: it tore through his hair, ripping the top of his brains out and plastering them on the wall behind. He was hurled backwards, his razor swept across Olga's throat, and she screamed.

Hargreave scrambled to her, horrified, and Olga screamed again – '*Behind you!*' Hargreave whirled, reeling, and saw Gregovich looming up, blood all over his shoulder, the truncheon on high. Hargreave gave another frantic roar and he fired again.

He fired at point-blank range into Gregovich's guts, and for an instant the man seemed to hang poised in mid-strike, shock all over his contorted face; then he was reeling backwards, arms upflung. He crashed against the table and sprawled across it. Hargreave crouched, wild-eyed, then he turned and scrambled to Olga. He grabbed her arm and heaved.

Olga lurched to her feet, one hand clutching her throat, blood oozing between her fingers: '*Only flesh!*' Hargreave turned desperately to Champion. He was trying to get up, clutching at his chest, face twisted in pain.

Hargreave dashed to him, grabbed his arm and heaved him to his feet. 'Are you okay? Can you walk?'

'Do I fucking look okay?'

Olga snatched her gun up off the floor.

'Come on!' Hargreave turned for the door, clutching Champion's arm. He looked wildly at Gregovich.

The man was groaning, eyes screwed up, clutching his stomach, blood welling between his fingers, flooding from his shoulder. Hargreave rasped:

'Don't die! I'm going to extradite you, and at the retrial I'll be giving evidence myself and the jury's going to hear all about today, every fucking thing you said, hear all about Tanya's breast in your refrigerator!'

'You're not going to kill him?' Olga cried.

Gregovich groaned: 'No . . . he's British . . . that's why I want him to work for me.'

'*Never!*' Olga rammed her pistol against his head – but she could not pull the trigger.

Hargreave snatched the gun aside. 'Leave him!' He dashed to the corpses of the guards and snatched up their guns. He thrust one at Champion. '*Come!*'

Champion lurched to the table and glowered down at Gregovich. '*Well I'm going to kill him –*'

'*No!* You want to be charged with murder?' Hargreave grabbed his arm.

Champion wrenched free and picked up the stun-truncheon painfully. 'Just one question.' He flicked the switch so the sparks crackled, then he jabbed Gregovich with it. Gregovich screamed. 'What's the name of the official in the Ministry of Defence who supplied the uranium?'

Gregovich had his eyes screwed up: '*General Karlov . . .*' he whispered.

'Jesus Christ! Come *on!*'

Champion gave Gregovich one more jab. 'Don't die yet,' he rasped through the man's scream.

Hargreave grabbed Olga's hand and plunged down the corridor to the door. Champion followed, staggering. '*What's the plan, Rambo?*'

'I've got a chartered plane waiting!' Hargreave peered desperately through the spyhole, then turned: 'Ready?' Olga nodded and took Champion's arm. Hargreave flung open the door.

They burst out into the corridor, looking left and right. They ran for the distant staircase beside the elevator, Champion lurching between them.

They were halfway to the stairwell when Olga remembered the moneybelt. '*Money!*' She let go of Champion, turned and ran frantically back to the apartment. She flung open the door, burst inside, and she screamed.

She screamed in horror at the wild-eyed Gregovich lurching at her, his face contorted in murderous rage, one clawed hand up to seize her, the other clutching a knife: Gregovich gave a crazed roar as Olga staggered backwards, and she fired. She fired blindly into the terrible face, and there was a splat of blood from his jaw as Gregovich spasmed. Then he reeled backwards, and crashed on to the floor, arms outflung.

Hargreave burst back through the door. He saw Olga standing over Gregovich, her eyes wild, trembling, her gun still pointed at him. '*Jesus . . . Come on!*'

Olga lurched to the table and snatched up the moneybelt. She turned back towards the door.

41

They came to a panting stop at the staircase. Olga was trembling, blood running down her neck. Champion was in great pain, clutching his chest. Hargreave peered desperately around the corner, nodded, and they began to descend. 'Do you know where we are?'

'No,' Olga whispered.

They came to the first corner. Hargreave stopped, peered, they hurried on down. The floor below was clear. They began the descent to the lobby. Hargreave stopped at the last corner, rasping, gun ready; the lobby looked empty. He looked feverishly at Olga, motioned her to stay where she was, and began to tiptoe down.

He came to the last step, gun up, and peered around the corner. The lobby was unoccupied. He looked out into the street, and his heart leapt; *there*, right outside the entrance, was his rented car where Sepov had left it. Nobody inside it. *Where was Sepov?* He held a warning finger up at Olga, then dashed to the entrance. He pressed himself against the wall, and peered out into the dark street.

Sepov was not to be seen. A few distant pedestrians were hurrying down the bleak avenue, cars were scattered down the kerb. Hargreave turned back to the stairwell and beckoned. Olga came down into the lobby, Champion following.

'That's my car.' Hargreave pointed. 'As soon as I've started it you *walk* out with Champion, normally, and get in the backseat.'

Olga nodded, the blood trickling down her neck. She grabbed his arm: 'I love you.' She put her fingertip on his bloodied cheek.

'I love you too.' Hargreave turned, walked unsteadily to the entrance, and stepped into the Moscow night.

Andreovich Sepov was sitting in his unmarked police car, with Sergei, a hundred yards from Hargreave's vehicle. They were not expecting any trouble: they were waiting to be summoned upstairs in due course to fetch Champion, drive him out of the city, shoot him and dump his body with Kerensky's. They certainly were not expecting to see Hargreave emerge unescorted from the building. They paid no attention when a man came out into the darkness and got into one of the cars parked up the street: they only did so when a woman hurried out moments later, helping a big man, then scrambling into the rear seats.

'*That's her!*' Sergei cried.

Hargreave let out the clutch before the door closed, and went roaring off up the street with a squeal of tyres. He was two hundred yards away before Sepov pulled the keys from his pocket and rammed them into the ignition: Hargreave had disappeared round the corner with another squeal of tyres before Sepov pulled away from the kerb.

'Which way to Tverskaya Street?' Hargreave rasped.

'East!' Olga blurted. 'We are in the west –'

'Which way is east?'

'Turn right!'

Hargreave swung the wheel and took the next corner with another squeal of tyres. Olga was looking frantically out of the rear window. They roared down the quiet street, apartment blocks flashing by, Sepov four hundred yards behind. 'Here they come –' Ahead was a major road, vehicles going in both directions, traffic lights on red. Olga cried: 'That's Smolensky Boulevard – turn left into it!' Hargreave raced towards the intersection, desperately praying that the lights would change. When he was thirty yards off they turned green and he trod the accelerator flat. He swung left into the intersection at fifty miles an hour, swinging wide out of his lane, the car heeling. He straightened and roared on up the boulevard. Olga looked back: '*They're coming!*' Sepov swung into the wide street midst an angry blast of horns. Ahead was another set of traffic lights, green, Hargreave raced towards them. '*Turn right!*' Olga cried. The lights changed to red as Hargreave swung right into Arbat Street, tyres squealing. '*He'll have to stop for this –*' But Sepov did not stop: he roared across the red light, his horn blasting, his tyres screaming, scattering traffic, and swung into line behind them. Hargreave pressed the accelerator flat again. Then a blue light started flashing on Sepov's roof, and the wail of a police siren rent the night. Olga screamed: '*He's pretending he's a policeman!*'

'He *is* a fucking policeman and I'm going to kill him!' Champion gritted.

'No shooting!' Hargreave cried.

'But we have a body in the boot!' Olga cried.

'*Oh Christ!*'

'He'll arrest us and say we did it!'

'No shooting in the streets!'

'He's not going to arrest us,' Champion rasped, 'he's going to kill us because I witnessed him shoot Kerensky – but that's only one reason I'm going to kill the sonofabitch!' He grimaced painfully and started rolling down his window to get his gun into position.

'Not in the streets!'

'Relax, Rambo, he's still too far away.'

'*Relax?*' Hargreave slapped his hand on the horn and rammed his foot down harder. Champion slumped back in the seat, his face in a grimace, eyes closed, muttering to Olga: 'Tell me when they're within fifty yards.' To Hargreave: 'I hope you're satisfied, Rambo.'

'Me satisfied? I didn't recruit fucking Sepov!'

'No, you just made a deal with the Mafia to fuck up my case!'

'That wasn't a fucking deal – that was a ploy to get Olga to Hong Kong! I had every intention of getting Gregovich convicted! You committed fucking perjury!'

'And you fucking suborned perjury!'

'*Stop fighting!*' Olga shouted.

Hargreave was driving as he had never done before, his mind gabbling *please God please God please God*, driving furiously, reckless of overturning, of traffic lights, of other traffic, reckless of everything to shake off this murderous bastard behind him. Ahead was the junction with New Arbat Street, the lights red; he kept his hand on the horn and he roared across it on to Boulevard Ring, the floodlit Kremlin flashing by on his right. '*How far behind?*'

'Two hundred yards, Rambo . . .'

He tore across Herzen Street, his horn blasting, then ahead was Tverskaya Street, the lights green. He glanced frantically in the rearview mirror, desperately hoping to see an almighty pile-up but all he saw was the flashing blue above Sepov's glaring headlights. The lights changed to amber as he swung wildly into Tverskaya Street. It was full of traffic converging on the lights. '*This time he must stop!*' But Sepov did not. He roared into the intersection after them, siren wailing, blue light flashing amidst screeching of brakes and blasting of horns. Hargreave bellowed, '*Please God stop him!*' and swung off the highway, on to the streets towards the airfield.

But God did not stop Sepov. Hargreave raced into the suburbs of north-east Moscow, the bleak apartment blocks flashing past, his horn blaring, people and cars scattering, and Sepov roared after him. Hargreave hurtled down the familiar roads, swinging left and right and left and right again, tyres screeching, desperately hoping for the sound of a godalmighty crash as Sepov wrote himself off on a corner. But Sepov did not, he came screaming round the corners, wailing, flashing, and now he was only a hundred yards behind. Then the suburbs of Moscow were thinning out, the apartments getting fewer. Champion twisted painfully in his seat and peered backwards; then he twisted the other way, leaned out of his window with his gun and fired. Sepov's windscreen shattered. 'That'll slow the bastard down!'

'*For Christ sake wait till we're out of town!*'

But it did slow Sepov down. He was five hundred yards behind when Hargreave swung on to the dirt roads leading to the airfield. His tyres skidded, grit flying, his steering wheel straining, the corner hedge racing towards him, then he corrected desperately and shoved his foot flat again. He roared down the narrow road, the hedges flashing past, and back at the corner Sepov's car went out of control.

Sepov skidded across the road at fifty miles an hour, across the verge, his rear mudguard smashing into the hedge, and he stalled. He cursed as he twisted the ignition key: the car restarted but his wheels spun on muddy grass. He bellowed and Sergei leapt out, gripped the rear bumper and heaved. The car inched off the grass, wheels churning. Then it was back on the road. Sergei scrambled in, and they roared off again after the diminishing tail-lights.

Hargreave's car was two miles ahead when it swung into the gate of the airfield. There was the Stardust hangar, light shining out of its huge open doors, there on the apron stood the aircraft. Hargreave kept his hand on the horn and roared down the row of huts. He slammed to a stop beside the aircraft as Chuck Hunter emerged from the hangar. '*Out! Get into that plane!*'

'Jesus, what's happening?' Chuck shouted.

'Get that plane to the runway!'

Olga was scrambling out of the car, clutching her gun, pulling Champion's arm. Chuck shouted, '*Jesus! No guns here, lady!*'

'Shuttup!' Champion came lurching out of the car, holding his bloody chest.

'*Christ!*' Chuck shouted at Hargreave, 'you can't do this to me!' Hargreave was letting out the clutch and swinging the wheel, roaring back towards the gate.

'*Where're you going?*' Olga cried as Champion swung his gun on Chuck: 'Get that fucking engine started!'

Sepov's car was half a mile away when Hargreave slammed to a stop across the gateway, blocking it. He rammed the car into reverse gear, scrambled out, locked the doors and started running.

He ran flat out up the side of the huts, out of sight of the road. He looked wildly at the aircraft, saw Olga clambering up into it, Champion standing groggily beside it. Hargreave ran out into the open. He looked back and saw Sepov's headlights stop at the gate, silhouetting his car. He looked wildly at the aircraft – the propellers started turning, Champion alongside it, looking back for him. Then the aircraft started moving. *'Get aboard!'* Hargreave bellowed but it came out in a rasp. He looked wildly back to the gate and saw Sepov and Sergei climbing over his car bonnet, silhouetted against the lights. Then their first shot rang out.

The gunshot cracked above the pounding of his feet and he cried out *'God help me!'* and swung his arm back, fired blindly and kept running. He looked again at the moving aircraft and saw Champion staggering towards him, his gun up, and a second shot rent the darkness. Hargreave flung his arm back, fired blindly again, bellowing *'Get aboard!'* He was still over a hundred yards from the aircraft, the propellers a blur; through his gasping he saw Olga leaning out of the door shouting, he saw Champion lower himself to one knee. *'Get aboard!'* Hargreave screamed again. Champion fired again, the gun held in both hands. Hargreave ran and ran, rasping, gasping, his heart pounding and his guts wrenching; now he was only eighty yards from the slowly moving aircraft, now seventy, now sixty, the propellers' whining above the pounding of his heart. Now he was only fifty yards off, and there was nothing in the world but the exhaustion wrenching at his guts. Then another shot rang out, and Hargreave sprawled.

All he knew was the blinding blow of the bullet on his leg, the shocking jolt, then the reeling, his arms desperately trying to recover balance, then he hit the concrete with a blinding crash. For an instant he lay there, stunned, then he tried to scramble up and his leg buckled and he collapsed on to one knee. Champion was bellowing at him. He looked wildly behind him and saw dark forms running at him. He staggered to his feet and tried to run again, lurching, towards the moving aircraft, gasping, the pain thudding in his thigh; then the plane stopped as Olga reached across and snatched out the ignition key.

Olga scrambled out on to the wing and leapt to the ground, gun in hand. *'Get back!'* Hargreave panted. She was running across the concrete, hair flying. Then Champion was lurching after her, bellowing *'Get back!'*

Hargreave fired blindly at the dark forms chasing him, and then reeled and sprawled again. He fell on to his side, he began to get up, then Olga was pounding up to him. *'Get up!'* She grabbed his arm. Hargreave clambered to his feet, exhausted, and then Champion was seizing his other arm. *'Run!'* And they tried to run together.

403

They staggered across the concrete, Olga frantically trying to pull Hargreave, Champion lurching behind them, looking over his shoulder. Hargreave hobbled desperately, trying to tell her to run for her life, exhaustion wrenching at his guts. Chuck's aircraft was seventy yards away. Hargreave looked wildly over his shoulder and saw the running forms just fifty yards behind: '*You run –*'

'*Come on!*' Olga shrieked. Champion lurched to an exhausted halt, clutching his bloody breast, turned to face their pursuers, his face screwed up in agony; he dropped to one knee again, raised his gun in both hands, and fired.

Sepov was only thirty yards away. The bullet smashed through his chest, and he lurched, a black shadow against the hangar lights, his arms upflung, his head thrown back. Then Champion fired again, at Sergei, a running figure against the lights, and the shot missed. Hargreave looked back, then a third shot rang out. It came from Sergei, and Hargreave saw Champion stagger; then he started to struggle up to his feet.

As if in slow motion he saw Champion make it to his feet against the hangar lights, Sergei crouched twenty yards beyond. Then a fourth shot rang out and Champion twisted, his big frame arched; for a moment he seemed about to fall, but he recovered his balance. Then there was a fifth shot: it came from Olga. Sergei shouted, scrambled up, turned and began to lurch away. He stumbled off into the lights, then he collapsed.

Champion was staggering across the concrete, clutching his guts: then he sprawled. Hargreave was hobbling frantically back to him. He slumped to his knees beside him. Champion was flat out on his back, blood flooding from his torso. '*Champ?*' Hargreave got his hand under his head and lifted. Champion opened his eyes and tried to focus.

'*Has Olga . . . still got the fucking money?*'

'Yes, sir,' Olga panted. She grabbed his arm to try to lift him.

Champion slid his eyes back to Hargreave: '*Watch it . . .*' he whispered.

Hargreave panted, 'Guard your tongue!' He got his arm under Champion's shoulder and heaved him up into a sitting position.

'That's rich . . . after fucking up my case . . .'

'You committed perjury! *Now get up!*' He heaved on Champion's armpit. He was a dead-weight.

'And you made a deal . . . with fucking Vladimir!'

'And fucking broke it! *Now get up!*'

'*Stop quarrelling!*' Olga cried. She heaved on Champion's arm.

'Bastard, fucking up my case. And you the Director . . . Public Prose-cutions.'

'*Was.*' Hargreave tried again to lift him. '*Get up or I'll kick your arse all the way to that aeroplane!*'

Champion closed his eyes. He sagged. 'Nice sitting here . . . Think I'll spend the rest of my life . . . just sitting here . . . Anybody . . . got a Band-aid?'

'*We're getting you to a doctor! So help us get you on your feet!*'

Chuck Hunter came panting up to them, wide-eyed, furious. '*Jesus* – what's all this about?'

'Shut up and call a doctor, Chuck!'

'Doctor's coming – phoned my protection boys, be here in ten minutes! What the fuck's this all about?'

'Hear that, sir?' Olga panted. 'Doctor is coming!'

'Will he . . . have a Band-aid? I want to go with Al . . . No official reports.'

'Like hell you are!' Chuck snapped. 'I don't want any stiffs in my plane, where do I dump your body in Helsinki?'

'Nice guy,' Champion groaned to Olga.

'There'll be no official reports! For Christ's sake – this is what I pay my Mafia for! The doctor'll fix you, then they'll get you out of Russia!' Chuck turned to Hargreave furiously: 'And as for you, sir – the price has just gone up! Double! Jealous husband, my poor achin' ass!'

'Does that include . . . all hush-money?' Champion grated.

'Of course! I don't want Russian cops around either!'

'Go for it . . .' Champion advised Hargreave. 'No cops . . .'

Of course Hargreave was going to go for it – he'd had enough of Russian cops too. 'Deal,' he said to Chuck.

'Then get aboard!'

Champion rasped, 'In Hong Kong you cover for me . . . I cover for you . . . Deal? No injustice. Did nothing wrong.'

The hell we didn't. But think of Tanya's tit. Think of Simonski. Think of that uranium. '*Deal.*'

'Clear conscience?'

'No.'

'Fucking lawyers! *Deal?*'

'*Yes, for Christ's sake!*'

'Then get aboard and wait for me!' Chuck snapped. 'I'll stay with him till my boys come!'

'The doctor must see Alistair's leg!' Olga insisted. 'Are you in pain, darling?'

'Clean exit wound, jab of penicillin will do till Helsinki.' Hargreave added: 'Getting used to getting shot.'

'Hell of a hero . . .'Champion gritted. 'Bastard. Fucking up my case.'

'He saved your life!' Olga cried.

'When? Thought I saved his.'

'In the apartment! Shot Gregovich and Vladimir! They would have killed you most cruelly!'

'Ah . . . Remember now. Got-Balls-Will-Travel Hargreave . . . So get aboard . . . Send the doctor over to give you a jab, blunt needle. Where you going?'

'Helsinki,' Hargreave said, 'then Hong Kong. Face the music.'

'Nervous breakdown, end of music . . . Early pension. Then?'

'Maybe go to the bar, make some money. Maybe help Jake McAdam and Martin Lee.'

'And when the Comrades . . . want to throw you in jail?'

'Caribbean. Sail the boat there.'

Champion winced at a wave of pain. 'Nice there . . . You sure . . . Olga's got the money?'

'Yes, *sir*!' Olga said indignantly.

'No cash, no dash,' Chuck said dangerously.

Hargreave jerked his thumb at Champion. 'What do I owe your doctor for this guy?'

'Mafia doctor. A thousand would help.'

'*Charming* . . .' Champion groaned. He turned painfully to Hargreave. 'Nice in the Caribbean . . .' He twisted his head to Olga. 'Look after this bastard . . . Good bastard, Al Hargreave . . . Got balls . . .'